Whispers and
WILDFIRE

A SMALL-TOWN ROMANCE

CLAIRE
KINGSLEY

Always Have LLC

Published by Always Have, LLC

Edited by Michelle Fewer

Cover design by Lori Jackson

ISBN: 978-1-959809-22-7

www.clairekingsleybooks.com

❀ Created with Vellum

Thank you to firefighters everywhere who risk their lives to save others.

About this book

He'll save her from the nightmare in her past.

Luke Haven has an adrenaline problem. As in, he can't get enough.

His squeaky-clean, nice-guy reputation in his small town isn't a lie. But it's not the whole truth, either. Although his real problem? He's not even sure what he's searching for.

Melanie Andolini never thought she'd be starting over in her thirties. But moving back to her hometown is exactly the fresh start she needs.

Until she runs into Luke Haven, and things get complicated. Really complicated. Although it feels like a lifetime since they dated in high school, sparks fly as soon as they're face to face—hot enough to light up the whole town.

Melanie blazes into Luke's life like wildfire—messy and chaotic, beautiful and tempting. But they played with fire once and both got burned. They're not going down that road again.

Except Melanie brought home a secret that still haunts her dreams. And when her nightmares turn all too real, Luke will risk everything to save her.

And make her his—this time, forever.

Author's note: a not-your-usual second chance romance with a fiery heroine and the hero who won't quench her flames—he'll bask in her heat. Family shenanigans, witty banter, page-turning suspense, and a wild happily ever after that will leave your heart full.

CHAPTER 1

Luke

ANTICIPATION THRUMMED THROUGH ME, a hint of life returning to my body. I could feel the pulse in my neck, tension rippling through my shoulders and back. The scent of gasoline, rubber, and dust filled the air, and the rumble of engines vibrated through me, heightening the sense of expectation.

It was the middle of the night, but the not-exactly-legal races still drew a crowd. Drivers, car enthusiasts, and groupies milled around, and street cars shined their head-lights, illuminating the old racetrack. It was about an hour outside my hometown—not in the jurisdiction of the Tilikum Sheriff's Department. An important detail when your brother was a sheriff's deputy, and your nosy family didn't know you still raced.

"How you feeling tonight?" Kyle, a guy about my age who'd been part of my unofficial pit crew for years, handed me my helmet. He wasn't asking because he cared. He was deciding how much money to put on me to win.

I took the helmet, my eyes never leaving the track. "Good. Focused."

He clapped me on the back. "That's what I like to hear."

For most spectators, the race was only part of the draw. They were there to gamble. Thousands of dollars—all cash—would change hands before the night was over.

I didn't care about any of that—the crowd, the groupies, the money. I was there for one thing and one thing only.

The rush.

Outside the track, in the normal routine of daily life, things were fine. I had no reason to complain. My custom auto shop was thriving. I owned my house, had money in the bank. Had my pick of badass cars to drive. I came from a good family—who thought I'd outgrown this particular habit. I was single, but I liked to think of it as being available. Open to possibilities.

So why was I so empty?

Not there. Not with the excited energy of the growing crowd, the rivalries with other drivers, the intense competition.

When I was on the track, I felt alive.

There was probably something wrong with me. Racing was dangerous—especially the way we did it. Not many rules. Certainly no organizational oversight. Just a bunch of guys with minimally modified cars in our backwoods version of showroom stock racing.

I'd started racing as a teenager and somehow managed to get by with only minor injuries, easily explained away. Every few years, I'd quit—for a while. But something about it always drew me back in. My day-to-day existence would get too gray. Too monotone.

Too boring.

Dangerous or not—stupid or not—I was there, my body beginning to buzz with adrenaline.

Breathing deeply of the exhaust-tinged air, I savored the sensation. The way my heart started to beat harder, the wave of anticipation that swept through me.

A girl in a black crop top and shorts that were hardly more

than bikini bottoms walked by, eyeing me as she passed. Her blond hair reached her lower back, and she somehow managed to walk in high heels on the uneven ground. She gave me a sultry smile. I tipped my chin to her.

The race on tap was the classics division, loosely defined as nothing newer than 1975. The cars were beasts—heavy and lacking a modern suspension. But that was what made it fun. Top speeds weren't what you'd get out of smaller, newer vehicles. But there was something about making an old school muscle car obey your commands that set a guy's blood on fire.

I loved it.

Drivers started getting in, so I went to my car—a 1966 Ford Mustang—got in and put on my helmet. That helmet and roll cage were the only real nods to my nocturnal activities in that car. No bright-colored racing jumpsuit with a sponsor's logo on the back. Just an old T-shirt and faded jeans. Some drivers wore gloves, but I liked my hands on the wheel with no barriers.

Dimly, I was aware of the roar of the engines as the other drivers started up. The crowd moving off the track. It was an irregular shape, modified from its original oval sometime after it closed, giving it a series of S-curves just after the first turn. Part dirt, part pavement. On a hot summer night, the dust cloud would be intense.

I turned on the engine and revved it. The throaty roar and low vibration rippled through me. It took another moment to get everyone out of the way, and my patience was wearing thin. I needed this. Needed the speed. The danger. The thrill.

Finally, a guy with a reflective vest climbed the ladder set up on the side of the track. A hush settled over the crowd, and it seemed as if we all drew a collective breath. He raised a gun into the air and fired a blank.

The shot was barely audible over the roar of engines, but it was enough. My foot slammed down on the gas, and I was off.

Tires squealed, dust and smoke from burning rubber rose in the air. I shot ahead but didn't take the lead. Not yet. Rookie drivers liked to do that—get out in front early on, thinking they could hold it. Took me a while to learn that lesson. But I wasn't a rookie anymore.

The race was five laps. No idea why, it was probably arbitrary. I hugged the first turn, letting a few cars get in front of me. I wasn't worried. I'd overtake them later. I was more concerned with not letting anyone clip me. A lot of those guys raced dirty.

More spectators were probably camped on the hill above the S-curves, but I ignored them. With intense focus, I drove, flying around the turns as I let the outside world fall away. Adrenaline coursed through my veins, fueling the high I was forever chasing. Bliss was always around the next turn, or the next, just slightly out of reach.

I drove harder, faster, until sweat dripped down my temples and only two drivers were in front of me. Four laps down. One to go.

My engine didn't purr, it roared like a lion. I flew past the starting line for the last time, my attention never wavering from the track and the drivers about to go down. A smile crept over my lips, and euphoria swept through me as I pushed my car to her limits, tires squealing on the turn.

I overtook the number two car, sneaking by him on the inside, and grinned at my glimpse of his shocked expression. He'd really thought he had me.

Dirt flew at my windshield as the driver in front of me hit the S-curves. The asshole had slowed down just enough to let his tires catch in the track, spewing debris behind him. Prick. Didn't matter, I wasn't slowing down. His taillights led me through the cloud, and in seconds, I was right on top of him.

No way was he letting me pass him on the inside, and I

only had two turns left. I wasn't going to fight dirty—I had no intention of crashing—but I needed the win.

Not for the money. Not even for the glory. It was all about the rush. I wanted the speed. The battle for the win.

I got behind him and faked like I was going to try for the inside. He moved over, and as soon as we hit the final turn, I floored it. My hands held the wheel in an iron grip and my muscles clenched tight as I fought my car to make the corner —as I bent her to my will.

"Come on," I growled.

The tires were going to slip. I was losing control. I could feel it.

Gritting my teeth, I held on. We came through the turn, and I shot ahead as soon as my tires straightened.

Seconds later, I crossed the finish line. Winner.

I came to a stop to the sound of cheering. It wasn't really for me. No one out there gave a shit about Luke Haven. They gave a shit about the money they'd just won betting on my win.

Still, the high lingered, and I got out smiling. Took off my helmet and lifted it over my head, letting the euphoria sweep me away.

People ran over to congratulate me with high fives, handshakes, and a few back-slapping hugs. The honest ones thanked me for winning them money. I laughed, still feeling the effects of the race. It was better than the most potent shot of liquor.

Kyle shoved an envelope of cash at me—my share of the winnings. I didn't bother counting it. Just leaned against my car and took a few deep breaths, inhaling the scent of fuel, dirt, and victory.

The woman in the crop top watched me from about ten feet away. Gave me the look. I'd seen it plenty of times. Knew exactly what it meant. She'd leave with me if I asked. Probably let me do all sorts of things to her, no strings attached.

I blew out a breath and looked away, the high already receding. The rush never lasted. I wanted to race again. To feel the tires almost leaving the pavement, their grip failing. I wanted imminent danger and the rush of knowing I'd cheated death. Again.

The cash, the girls, they were just... there. I didn't care. It didn't matter what the girl in the crop top looked like, I wasn't interested. A younger me would have thought I was an idiot. How could I pass up such an obvious yes?

But I was already sinking, the darkness swirling around me, churning like a river at the height of the spring snow melt. Ignoring the girl, I got back in my car and tossed my helmet on the passenger seat.

The party around me was just getting started, but I wanted out of there. I'd already gotten what I came for.

I had to roll slowly to get through the people, but soon enough, I was making my way down the dirt road that led to the highway. A cloud of dust rose in my wake, and the exhilaration that brought me out to race again would soon be gone.

That was how it worked. Nothing I could do about it except wait it out and chase the next high.

Although it made me wonder if I was ever going to find what I was looking for.

CHAPTER 2
Melanie

THE HOUSE WAS SUCH A DISASTER, I didn't even know where to begin.

Glancing around, I took a crunchy bite of my dill pickle. The mess was partially my fault. I could admit that. I'd known moving day was coming, and I'd let things pile up—quite literally. I'd take twenty-five percent of the blame. It was only fair.

My phone rang. There was the other seventy-five percent.

More specifically, his lawyer.

Eighty percent his fault. At least.

I took a breath. I was going to answer the call calmly and rationally. My voice would remain steady. I wasn't going to yell, not even a little bit.

I let my breath out, then answered, purposely using my maiden name. "Melanie Andolini."

"Hello, Mrs. Davis… Excuse me, Ms. Andolini."

I let that slip go even though I was convinced he did it on purpose. "Mr. Traver."

"I'm calling to confirm you'll be out of the house by this afternoon."

I glanced at the chaos. It didn't look good, but I also didn't have much choice. "Why? Is Jared afraid I'll be here when he finally comes to get his things?"

"That is a concern."

I rolled my eyes. "And he says I'm dramatic."

"Ma'am, the last time you two were in a room together, you called him… a bulbous pustule of duplicity." It sounded like he was reading from his notes. "As well as a deceitful scumbag. And you made it clear if he were to enter the home in question, he would, and I quote, 'regret it with every ounce of his maggot-infested soul.'"

"So what you're saying is, my ex-husband is afraid of me."

He sputtered. "No. I wouldn't say that."

"Can that be added to the divorce decree? I don't care where, even a side note. I'd like that to be on the legal record."

"Ms. Andolini, the issue is whether you are vacating the house and what time Mr. Davis can arrive to retrieve his share of the belongings."

This wasn't about Jared's stuff. He'd moved out a year ago. There was nothing in the house he actually needed. He was mad that I hadn't rolled over and capitulated to his ridiculous terms and was trying to make me pay for it.

I hadn't wanted anything extraordinary. Just half. He was the one who'd walked away from our marriage and then had the audacity to suggest he should get the majority of our assets. Why? Because he was a high and mighty attorney who thought the years he'd spent in law school made him special. And more important than the woman he'd married.

The worst part was, most of the value of those assets had already been eaten up by debt—his, not mine—and the rest was going to the never-ending legal fees. I was freaking broke.

"I have until four. And if he's so terrified of seeing me

again, tell him not to get here at three fifty-nine. I'm going to need every minute."

"Noted. Thank you for your time."

I wanted to say *you're not welcome because you've been awful to deal with, and I hope I never have to hear your slimy voice again.* But he hung up.

Slightly disappointing, but probably for the best.

Slipping my phone into the back pocket of my jeans, I looked around again and took another bite of my pickle.

I'd met Jared when I was living in LA, but his career had taken us to Seattle a few years after we got married. Not my first choice of cities, but the house had been a dream. It was big, airy, and beautiful. But its pretty exterior and expensive finishes were just a facade. The reality of my life in it had been anything but a dream.

A nightmare? That was a little much. It hadn't been a nightmare, but it hadn't been good. Especially when Jared had declared that he was leaving me to shack up with one of his twentysomething paralegals.

Wives weren't usually cast aside until they were middle-aged, right? I was still in my thirties. Hardly the frumpy and sadly underappreciated woman who'd given her best years to a man who decided to go through a midlife crisis and trade her in for a newer model. We hadn't even gotten that far.

Obviously, it was for the best. I wasn't sad about my marriage ending. I wasn't even angry—not anymore. I had been at first, but a few weeks into life on my own, I'd realized how inevitable—and necessary—the end of our relationship had been.

So there I stood, in the middle of a giant mess of boxes, half-sorted and half-packed stuff, on my last day in the house we'd shared. And I laughed. Hard.

I burst out in a fit of laughter that shook my shoulders and made my stomach cramp. Clutching my middle, I doubled over, gasping for breath. I probably looked ridiculous, but I didn't care. No one was watching. And I would have laughed just as much either way.

The heady sense of freedom almost made up for the fact that I had days' worth of work to do before the movers arrived and only a few hours in which to do it.

Pushing aside the temptation to just burn the whole house down and be done with it, I finished the last bite of my pickle, then gathered my long dark hair into a ponytail and cinched it with a hair tie.

I hadn't meant to procrastinate so much. I'd honestly thought I could sort and pack everything in plenty of time. It was possible time management wasn't my best skill. But hey, I was an actor. Weren't creative types supposed to get a pass when it came to organizational skills?

There was a knock on the door, and I shot a glare across the house, as if the door itself had insulted me. It couldn't be the movers already. I had three more hours. How dare they?

I went to answer it, ready to beg them for more time, but it wasn't the movers. It was my older brother, Nathan, and his wife, Sharla.

Although we were five years apart, Nathan and I were often mistaken for twins. We had the same brown eyes and olive skin that tanned in about five minutes, thanks to our Italian dad, but Nathan had a sprinkling of gray at his temples, where I was all dark brown, thank you very much.

Sharla was athletic, with a sporty blond pixie cut and a butterfly tattoo on her ankle that she openly regretted. She and Nathan were the type of weirdos who loved to run marathons. For fun.

They also lived a couple hours away in Tilikum, the small town in the Washington Cascade mountains where we'd grown up.

"What are you doing here?" I asked.

"You said you had to be out by today," he said with a casual shrug.

"And we figured you'd need help," Sharla added.

"You didn't have to come all this way." I stepped aside so they could come in. "I've got this."

Sharla craned her neck to look deeper inside at the chaos of boxes and stacks of stuff that still needed to be packed. "When do the movers arrive?"

"A few hours, but I'll be fine."

She put a hand on my arm. "You don't have to do everything alone."

"I know," I said, injecting a bit of affront to my voice.

Nathan raised his eyebrows at me.

"What?"

"You suck at asking for help." He walked past me straight into the house.

Following him to the kitchen, I rolled my eyes, but he wasn't wrong. I was terrible at asking for help.

Time for a change of subject. "Where are the kids?"

"With Mom and Dad." He picked up a pizza cutter sitting on the kitchen counter.

"That's Jared's."

He let it drop.

Nathan and Sharla had three kids, Lucia, Zola, and Nico. My nieces and nephew were a big part of why I'd decided to move back to Tilikum. The whole starting over thing was daunting, but at least I'd be there for birthday parties, school plays, and soccer games.

I'd missed too much already.

Sharla put her hands on her hips and looked around. "Where should we start? I take it everything isn't yours?"

"No, Jared's stuff is here, but I don't know what he's planning to do with it. He won't speak to me directly anymore."

"What?" Sharla's voice was incredulous. "What do you mean, he won't speak to you directly?"

"We have to go through our lawyers. As if I have money

to burn and want to pay my attorney a million dollars an hour to forward his attorney's emails."

"Why would he do that?"

"Because he's a dick," Nathan deadpanned.

"True." I paused and twirled a lock of hair from my pony-tail around my finger. "And it might have something to do with the fact that I called him a bloodsucking tick on the ass of humanity who wouldn't know integrity if it hit him in the face with a shovel."

"Good one," Sharla said.

"And also a festering boil." I started ticking off insults with my fingers. "A lying toad, a craven weakling, a stinking pile of dung, and a disgusting excuse for a man who's an embarrassment to his parents and men everywhere."

"You're not wrong," Nathan said.

I looked around, wishing I had another pickle—they're my comfort food, don't judge—not sure if even three people were enough to get things under control by the time the movers arrived. "Maybe we just burn it down, and I buy all new stuff. How about this? I cook bacon, get the grease good and hot. It catches fire, then I throw water on it and claim I didn't know how to put out a kitchen fire."

"Or we just pack what's important and leave the rest for the shithead," Nathan said.

Sharla patted her husband's arm. "I like this plan."

"Are you sure? I think there's some bacon in the fridge."

"We're not burning the house down," she said.

"Fine. The important stuff is my recording equipment. That's all packed." I worked as a voice actor, and since I had my own setup, I was able to work from home. It wasn't a bad gig, although jobs could be few and far between. "It's the rest of it that's the problem. His attorney sent over an inventory list. I'm supposed to stick to that."

Nathan picked up the printed-out list. "What a tool."

I waved it off. "I don't care about most of it. If he wants the pizza cutter and all the bar glasses, he can have them."

"What about the furniture?" Sharla asked. "Are you keeping the bedroom stuff? I feel like that would be weird."

"I slept on that bed alone more than with him, but no, I'm not taking it. He can get rid of it."

"Fair enough." She rubbed her hands together. "Let's get started."

Nathan's brow furrowed as he read over the inventory list. His eyes moved to a glass sitting out on the counter. "Bar glass?"

I nodded.

His face expressionless, he batted it like a cat, right into the extra-deep farmhouse sink. The sound of breaking glass tinkled.

It was music to my ears.

"Don't make a mess," Sharla said. "You're going to get her in trouble."

The corners of his mouth lifted in a slight grin.

"Come on." She grabbed his arm and tugged him out of the kitchen. "Let's pack some boxes."

We got to work, sorting through what Jared and I had accumulated over roughly a decade. The more we packed, the less I decided to keep. So little felt untainted by the ups and downs—mostly downs—of our relationship.

The movers arrived before we finished, but they were able to get started loading the truck while we madly sorted through books, kitchen items, and a closet we'd totally missed. Part of me wanted to take the curtains, bathroom mirrors, toilet paper holders, and light fixtures simply because they weren't on Jared's inventory list. But I opted out of that level of pettiness and settled on taking all the tools in the garage since Jared had neglected to divide them up.

His loss. And a girl never knew when she might need an electric drill with three sets of drill bits.

After the movers loaded everything, they shut the truck door with a bang. I stood on the front step, gazing at the moving truck with the contents of my life stuffed inside. Sharla sidled up next to me and put an arm around my waist.

"Are you okay?" she asked.

"Yeah. I really am. I mean, I'm broke and about to move back to my hometown to completely start my life over. But I'm okay."

"I think it's going to be great. The kids will love having you close. When does the truck drop off your stuff?"

"Tomorrow afternoon." I paused. "I just hope it's not weird living in Tilikum again. It's been so long, I hardly remember what small-town life is like. I haven't been back for more than a summer since I left high school."

"It's the same, but different. But the same."

Wordlessly, I nodded. I was going back to the beginning for a new beginning. There was something poetic about that. I certainly had plenty I was ready to leave behind, and not just my ill-fated marriage.

And most of my memories of Tilikum were good ones. Not all. But most. And the ones that weren't?

I'd just have to avoid them.

CHAPTER 3
Luke

UNCLE TIME WAS one of my favorite things. My sister, Annika, had asked me to come over and hang out with her kids for a while so she could get some work done. I was more than happy to help. I stood outside in her backyard, watching my nieces and nephews run through a sprinkler, their squeals of laughter filling the air.

I could think of worse ways to spend a hot summer afternoon.

Annika and her husband Levi Bailey were at the forefront of the Haven family baby explosion. They had four kids—eleven-year-old Thomas, seven-year-old twins Emma and Juliet, and four-year-old Will.

Thomas had a sperm donor out there somewhere, and if that shithead ever showed his face in our town, he'd be facing a wall of Haven—and Bailey—brothers, ready to rearrange his face. But Levi had stepped up as a dad to Thomas from the beginning—a lot like my parents had with each other's kids when they got married.

My dad, Paul Haven, had three boys—Josiah, Garrett, and me—and my mom, Marlene, had three—Reese, Theo, and Zachary. Then they had Annika together. If someone asked, I actually had to stop and think about who was biologically related to who. We'd all been a family for so long, no one even thought about it anymore.

Annika and Levi were like that—they were just a family. The fact that Levi wasn't Thomas's biological father didn't matter. Levi was his dad.

I admired that about them. Hell, I admired that about my parents. They'd taken a shitty situation and turned us into a family. Granted, we'd driven them crazy—six little boys so close in age would do that. But we were probably a lot less screwed up than we could have been.

Okay, so I was kind of screwed up. But it could have been worse. At least I wasn't Reese. Our oldest brother had bailed, taking off for who knows where, and no one except Mom had heard from him in years.

Jerk.

"Careful, Juliet," Thomas said as his sister did a cartwheel through the spray of water.

"I am being careful."

I just smiled. Thomas was the mini-dad of their family, always looking out for his younger siblings. I doubted they appreciated it, but I thought it was pretty cool.

"Who wants a popsicle?" Annika called as she opened the sliding glass door.

My hand shot into the air.

She rolled her eyes at me. "Okay, Uncle Luke, but we'll go in reverse age order."

"Me! Me! Me!" Will chanted, jumping up and down in his bright red swim trunks.

Annika handed him a popsicle, and he immediately tore open the wrapper and bit the entire top off. The other kids took theirs in turn, and she held up the last two. "These might both be orange, or maybe one is red."

I grabbed the one in her left hand. "Either one is fine. Thanks, Sis."

She unwrapped hers. Red. "No problem. Thank you so much for coming over. I actually got some work done."

"Happy to." I set my wrapper on the patio table and had a taste of mine. Orange. Not bad. "They're pretty much entertaining themselves out here anyway."

"Nothing like a sprinkler on a hot day." She tilted her head as she ate her popsicle. "Imagine what it will be like when the babies are all running around in a few years."

"Chaos," I said with a soft laugh. "Beautiful chaos."

The babies referred to the second round of the Haven family baby explosion. Back in March, Garrett and Harper welcomed their surprise baby girl, Isla, making Garrett's teenage son Owen a big brother. Only a couple of months later, Zachary and Marigold had their first baby, a little girl named Emily. And rounding out the baby-splosion was Josiah and Audrey's baby girl, Abby, born just a few weeks after Emily.

I figured that was just what happened when three of your brothers got married in the same year.

It looked like the weddings-and-babies phase had died down, and everyone seemed to be enjoying a relatively uneventful summer. I didn't want to say it was too uneventful, considering the alternative in my family seemed to be the opposite. Between Audrey's stalker, Marigold's abduction, and Garrett's cold case turning deadly, we'd been through a lot in the past couple of years.

I certainly wasn't going to wish for another bad guy to mess up our lives, but I still felt restless, even after racing the other night.

We hung out for a few more minutes while the kids finished their popsicles, then Annika ushered them inside to clean up and dry off. I went in after them, and she put me to work chopping tomatoes and cucumbers while she helped the kids get dressed and set them up in the living room with a show.

"Thanks again," she said when she came back in the kitchen. "I probably should have invited you to stay for dinner before I gave you a job."

"No worries. Levi must be on duty?" Her husband was a firefighter with the Tilikum Fire Department.

She nodded. "Until tomorrow morning."

The sound of the TV carried in from the other room, and a female voice caught my attention. It was sultry, almost raspy, but feminine. My heart rate picked up, and I felt a hint of adrenaline. Not the high of a race, but a familiar buzz flowed through my body.

That was weird.

"What are they watching?"

"It's a cartoon called *Enchanted Hollow*. They're obsessed. I thought the girls were past their watch-the-same-thing-eight-hundred-times-in-a-row phase, but apparently not."

The voice came again. I couldn't quite make out what she was saying, but the laugh made it clear she was the villain. I found myself cracking a smile.

Annika was busy prepping the rest of the meal, so I didn't resist the strange magnetism of the voice. I wandered into the living room where Juliet and Emma sat on the couch with Will wedged between them. Thomas sat in an armchair.

"What are you watching?" I asked, nodding toward the TV.

Juliet's eyes were glued to the screen. She didn't even blink. Will was similarly mesmerized.

Emma tore her gaze away. "*Enchanted Hollow*."

"Yeah? Is it good?"

She smiled. "It's my favorite. There's princesses, and they're twins like me and Juliet."

"And the bad lady," Will said, pointing at the screen.

I glanced at the TV. The bad lady, as Will called her, was the character with the voice that had caught my attention. She was drawn with an otherworldly but severe beauty, full of contrast. Dark hair that was long and flowing, alongside sharp cheekbones and a prominent jawline. Big blue eyes, dark red lips, and she wore a black gown that seemed to float around her.

"Soon, they'll see their mistake," she said. Her mesmerizing voice wrapped around me like smoke. "They'll pay for their disrespect."

"She's so scary," Juliet whispered.

Emma's eyes were wide as she nodded in agreement.

The character gestured with her hands, casting a spell, and mist swirled around her until she disappeared.

It was oddly disappointing.

I glanced at Thomas. "You like the show too, or do you just put up with it?"

"No, it's good. Queen Ione turns into a dragon in one of the episodes. It's cool."

"Shh," Emma said, putting a finger to her lips. "Don't tell. Uncle Luke hasn't seen it before."

"That's okay, kiddo," I said. "I don't mind spoilers."

Suddenly, Thomas jumped up from his seat. "I almost forgot! Wait here."

I sat down next to Juliet while Thomas hurried down the hall to his room. A moment later, he came out with his hands behind his back.

"We got you something," he said. "It was supposed to be for Christmas last year, but Will was playing with them and lost them."

"I did not," Will protested.

Thomas raised his eyebrows at him.

Will grinned. "Oh yeah, I did. Sorry."

"Anyway," Thomas said with a slight roll of his eyes, "I found it the other day. Here."

He handed me a small blue pouch that cinched with a drawstring. I opened it and emptied the contents into my hand. There was a little toy sports car—cherry-red—a pocket-sized flashlight, and a small plastic compass.

I held up the car. "Do you know what this is?"

"A cool sports car."

"It's a very cool sports car. This is a Lamborghini Essenza SCV12. They only make them for racing."

"Have you driven one?"

"Afraid not. Those bad boys cost over two million dollars."

His smile faded, and a look of seriousness passed over his features. "This didn't cost that much."

I laughed as I put everything in the bag and cinched it closed. "Of course not. This is awesome, buddy. Thank you."

"There was another car in there. A black one. But, Will." He rolled his eyes again. "If I find it, I'll give it to you."

"I didn't know it was Uncle Luke's," Will protested.

"It's all good, buddy," I said. "I have my Lambo."

I set the bag near the door so I wouldn't forget it when I left, then went back to the kitchen to help Annika finish dinner while the kids watched their show. The evil queen came on again. It was the strangest thing, but hearing it gave me another burst of adrenaline. What was it about that voice?

Was it weird to have a crush on a cartoon character?

My curiosity was soon forgotten as we all sat down for dinner—oven-baked chicken and salad. I stayed long enough to help clean up, then spent the next twenty minutes saying goodbye and giving Emma and Juliet each "just one more" hug.

Before I pulled away from the house, I put the bag with Thomas's gift in the glove box of the blue 1970 Chevelle I'd restored the year before. A mild sense of restlessness made me antsy. It was still early, and I thought about going to the Timberbeast Tavern for a drink, but that didn't sound appealing.

Maybe I'd just go for a drive. It was a nice evening. A haze of smoke from wildfires deeper in the mountains had lingered for the past several weeks, but it had cleared up after a hard rain the other day, leaving the sky clear and blue.

After leaving my sister's neighborhood, I headed through town. Summer was tourist season, and the side-walks were alive with activity—families, visitors, kids skate-boarding. I passed Lumberjack Park, where evening picnickers sat on blankets, and someone threw a ball for their dog.

I kept going, passing the turn that would have taken me to my house, and headed toward the highway. As I came around a bend, a car drove right out in front of me.

Adrenaline surged through me, and my instincts kicked in as I hit the brakes. I swerved enough to miss the other car without losing control and winding up in the ditch.

Whoever was driving the second car overcorrected, tires squealing on the asphalt. I caught a quick glimpse of a woman with a dark ponytail as she spun and wound up facing the other direction.

Instead of driving off, I pulled over. I wasn't mad. Not really. I wasn't about to admit—not even to myself—how much I liked the surge of adrenaline. How much more alive I felt after that near miss. And even though she'd obviously pulled out in front of me without looking, she hadn't hit me. But she'd stopped in the middle of the road and hadn't moved. I just wanted to make sure she was all right.

My car faced her passenger side. I got out and hesitated. Was she going to get out? Drive away?

Her door opened, and she got out, hurrying around the front of her car.

And giving me another hit of adrenaline, potent and intoxicating. My eyes widened, my heart thumped hard in my chest, and it almost felt like someone had kicked the air out of my lungs.

Melanie Andolini.

"Oh my gosh, I'm so sorry." She stopped dead in her tracks, right in the middle of the road. "Luke?"

I couldn't keep the shock out of my voice. "Melanie?"

We stared at each other for a second or two. Although I saw her family around—small-town life—I hadn't seen her in years. Especially this close.

The fact that she was still the most beautiful woman I'd ever known could have swept through me like a late summer breeze, stirring pleasant nostalgia. Even latent attraction.

Maybe if she had been anyone else, it would have.

But she was Melanie Andolini, my high school girlfriend and first love. And if there was anything she was good at, it was pissing me off. Even after all those years.

"What the hell?" I snapped. "You almost ran into me."

Her expression shifted from surprise to defiance. "What? No. *You* almost hit *me*."

"Mel, you pulled out in front of me without looking."

"How do you know where I was looking?"

"Obviously not where you were going. Otherwise, you wouldn't have pulled out like that."

"You came out of nowhere." She gestured emphatically to the road. "How fast were you going?"

I ran my tongue over my teeth. Probably too fast, but that wasn't the point. "I wasn't going light speed. If you'd have looked, you would have seen me."

"I did look. You were speeding."

The truth was, we were probably both in the wrong. And no harm had been done. I could have pointed that out. De-escalated the situation and had us both going calmly on our way.

But I didn't.

"If we'd been in an accident, you'd be getting the ticket," I said, not bothering to keep the smugness out of my tone. Because I was right, damn it.

"Well, we didn't get in an accident, did we?"

"Because I prevented it."

"Aren't you the big hero." Her voice dripped with sarcasm.

It figured that the first time we saw each other in forever, we'd start fighting. "You haven't changed at all, have you? Still a pain in my ass."

Her eyebrows lifted, and she planted her hands on her hips. "Oh yes, I'm definitely the unreasonable one."

"I didn't say you were unreasonable. I said you were a pain."

"What's the difference?"

Tension rippled through my shoulders and back. She was so aggravating.

My eyes flicked to her mouth, and I was suddenly filled with the memory of what those lips tasted like.

Fuck.

Anger surged through me like a hot wave. I opened my mouth to go off on her, but a car pulled up on the other side of hers and stopped.

"You're blocking the road," I snapped.

"Thanks, I couldn't see that." She spun around, whipping her ponytail, and stomped back to her car.

So dramatic.

I stepped back so I wasn't on the road while she got in her car and backed up enough that the other guy could get around her. I gave him an apologetic wave, and he nodded as he drove by.

Melanie backed up a little farther, then seemed to change her mind about which direction she wanted to go. She cranked the steering wheel in one direction, pulled forward a couple of feet, then hit the brakes.

Her scowl of frustration as she tried to correct made me chuckle. Served her right.

For what, I didn't know, but that wasn't the point. She just pissed me off.

Crossing my arms, I watched her go. She shot me a glare as she passed, as if the whole thing was my fault.

"Great to see you again, Mel," I called out.

She flipped me off through the window.

That made me laugh. Fucking Melanie.

Her car was out of sight, but the heady buzz of adrenaline hadn't abated. I still felt the tingle in my limbs, and my heart thumped in my chest. I wasn't sure what that was about. A close call on a side street wasn't a big deal.

Seeing her wasn't a big deal either. She was probably in town visiting. Last I'd heard, she lived in Seattle and was married to some lawyer guy.

She'd go back to her life, and I'd go back to mine. I wouldn't think about her again.

And when I got in my car, I actually believed that was true.

CHAPTER 4
Melanie

OF ALL THE people who could have almost hit me—fine, I'd almost hit him—it had to have been Luke Haven.

Seriously, universe? There were like eight hundred Havens in Tilikum. Why did I have to pull out in front of that one?

A fiery mix of emotions swirled through me as I drove away. Why did he have to be so aggravating? I hadn't seen him in years. You'd think we could have handled a chance encounter like adults instead of immediately launching into an argument. But he made me so mad.

Flipping him off had been satisfying, though.

I shook out my hands and rolled my shoulders, hoping to release some of the tension. Seeing Luke Haven—even almost crashing into Luke Haven—should not have made me feel anything, let alone the overwhelming combination of frustrated, flustered, and, dare I say it, aroused.

But could anyone blame me? He'd always been a masterpiece of masculinity. Thick hair, strong stubbly jaw, broad shoulders, and those hands. They were probably still rough and calloused. He'd always been full of contradictions—easygoing but opinionated, calm but stubborn, rough around the edges with a soft heart.

"What have you done to me, Luke Haven?" I said, slipping into my Queen Ione voice. I fully admit that one of my weirdest habits was talking to myself as characters I've voice acted. "Your presence is a thorn in my foot. One that I will pluck out and cast aside."

A thorn in my foot. The made-up line made me laugh a little. It sounded like something Queen Ione would say. The writers had created her to be a quintessential evil queen—powerful and haughty, jealous and angry. She was fun to portray.

Luckily for me—and everyone else involved—*Enchanted Hollow* had been renewed. At first, it had flopped. Ratings and reviews were great, but that didn't matter if no one was watching. Somewhere along the way, about two years after the show originally aired, it took off. Kids started watching, and so did parents.

I'd since been contracted to reprise my role as Queen Ione in seasons two, three, and four. It was amazing news and almost in the nick of time. But not quite. Things were moving slowly, and I wasn't set to start recording for another couple of months. Which meant I wasn't getting paid for another couple of months. And that was if there weren't any delays.

There were always delays.

The bank account situation was a much bigger issue than almost crashing into Luke Haven, no matter how jittery or frustrated or whatever it was he'd made me feel. Granted, the encounter had been inevitable. Tilikum was too small for me to avoid him forever.

Besides, he was just my high school ex-boyfriend. That wasn't a big deal. It had been so long, I hardly remembered anything about our relationship.

Okay, fine, that was a lie. There was plenty I still remembered.

But I wasn't going there.

What I really needed had nothing to do with Luke. I needed a temporary job. I'd signed the contract for *Enchanted Hollow*, and it included a noncompete. That meant I couldn't take on any other voice acting jobs until I'd finished recording for them. Studios didn't always do that, but in this case, it would be worth it—once I finally started getting paid. After all the lawyer fees and moving expenses, things were looking bleak.

I slowed and took a right, heading to my parents' restaurant. Eight or nine years ago, they'd become the proud owners of Home Slice Pizza. They'd bought it from Freddie Haven, one of Luke's uncles, and called it their preretirement project.

Yes, the part-Italian family owned a small-town pizza place. It was so cliché, it was adorable.

A squirrel ran out in front of me, and I slammed on the brakes to avoid squishing it. It darted across the road, oblivious to its brush with death.

"Vile creature," I said, using my Queen Ione voice again. "You're lucky I didn't crush you into oblivion."

The squirrel disappeared into the brush on the other side of the street, so I kept going. At least I hadn't hit it. No Luke necessary to prevent that little incident, thank you very much. My reflexes were just fine.

That thought made me roll my eyes. "Get out of my head, Luke."

Home Slice Pizza was downtown, in a quaint building with a pitched green roof and a big sign above the front door with the Home Slice logo. It was a little faded, but they'd kept the original, well-loved logo when they bought it. I parked outside and went in.

The aromas of oregano, tomato sauce, and browned cheese greeted me. A small lobby area at the front had a few chairs and a counter for customers to place and pick up to-go orders. A swinging door behind the counter led to the kitchen, and tables with white paper tablecloths that kids could color on took up the rest of the space. A short hallway at the back was lined with old arcade games and led to a banquet room that could be reserved for parties.

"I'll be right out," my mom called from the kitchen.

"Just me," I called back.

A man came in, dressed in a bright orange shirt and jeans. I stepped aside and gestured for him to go ahead. He was probably there to pick up an order, and I hated having people stand behind me.

My mom came out dressed in a black blouse and slacks. I loved that she dressed like her restaurant was a fine dining establishment and not a small-town pizza joint. It was so her. If her shoulder-length brown hair had even a single strand of gray, it was a secret known only to her hairdresser, and her magenta lipstick was as bold as her personality.

"Can I help you?" she asked the man. Her eyes flicked to me, and she winked.

I waited while she retrieved his to-go order, a stack of four pizzas plus breadsticks and dipping sauce. As he was leaving, I held the door for him. He said a muffled thank you from behind his stack of pizza.

Letting the door shut behind him, I went back to the counter.

"How's everything?" Mom asked. "Getting settled?"

"Yes and no. I have a place to sleep and a semi-functional kitchen. It's a start."

"A good start. Have I told you lately that I'm proud of you?" She reached across the counter and booped my nose.

"Thanks, Mom."

"Where's your father?" She turned toward the kitchen and raised her voice. "Anton! What are you doing back there? Melanie is here!"

Dad's muffled reply came a second later. "In a minute."

"It's fine. He can take his time."

Tristan, one of their teenage employees, came out from the kitchen carrying several large pizza boxes. He slid them into the warmer.

"Anton!" she called again in a robust but semi-singsong voice.

Tristan didn't seem fazed. He just clipped the order receipt into the top of the warmer and went back to the kitchen.

"Mom, I'm early. Let him finish what he's doing."

"An—"

He interrupted her by stepping through the swinging door. "Krista."

"There you are. What have you been doing back there?"

"Pizza." His voice was soft, without a hint of irritation at my mom's impatience. "We have orders to fill."

"I know, I know." She waved her hand. "Although it's shaping up to be a slow night. Maybe that's a good thing. Melanie's here. Nathan and Sharla and the kids should be here any minute."

Italians had a reputation for being loud, but it was my Polish-German mother who talked with her hands and didn't have an inside voice. She was a force of nature. My Italian father, on the other hand, was calm and reserved—probably why they were so good together.

"Hi, Dad."

He smiled, his brown eyes crinkling at the corners. Although he was average height, he towered over my less-than-average-height mom, and his dark hair was peppered with gray.

"Are you going to have time to eat with us?" she asked him. "I was hoping we could all sit down together. Tristan can help, can't he? I keep saying we need to hire another pizza maker. You work too hard."

"It's pizza, not brain surgery," Dad said. "Of course he can help. I've been showing him everything."

"Good." Mom clapped her hands together with a bright smile. She seemed to be about to say something else, but another customer came in to pick up their order.

Dad took the opportunity to slip back into the kitchen while Mom wasn't looking. I pressed my lips together in a smile. Mom talked a lot, but Dad always did exactly what he wanted, when he wanted.

"Do you need any help back there?" I asked once the customer had gone. "Not that I know where anything is."

She waved her hand again as if batting my offer out of the air. "No, no, we're fine. Like I said, it's shaping up to be a slow night. Some days are like that. If it was a Friday, we'd have a line out the door."

"But business is going well?"

"It is." Her voice was emphatic. "This is a pizza-loving town, and thank goodness for that. How about you go push some tables together before your brother gets here."

"That, I can do."

I chose two tables near the front counter in case either of my parents needed to jump up and take care of customers while we ate. After moving the chairs, I went behind the counter to grab cups of crayons for my nieces and nephew. They loved to draw on the paper tablecloths while they waited for their dinner.

Despite my need for a job, working for my parents at Home Slice was so not an option. Mom had offered when I'd first told her I was moving back to Tilikum, but I'd politely refused. And even she seemed to realize that wouldn't have been good for our relationship. We got along just fine, but we both had strong personalities, so working together would probably push us both past our breaking point.

I'd just set the crayon cups on the table when the feeling of someone coming up behind me made me jump, and I knocked one over, spilling crayons all over the floor.

"What's the matter?" Mom asked.

"You startled me." I crouched to pick up the crayons.

"Honey, I'm sorry. I thought you heard me coming. What's wrong? Why are you so jumpy?"

"Have you met me?" I put the crayons back on the table. "I'm always jumpy. It's nothing."

"Ah!" She pointed at me. "It's nothing means it's something. Come on, talk to your mama. Is it, you know?"

"No, it's not that. That's over. I don't want to talk about it."

"All right, all right. Then what is it?"

I rolled my eyes. "It really is nothing. I just ran into Luke Haven. Almost. I didn't hit him. Just came close."

"Didn't hit him with a fist?" She clenched her hand, as if to demonstrate. "Or are you talking about with your car?"

"Both, I guess, although I wasn't close enough to punch him."

"Well, that's something. Luke's a nice man. You shouldn't punch him."

That made me roll my eyes again, although I didn't try to argue with her. "Anyway, I made a left turn, and he was right there."

"How fast was he driving?"

"Exactly!" I threw my arms up. "See, everyone knows he drives too fast. And then he blamed it on me. I mean, sure, I did pull out right in front of him, but if he hadn't been going so fast, I wouldn't have almost hit him."

"How is Luke, anyway? I haven't seen him in a while."

I blinked at her. "I don't know. He was yelling at me on the side of the road, not telling me his life story."

"Did you yell back?"

"Yeah. And I flipped him off when I drove away."

She laughed softly. "Oh, honey."

"What? He deserved it."

"I'm sure he did."

I couldn't tell if she meant that or was just humoring me. She'd always liked Luke, even after we'd broken up, and she and my dad were still friendly with his parents. I didn't mind —it was all ancient history anyway.

The door opened again, and a whirlwind of children tumbled inside, followed by Nathan and Sharla.

My nieces and nephew were a fascinating study in genetics. Ten-year-old Lucia had dark hair, blue eyes, and tanned skin from a summer spent outside. Eight-year-old Zola was platinum blond with ice-blue eyes and skin that burned in about five minutes of sun exposure. Nico, the baby of the family at six, was a carbon copy of his dad, with brown eyes, dark hair, and an olive skin tone.

Same two parents, three different looks. Although their features—eye shape, noses, and facial structure—made it obvious they were siblings.

"My sweet darlings!" Mom scooped them each in a hug and kissed the tops of their heads. "How are you? Ready for pizza?"

"Yeah!" they answered in unison.

As the kids took their seats at the table and started coloring, I helped my mom bring drinks, plates, and napkins. Dad brought out the pizza to applause from everyone, and it suddenly hit me that I was home.

So much of what I'd been missing all the years I was married wasn't just a good relationship—although that was a big part of it. Jared hadn't liked Tilikum and hadn't particularly liked my family, so we'd rarely visited. I'd missed years of pizza nights because I'd married the wrong man.

I wasn't going to blame him. Okay, yes, I was. It was totally his fault, the jerk. But it wasn't like he'd held me captive. I'd been too wrapped up in my own life—my own stuff—to make time for my family.

That was over. I was home.

And Luke Haven? He and I would just have to get used to living in the same town. We were both adults, and our breakup had been ages ago.

How hard could it be?

CHAPTER 5

Luke

I WAS NOT in a good mood.

I'd started my day working on my latest restoration project—a 1955 Ford Thunderbird—but nothing was going according to plan.

Andrea, my receptionist, was out on maternity leave. Great for her, but not so great for me. I'd hired a woman named Stephanie as a temporary replacement, but she hadn't shown up for work. Again. That meant I kept having to stop to deal with customers, and now I was missing a part I needed and couldn't find a copy of the order form.

The noise of power tools drifted from the garage into the lobby as I shuffled through stacks of paperwork on the cluttered front desk. The lobby was small, just the tall wooden desk and a couple of chairs next to the front door. The walls were decorated with photos of cars we'd rebuilt and restored —some of the highlights of our work. We'd done everything from muscle cars like the '69 Charger to an old Ford Model T. One of my personal favorites was the cherry-red 1952 Corvette. Such a hot car.

Behind the desk were old black-and-white racing photos,

most from the early 1900s. I'd inherited them when I'd taken over Haven Auto Restoration from my great-uncle in my early twenties. Since then, I'd grown the business from a one-mechanic shop to an award-winning restoration garage.

Over the years, I learned that there was a lot more to being a business owner than knowing your way around an engine. And some days, when all I wanted to do was get my hands greasy, a million other problems seemed to come out of the woodwork.

Like what had happened to that order.

And where the hell was Stephanie?

With a frustrated groan, I dropped into the chair and pinched the bridge of my nose against the headache threatening to split open my skull. That was why I was so grouchy. Work stuff, and my head hurt. It had absolutely nothing to do with unexpectedly seeing my ex-girlfriend the other day.

Why? Why did she keep popping into my head like that? So she'd almost hit my car. I'd avoided the collision. There was nothing else to think about. I didn't need to keep wondering why she was in town. Her family lived in Tilikum, that was explanation enough. I didn't need to keep thinking about her.

Or her mouth and the curve of her hips.

What I needed to do was figure out why Stephanie wasn't at work.

I found Stephanie's number and called. It rang a few times, and I thought I was about to get her voicemail when she answered.

"Hello?"

"Hey, Stephanie, it's Luke."

"Hi, Luke." Her tone was cheerful.

That was odd. Did she not realize she was supposed to be at work?

"So, are you coming in today, or…"

"Oh, about that. I'm not."

"Why not?"

"I don't want to."

I hesitated, not sure how to respond to that. "You don't want to?"

"My best friend from high school just got back into town. We're getting mani-pedis and then probably going shopping."

"But you're supposed to be here."

"You can't expect me to blow off my friend. She's my bestie."

I shook my head in frustration. "I can expect you not to blow off work."

"That reminds me. I won't be able to come in tomorrow either."

"I think maybe there was a miscommunication. I hired you to come in regularly, not just when you feel like it."

"Seriously?"

"Yeah. That's how jobs work."

"Well, that's definitely not going to work for me. I have too much going on."

"Okay, if you have too much going on to come in to work, I'll have to find someone else."

"So should I come in next week?"

I blinked a couple times before answering. "No."

"Really? Oh well. I guess it wasn't meant to be."

"I... guess not."

I didn't bother saying goodbye. Just ended the call.

Pinching the bridge of my nose again, I let out a frustrated breath. When I'd interviewed Stephanie, she'd given me the impression that she might be a little flighty, but I'd hoped she just needed a chance. Bad call on my part.

The door opened, and I looked up to find my older brother Garrett in his sheriff's deputy uniform and a pair of slightly cliché, but admittedly very cool, aviators. He swiped the sunglasses off his face as the door shut behind him.

"Hey, bro," I greeted him. "What's up?"

"Just out following up on a few things."

"Not another murder case, I hope."

"No, nothing like that."

Last year, some crazy shit had gone down with Garrett's investigation of a cold case murder. He'd almost gotten himself killed. I'd been there—saw the whole thing in real time. I'd always respected my brother, but after watching him go through hell to save his wife, Harper, and his son Owen, I was in awe of him.

He was a freaking badass.

"I'd say let's grab some lunch, but I'm buried," I said. "Andrea is on maternity leave, and her replacement fell through."

"That's okay. I actually stopped by to ask you about something."

I glanced up.

He had his cop face on. Serious, stoic, responsible. "Is something wrong, Deputy?"

"Do you know anything about the underground racing that's been going on down at the old Cascade Speedway?"

Shit. "Why?"

"You know, rumors. Things get around."

"Come on, you know better than to trust the gossip line. People say all kinds of wild stuff in this town."

"I know."

"Most of it's bullshit."

"Yeah."

"Then what are you worried about?"

"You."

I leaned back in the chair. "You don't need to worry about me."

"Or the roll cage in your Mustang?"

I grinned a little. "Safety first."

Garrett glowered at me. Apparently, he didn't find that amusing. "I thought you quit that scene a long time ago."

"I did." That wasn't a lie. I had quit. I just hoped I could leave out the part where I'd started up again.

"Look, forget the uniform for a second. Officially, I'm not here talking to you about this. But unofficially…"

"Unofficially, what?"

"Someone saw you and let me know. Not to rat you out. They figured I'd want to know first so I could keep you out of trouble."

"Not to rat me out, my ass. Who was it?"

"Doesn't matter."

I glanced away. "It's not a big deal."

"You sure about that?"

Out of all my brothers, Garrett was the last one I wanted to know I'd gone back to racing. He was a cop. But he was also the last one I'd ever lie to. Especially after everything we'd been through. He'd trusted me when it mattered. That meant a lot.

"Okay, truth. Yeah, I race sometimes. But it's just to blow off steam. No street racing, only on a track. And hell, it's not even in your jurisdiction."

"Blowing off steam is fine, but when you're risking your life on a closed track in an illegal and unregulated race, that's a problem. Don't even get me started on the rest of it."

"Rest of what?"

"The illegal gambling. That could be a felony."

"I don't do it for the money."

"But you take the money."

Groaning, I ground my teeth together. "I'll donate it or something."

I don't know why that made him laugh, but it did. "You're killing me. Couldn't you find a hobby that's not likely to get you killed? Or arrested?"

"Which one worries you more?" One corner of my mouth lifted. "Be honest."

"I've arrested Zachary. Don't think I won't arrest you."

He was half joking about arresting me, but only half. And he had arrested our brother Zachary. Probably more than once.

I was too old not to know he was right. Of course he was. Twenty-year-old me might have gotten a pass for being young and idiotic, but I was in my thirties. Illegal racing was stupid and dangerous, and I knew it.

But it was also addictive.

"I don't want to lie to you," I said.

"Then don't."

"You're right. It's stupid. I should find a better hobby. And if I tell you I won't do it again, I'll mean it right now."

"But?"

"But I don't know if I can promise to never do it again."

"Have you tried skydiving?"

"Dude. I'm not jumping out of a perfectly good airplane."

Shaking his head, he chuckled. "Killing me. You should have gone into law enforcement. Plenty of excitement there."

"I don't think I could do your job."

"Fair enough. Just… be careful. I don't want to see you get hurt."

I nodded. "Thanks."

He turned to leave but paused at the door and looked over his shoulder. "You know what you really need?"

"Other than someone to fill in for Andrea?"

"Yeah."

"What?"

He smirked at me. "A good woman."

I wadded up a piece of paper and tossed it at him.

He just grinned and walked out the door.

A good woman. That was even less likely than me quitting

racing for good. I was pretty sure I was cursed when it came to women.

Dramatic? Maybe. But true. My track record spoke for itself.

Besides, he was wrong. I didn't need a woman in my life.

So why was I suddenly picturing Melanie Andolini? She was like a song I couldn't get out of my head, the lyrics running through my mind in an endless loop.

If I did need a good woman in my life, it was *not* her. I was a pretty easygoing guy. Usually got along with everyone. But Melanie? Not so much. Our relationship had had more ups and downs than a roller coaster. Granted, we'd been young. I'd mellowed out since my teens, so maybe she had too.

Actually, I doubted it. Mellow wasn't in her vocabulary.

It didn't matter, anyway. We'd run into each other. So what? Tilikum was a small town, and her family still lived here. It had to happen occasionally.

Although it was odd that it had been so long. Her family *did* live in Tilikum, and it *was* a small town. Why had it been so long since I'd seen her? Where had she been? What was going on in her life?

I shook my head to clear it. None of my business. I didn't need to know.

What I needed was a temporary employee. That was my current problem, not my high school ex-girlfriend.

I figured I'd call my sister, Annika. She worked for me before our brother Josiah stole her away. Maybe she had time to help me out for a few months.

And maybe she knew why Melanie was in town. They'd been friends back in the day. Did they keep in touch?

I groaned. How was Mel still so frustrating? She wasn't even around. But there she was, invading every freaking thought in my head.

I pulled out my phone and called Annika.

"Hey, Luke."

"Hi. Listen, I'm in a bind at the garage. Andrea went on maternity leave, and the gal I hired to fill in flaked out on me."

"That's frustrating."

"Yeah. I know you're busy already, but could you find a way to come in for a few hours a day? Just temporarily."

"I would love to help, but I can't. I'm sorry, I just don't have time."

"Come on, it's not like you have kids and a job and everything." My voice was tinged with humor. "You can't be that busy."

She laughed. "Nope, not at all. Speaking of, hang on." Her voice got quieter, as if she'd moved the phone away. "Will, stop right there. Don't come in the house yet."

"Is he okay?"

"He's covered in mud." Her tone was matter-of-fact, as if that were an everyday occurrence. "I need to go hose him down."

"Fair enough. Before you go, do you know anyone who's looking for a part-time gig? Ideally someone who might actually show up to work?"

"Not off the top of my head, but if I think of anyone, I'll let you know."

"Thanks."

"I have to go take care of my little mud monster. Oh good, the girls are covered too."

"You're an awesome mom."

She laughed again. "Thanks. I just know when to pick my battles. Kids get dirty. It's fine. I'll talk to you later."

"Bye."

I ended the call and put my phone down. Well, that sucked. Annika would have been the perfect solution. Not that I blamed her for saying no. She had her hands full.

Who else did I know who might be available? I had a great crew, but their skills were out in the garage. I was pretty sure Ollie was allergic to paperwork, and although Patrick was a genius with bodywork, he had the personality of sandpaper. Not the kind of guy to fill in at the front desk, even for only a few hours a day.

I'd just have to do my best to keep up with everything. And maybe being slammed at work was exactly what I needed to shake off the effect of seeing Melanie again.

CHAPTER 6

Melanie

CLASSIC ROCK SPILLED out into the night as I opened the door of the Timberbeast Tavern. My lips curled in a smile. Some things never changed, and the Timberbeast appeared to be one of them.

I stepped inside and back in time—to college summers spent in my hometown, finally old enough to enter the coveted hangout—when a night in a tavern with sticky floors, ice-cold beer, and a bunch of burly men in flannel had been the best sort of evening.

My smile fell at the memory of Luke, chatting up some cute out-of-towner at the bar. Or maybe even a Tilikum girl—someone we both knew. I'd have pretended not to notice, except to shoot him the occasional glare just for being in the same place as me.

How dare he?

Small-town breakups were complicated.

Fortunately, I was past all that.

I was about to take a seat at the bar when a familiar face caught my eye. Theo Haven sat alone at a small, round table strewn with papers and a clipboard. His hair was slightly shaggy, like he was overdue for a haircut, and he wore a dark T-shirt.

He took a drink of his beer without looking up from whatever he was doing. I remembered him as the jock of the family, always playing sports or watching them. Technically, he was Luke's stepbrother, although no one ever made that distinction—least of all them.

And I couldn't explain how or why, but all the Haven brothers looked alike, as if their family culture was more powerful than their genes.

Bypassing the bar, I went over to his table to say hello. "Hi there, stranger."

His eyes widened slightly as he glanced up. "Well, holy shit. Melanie Andolini."

"The one and only."

"I heard you were back in town."

"Did you?"

He lifted his shoulders in a casual shrug. "Gossip line. You know how it is."

I'd barely known my neighbors' names in Seattle, let alone anything about their personal lives. Everyone knowing my business—whether or not it was any of theirs—would take some getting used to.

"Of course. Tilikum at its finest." I touched the empty chair. "Mind if I sit?"

His eyes flicked around the bar for a second. "Sure."

"I won't if you're meeting someone. Do you have a date?"

He barked out a laugh. "No."

I sat and hung my purse on the back of the chair. "Why is that funny?"

"I don't date."

"Ever?"

"No."

I nodded, mildly impressed. "Good for you."

He raised his eyebrows. "Really? Usually, people try to tell me I'm wrong."

"I mean it. I assume you have your reasons. I don't date either, and I have reasons of my own. Although, I'll be shocked if my mother doesn't play matchmaker sooner rather than later. And knowing her, she'll manage to talk me into it. But enough about me. How are you?" I pointed at the papers in front of him. "Working?"

"Football camp is coming up soon. There's a lot of planning."

"That's right. You're a coach, aren't you?"

The corners of his mouth lifted. "Yeah. It's a great gig. I teach, too."

"High schoolers? That's brave. What do you teach?"

"Math and science."

"Ew, math," I said with a slight smile. "Didn't you play pro football for a while?"

"Until I got injured."

I winced. "Sorry. Any other painful subjects I could bring up while I'm busy making things awkward?"

The subtle grin didn't leave his face. "No, I think my career-ending injury is about it."

"Oh! We could talk about my frustrating divorce. Would that even things out?"

"Don't worry about it. We're good."

Theo's eyes moved to something—or someone—behind me, and I caught the subtle scent of cologne mixed with a hint of rubber. I had a feeling I knew exactly who it was. A tingle swept across my skin, and my stomach fluttered, but I couldn't tell if it was from excitement or loathing.

"That's my seat." Luke's voice was flat as he moved to stand next to the table.

I lifted my gaze, batting my eyelashes, and when I spoke, I dropped into an exaggerated Southern accent. "And what a gentleman you are for lettin' me keep it."

"That's not cute."

"I daresay I disagree," I said, keeping the accent and putting a hand to my chest. "I'm cute as a button and sweet as strawberry rhubarb pie."

"And also delusional." His tone was controlled, but I knew him. I could hear the undercurrent of ire.

"What? I'm a delight."

"Can you just use your normal voice? The world isn't your stage."

I almost kept the Southern belle act going just to push his buttons, but I let it go and returned to my natural voice. "My friend Shakespeare would disagree."

"All the world's a stage, and all the men and women merely players," Theo recited.

Luke and I both turned to look at him.

"What?" he asked.

My gaze swung back to Luke's. Eye contact with him was disconcerting, but I wasn't about to let that show.

"Why are you even here?" he asked.

"It's a bar. I came in to get a drink."

"They're out. You can go now."

"Out of drinks?"

He nodded once.

"I doubt Rocco ran out of alcohol." Did Rocco still own the place? I glanced at the bar, and, sure enough, there he was, the burly lumberjack bartender himself.

"That's not a thing, dude," Theo said.

Luke side-eyed his brother.

"I have as much right to be here as you do," I said.

"But why are you here?"

"I just answered that question."

"No, not here at the bar. In this town. Why are you in Tilikum? Don't you live… I don't know, somewhere that isn't here?"

"Not anymore."

His jaw hitched, and nothing about the hard look he gave me was sexy. Absolutely nothing at all.

I was such a liar. He dripped sex appeal, which only made me angry.

"What do you mean, not anymore?" he asked through clenched teeth.

"I mean, I'm at the Timberbeast because I wanted a drink, and I'm in Tilikum because I live here."

He stared at me for a few seconds, unblinking, as if he were too shocked to reply.

"Luke?"

"Great. This is fantastic." He gestured to my seat. "You steal my chair and my town?"

"Your town? I don't think you own Tilikum."

"I don't have to own it to have dibs."

"Oh boy," Theo said.

Luke glared at him. "Don't take her side."

Theo put his hands up in a gesture of surrender. "I'm not getting involved."

"You can't call dibs on an entire town." I leaned back in my seat as if making myself more comfortable. "Or a bar. If I want to sit with Theo and have a drink, I will."

"I was here first."

"You didn't save your seat."

The fact that this was practically devolving into play-ground taunts like we were nine probably should have calmed the situation—made us both laugh. From the outside, we undoubtedly sounded ridiculous.

But he'd riled me up, and I wasn't going to be the one to back down.

He crossed his arms. "Go have a drink with your own brother."

"Don't tell me what to do."

"I'm not. I just want my seat."

"And I want to catch up with Theo. It's been a long time."

"Oh look, something over there." Theo shuffled his papers into a pile, grabbed his beer, and stood. "Why don't you sit here, and I'll go… anywhere else."

"Way to make it awkward," I said to Luke as Theo went to the bar and slid onto a stool.

"Me?" He dropped into the chair Theo had vacated. "You're the one too stubborn to move."

"Says the man who just took his brother's seat."

"Because you won't leave."

I narrowed my eyes. "What is this all about? Are you still mad about the other day?"

"What, when you pulled out into traffic and would have caused an accident if I didn't have lightning-fast reflexes?"

"No, when you were driving too fast—as usual—and almost hit me."

"How would you know how fast I drive?"

"I know you."

It was his turn to narrow his eyes. "No, you don't."

"I beg to differ."

"What could you possibly know about me? You left a long time ago to live your fancy life with your fancy husband. You don't know the first thing about me or my life. Or this town."

"Ex-husband."

"What?"

"He's my ex-husband." I held up my hand, palm facing me, to demonstrate my lack of wedding ring.

A flicker of emotion crossed his features, but despite my claim to still know him, I couldn't read it. Was it anger? Satisfaction? Triumph? It irritated me that I didn't know.

"Is that why you're back?" he asked.

"Yes, and that obviously bothers you."

"It doesn't bother me."

My lips turned up. "You're such a liar. You just called dibs on the entire town."

"It is my town."

"And you don't want me in it?"

Glancing away, he blew out a breath. His crossed arms accentuated his broad shoulders and toned biceps.

Not that I noticed.

Fine, yes, I did.

"I'm not that much of a jerk."

I choked back a laugh.

His tongue slid across his teeth. He'd always done that when he was mad. It was frustratingly sexy.

He uncrossed his arms, but despite his attempt to look nonchalant, tension snapped between us. "You aren't getting under my skin, Mel. It's not gonna happen."

"What makes you think I'm trying to get under your skin?"

"I know you."

My mouth dropped open. "Are you kidding me? I don't know you because I left with my fancy husband. But you have the audacity to claim you know the first thing about my life?"

"No, I don't." His voice started to rise. "I don't know anything about your life. How could I? I haven't seen you in years. Which is fucking weird, because your family lives here and this town is so damn small, we trip over each other when we walk out the door. But whatever, people move on, that's fine."

I opened my mouth to reply, but he pointed a finger at my face and kept talking.

"But I do know *you*. And I know how much you love to get in my head and mess with me."

"No, I don't."

He stood so fast his chair almost tipped backward. "Yes, you do. You waltz into my town, full of sass, and suddenly, I'm arguing with you over a seat in the bar. But it's not happening. Not this time, Melanie. Not this time."

He backed up a step, then turned and stalked out the door.

I blinked a few times. And people said I was dramatic.

Our little… we'll call it an incident… had garnered the attention of the other Timberbeast patrons. Most of them turned back to their drinks once the door closed behind Luke. Rocco eyed me from behind the bar, but he didn't say a word.

Theo tapped his stack of papers on the bar and clipped them into his clipboard. He tucked it under his arm and followed Luke outside.

Seething with frustration, I glared across the room at absolutely nothing. Who did he think he was? I didn't mess with his head. If anything, he messed with mine. And sass? Okay, that was fair, I had an attitude. But he brought it out in me like no one else did. I hadn't stolen his chair, and I certainly wasn't trying to get under his skin.

But what made me really mad was how easily he was getting under mine.

CHAPTER 7

Luke

WHAT THE HELL was wrong with me?

I stalked out to my car, blood simmering with rage. All I'd wanted to do was chill out and have a beer after a long day. And there she was, sitting in my seat, taking up space in my bar. Antagonizing me just by existing.

What was it about her? If it had been anyone else in the world, I would have just pulled up another chair. No big thing. I was an easygoing guy. I could go with the flow.

Not when she was involved.

It had been the same when she'd almost hit me with her car. If that had been any other person, I would have made sure they were all right, then been on my way. No harm, no foul. But Melanie? The woman made me crazy.

I opened my car door but Theo's voice made me pause.

"Dude, what was that about?"

"Nothing."

"It looked like something."

I turned to face him and gestured toward the bar. "She was in my seat."

"You know how childish that sounds, right?"

"It's not childish, I—" I shut my mouth because he was

right, it was. And my desire to argue was already cooling off. "Did you follow me out here?"

"Obviously I need to find out who you are and what you did with Luke."

I shook my head. "I don't know, man. She messes with my head."

"Still?"

"I know. It's idiotic, right?"

"Yeah. It is."

I scowled at him. "Thanks."

"You said it. Besides, why are you letting her get to you?"

That was an excellent question. Why *was* I letting her get to me? "I don't know. I just didn't expect to see her."

"Sounds like you better get used to it."

"That's the thing. Why did she have to move back to my town?"

"There you go again with the *my town* thing."

"You know what I mean."

"Not really."

I blew out a frustrated breath. "She just shows up after all these years and…"

"And?"

"I don't know. Pisses me off."

"You're both adults. I'm sure you can find a way to live in the same town."

Could we, though?

"It's fine. I'll just avoid her."

"That's a healthy option."

"Nice sarcasm."

He grinned. "Always."

The longer I stood outside in the cool evening air—and away from her—the calmer I felt. Avoiding her wasn't unhealthy, it was smart. We'd always been volatile when we were together, and clearly that hadn't changed.

"I should expect a call from Mom about this tomorrow, shouldn't I?"

"She won't hear it from me," Theo said. "But you know she'll hear it from someone."

That was true enough. I'd just caused a scene. And I wasn't the Haven brother who usually caused scenes.

"Nothing I can do about it now."

"I'm going to head out." His brow furrowed. "You sure you're okay?"

"Yeah, I'm fine."

He nodded and went to his truck, although I wasn't sure if he believed me.

I glared at the door to the Timberbeast and got in my car. *Thanks for screwing up my night, Mel.*

Restless and dissatisfied, I headed home.

———

I poured a cup of the sludge Patrick considered coffee and took a sip. The garage was busy, as usual. The Dodge Patrick was working on would be ready for paint soon. That would make the client happy. And Ollie was in a pair of coveralls, head buried in the engine compartment of what had once been a 1964 Jeep Gladiator pickup. We'd scored that job from a guy down in California. It needed a lot of work, but it would be killer when it was done.

The dark roast had been brewed too strong, but I drank it anyway. I needed the caffeine. After the previous night's run-in with Melanie the human hurricane, I'd slept like crap. Although my initial rush of anger had worn off, I'd gone home still amped with adrenaline. It had taken hours to come down.

My phone buzzed in my pocket, so I went into my office where I'd be able to hear. It was my mom.

I groaned. I loved my mom, and we got along fine. But I

wasn't looking forward to her questions about a certain ex-girlfriend.

"Hi, Mom."

"Hi, honey. Sorry to bother you at work."

"That's okay. What's going on?"

"Well, I was just at Nature's Basket and ran into Doris Tilburn. She said she heard you got into a bit of a quarrel with someone at the Timberbeast last night. Is everything all right?"

"Yeah, everything is fine."

"Was it Melanie?"

"It was."

"How is she? I haven't seen her in so long."

I blinked in confusion. "I guess she's fine, although we weren't hanging out to catch up."

"I'll have to reach out to Krista."

"Okay…" I didn't really care if my mom talked to her mom, but I didn't know why she seemed concerned. "Is that why you called?"

"I'm not trying to be nosy. I just wondered what happened. Doris heard there was quite a commotion, and that doesn't sound like you."

"That's just the gossip line blowing things up, as usual. There was no commotion."

"Good to hear. Okay, honey, I'll talk to you later."

"Bye, Mom."

I slipped my phone back into my pocket and rolled my eyes. Commotion? Come on, we hadn't caused a commotion.

Much.

Ollie knocked and poked his head into my office. "Someone in the lobby to see you."

I tipped my chin to him in acknowledgment and went to see who it was.

Pausing just inside the lobby, I suppressed a groan. The

petite old lady in a lime-green velour tracksuit was not who I'd been hoping to see.

Aunt Louise.

She had silver hair she'd recently cut short that curled at the nape of her neck, and a large blue quilted handbag hung from her elbow. She took slow steps, gazing at the photos on the wall.

Don't get me wrong, the almost-groan wasn't because I don't like my aunt. I like her fine. I just avoided her as much as possible because she'd appointed herself Haven family matchmaker. She was forever on a quest to get me and my brothers married off. I'd been subjected to her matchmaking attempts often enough that I knew better than to say yes. Ever.

"Hi, Aunt Louise," I said, getting her attention.

She turned with a big pink-lipstick smile and took a pair of oversized sunglasses off her face. "Hi there, dear. You're just the man I wanted to see."

"Do you have a car that needs to be restored?"

"No, no, nothing like that."

I knew she wasn't there about a car. She drove a beige Buick that my uncle George kept in pristine condition for her. There was only one reason Aunt Louise ever appeared, and I needed to head her off before she got too deep into her ask.

"I didn't think so," I said. "Before you say anything, I love you, but the answer is no."

"No to what? I haven't asked you anything."

"But you were going to."

"Hear me out first. You're going to love this."

"I don't care who she is. This isn't a good time."

"Who, who is?"

"The girl you're trying to set me up with."

She blinked in confusion. "I'm not trying to set you up with a girl."

"You're not?"

"No, of course not."

I resisted the urge to facepalm. "Don't sound so shocked. You're usually trying to set me up with someone."

She waved that off. "Another time. I'm here about the Squirrel Protection Squad."

I didn't know what was weirder—that my aunt was forever trying to set up her nephews on dates or that I lived in a town with an organization called the Squirrel Protection Squad. And they were completely serious.

They'd formed when someone was stalking my now sister-in-law Audrey and left a dead squirrel outside her house. Somehow, they'd morphed from protecting wildlife to a civilian security detail.

"What about the SPS? I think they have plenty of volunteers."

"They certainly do. Which is why they need a headquarters."

"Headquarters? Wow."

"It's going to be fantastic. Plenty of space for meeting with new recruits, and they'll be able to hold first aid and CPR classes—for humans and squirrels."

"CPR for squirrels?"

She nodded. "Mm-hmm. You know the empty storefront in that old strip mall? The one next to the Knotty Knitter? They got a great deal from the owner, which is why the whole thing is possible. Josiah and your dad already volunteered to help with any necessary renovations. But there's still more to be done, which is where I come in."

"You need more help with renovations?"

"No, no. Doris Tilburn and I are planning a fundraiser. It's going to be very fancy. The Grand Peak Hotel donated their ballroom."

"So you're looking for donations or sponsors or something?"

"That would be wonderful, but it's not why I came. I need your help with the event itself."

Help with a fundraiser? That didn't sound terrible. But I still hesitated, my instincts telling me she was up to something.

What was the catch?

"What kind of help?"

She clasped her hands together. "Are you ready for this? I'm so excited. It's going to be such a treat. We're holding a bachelor auction."

"Oh no."

"Oh yes!" Her eyes were bright, and she smiled as she spoke. "Isn't that the most delightful idea? I came up with it."

"I'm not surprised."

"I knew you'd love it."

"Hmm. Don't think I love it, to be honest."

"Oh, don't be a fuddy-duddy. It's for a good cause. The winner will get an evening with their bachelor, nothing scandalous."

"Can't you get Theo to do it?"

"He'll be there too."

I eyed her with skepticism. "Does he know that?"

"I haven't had a chance to ask him yet, but I'm sure he will. Besides, I only have the two of you left. The Havens need to make a good showing."

"This isn't your newest way of trying to set me up with someone, is it? It's actually a charity auction, and anyone who bids has the chance of winning?"

"Luke, if I wanted to set you up, I'd just do it. I wouldn't go to all this trouble just to get you a date. Believe it or not, I have other interests besides the love lives of my nephews."

I raised my eyebrows in disbelief.

She didn't seem to notice. "Wonderful. I knew you'd agree. Thank you, honey." She slipped her sunglasses back on and hurried for the door. "Ta-ta for now. I'll be in touch with details."

My mouth hung open as the door closed behind her. Agree? When had I agreed?

For a second, I thought about chasing her down. I didn't want to be auctioned off for charity. Although she was right, the SPS was a good cause. They did a lot for our community.

I took a drink of coffee and headed back to the garage. It was probably easier to just let it happen. I'd have to make sure Theo agreed to go too. I would not be the only Haven brother on the chopping block.

In the meantime, I had too much work to do to worry about Aunt Louise's shenanigans. Besides, she hadn't tried to set me up on a date, so I had that going for me.

CHAPTER 8

Melanie

THE DARKNESS WAS SO THICK, I couldn't tell if my eyes were open or closed. Which way was up? I reached out my hand, hoping to find something solid to help me get my bearings.

Nothing. Just empty space.

My heart beat uncomfortably hard, and my jaw hurt from clenching my teeth. Fear surged through me in time with my pulse. I wanted to run, but I couldn't see.

In fact, I couldn't even move.

What was happening? Where was I?

My arms and legs were suddenly useless. Was I still standing? The world spun in a disconcerting whirl. Up was down, down was up, nothing made sense. I couldn't move—could hardly breathe.

Someone was near. I could feel him. Feel his breath on the back of my neck. His cold hands about to touch my skin. I opened my mouth to scream, but nothing came out. I was trapped, and he was—

With a gasp, I sat up in bed. My heart still raced, and my tank top was drenched with sweat. I flipped on the light to chase away the grasping darkness and blinked at my surroundings to ground myself in reality.

A nightmare. Just a dream.

I sat for a long moment, catching my breath and waiting for my heart to slow. My body tingled with fear and adrenaline, frightened by the monster who lived inside my head. And in my past.

"Just a dream," I said aloud, as if speaking it would make it more true. "It wasn't real."

Pressing my palms into the mattress, I felt the reality of it —the solidity. I swung my feet to the floor and stood, pausing to press my toes into the carpet. That was real, not the swirling confusion of my recurring nightmare.

So was my clammy skin and sweat-soaked tank top.

Gross.

"Hot flashes will be a breeze after this," I muttered as I stripped off my damp clothes and tossed them in the hamper. I changed into a clean tank top and stumbled into the hallway to find a fresh set of sheets. It certainly wasn't my first middle-of-the-night bed-changing session, but I didn't usually have to search through a half-unpacked house to find what I needed.

By the time I'd put on clean bedding, I was wide-awake. Still tired, but I knew better than to think I'd fall asleep again.

Which was fine. I didn't particularly want to.

Stupid nightmares.

Instead, I went to the kitchen to make a cup of tea. That would give me something to do while I waited for the sun to come up.

———

Several hours later, I was dressed and looking cute, with renewed gratitude for good concealer that could mask the dark circles beneath my eyes. The summer weather was hot, so I'd chosen a pink-and-orange sundress with strappy beige sandals. I'd painted my own toenails—this broke girl didn't have the budget for a proper pedicure—but I figured no one was looking that closely at my feet anyway.

I left the little house I'd rented feeling optimistic, hoping my quest to find a part-time job would push the previous night's unpleasantness from my mind. The nightmare wasn't new. I'd suffered through it more times than I could count. It had been a while since the last one, though. I chalked it up to sleeping in a new place. Once I got used to my surroundings, I was sure the bad dreams would go away.

The past couldn't haunt me forever. Even though it seemed intent on trying.

I headed downtown and parked at Home Slice. My plan was probably a bit old-school. Job applications were usually submitted online, but I thought a bit of personal contact couldn't hurt. I'd stop in the businesses that looked like the sort of places that might need part-time help, introduce myself, and see if they were hiring.

The Copper Kettle didn't need anyone, but Rob, the owner, did take my information and promised to get in touch if anything changed. Not ideal, since I needed a quick turn-around, but better than a hard no. I checked the pet store, Happy Paws, and got a vague maybe. Same with the florist, Blossoms and Blooms, the little soap and candle shop, a housewares store, and a clothing boutique I didn't remember seeing before.

Undaunted, I tried a few more but had no immediate luck. How was that possible? It was summer, which meant tourist season throughout the mountains. The shops were bustling, the sidewalks full of people. How could no one be hiring?

I stopped outside the Steaming Mug. Growing up, I wouldn't have set foot inside that coffee shop. In the days of the Haven-Bailey feud, it had been enemy territory. I'd been on the Haven side—particularly because I'd dated Luke—and frequenting the wrong business was something you just didn't do.

But the feud had ended years ago and the rift that had divided Tilikum for generations had gradually mended. Which meant the Steaming Mug was an option, both for a midday caffeine boost and as a potential source of employment.

I walked in to the scent of espresso and acoustic guitar music in the background. A large black chalkboard with the menu hung on an exposed brick wall behind the painted teal counter. Round tables and a few armchairs gave the place a homey, comfortable vibe.

After waiting in line, I ordered a latte and struck out again when the barista said they had just hired two new people and weren't looking for anyone else.

While I waited for my drink, I indulged in a brief fantasy of one of the new baristas angrily dumping scalding-hot coffee on her ex-boyfriend—a guy at one of the tables working on a laptop played the part in my head—only to be immediately fired. Cue Melanie jumping in to save the day and being rewarded with a job on the spot.

"Melanie," the barista said, sliding my latte across the counter.

"Thanks." I smiled as I picked up the cup, only feeling a tiny bit guilty that I'd been low-key wishing she'd get herself fired in dramatic fashion.

Another voice from behind me said my name. "Melanie?"

I turned, and a familiar face appeared. Luke's sister, Annika, stepped through the people in line. Her dark blond hair was cut shoulder length with curtain bangs, and she wore a tank top and shorts.

"Annika Haven," I said. "Sorry, you're Annika Bailey now. My bad."

From what I'd heard, she and Levi Bailey were the reason

I stood in what had once been an off-limits coffee shop. Their love had ended the feud.

She stepped in for a hug, and I happily hugged her back. In what felt like another life, she and I had been good friends.

"It's been Annika Bailey for a while. I heard you were back in town. How are you?"

"Well, I'm hot off a divorce, broke, can't seem to find a job, and slightly overwhelmed by life." Small talk was beyond my capabilities. I either conversed about real things or nothing at all. "But other than that, I'm actually doing pretty well. How about you?"

Her lips parted in surprise. "I'm fine. Sounds like we have a lot to catch up on. Are you staying? We have a table in the back."

"We?"

"My sisters and I."

I drew my eyebrows in. "Sisters? Annika, you have like forty-seven brothers."

"Sisters-in-law." She shifted so I could see past her. "I have tons of them now. Bailey sisters, Haven sisters. It's my Haven sisters-in-law today, though."

Three women, all holding young babies, sat at a table near the back. Two I didn't recognize. The first wore a blue tank top and had long blond hair tied in a low ponytail. Her baby had a tuft of blond hair with a pink bow and looked just old enough that she could keep her head up without flopping around.

The second woman had dark hair and a friendly smile. The baby in her arms was asleep, but I could see a full head of brown hair.

But it was the third woman who made my eyes widen and my mouth drop open. "Marigold Martin! She's your sister-in-law? How did that happen?"

"I know. It's wild, right?" Annika said. "She married Zachary last year."

That was wild. Zachary hadn't seemed like the marrying type. And to sweet Marigold? That was not a piece of news I'd been prepared to discover.

Pushing aside the familiar pang at seeing new moms with their babies, I picked my way through the crowded shop to their table. Marigold also held a baby, but hers was sleeping in one of those wrap things that left her hands free.

"Don't get up," I said. "But hi, it's so good to see you. You look absolutely beautiful. And Zachary? Really? I knew I was out of touch, but I think this might be more surprising than the end of the feud."

Marigold smiled. Her brown hair was styled in perfect loose waves. I remembered her as a quiet bookworm, but she'd blossomed since high school.

"Yes, really, Zachary. And this is our daughter, Emily."

"I'm sure she's beautiful even though I can only see the top of her head." I turned to the other women at the table. "Sorry, I'm Melanie. I used to live here, and it feels like thirteen lifetimes ago."

"We have an empty chair," Annika said. "You should join us. And let me introduce you. This is Audrey, Josiah's wife, and baby Abby. And this is Harper, Garrett's wife, and this little bright-eyed beauty is baby Isla."

They smiled and said hello.

Out of nowhere, I almost panicked.

This wasn't just a table of women. It was a table of Haven women. Luke's sister and sisters-in-law.

Was it weird?

No, why would it be weird? I'd been friends with Annika before I'd dated Luke. And as I had reminded myself no less than eight thousand times, high school was ages ago. My identity was not Luke Haven's ex-girlfriend.

"I'd say I don't want to intrude, but I absolutely do." I took the chair she offered and sat with my coffee. "Harper? You look familiar. Do we know each other? And if you married Garrett, that must mean he's no longer with what's-her-name. I hope you all popped the champagne when that ended." I paused. "I'm so sorry. I have no filter."

Harper laughed, and her baby smiled. "That's okay. Whatever happened with Garrett's ex was before my time. I don't think we know each other, but I used to visit Tilikum when I was growing up. My aunt is Doris Tilburn."

"I remember Doris. Angel Cakes Bakery?"

"Yep. I run the bakery now."

"And she's a cookie genius," Annika said. "But you have to tell us about you. My mom mentioned hearing you'd moved back, but you never know what to believe in this town."

"I heard you won the lottery and were planning on buying the Grand Peak Hotel and turning it into a giant mansion," Marigold said. "But obviously, I didn't believe that. I get all the gossip at the salon."

"Won the lottery would be rather helpful right about now, but no," I said. "Kind of the opposite, actually. My marriage fell apart, and my ex immediately moved on with a younger woman, leaving me to deal with the house and all the debt, and then tried to weasel his way out of dividing things fairly, which did nothing but cost me an exorbitant amount in attorney fees. But, silver lining, I'm no longer married to a man with delusions of adequacy."

They all looked at me with raised eyebrows.

"Sorry. See? No filter. I'm somewhat of an expert at making things awkward."

"Oh, me too," Audrey said. "It's nice not to be the only one."

"I'm sorry about your divorce," Marigold said, patting Emily gently. "But it sounds like it was for the best. And it's so lovely that you're back in Tilikum."

"Thanks," I said with a smile. "I've missed it."

"Speaking of making things awkward," Annika said, her voice hesitant. "Does Luke know you're back in town?"

Marigold raised her eyebrows, a look of curiosity on her face.

"Oh, come on, that's not awkward." That was a lie. Just the mention of his name made me want to squirm. "We dated a million years ago. And yes, he knows. I almost ran him off the road. But in my defense, I didn't hit him."

"Um…" Audrey paused. "Why did you almost run him off the road?"

"He drives too fast."

She opened her mouth again as if she wasn't sure what I meant by that.

"Oh!" I laughed. "You thought I meant I did it on purpose. No, it was an accident."

"Sorry," Audrey said.

"It's okay. I probably seem like someone who'd run her ex-boyfriend off the road."

That made all four of them laugh.

I was being flippant about Luke. And not because seeing him hadn't made an impact—it had. I'd been looking over my shoulder everywhere I went, wondering if, or maybe when, I would see him again. But I wanted—or maybe needed—to pretend I didn't care. That our relationship was in the past and I didn't feel a thing.

In reality, I felt about a million things. But, despite my lack of filter, I wasn't prepared to admit to any of it.

Because, honestly, what was wrong with me? Why were a couple of chance encounters with my high school boyfriend bothering me like a splinter in my toe I couldn't remove?

"I saw Theo at the Timberbeast the other night," I said. "That was fun. Until Luke showed up and called dibs on Tilikum and then stormed out."

"Luke stormed out of the bar?" Audrey asked. "That doesn't sound like him."

I took a sip of my coffee. "It doesn't? It sounds very much like him."

"Are we talking about the same Luke?" Harper asked. "Luke Haven? Because he seems so easygoing."

"He usually is," Annika pointed out.

"I probably bring out the worst in him," I said. "But it's only fair because he brings out the worst in me. Kudos to the three of you for tackling Haven men. I tried that once, and it was a disaster."

"You were both so young, though," Annika said. "We're all idiots in high school."

I shrugged. "Maybe. But he and I don't seem to have gotten any better at not wanting to murder each other."

"Anyway, enough about Luke." Annika waved her hand. "Sorry for bringing that up. New subject. What do you do?"

"I'm a voice actor."

"Really? What kinds of things do you work on?"

"Whatever I can get. I've done commercials, some low-budget documentaries, a cartoon series."

"That's amazing." Marigold turned to Audrey and Harper. "Melanie was so good at theater. She always got the lead. Do you still do theater, or just the voice acting?"

"I did theater for a while, but I transitioned to voice acting."

"I love that," Annika said. "What's the cartoon series?"

"It's called *Enchanted Hollow*."

Annika's mouth dropped open. "You're kidding. My kids are obsessed with that show. Who do you play?"

I cleared my throat and continued in my Queen Ione voice. "The magnificent, illustrious Queen Ione."

Annika gasped. "No. Way. She's the best part."

"Aw, thank you," I said in my natural voice. "It's a great role. Unfortunately, there's been a hiatus between seasons, and with the whole broke-after-divorce thing, I'm looking for a temporary job. Speaking of, are any of you hiring?"

They all shook their heads.

"Well…" Annika paused. "Okay, don't say no."

"That makes me want to instantly say no."

"I know, I know. But hear me out. Luke's front desk person is on maternity leave, and he needs someone to cover for her until she comes back."

"You can't possibly be suggesting what I think you're suggesting."

"Why not?"

"Because we can't be twenty feet from each other without fighting. But you think we should work together?"

"It's not as out there as it sounds. I used to work for him, and he's always busy in the garage. You'd hardly see him."

I eyed her with skepticism.

"You need a temporary job," she continued, "and he needs a temporary employee. It's a win-win."

"Until we kill each other."

She laughed. "I don't think you'll kill each other. Like you said, you dated a million years ago. I'm sure you could at least tolerate each other."

It sounded so reasonable when *she* said it. It had been a long time, and it wasn't like we still had feelings for each other.

Okay, so we did have feelings—fiery ones—but they weren't romantic.

Maybe it could be like a type of exposure therapy. If we were forced to interact and be on our best behavior, we'd move past whatever seemed to rile us up.

"I don't know. I'm sure I could do it, but I don't know about him." I pressed my lips together and shook my head. "Yeah, I'm not sure I could do it either. But you do have a small point about my need for a job. Although I highly doubt he'll go for it."

"He might." She shrugged. "I'll talk to him."

I gave her my number so she could get in touch after

talking to Luke and we could make plans to hang out again. Despite my less-than-charitable feelings for her brother, I liked Annika. I always had. And I was glad my status as her brother's ex-girlfriend didn't appear to preclude a friendship.

Work for Luke Haven? That had to be a terrible idea. So why was I considering it? I was a little bit desperate for a job, and something temporary was proving hard to come by. But was I desperate enough to subject myself to hours of *him* every day?

Living in the same town was one thing. Working together was quite another.

Maybe he'd be the one to say no.

That got my hackles up, and it was only theoretical. But what if he did say no? I knew myself well enough to know I'd be insulted. I could feel my propensity for being dramatic bubbling to the surface. How dare he not give me a chance?

And somehow, by the time I left the coffee shop, I was convinced I needed to get that job just to show him who was right.

CHAPTER 9

Luke

"NO."

Annika sighed. "You didn't let me finish."

"You don't need to finish. It's a hard no."

I leaned back in the chair and nodded to Ollie as he walked through the lobby to the garage. A sense of longing tugged at me. I wanted to be out there, getting my hands dirty, not stuck behind a desk.

Annika leaned forward, her elbows on the front counter, her eyes imploring. "She'd be perfect. You need someone to fill in. She needs a temporary job. She's smart and capable. You could probably teach her everything she needs to know in a day, and she'd be off and running. You could get back to your job."

I did want to get back to my job, but Melanie was not the answer. "It would never work. We can't stand each other."

"It was just the shock of seeing each other for the first time in a while. You'd get over it."

"If we were going to get over anything, you'd think we would have by now."

"I admit, you two seem to have some unresolved feelings—"

"No, we don't."

She tilted her head. "Are you sure about that?"

"Absolutely. I don't have any feelings for Melanie. Except loathing."

"What are you even mad about?"

That was a great question. What was I mad about? "I'm not mad about anything. Except that she moved back to my town, almost hit me on the road, and then took my seat at the bar."

Annika blinked a few times like she was confused. "Or something happened between you all those years ago, and you've never resolved it?"

I scoffed. "That's ridiculous. I don't even remember what happened."

"Liar."

"Come on, you know me. When have I ever held a grudge?"

"Two words. Evan Bailey."

I started to argue, but she wasn't wrong. Evan and I had been sworn enemies when we were younger. "We get along great now."

"But you didn't for a long time. And don't say it was because of the feud. You two took the feud to another level."

"Okay, you have a point about Evan. But he doesn't count anymore. We're friends."

"Which proves my point." She gave me a triumphant smile. "If you can become friends with Evan Bailey, you can learn to get along with Melanie."

I opened my mouth, but nothing came out. Freaking sister logic.

"I know she's…" Annika trailed off, as if trying to decide how to describe her.

"Dramatic? Full of sass? Frustrating as hell?"

"A little bit extra. But she's also very smart, and sweet, and personable."

"I agree she's smart, but I take issue with sweet."

"She is. She's nice."

I raised my eyebrows in disbelief.

"Fine, she's… spicy nice."

I tried to hold back a chuckle. Spicy nice. That was Melanie. "She's probably personable around anyone else, but around me, she's nothing but a spitfire."

"And I'm sure you don't do a thing to antagonize her."

"She antagonizes *me*!" I placed a hand on my chest. "Why do you assume it's my fault?"

"I'd bet money on it being mutual."

I scowled. "Whatever. I'm not—"

The door opened, and I forgot what I was about to say. Melanie swept in, dressed in a dark gray suit jacket and skirt with bright red heels. Her hair was up in some kind of twist, and her lipstick matched her shoes.

I gaped at her. What was she doing there? And why was she dressed like that?

"Well, isn't that perfect timing," Annika said cheerfully.

"Did you know she was coming?" I asked.

"No." Annika smiled and shouldered her purse. "But it looks like my work here is done."

She hugged Melanie on her way out. Fantastic, my sister and my ex-girlfriend were friends again. As if that hadn't been frustrating enough back in high school.

"What are you doing here?" I asked as the door shut behind Annika.

"Ooh, déjà vu. Is there a glitch in the matrix?"

"What?"

"You asked me that question in the bar the other night. Anyway, I'm here for my interview."

My eyes swept up and down, taking her in, and a pulse of arousal burst through me. I didn't want to notice the curve of her hips or the way her hairstyle showed the soft skin of her neck. I didn't want to, but I did.

"Since when do you have an interview? I don't remember calling you and asking you to come in."

"You didn't, but I figured I should be proactive in case you decided to be stubborn and refuse to call me."

"I was going to refuse to call you."

"Exactly," she said with a smile. "Should we do it here, or do you have an office?"

Heat swept through my veins, and a shot of adrenaline made my whole body buzz. I could do a lot of things to Melanie in my office.

No, no, I couldn't.

I slid my tongue along my teeth, feeling like I teetered on the edge of a knife. I could tell her to leave—burn that bridge all the way down to ash. We had to live in the same town, but that didn't mean we had to get along. There was no good reason for me to extend an olive branch.

Except the tiny glimmer of hope in her eyes tugged at something in my chest. I didn't want to acknowledge that I could have feelings for Melanie—other than antipathy—but for a moment, there was something else there. Something I'd tried to bury a long time ago.

"Fine. Let's go."

I led her through the garage to my office. There was a leather couch that I rarely used, a large desk, and the walls were covered in pictures of restorations I'd done. I sat at my desk and gestured for her to sit in one of the extra chairs. She sat, crossing her legs at the ankle and folding her hands in her lap.

"I was going to send you my résumé, but I don't have your email address," she said. "And I would have printed it, but my printer broke in the move."

"That's all right." I was trying to act like this was a real interview—and I wasn't distracted by her sultry cadence or how her lips moved when she talked. I cleared my throat. "What can you tell me about your recent job history?"

"I'm an actor. I've done it all. Waitressing, tending bar, answering phones."

"Do you still act?"

She nodded. "My real career is as a voice actor. But I'm waiting for my next gig to start. Hence, the need for a temporary job."

"Voice acting, huh?" She'd always been an incredible actress. "Do you still do theater?"

"Not really. I did for a while, but voice acting felt… I don't know, safer."

I met her eyes. Safer? Something in her tone tugged at my chest again. I wanted to know why she'd ever felt unsafe. Maybe even fix it.

Clearing my throat, I glanced away. What the hell was wrong with me?

"So, you're waiting for your next voice acting job to start. When will that be?"

"At least a couple of months. Maybe more." She shrugged. "Divorce and moving are expensive, and I'm bound by a noncompete until my contract is finished. That means I can't line up another voice-acting gig to fill the gap. I could use something temporary so I don't have to go back to eating ramen noodles and searching out the almost-expired discount section at the grocery store. Not that I need a handout. Or your sympathy."

"I know you don't need my pity."

"Nor do I want it."

"Obviously, Annika already talked to you about the job, but I don't know if she told you any details."

"Not much. Just that your front desk person is on maternity leave, and you need someone to fill in. I assume that means things like greeting customers, answering the phone, maybe some admin work."

"Yeah, pretty much."

"I've had jobs like that."

I nodded. What was happening? Was I actually considering this? I couldn't hire Melanie.

Could I?

"Look at us, having a civil conversation," I said.

"I'm proud of us. I wasn't sure we could do it."

I grinned. "Me neither. Helps that you're not in my chair."

Her lips turned up in a smile.

Okay, maybe Annika was right. Maybe it had been the shock of seeing each other for the first time in a while, and we could learn to get along.

"Were you always so territorial?" she asked.

"Probably. I get a little possessive."

There was a flash of something in her eyes. Heat? Interest? I couldn't tell. I expected her to say something snarky, but surprisingly, she didn't.

"You haven't offered me the job, but obviously, you will. I just have one question."

"What makes you so sure I'm going to offer it to you?"

"I'm your best option. There are only so many people in this town. If there was anyone better, he or she would be sitting at the front desk right now and I'd be home trying to decide which bills I can safely ignore this month."

"Okay, so what's your question."

"Do I have to be me?"

"What do you mean?"

"I was just thinking, I could be someone else to make it more fun." Her voice changed to the Southern drawl she'd used the other night. "I doubt you'd care for this one since you didn't appear to find it amusing at the bar." She shifted to a British accent. "But perhaps you'd be interested in hiring a fine young lady from London. She does sound sophisticated, don't you think?"

I shook my head. "How about just Melanie?"

"But Melanie is so boring, mate." She started off

Australian, then pitched her tone higher. "Or a little forest pixie. That's cute, right?"

She was good. Not that I was going to tell her that. But she was.

"No forest pixies."

"You're no fun," she said in her natural voice. "I think your customers would get a kick out of it."

She was right. They probably would. But she was brushing up against something inside me—something that made me want to ensure she didn't win. "Maybe, but you'll drive the rest of us nuts."

"That sounds like a you problem."

Don't get mad. Don't get mad.

"Do you want the job or not?"

"I mean, do I *want* the job? That's a complicated question. It's not exactly my dream to work the front desk of my ex-boyfriend's auto shop. But I suppose dreams don't have much to do with anything when you move back to your hometown to start your life over."

I leaned forward. "Now you're trying to get a rise out of me."

"I'm not."

"Yes, you are."

She crossed her arms. "I'm not. Sometimes I just… don't know when to stop talking."

"Or when the performance is over, and real life begins."

"This is an interview. What is it if not a performance?"

I hesitated. "This is a bad idea, isn't it?"

"Oh, undoubtedly."

Her expression felt like a dare. *I dare you to let me in your space and not let me affect you. Not let me get under your skin.*

I could handle it. If anyone in the world could handle Melanie Andolini, it was me. I knew what I was getting into. She was a handful, but I could give it as well as she could.

This was a challenge. I wasn't sure what beating her meant, but I was absolutely going to win.

I locked eyes with her. "Do you want the job?"

"I'll take it."

Released

ROSWELL MILLS

TEN YEARS. Ten long, frustrating years were coming to an end.

Finally.

I hated every person in that stinking prison. The other inmates were nothing but lowlife scum. Idiots, all of them. The staff? Hypocrites. The guards? Bullies and overbearing tormentors.

Not a bit of that showed on my face. It never had. I'd made friends. Formed alliances. Given favors and gotten them in return. None of them saw the depths of my hatred. None of them knew I'd sooner slice them all open with a box cutter than listen to their sniveling voices.

Courting their favor had suited my purposes. I was good at doing what needed to be done to survive.

But finally—finally—it was over. My sentence complete.

I walked out wearing a used T-shirt and jeans that didn't fit, carrying the few belongings I'd accumulated during my stay in a brown paper bag labeled with my name—Roswell

Mills. There wasn't much. A few books, a hooded sweatshirt, my wallet, an extra pair of shoes.

My shoulders hunched forward as I shuffled behind the guard toward the exit. The posture of a penitent. I was sorry, yes, so very sorry, for my crimes. I kept my eyes downcast, a man beaten down and contrite. Quiet, unassuming. Not a danger to anyone.

"Nice day," the guard said as he opened the door to my impending freedom.

The clear, blue Tennessee sky stretched above the prison, a stark contrast to the ugly walls and barbed wire.

"Beautiful," I mumbled.

He led me through the outer gate, and without meaning to, I stopped. They were actually going to let me go free? After ten years, I could walk outside… unencumbered?

The guard glanced over his shoulder. "It's okay. Everybody stops there."

Impotent rage poured through me. I wasn't everybody. I wasn't like the other prisoners—thieves, thugs, drug dealers. I was better than them.

Or maybe worse.

I bottled up the rage, shoving it down so it wouldn't show. So nothing would show. So I'd stay invisible.

"Just glad to be going free," I said, not looking up.

"Of course. I'm happy for you, man."

His voice held nothing but sincerity, but it was probably misplaced. If they knew what I was going to do, they'd have never let me out.

But that was simply because they didn't understand.

The guard kept walking. My feet moved, and I followed him, eyes still on the ground. Words ran through my mind in a hideous whisper.

They still don't see you. No one does.

With a shudder, I pushed the whisper away and kept walking.

Of course they didn't see me. Didn't really know who I was. How could they? I'd served time for credit card fraud. My sentence had been so long because I'd stolen more than sixty thousand dollars—a Class B felony in Tennessee.

I looked like nothing more than a petty thief—just greedy. A guy who found a way to make a quick buck and got caught.

My lips turned up in the hint of a smile. They had no idea.

"You have a ride coming to meet you, right?" the guard asked.

"Yes. My mother."

"Hey, man, that's great. Not everyone who gets out has family to go to."

He led me through another gate and out to the sprawling parking lot. A worn-out white Dodge caravan was parked in one of the visitor spots, the engine running.

The driver's side door opened, and my mother stepped out. The past ten years had not been kind to her. She had saggy, wrinkled skin and a thicker middle than I remembered.

"Is he free to go?" she asked the guard.

"Yes, ma'am."

"Let's go, then. I've been waitin' an hour."

The pity in the glance the guard cast my direction made me want to rip his insides out.

I pretended not to notice his expression as I walked to the van's passenger side and got in. An air freshener hanging from the rearview mirror did little to mask the smell of cigarette smoke.

Mom got in and shut her door. "Well, you learned your lesson, I'm sure. You won't hear more about it from me."

"Thanks."

"Your uncle Glen passed. Did I tell you that? Couple of years ago."

"You did, yes."

She kept talking as she pulled out of her parking spot and drove through the outer gate, droning on about neighbors and relatives. It was odd how she'd adopted a Tennessee accent. Granted, she'd lived there for about fifteen years, but adults didn't always change their speech when they moved to a new place.

It irritated me, as did her litany of updates about people I didn't care about.

But I kept quiet, nodding along as if I were interested. It was easier that way. Not because I felt any particular affection for her. An accident of birth didn't mean I owed her anything, least of all some sort of emotional attachment. It simply served my purposes to stay in her good graces.

She had something I needed.

The drive to her house took several hours. Eventually, she ran out of things to talk about. We stopped for fast food, and the salty, oil-soaked fries, cheap burger, and processed cheese were so good, I almost moaned while I ate. Prison food had left a lot to be desired.

My restlessness increased as we got closer to her house. She'd kept my things, and I had no reason to believe they wouldn't be there. She lived alone, hadn't moved, and had no reason to get rid of what I'd asked her to store. Even if she'd gone through my belongings, she'd never know how important it was. Never know the significance of what she kept.

Finally, we arrived. Her little house looked faded—in need of fresh paint—and the grass was brown. She started talking again, but I hardly listened. I had to get to it. Had to make sure it was there.

Had to see it, hold it in my hands.

"Everything's where you left it," she said as we walked inside, gesturing down the hall to the spare bedroom. "Probably a bit dusty. I only go in there to vacuum once in a while."

"That's fine. I'll clean it up."

"I know you just got out and all, but they gonna help you

get a job or somethin'? There must be programs out there to help guys like you."

Guys like me. Criminals.

I lifted my eyes to meet hers. Like usual, my voice was soft. "Don't worry about that. I won't be staying long."

"I'm not gonna kick you out or anythin'. I just think you should have a plan."

"You're right." I resisted the urge to fidget with my hands, but the need to see it was quickly becoming too much to contain. I needed to reassure my mother so she'd leave me alone. "There are programs. They gave me all the information I need. I have a plan."

She nodded. "Good. Glad to hear it. I'll let you get settled."

Finally.

Carrying the brown paper bag of useless garbage I'd brought from prison, I went to the spare room. I'd been living there when they caught me. Hiding out. Regrouping.

The air was stale, and a sheen of dust covered the furniture. The mattress was bare, and a now-obsolete computer sat on the desk right where I'd left it.

Absently, I dropped the bag and went to the closet. My heart sped up, anticipation making my blood run hot for the first time in years. Just the thought of it—of her—aroused me. Made my groin ache.

The plastic box with a lid that latched closed was exactly where I expected it to be—on the floor of the closet, buried beneath winter sweaters and a thick coat. She hadn't touched it, didn't know.

Reverently, I uncovered the box and slid it from its place of secrecy. The lid snapped off, confirming the only things I cared about—my most treasured possessions—were still inside.

There was money, thick rolls of bills I'd managed to keep hidden. I set those aside. The childhood photos, old report cards, and my first driver's license were a ruse. I didn't care about them at all. But if anyone had opened the box, the important items—the real reason I kept it—wouldn't stand out. No one would notice.

With a slight tremble in my hands, I pulled out what I'd been longing for—a yellow manila envelope with the photos I'd taken and printed myself.

It was her.

Laying them on the floor, I lined them up in chronological order. The first photos I'd taken of her were from a distance. I hadn't dared get too close. She was talking to friends or colleagues. In line to order a coffee. Getting into her car.

Another was at night, but closer, the outline of her face visible in the glow of the bar. There were more like that, taken without her knowing. Moments when I watched her, unseen.

But my favorite, the picture I coveted above all others, showcased my glorious triumph. And reminded me of my failure.

I'd managed one picture of her that night. Tied up in the trunk of my car. Gagged, bound hand and foot. All that fire in her, all that spirit I loved so much, restrained and controlled. By me.

Everything should have gone according to plan, but I'd made a fatal mistake. I'd underestimated her. And she'd gotten away.

I wouldn't make the same mistake again.

Fortunately, I hadn't been caught. Not for that. Credit card fraud was nothing—even with a ten-year sentence. I didn't know where she was—where she lived or what she'd been doing for the past ten years—but I wasn't worried about that. I'd find her.

And when I did, I would finish what I'd started all those years ago. She was the one who got away.

I was going to take her back. And she'd finally be mine.

CHAPTER 10
Melanie

SO FAR, the job was not the worst decision ever.

Granted, I'd only been working at Haven Auto Restoration for a few days, but I was already getting the hang of things. Luke was back doing whatever it was he did in the garage or sometimes in his office—not that I was keeping track—and we hadn't fought once.

Okay, so there had been some snide comments here and there. But we'd poked at each other like that when we'd been dating. A little sarcastic banter was how we'd always communicated.

I'd toned down my outfit from the suit I'd worn to my so-called interview. It was a garage, not a corporate office. When I asked Luke if there were expectations regarding dress, he shrugged and said he didn't care. That made me want to wear either a suit and heels every day or dress like the mechanics in old jeans and faded T-shirts.

Instead of using my wardrobe to provoke Luke, however, I'd decided on a business casual vibe. It was hot out, so I was wearing a lightweight blouse and linen pants, and my hair was up to get it off my neck.

The phone rang, and I answered with exaggerated cheer-fulness. "Haven Auto. How can I help you?"

Luke had told me to be myself, but I'd taken some liberties with what that meant and came up with a character to play while I worked. I called her Receptionist Melanie. She essen-tially had my natural voice—no accent at least—but she was a lot friendlier than the real me. One might even call her bubbly.

It made the job a lot more entertaining.

"Uh, yeah, do you guys fix mufflers?" a male voice on the other end asked.

"Hmm, that depends. What kind of car?"

"It's a 2017 Honda Civic."

"Oh my goodness, no. We only deal with cool cars here. But you can try Dusty's Auto. They work on the nerd mobiles."

"What?"

"Thank you for calling!" I hung up and smiled. "I'm good at this."

The UPS guy came in the front door with a small box. He set it on the counter in front of me and tipped his chin.

"Thank you," I said with a wide smile.

His forehead creased like he wondered what was wrong with me. "Have a good day."

I toned down the smile and lowered the pitch of my voice just a little. "Thanks. You too."

Characters were always a work in progress.

The delivery was for Patrick, one of the mechanics. I wasn't sure what I was supposed to do with it—if anything—but bringing it to him seemed like a logical choice. It wasn't large, so I picked it up and took it into the garage.

There were four large bays, and all but one of the doors were open. Industrial fans kept the air moving, cutting down on the worst of the heat. They had several cars undergoing restorations. I'd never been much of a car person, but the convertible on the far side looked like it would be fun on a summer evening.

I hesitated for a second, trying to remember which one was Patrick. Was he the one with the beard or the guy with the battered baseball cap?

My eyes locked on a pair of jeans. Or rather, the backside in those jeans.

Luke leaned over a black car with the hood up. I blinked, and I wasn't in the large garage anymore but in the shop behind his parents' place. I'd come over without calling first, wanting to surprise him. It had been a hot summer day, and I'd been dressed in nothing but a bikini top and denim shorts, hoping he'd get the hint and take me out to the lake.

I'd walked in while he was working on his car. That was nothing new. He was always working on his car. In those days, it had been a 1960s Chevrolet something or other. I'd teased him that he loved that car more than me.

Turned out, he probably had.

But that day, I'd opened the shop door and stopped to take him in. The way his jeans hugged his body. The stretch of his T-shirt across his shoulders and back when he straightened. The way he'd turned, and the smile that had hooked his mouth when he saw me.

The smile that said *there's my girl*.

There'd been a time when being Luke Haven's girl had been all I ever wanted. I'd thought I had it all.

Luke straightened, and I looked away so he wouldn't catch me staring. I quickly checked the rest of the garage to make sure no one noticed me watching him. It had only been for a moment, but it was long enough that it would have been obvious. Thankfully, it didn't look like anyone was paying attention to me.

I didn't want to have to ask Luke which mechanic was Patrick—and what I should do with his delivery—but considering I was coming up blank, I probably didn't have a choice.

I was about to suck it up and admit I needed his help—cue the heaviest of sighs—when a car pulled up in front of the open garage bay, and a woman got out.

A very attractive woman.

She wore a fitted tank top and a pair of shorts that made her tanned legs look a mile long. Her dark blond hair was long and thick, styled in the type of loose curls I could never seem to get right. She approached the garage with a smile.

Luke sauntered over to her, all casual confidence, and the way he said, "Hey," made me wonder if he knew her.

My eyes narrowed. Who was she, and what was she doing there? Was she a customer? Or something else?

Was Luke dating her?

Was Luke *dating*?

I didn't know why that thought made me so furious. Our relationship had ended ages ago. We'd both dated other people. I'd married one. I had absolutely no right to be seething with jealousy over Luke talking to another woman.

She wasn't even *another* woman. She was just *a* woman.

A very beautiful woman. Maybe even the type of woman Luke Haven would want to date, if he wasn't already.

She smiled and nibbled her lower lip. That was a flirtatious move if I'd ever seen one. How dare she? The audacity! The nerve of her!

I needed to turn around and walk away before I did something extraordinarily stupid. Like interrupt them.

Interrupt them. Now there was an idea.

I needed Luke's help anyway.

I'm not ashamed to admit I straightened my shoulders to emphasize my boobs and swayed my hips a little more than necessary as I walked over to Luke. Especially once he caught a glimpse of me out of the corner of his eye and turned.

"So sorry to bother you," I said with a smile. "Are you with a customer?"

"Um…" Luke hesitated. "Jenna just had a few questions."

"If it's about scheduling, don't bother Luke with it. He's hopeless with the calendar. But I can help if you'd like."

"Oh, that's okay," Jenna said. "I was just asking about an old car my grandpa has."

I wanted to tell her that maybe her grandpa should be the one to talk to Luke, if it was his car. But jealous ex-girlfriend isn't a good look, so I bit back my reply.

Besides, I wasn't jealous. Not even a little bit.

"Sounds good. Luke, when you have a second, I have a question."

"Sure, Mel."

I turned and walked back into the garage, willing my ass to look amazing. And wishing I'd worn something sexier than linen pants.

But why? I wasn't trying to impress Luke Haven. That was just silly.

So what was I doing, swaying my hips as I walked, hoping he was watching?

By the time I got back to my desk, I was livid. At myself. At Luke. At Jenna. At my pants for not making my butt look good. I dropped into my seat with a huff and set the box down.

A few minutes later, the door opened and Luke poked his head in. "Hopeless with the calendar?"

"I wasn't making that up. Annika forewarned me."

He rolled his eyes. "Did you really have a question?"

I swiveled the chair so I was facing him. "Of course I had a question. Why else would I have said that?"

He stepped into the lobby, and the door swung shut behind him. The little smirk on his lips made me want to smack it off him.

Or kiss it off him. Once upon a time, that's exactly what I would have done.

"I don't know." He shrugged. "I thought maybe you were…"

I raised my eyebrows and blinked a few times. "Yes?"

His smirk grew, as did my annoyance. "Never mind. What do you need?"

"I…" I glanced away, suddenly reluctant to admit I needed anything from him. The irrational, jealous part of me wanted to cross my arms and tell him, *'Nothing, go talk to your hot new customer.'*

But that would have been immature, and I knew it. If I was going to get mad at Luke, I ought to at least wait until he did something that deserved my sass.

I took a quick breath. "Patrick got a package, but I wasn't sure what I'm supposed to do with it. Or which one is Patrick."

"Oh," he said, as if that surprised him. Apparently, he'd been expecting to get my sass. "No worries. It usually takes me a while to remember names, too."

"Really?"

"Yeah. No big deal. Patrick is the one with the beard. Or you can always just open the door and shout. They'll answer."

My lips turned up in a small smile. "Thanks."

"Sure." He pointed at the box. "Is that the package? I can take it."

I picked it up and handed it to him. "Great. Thank you. Again."

"You're welcome."

Although I'd gone from ready to spit fire to perfectly calm in the space of our short conversation, I didn't have emotional whiplash. He hadn't taken the wind out of my sails so much as lowered them, so the wind wasn't buffeting me so badly.

A pleasant feeling filled my chest, and my cheeks warmed under his gaze. His voice echoed in my mind, saying those words I'd loved hearing so long ago.

There's my girl.

I spun the chair back to the desk and coughed a little to

clear the lump in my throat. I could still see him from the corner of my eye as he opened the door, the brown box tucked beneath one arm.

"Mel?" His voice was soft.

"Yeah?" I didn't turn to look at him.

"Her, um… her grandpa really does have an old car."

"Yeah, I know. That's what she said."

"I just mean, I'm not… there wasn't anything…"

Old wounds that should have healed a long time ago flared with pain. As did my instinct to protect myself. I swallowed hard and put on a smile. "It's fine. I just work here."

He let out a frustrated breath. "Right. Yeah. Never mind."

With my eyes on the desk, I bit the inside of my lip as he walked out into the garage.

A confusing tangle of feelings ate at me from the inside. That was what I got for reminiscing about the good times with him. A stark reminder that he might have been my first love, but he'd also broken my heart.

Maybe he was single now, but living in Tilikum meant I was going to have a front-row seat when that changed. It shouldn't have mattered. I should have been able to handle it.

But I wasn't so sure that I could.

CHAPTER 11

Luke

THE PINE TREES that surrounded my parents' place shaded us from the worst of the summer heat. They lived just outside town, up a long gravel driveway, in a log home my dad and uncles had built with their own hands.

Theo threw a football, and our nephew Owen caught it. It had been an all-football-all-the-time summer for those two. Owen had played for Theo the prior year and wound up a starter as a freshman. No nepotism involved. He was a badass athlete. Probably had at least a college scholarship in his future, if not a shot at the pros, just like Theo.

I decided to take a break from the endless game of catch to grab a beer from the kitchen.

"Want anything?" I asked Theo, jerking my thumb toward the house.

"I'll take a beer."

"Owen?"

A grin crept over his face, and I had a feeling I knew what he was going to say.

"Not a beer." I pointed at him. "Don't try to get me in trouble with your dad. Or Coach Haven over there."

Owen put his hands up. "I know, I know. I wasn't going to ask for a beer."

"You better not." Theo threw the ball directly at Owen's midsection, making him grunt when he caught it. "No drinking."

"I won't."

Theo gave him a stern look.

"Don't worry, Coach," I said. "He already figured out a life of delinquency isn't for him."

Owen groaned. "Are you guys ever going to let that go?"

More than a year before, Owen had been caught shoplifting from Angel Cakes Bakery. He had no idea at the time that he'd stolen from his future stepmom. Fortunately, it had been a one time thing, and he was generally a great kid.

"Have you met us?" I asked. "This is what happens when you start to grow up."

"You tease me mercilessly about every little thing?" he asked.

"Pretty much."

"Yeah, that tracks," Theo said. "Luke still gives me crap about the bologna sandwich incident. I was probably your age."

"Never gets old." I looked at Owen. "Lemonade?"

Owen caught the ball again and held it. "What's the bologna sandwich incident?"

"Don't ask," Theo said.

Owen shrugged and threw the ball. "Yeah, lemonade. Thanks, Uncle Luke."

"You got it."

I headed for the side door and held it open for my dad, who was on his way out with a tray full of raw burger patties. A man of few words, he nodded his thanks. I did a quick double take at his Squirrel Protection Squad T-shirt. It was almost too small for his broad chest and muscular arms.

Inside, my parents' house was comfortable and familiar.

The living room had a denim couch and armchairs draped with blankets my mom had knitted. Family photos adorned the walls, a reminder of the days when their house had been full of six rough-and-tumble brothers and one baby sister.

Mom was in the kitchen, loading another tray with condiments and buns.

"Need help?" I asked.

"No, I've got it. I just hope your dad made enough burger patties."

"Why? Are Garrett and Harper coming over too?"

"No, Isla has the sniffles, so they're home with her. Theo brought Owen. I just know how these things work. Someone else is bound to show up."

"Well, Dad had enough burgers to feed an army. I think you're good."

I poured lemonade for Owen and grabbed three beers out of the fridge—figured Dad would want one too—and went back outside.

Mom was already arranging things on the picnic table. Dad glanced at her and, with a subtle grin, grabbed her backside. She jumped and playfully smacked his arm. I pretended not to notice.

After passing out drinks, I opened my beer and took a sip. Theo wandered over and stood next to me.

"How's work?" he asked.

I hesitated before answering. "Fine, I guess. I don't know, man. This whole Melanie thing is driving me nuts. She does the job fine; it's not that. But she just…" I made a fist. "You know?"

"I was just wondering if you were working on any cool cars."

"See? This is what I'm talking about."

He glanced at me with his beer halfway to his lips, like he had no idea what I meant.

"Why am I answering your question about work by talking about her?"

"I don't know."

"This is what she does to me. It's like the other day. This woman came to the garage to ask some questions about a car her grandpa has sitting out at his property. And not just a woman, a hot woman, and I'm telling you, she was flirting with me."

"And this is bad because?"

"Because Melanie."

"What does she have to do with it?"

"That's exactly my point. She shouldn't have anything to do with it. I was standing there talking to her, thinking she wanted me to ask her out. And any other time, I would have. Because why not? I'm single. She seemed to be single. There could be something there. But did I?"

"I'm guessing no, based on how annoyed you are right now."

"No. No, I didn't. And do you know why?" I didn't wait for him to answer. "Melanie, that's why. I felt guilty. Why should I feel guilty? I'm not dating her. I don't even like her."

"Then there's no reason for you to feel guilty."

"I know. But I did. Then I realized she was watching, and I felt even worse. Like I'd been caught doing something wrong."

By the face Theo made as he nodded, I could tell he had no idea why I was so riled up.

Neither did I.

"Think of it this way," Theo said. "Maybe she inadvertently saved you from a disaster."

"Who? Melanie?"

"Yeah. If she hadn't been there, you might have asked the woman out. And let's be real, she's probably terrible for you."

"Excuse me?"

"You always date women who are awful for you."

"I do not."

"You totally do."

My brother Zachary seemed to appear out of thin air, eating a cookie. Baby Emily slept against his chest, secure in her carrier. "Actually, that's true, dude."

"Where did you come from?"

"I got here like five minutes ago."

"Have you just been standing there listening to our conversation?"

"It's not my fault you didn't see me." He popped the last bite of his cookie into his mouth. "And we all know you have a broken radar."

"Yeah, that's exactly it," Theo said.

"What?"

"Let me put it this way." Z patted Emily and swayed back and forth as he talked. "If you walked into a bar with a hundred single women, you'd find the one guaranteed to end in disaster. It's like you're attracted to the hot messes who are totally wrong for you. And don't get me wrong, I'm not judging girls who are hot messes. I'm a hot mess."

"But you're not bad for Marigold," I pointed out.

"Indeed, I'm not. My wifey is a lucky woman." He glanced over his shoulder and winked at Marigold, who was chatting with our mom by the grill.

Theo groaned. "You're lucky she puts up with you."

Z chuckled. "No, you're right, that's totally true. I'm the lucky one."

"I don't know what you're getting at," I said. "Sure, I've had relationships that didn't work out. But who hasn't? Look at you guys." I pointed at Theo first, then Zachary. "You're still single, and you just got married last year. It's not like either of you are paragons of long-term relationships."

"No, but you have a specific talent for dating women who are clearly bad for you," Theo said.

I opened my mouth to keep arguing, but a part of me

wondered if he was right. I didn't have the best track record when it came to dating.

"It's a thing," Z said with a casual shrug of his shoulders. "If you bring someone home, we already know it's doomed."

Instead of answering, I took a drink of my beer.

"Don't be grumpy." Zachary nudged me with his elbow. "You just need to find a woman who's the right kind of bad for you."

"What does that even mean?"

"I don't know, but you'll know when you find her."

"That actually makes sense," Theo said.

"Neither of you makes sense," I said.

"Burgers are done," Mom called.

Glad for the interruption, I went to the picnic table. Everyone dished up on paper plates, and even with the arrival of Zachary and Marigold, there was plenty to go around. I loaded up my cheeseburger with condiments but paused before adding pickles.

Melanie loved pickles. Wrinkling my nose, I skipped them.

There wasn't enough room for everyone at the table, so Theo and I pulled a couple of camping chairs closer, angling them so the sun wasn't in our eyes. Marigold offered to take Emily, but Zachary said he'd just eat standing.

"So what's new?" Mom asked, looking around. She paused on me like she expected me to be the one to answer.

I took a bite of my burger to avoid replying.

"Other than Luke hiring his ex-girlfriend to work at the garage?" Theo asked.

I shot him a glare.

"Luke, I think it's great," Mom said. "I saw Krista Andolini yesterday, and she said it's going well."

Dad snorted.

She turned to him. "What was that for?"

He shook his head and took a bite of his burger. I understood his meaning—

what the hell were you thinking?

"It's just temporary," I said, more to answer my dad's unspoken question than in response to my mom's curiosity. "She needed a job, and I needed someone to fill in for a while. Not a big deal."

"I'm so glad to hear that," Mom said. "It sounds like she's been through a lot."

Had she been through a lot? How was I supposed to know? She'd made it clear she just worked there. "Maybe. I don't really know. Her personal life isn't my business."

"If you hear that she's hiding from the FBI, don't listen," Mom said. "It's just the gossip line getting out of control again."

"That doesn't even make sense," Theo said. "If she were hiding from the FBI, she wouldn't come here, where everyone knows her."

"Or use her real name," Owen added.

Theo held out an open bag of chips for Owen to take some. "Exactly."

"I haven't heard anything about hiding from the FBI," I said. "Although you never know with her. She could be the head of an organized crime ring."

Theo nodded thoughtfully. "You know, I can kinda see it."

"Stop," Mom said with a laugh. "Melanie Andolini is a sweet girl from a very nice family."

There went someone calling her sweet again. "Do you actually remember Melanie, or are you mixing her up with someone else?"

"Of course I remember. I know things didn't work out between the two of you, but that doesn't mean I have to dislike her."

"That's not what I'm saying."

"You should invite her for dinner," Mom said.

"Why would I do that?"

"I can't remember the last time I saw her. I'd love to catch up."

I looked at my dad, hoping he'd tell her that was a terrible idea. He just grunted and shook his head as if to say *I'm not getting involved.*

"Thanks, Dad."

"I didn't say anything."

"Exactly." I sighed. "Mom, I don't think inviting her over for dinner is a good idea."

"Wait, I'm confused," Owen said. "Who's Melanie?"

"Luke's girlfriend from high school," Theo answered.

"And she works at the garage?" Owen continued. "But she might be the head of an organized crime ring?"

"No, her only crime is driving me crazy," I said.

"Be kinda cool if she was," Owen said with a grin. "I mean, not really, because my dad would have to take her down. But it would make a good story when it was over."

"I don't know, I think our family has enough good stories," Theo said. "We don't need to add Luke dating the head of an organized crime ring."

"I'm not dating Melanie," I snapped.

"Dated," Theo said. "I meant dated."

Zachary chuckled. I glared at them both.

"How are things shaping up for football this season?" Dad asked Theo.

I glanced at Dad, and he gave me a quick wink.

Holy shit. My dad had changed the subject for me. I subtly tipped my chin to him so no one else would notice.

Dad's subject-change diversion worked. Theo launched into his favorite topic—football. He had plans for their summer camp and the upcoming season. Owen had plenty to add, especially when it came to Tilikum's rivalry with neighboring Pinecrest. Back in our day, some of that competitiveness would have been harnessed for pranking the Bailey brothers. But with the feud over, the kids of Tilikum had to do what normal small-town teenagers did and trash-talk their rival schools' sports teams.

I finished my burger and my beer, glad no one was talking about Melanie or my apparently failed love life anymore.

Despite the shift in the conversation, I found myself thinking about her. What did it mean that her mom said her job was going well? Was Mel happy working at the garage? Was it all in my head that she'd seemed irritated with me for talking to Jenna?

And why did I care? It didn't matter what she thought.

My family kept chatting, and I got up and went inside to get another beer. As I opened it, my phone buzzed with a text. It was Kyle. A race was on.

Knowing full well I shouldn't race on a Sunday night—I'd be dragging ass the next day—I texted back that I'd be there. The temptation was too strong. I wanted the rush.

And maybe it was just what I needed to get Melanie out of my head.

CHAPTER 12

Luke

DESPITE KNOWING I'd be dragging after going out the night before, I was still grumpy about it. I'd snoozed my alarm three times and groaned like my old man getting out of a chair as I hauled myself out of bed. Even after some very strong coffee, I was struggling.

Racing had been what it always was. A temporary fix. Exhilarating high one moment, crashing back to reality the next. I'd skipped the after-party as usual, but I'd still been out half the night.

I drove to the garage with the windows in my Chevelle down, dark sunglasses cutting down the sun's glare. It was hot already. Apparently, summer had no intention of letting up. My mind drifted to the days when my brothers and our friends and I would have congregated at the lake, beating the heat in the chilly water. Staying to sit around a fire as the sun went down.

When was the last time we'd done anything like that? It seemed like life—or maybe adulthood—had gotten in the way.

Chasing away thoughts of summers spent at the lake, I

parked and got out. I had a hell of a lot of work to do, and I was already behind.

A zing of adrenaline perked me up more than my coffee as I entered the lobby. Melanie sat at the front desk, talking to someone on the phone. Thankfully, she was using her regular voice—no random accent. Her dark hair was up, and it irritated me the way her red lips twitched in a hint of a smile as our eyes met.

I was going to walk by and head straight for my office, but something about her was magnetic. She pulled me in against my will.

She said goodbye and hung up the phone. "Morning."

"Morning."

"Why so glum?"

"Glum? Who uses that word anymore?"

"Me, obviously. I was trying to be nice, but since that failed, why do you look like you slept in a dumpster?"

I glanced down at myself. "I don't look like I slept in a dumpster."

"Fine, someone's couch, then."

"I slept at home. Not that it's any of your business."

"Of course it isn't. Let's try this again." Pausing, she took a breath, then gave me a too-big smile. "Good morning, Mr. Haven. There's fresh coffee if you'd like."

"Is that your receptionist persona?"

She kept smiling. "I thought it would be appropriate."

"Can you just be… you?"

"Well, you don't like me, so…"

Glancing away, I rubbed the back of my neck. "I don't not like you. And before you make fun of me for the double negative, you know what I mean."

"I wasn't going to."

"Sure, you weren't."

Her lips turned up in a grin again. "Coffee?"

"Are you actually trying to be nice, or do you keep offering me coffee because I look like hell?"

"Both."

I backed away from the counter. "You drive me nuts. You know that, right?"

"Sorry. You look fine. You work in a garage, no one will notice."

"Exactly." I turned, pushing away the temptation to keep arguing with her, and went into the garage. I actually wanted a cup of coffee, but I couldn't get one after that. Not from up front, at least.

Fucking Melanie.

I went to my office, dropped into my chair, and raked a hand through my hair. A not-so-pleasant scent caught my attention. What was that? It smelled like dirty laundry. I sniffed the air again. Where was it coming from? Had I left something in my office? It wasn't exactly tidy, but there shouldn't have been anything that foul.

Wait.

Leaning down, I sniffed my armpits.

It was me.

I grabbed the hem of my shirt and pulled it down. Dirty. Visibly dirty. Sliding my chair back, I straightened my legs to inspect my jeans. They didn't look clean, either.

Apparently, I hadn't been paying attention when I'd grabbed my clothes. I must have taken them from the dirty basket, not the clean one.

Yes, I had a clean basket. Don't judge. At least my clean clothes weren't on the floor.

I really did look like I'd slept in a dumpster.

The last thing I was going to do was admit to Melanie she'd been right. I'd avoid the lobby and live with Patrick's barely drinkable coffee. And I was not changing my clothes. I'd just work on one of my restoration projects and get even dirtier. I was a mechanic, after all. Who needed clean clothes when you worked on cars all day?

My phone buzzed, so I swiped the screen to check. It was a text from someone who wasn't in my contacts.

Hey, it's Jenna. I was hoping you could come take a look at my grandpa's car.

She didn't just want me to look at her grandpa's car. I'd have bet my entire garage and every car in it. She wanted me to ask her out.

And why not? She was cute. I hadn't dated anyone in a while, so maybe it was time. I could look at her grandpa's car, then take her out. See if we hit it off.

Frustrated, I dropped my phone on my desk. I couldn't do it. It was the stupidest thing. She was attractive, and there might have been some chemistry between us. Or there should have been.

But somehow, the thought of going out with Jenna was strangely repulsive.

What was wrong with me?

I was tired and grumpy. That was all. I decided to wait and text Jenna back when I wasn't in such a crappy mood.

Leaving my phone on my desk, I went out to the garage in search of coffee. Unfortunately, the pot was empty. With a sigh, I decided to suck it up and go back to the lobby and the fresh—and undoubtedly better—coffee Mel had made.

Melanie's voice carried through the door that led to the lobby. I paused, listening. She wasn't using an accent or character voice, but there was something in her tone—a barely concealed sharpness. Who was she talking to?

I pushed the door open just enough to peek through and almost groaned. Gary Boggs stood in front of the counter wearing his typical sour expression. He was a local classic car enthusiast who did a lot of business with my garage. That should have been a good thing, but I wasn't sure if dealing with him was worth it. He was never happy.

"I've been waiting for an update," he said. "Tried calling a few times. Still nothing."

"I'm sorry about that. Our usual front desk person left on maternity leave, so I think a few things have fallen through the cracks."

"How is that my problem?"

"I don't suppose it is, although I'd think knowing the reason might lead to understanding."

"I understand, all right. It's always the same with him. Lazy as all hell. Luke Haven is unreliable and always has been."

I rolled my eyes. He was such a dick. I put my hand on the door and was about to saunter in and put him in his place when Melanie started to laugh.

It wasn't just any laugh. It had a hint of cartoon villain to it, which was oddly arousing. I hesitated, holding the door ajar with my foot.

"Oh, my friend." She slowly stood. "What was your name again?"

"Gary."

"Of course, Gary. You think Luke is lazy and unreliable?"

"That's what I said."

"Interesting. Because last I checked, customers are lined up to have him restore their cars. There's a mile-long waiting list and an even longer list of happy customers. You seem to be the anomaly, Gary. Which makes me think this is a *you* problem."

"Excuse me?"

"I think I was clear. If Luke owes you an estimate, and it's actually late, then I apologize for the inconvenience. But I have a feeling you were just looking for something to complain about today, and this happened to come up first on your list. Or maybe you were driving by, saw our sign, and thought, damn it, that Luke Haven." She dropped into a remarkable impression of Gary. "He didn't give me what I wanted exactly when I wanted it. I better go give him a piece of my mind. And while I'm at it, I'll be unnecessarily rude."

"Rude?"

"Yes, rude. You didn't have to waltz in here with insults on your tongue."

He crossed his arms and narrowed his eyes at her. I clenched my fists, tension rippling across my back. If he snapped at her, I was going to rearrange his face.

"Fair enough," he said, chastened. "My apologies."

Her expression softened into a smile. "Thank you, Gary. Apology accepted. And I'll find out about your estimate and make sure someone gets back to you as soon as possible."

"All right. I'll be expecting a call."

"Absolutely."

He nodded once and turned to leave.

"Enjoy the rest of your day," she said.

"I will. Thank you."

He left, and Melanie flipped him off as soon as the door closed behind him. "Asshole." She kept mumbling as she took her seat. "What a jerk. Lazy. Whatever. Unreliable. You're unreliable, Gary."

Stepping back, I carefully turned the knob so she wouldn't notice the door closing. It was hard not to laugh. She'd handled him like a pro, somehow telling him off and getting him to apologize in one fell swoop. I'd never heard Gary Boggs apologize for anything in all the years I'd worked with him.

But the almost-chuckle died on my lips as what she'd just done hit me square in the chest. She'd stood up for me. Not that I'd needed her to. Gary wouldn't hurt my feelings, no matter what he said about me. And she knew me well enough to know that. But she'd done it anyway.

Granted, maybe he'd just irritated her, and it didn't have anything to do with me.

But it wouldn't have been the first time.

A flood of memories came rushing back. The time our science teacher decided to give a surprise test right before finals week. Melanie had campaigned to get the grades removed, citing it as unfair to the students—not because she'd bombed that test but because I had.

Or when Harry Montgomery had accused me of crashing into his fence and letting his goats out. Melanie had mounted a defense every bit as good as a lawyer to prove it hadn't been me. I cracked a smile at the memory. She'd been incensed at the accusation. She'd even risked getting herself in trouble, considering I'd been with her that night, and we'd been out after her curfew.

Spicy nice. Annika had been right about that. And there'd been a time when Melanie's version of nice had been appealing. Not that I'd needed my girlfriend to defend me—I could have stood up for myself just fine—but she'd done it anyway. Because that was how she cared.

A very troubling thought crossed my mind. Had she stood up for me to Gary because she cared about me? Or had he just pissed her off? If he'd been complaining about Ollie or Patrick, would she have reacted the same way?

Probably. It couldn't have been because she cared about me, specifically. He'd just riled her up, which, let's be honest, wasn't hard to do. Melanie had a lot of buttons, and it was all too easy to push them.

Still, the thought was there, and I couldn't shake it. I went back to my office, trying not to think about a version of Melanie Andolini who still cared, and what it meant if she did.

Located

ROSWELL MILLS

THE LIBRARIAN DIDN'T LOOK up as I walked by. Either she didn't notice that I'd come in or she didn't care enough to raise her eyes. That was good. I wanted to go unnoticed.

But it also made me furious.

Shoving my hands deeper into the pocket of my hoodie, I appeased myself with a brief fantasy of strangling her—watching her face turn purple and her body twitch as it struggled for air.

I'd never killed anyone, although I'd fantasized about it often in prison. But I didn't imagine it would be difficult.

The bank of computers was mostly empty. An older man sat in front of one, leaning forward and adjusting his glasses as if he were having difficulty seeing the screen. I chose a workstation a few chairs down and sat. He didn't notice me, either.

I again reminded myself that was good. Invisible. Quiet. That was what I wanted, even though I hated it.

I wouldn't be invisible to her. She'd be the one to see me.

The library silence was briefly broken by the shrill cry of a brat in the children's section. The noise crawled up my spine, making my shoulders tighten. I didn't want to be there—didn't want to do my work in a public place. But it was safer that way. Fewer clues would lead them to me.

My stint in prison taught me a lot, particularly about how not to get caught. I'd listened, taking in the stories of the other inmates. Absorbed lessons they hadn't meant to teach. I'd benefit from their mistakes.

A thrill of anticipation invaded my chest when I touched the mouse and clicked to open an internet browser. I didn't anticipate difficulty in finding her. By now, she'd have let her guard down. But it made me wonder what she looked like. How had she changed? Was her hair different? Her choice of clothes?

I'd been in prison for ten years, and even before that, it had been a while since I'd seen her. After our encounter had ended so badly, I'd fled—not just the scene, but the state. I'd left Los Angeles and taken refuge with my mother in Tennessee.

I'd expected them to come. The police, the FBI, some law enforcement agency. But they hadn't. No one had come for me. Not because of her, at least.

I'd gotten sloppy later with the credit card thing. Too confident. Another mistake I wouldn't make again.

One side of my mouth curled in the hint of a smile as I got to work. Social media. What a glorious invention. People posted everything. All the seemingly meaningless shreds of their lives, right there for all the world to see.

I found her accounts on several different sites, but they didn't contain much by way of personal information. There were photos, but they were carefully curated. Posts, but all related to her profession as a voice actor. She wasn't a habitual social media user or even a casual one. It was all business—almost nothing personal.

Clicking through her profile, I found some older photos

with a man. My eyes narrowed. Him. I remembered him. The lawyer. So much of what I'd done had been his fault. He'd been in the way.

Interesting that there were so few of them together, and none of them recent. Maybe he was already out of her life.

Not that it mattered. She belonged to me. She just didn't know it yet.

I found contact information but no physical address or location. She didn't post enough photos to make it clear where she lived. I wondered if she was so private online because of me. It would have been gratifying to take credit. To know she still feared me enough to be careful.

The voice in my head whispered again. *She forgot about you. You're nothing to her.*

Gritting my teeth, I ignored it.

I modified my tactic and searched for her last name. Family might give me a clue. I didn't know who they were, so it took me a while to narrow down the possibilities. But finally, there she was.

Someone had posted a photo of her with three young children. But it wasn't the picture that made my lips turn upward. It was the caption.

Auntie Melanie is home! The kids are so excited to have her back in Tilikum.

Tilikum. I looked it up. A little scrap of nowhere nestled in the Cascade mountains in Washington state. It was well over two thousand miles from where I was, but the distance didn't matter. She could have been in Antarctica, and I would have found a way.

Reaching out, I touched a finger to the screen, right on her face.

I know where you are. And I'm coming for you.

CHAPTER 13
Melanie

THE BANQUET ROOM at Home Slice was getting full, and I didn't know who half the people were. Nathan and Sharla were there with the kids, as were another family with kids of similar ages. My parents' longtime neighbors, Ed and Linda, sat at the long table, chatting with a couple I hadn't met yet.

Another family with two teenage girls sat at the other end of the table next to Heidi, who worked at the Copper Kettle Diner. I'd heard someone say the woman sitting next to Heidi was a kindergarten teacher, and a guy in scrubs had obviously come straight from work.

Covering my mouth with my hand, I tried to stifle a yawn. Thanks to a particularly vivid nightmare, I hadn't slept much the previous night.

I moved to stand closer to my brother so he could hear me over the din of conversation. "So, what's going on? Mom said to come for dinner, but she didn't tell me it was a party."

"It's the annual pizza tasting."

"What's the annual pizza tasting?"

Nico ran by, and like the expert dad he was, Nathan

slowed him down with a hand on his chest. "Dad likes to keep the menu fresh, so he brings in a bunch of people to taste his new pizza ideas once a year."

"That's… cute, actually."

"Yeah." He sounded skeptical. "Just be forewarned, it can be a little hit or miss."

"Uh-oh."

"The oyster pizza was pretty memorable. And not in a good way."

I made a face. "Oysters?"

"His attempts at seafood pizzas haven't been his best. The banana curry was pretty terrible, too."

"Banana on pizza?"

He shrugged. "Apparently, it's a thing in some countries."

"What are we in for tonight?"

"No idea."

"I don't have to pretend I like something if it's terrible, right?"

"Nah, they know who they invited."

"Good."

Several more people came in, including a guy around my age. Nathan went over to talk to him, and they shook hands. They clearly knew each other. I might have thought about the fact that he was attractive and wondered who he was, except the next couple who came in captured my full attention.

Paul and Marlene Haven.

My breath caught in my throat. I had yet to see Luke's parents since I'd moved back to town. I knew my parents were friendly with them. Always had been. The fact that their kids had dated—and broken up—in high school hadn't changed anything.

That didn't bother me. The Havens were nice people. But I still felt a twinge of nervousness as they made their way into the banquet room and started chatting with Ed and Linda.

Paul Haven had broad shoulders and a thick beard. There was more salt in his salt-and-pepper hair than I remembered. Marlene still had the same friendly smile and blue-rimmed glasses. Her hair was cut in an above-the-shoulder bob that looked cute on her.

"Auntie Mel, Auntie Mel!" Lucia and Zola collided with me, one on each side. "Do the voice! Do the voice!"

I looked down and gave them my best slow, evil grin, then dropped into my Queen Ione voice. "Who are these little peasants? How dare you touch me. Begone, insolent brats!"

Laughing, they both hugged me.

"We're not peasants," Lucia said. "We're secret princesses!"

I gasped and grabbed them each by the wrist. "Guards! The princesses have infiltrated my stronghold. Take them away!"

Nico marched up to us with a stern expression. He was smaller than both of them, but apparently, he was the guard. I handed them over, and he took his sisters' wrists, one in each hand. "Let's go."

"Princess magic!" Zola exclaimed and pulled her arm away.

Lucia did the same, only with a twirl.

"Curse you, princesses!" I shook my fist. "You won't escape so easily next time."

In a fit of giggles, they scurried away.

"That was cute."

I turned to find Marlene standing next to me and smiled. "Hi, Mrs. Haven."

"None of that. It's Marlene. It's good to see you." She held her arms out.

I stepped into her hug. "It's good to see you, too."

"How have you been? Getting all settled, I hope."

"I'm working on it. It's a process."

She gave me a warm smile. "I'm sure it is. I hear you're working at Luke's shop. How's that going?"

"The fact that you have to ask seems like a good sign. Maybe that means Luke hasn't been complaining about me."

"Not at all."

"That's a tiny miracle. But it's going fine. And it's temporary. He just needed someone to fill in for a while, and I needed a job to tide me over until my next voice acting gig starts."

"Voice acting? Is that what the voice was about just now?"

"She's a character I play in a cartoon."

"What's it called?"

"*Enchanted Hollow*. I play the villain, Queen Ione."

"I thought I recognized the voice. That's my grandkids' favorite show."

"Is it? That's great."

"Oh my goodness, they love Queen Ione even though I think they're a little scared of her."

I laughed. "That's kind of what the writers are going for. Scary, but not too scary."

The banquet room door flew open. My mom sashayed in and held her arms open wide. The small crowd immediately silenced.

"Family and friends," Mom said, her arms still out like she was going to hug the entire room at once. "Thank you for joining us for Home Slice's annual pizza tasting."

She paused and glanced around. I got the hint first and started clapping. She nodded a few times as the room gave her a polite round of applause.

Holding up her hands as if she needed to quiet us down, she continued. "Thank you. We appreciate you coming. You are in for a treat. Anton has been hard at work with a variety of brand-new recipes." She clasped her hands to her chest. "I can't wait for you to try them."

Stepping aside, she swept an arm out to usher in my dad. Her raised eyebrows indicated we were supposed to clap again, so I started the applause. Dad just shook his head a little as he set the first piping-hot pizza on the table.

Behind him came Tristan and another employee whose name I didn't remember, each with a pizza. They set them down next to the first. The three of them left, and Mom held up her hands, indicating we had to wait. A moment later, they came back with three more pizzas.

"All right, everyone." Mom's words carried above the rising conversations, and we all quieted again. "If you haven't joined us before, this is how it works. We have plates and napkins here. The pizzas have been sliced into small portions, so please try one of each. When you've tried them all, let us know what you think. Be kind, but we do want your honest opinion."

"What do we have here, Dad?" Nathan asked.

Dad pointed at each pizza in turn. "The first is an arugula and mushroom breakfast pizza, topped with fried eggs. Then we have loaded baked potato, asparagus and herbed cheese, hummus and sun-dried tomato, kimchi pizza, and finally, the Melanie. Fried pickle."

I gasped. "You made a fried pickle pizza? Best dad ever."

Nathan gagged. "Dad. No."

"Quiet, peasant," I said in my Queen Ione voice. "This is the greatest pizza flavor of all time. Fit for a queen."

"Okay, weirdo," Nathan said. "It's all yours."

"Try a piece, Nathan." Mom wagged her finger at him. "You know the rules. Try one of each."

"Mom."

"Don't test me."

Shaking his head, he chuckled softly. I noticed Sharla meet his eyes and give him a subtle wink. She knew how much he hated pickles. She'd have his back and take his slice for him.

What a great wife.

There were several small stacks of plates, so people moved forward haphazardly to dish up. The noise of conversation grew once again as people chatted while they sampled. I went straight for the pickle pizza, already knowing I would love it. I had yet to meet a pickle I didn't like.

Right as I took a huge bite, my mom appeared in front of me, smiling her big magenta smile.

"Mel, I want you to meet Hank." She yanked a man over by his arm.

It was the guy Nathan had greeted when he'd first come in. He looked about my age, attractive, dressed in a button-down shirt with the sleeves cuffed to the elbows.

It took me a second to swallow my bite before I could say anything. "You do not look like a Hank."

"Melanie, please," Mom scolded.

"What? He doesn't look like a Hank. That's not an insult. It's just my impression."

"It's fine," he said. "I actually get that a lot. My parents were country music fans."

"There you have it." I gestured to him and turned to my mom. "I was going to ask if his name was music-inspired before you interrupted me."

She huffed and rolled her eyes. "Don't be put off by my mouthy daughter. She's really quite charming when she wants to be."

"Mouthy? What am I, eleven?"

"She's a voice actor," she continued, clearly ignoring me. "Melanie, Hank teaches at Tilikum College."

"What do you teach?" I asked.

"Literature. My specialty is Shakespeare."

Mom turned to me, acting overly impressed. "Shakespeare, Melanie. You two must have so much in common."

That was when I realized what this was. She was trying to set me up with Hank.

Uh-oh.

"Um…" I hesitated, suddenly feeling flustered, although I had no idea why. "Shakespeare. That's interesting."

"His work has always been a passion of mine. Especially when it's performed on stage. Reading Shakespeare just doesn't have the same impact."

"See?" Mom nudged me and lifted her eyebrows a few times. "Theater."

"Mom, I don't think Nathan has had the pickle pizza yet." Yes, I was throwing my brother under the bus. But I was sure he'd done something mean when we were kids and totally deserved it. "You better make sure he tries it and doesn't give his piece to Sharla."

Mom looked around, her face lighting up when she spotted him. "Oh, Nathan!"

I let out a breath as she wove her way through the crowd to accost my brother with pickle pizza.

"Sorry," I said. "My mother is excellent at making things awkward."

"Not a big deal. So, voice acting? How did you get into that?"

"I did a lot of live theater when I was younger. But I sort of moved on from that." I kept it vague. I didn't like talking about that period in my life. "I tried some voice-over stuff, and it was a lot of fun. I guess the rest is history."

His lips turned up in a grin, and he took a small step closer. "That's great."

I felt a little flutter in my stomach, but it wasn't a pleasant one. Or was it? Maybe it had been so long since a man had seemed interested in me that I didn't remember what it felt like.

"So, your mom tells me you just moved back to Tilikum," he said.

"How do you know my mom?"

He blinked as if surprised by my question. Of course, I

hadn't answered his. "I did a community workshop on Shakespeare's comedies last summer. She was in the class."

"Oh, I see. And yes, I just moved back. Divorced." I shrugged. "My ex was a jerk, so we didn't visit very often. Makes it feel like I've been gone for a hundred years, and half the town is exactly the same, while the other half is unrecognizable. Where are you from?"

He hesitated again. Not everyone had an easy time keeping up with me. "I grew up in Oregon, just south of Portland. But I went to college in Boston."

"And here you are in funny little Tilikum."

"It's a great place to live."

"Even with all the squirrels?"

He laughed a little. "Yes, even with all the squirrels."

"Sorry to interrupt." Mom sidled up next to me. "Have you tried all the flavors?"

"No, I haven't."

"Well, don't let me get in your way." She tried to push me closer to Hank. "You two keep getting to know each other. But also try the pizza."

She disappeared again into the crowd.

I gestured to the table. "I should try the other flavors."

"She seems very serious about that."

"Apparently, the annual pizza tasting is a big deal."

He smiled. "I won't keep you from the experimental pizza. But would you like to go out sometime?"

My heart seemed to stop for a second. Did I want to go out with Hank? Why not? He was attractive and well-spoken. My mother hadn't scared him off. Of course, my mother had clearly invited him to introduce us, which meant if I said yes, I was trusting her judgment, and that was slightly terrifying. But still, just one date?

"Sorry," he said. "If it's too soon for you, I totally understand."

"No, it's not really. My ex and I split up over a year ago. I'm just… Sorry, I haven't… This is the first time that…"

He nodded along as I babbled, then hesitated, like he was waiting to see if I was finished. "The first time after divorce is probably difficult. I've never been married, but I'd imagine it's tough."

I appreciated his understanding, but it wasn't my divorce holding me back. So what was it?

This guy? Really, Mel? The voice in my mind sounded suspiciously like Luke Haven.

Luke. Freaking. Haven. He really needed to get out of my head.

Although I knew it wasn't Luke talking to me telepathically, the fact that he was invading my headspace when a nice, good-looking man was asking me out infuriated me. A burst of hot anger swept through me like a spark igniting dry tinder.

"Hank, I would love to go out with you," I said, my voice both cheerful and decisive. "That would be wonderful."

"Great," he said with a smile.

Triumphantly, as if I'd just won a victory over Luke, I gave Hank my number and put his in my contacts. We set a date. Dinner, maybe drinks afterward.

I went for a slice of the loaded baked potato pizza and took a hearty bite. That would show Luke. Not that he'd actually done anything. But still. I had every right to go out with Hank. Luke and I were… nothing. He was my temporary boss. So what? He wasn't going to care who I dated.

I tried the arugula and mushroom pizza. It was awful, so I tossed it and took another slice of pickle. Everyone else seemed to be avoiding it, but that was their loss. I scarfed it down, and I was absolutely not eating my feelings.

Okay, maybe a little.

Because what if Luke didn't care who I dated? What if he was completely indifferent?

Obviously, he was supposed to be indifferent. But his imaginary nonchalance about my potential love life made me angrier.

So I ate another piece of pickle pizza.

I'd go on a date with Hank, and it would be wonderful. And there wasn't a thing Luke Haven could do about it.

CHAPTER 14

Luke

MY STOMACH RUMBLED at the smell of fries while Evan Bailey and I waited for our food. The Zany Zebra was great for greasy burgers, fries, and milkshakes. I was starving, so it was going to hit the spot.

The guy at the counter handed us each a tray with our orders, and we found an empty table.

Evan Bailey was a big dude with a perpetual scowl. The fact that he and I were friends was only slightly less shocking than my sister marrying his brother, Levi. Annika and Levi had ended the feud that had raged between our families for generations. But the rivalry between me and Evan had gone beyond the feud. It was personal. We'd hated each other.

Funny how things could change. Once he and I grudgingly admitted we respected each other—at least on a professional level—we'd started to run out of things to hate each other for. He was a good guy, and we had a lot in common. Like me, he restored classic cars, and we could spend hours talking shop.

He'd asked me to go with him to take a look at a car he was interested in down in Wenatchee. It was a 1969 Camaro—

a favorite of both of us—and the news had been good. The car was in rough shape but definitely salvageable, especially if he could get it for a decent price.

We'd decided to stop at the Zany Zebra for food on our way back into town.

I was about to sink my teeth into my double bacon cheese-burger when the door opened, and *she* walked in.

My heart rate picked up, and a burst of heat ran through my veins. In a sleeveless black dress with her hair up, she looked amazing. Damn it. Why did she have to show up everywhere I went? Having her at work every day was one thing—I was getting used to that—but it was starting to feel like I couldn't go anywhere in town without running into her.

I took the bite, ready to ignore her, when some guy walked in behind her.

No, he wasn't behind her. He was *with* her. And by the way he put a hand on the small of her back, he was her date.

My eyes met hers and I caught a glimmer of surprise in her expression. She glanced at her date—whoever the fuck he was—and back at me.

Really, Mel? That guy?

Evan raised an eyebrow and looked over his shoulder. I ignored him, narrowing my eyes at Melanie. She narrowed hers at me. We were like a couple of gunslingers facing off, ready to draw as soon as the other one twitched.

Her date didn't seem to notice. With his hand still on her back, he led her to the counter to order.

She watched me as she walked, her glare deepening, until the guy said something, and she tore her gaze from mine to reply.

Evan's mouth turned up in a slight grin.

I had to swallow the bite I'd taken. "What?"

"Is that Melanie Andolini?"

"Yeah."

"Huh."

"What does that mean?"

He popped a fry in his mouth. "Nothing."

I scowled at her back—and the back of the fucking guy she was with. "It's not a big deal."

"Yeah, I can see this doesn't bother you."

I turned my scowl on Evan. "It doesn't."

"Okay, sure."

They ordered something, and I ate a few fries without really tasting them. "Who over the age of seventeen brings a woman to the Zany Zebra on a date? Cheap-ass."

"Maybe it's not a date."

The guy leaned in close to her ear and said something. She laughed. I glared harder.

"Do you know who he is?" Evan asked.

"No. He looks familiar, but I don't know him."

The kid working the counter gave them two milkshakes. With his hand on her back again, the guy led her to a table on the other side of the restaurant, and they sat across from each other.

He really needed to stop touching her.

But why? What right did I have to be mad that she was out with someone?

She wasn't mine anymore.

That thought hit me square in the chest. And hurt more than I wanted to admit.

Evan glanced over his shoulder again. "That does look like a date. Sorry, man."

Clearing my throat, I hunkered down with my food. I just needed to ignore them.

"So, what are you going to do about it?" Evan asked.

Drag him outside and punch him in the teeth? "Nothing. It's not my business."

"True." Evan paused. "But you want to hit him, don't you?"

"It would be satisfying."

He chuckled and ate another fry. "Do you want to know what I would do?"

"Sure."

"Make a statement. Prove you want her more."

I hesitated. "You're speaking from experience, aren't you?"

"There was a time when you tried to take my girl."

"Come on, man, she wasn't your girl then."

He tipped his head. "Fair enough. She wasn't. And I should probably thank you. Because as soon as I found out you made a move on her, I made a bigger one."

Laughing softly, I shook my head. He was right. Before he and his wife Fiona had gotten together, I had made a move on her. Her rejection had stung at the time, but she'd hurt my ego more than my feelings. She was great—especially for Evan—but my attraction to her had been mostly superficial.

However, this wasn't about Fiona. This was about Melanie. And Evan had the wrong idea.

"That might be good advice if I wanted her, but I don't, so I don't have anything to prove."

"You just don't want him to have her?"

My eyes flicked to them again. "No. That would make me a dick."

"Yeah, kinda."

They were too far away for me to hear what they were saying, but Melanie laughed. I rolled my eyes.

"What does she want with a guy like that, anyway? He's all wrong for her."

Evan smirked. "Oh yeah?"

"Look at him." My eyes flicked toward their table. "Clean shave. Probably ironed that shirt. I bet he has soft hands."

Evan nodded, but I had a feeling he was just humoring me. And what was I talking about, anyway? I didn't want to be with her. She drove me crazy. So why did I care that she was out with some guy?

Some guy who was obviously wrong for her.

That was the problem. This wasn't about me. It was about her. She'd just been through a divorce. For all I knew, the jackass she'd been married to was a guy like that—who shaved every day and ironed his shirts and wouldn't know the difference between a torque wrench and a socket set.

"It's not that I want her," I said.

"No?"

I shook my head, confidence in my explanation growing. "She just got divorced, and I don't want to see her get hurt again by the same kind of asshole who hurt her before. That's all."

"That's very gentlemanly of you."

"Quit with the sarcasm, you dick."

"I'm serious."

"Yeah, you're not. Why am I even talking to you? If I want someone to give me crap, I'll call Theo."

Evan shrugged. "Fine. You don't want your ex-girlfriend back. You're only plotting the guy's murder in your head because you don't want her to get hurt again."

"Exactly."

From the corner of my eye, I glanced at Melanie and her date. Did she like him? Was she having a good time? I wondered if it was their first date and what he had planned after they had their milkshakes.

He didn't think he was going home with her, did he?

"You're glaring," Evan said.

I scowled at him. Again.

"I get it," he said. "Before Fiona, if I had to see my ex all the time, it would have driven me crazy. And not because I wanted her back."

"It wouldn't drive you crazy now?"

"No. She doesn't matter anymore."

That was how I should have felt about Melanie. Indifference. She could do what she wanted—date who she wanted —and it shouldn't have mattered to me.

But being there, sitting in a restaurant while she was on a date with some jackass, was absolutely driving me nuts. I couldn't hide it. Anger consumed me. I wanted to grab the guy, drag him outside, and beat the crap out of him.

That wasn't me. I'd never been one to start shit. Even when Evan and I had been cutthroat rivals, I'd never been this angry at him over anything. Not when he beat me out to get a client I'd wanted or a car I'd been hoping to buy and restore. Not even when Fiona chose him—definitively —over me.

I didn't even know who I was mad at. The guy for taking Melanie on a date? Or at Melanie for... for what exactly? For being in my head and pissing me off?

I was angry at her for making me mad. That made a ton of sense.

My appetite was gone, so I crumpled up the wrapper with what was left of my burger in it. "I should get going."

"Yeah, me too. Fiona and the kids will be home soon."

My phone buzzed with a text. It was Jenna. Standing, I slipped it in my back pocket and gathered up my trash. Why had I been so hesitant about Jenna? It couldn't have been because of Melanie. That made about as much sense as being angry at her because she made me mad. I didn't have feelings for Melanie—not those kind, at least. She could do whatever the fuck she wanted.

So I would too.

I followed Evan outside and said a quick goodbye, then got out my phone.

Jenna: *Hi! Just wondering if we could get together soon. My grandpa lives right up the street from me, so you could just come here first.*

Me: *How about I pick you up Friday at 6? I can look at the car, then we can go out.*

Jenna: *I'd love to. That sounds great!*
Me: *See you then.*
I cast a glare at the Zany Zebra. *Have a nice date, Mel.*

CHAPTER 15

Melanie

I SUCKED my chocolate milkshake through the straw, not really tasting it. It had sounded good when we'd decided to stop at the Zany Zebra after dinner, but Luke had ruined it.

He ruined everything.

Fortunately, he'd left. And Hank had been oblivious to his presence, and the fact that it had taken every ounce of my self-control to keep from telling Luke to stop messing with my very nice date. In my outside voice.

Because it had been a nice date. A great one, as a matter of fact. Hank was awesome. He was smart, interesting, funny, attractive. Great hair, warm brown eyes, chiseled jaw, nice smile. He clearly spent time in the gym. He looked fit and strong.

So why was the fact that he was objectively handsome doing absolutely nothing for me physically?

This was a problem. I wondered if I was broken. Had it been so long that my hormones had decided I was finished with things like attraction and arousal? Were my lady parts planning an early retirement?

We'll just ignore the rush of heat I felt when I walked in and saw Luke. Nope. Didn't happen.

The man who should have been giving me pleasant, tingly feelings was sitting across from me. And he just… wasn't.

"Are you done?" Hank asked.

I lifted my half-full milkshake. "I guess I overestimated how much room I had left after dinner."

He grinned. "Me too. Ready to go?"

I nodded, and we both stood. He threw our cups in the garbage and led me out to his car—a Toyota RAV4. A perfectly sensible car and much more comfortable than the muscle cars Luke always drove.

We chatted a little more on the way to my house, and it was… nice. He made me laugh, and his smile was charming.

But the fire inside me wasn't for Hank. It was indignation at Luke for being at the Zany Zebra. The whole thing had to be his fault. He'd been sitting there in his faded T-shirt that stretched over his broad back and muscular arms, with that stupid scowl on his stupid handsome face. And all I could think about was that groove he got between his eyebrows when he was mad and how much it looked like the expression he wore when he—

No. I wasn't going there. I didn't even remember the face he made when he—

No. Again.

And there I was, blood boiling as we pulled up to my house. Hank got out to walk me to my door, and I tried as hard as I could to smooth out my features. But my face had a way of talking out loud, whether I wanted it to or not.

"Are you okay?" he asked, his brow creasing with concern.

"Yes. Sorry." I took a deep breath. "It's just work stuff. Something popped into my head that I have to deal with tomorrow, and my face doesn't have an inside voice."

He chuckled. "Fair enough. I had a good time tonight."

"Me too."

Leaning in, he brushed a quick kiss on my cheek. "Thanks, Melanie. I'll call you?"

"That would be great."

While he walked back to his car, I unlocked the door. He paused before getting in, as if waiting to make sure I made it inside okay. That was polite of him. I waved, then went in the house and shut the door.

I let out a long breath. I had no idea how to feel. Hank seemed like a good guy, and it had been a perfectly decent first date. What did I expect? Fireworks? To fall head over heels in love with someone over dinner and milkshakes?

And how would I manage to date anyone when Luke Haven seemed to be everywhere? What was next? Dinner seated at adjacent tables?

I shuddered.

Living in my hometown was turning out to be more complicated than I'd thought.

And what was going to happen at work tomorrow? I groaned. That was going to be awkward.

———

Apparently, I'd been wrong about the awkwardness at work. It wasn't. Because Luke wasn't there.

Where was he? It was irritating that he wasn't there, and just as irritating that I was irritated. I wasn't his keeper. I didn't need to know where he was every second of the day.

Ollie walked into the lobby from the garage, his battered baseball cap on backward. "Hey, Mel."

"Hi, Ollie." I started to ask if he knew where Luke was but pressed my lips together to stop myself. I didn't need to know.

Didn't even care.

He grabbed some mail off the desk and went back to the garage.

I checked the clock again. I still had a couple hours before it was time for me to go home. I needed to get out of there and stop pouting about the fact that my ex-boyfriend-turned-boss hadn't been in to work yet.

My cell rang. It was my mom, so I answered. "Hi, Mom."

"How was your date?"

I shook my head slightly at her bluntness. "It was fine."

"Fine? Just fine? What do you mean by that?"

"I mean it was good. We had a nice time."

"And…?"

"And, what? Do you think I'm going to give you the details of any post-date bedroom activities? There were none, by the way, but why are you even asking me that?"

"Why not? We're adults. Melanie, this may come as a shock, but I know you're not a virgin."

"That doesn't mean I want to discuss my sex life with my mother."

"Mother? Why do you have to be like that? You know I hate being referred to as 'mother.'"

"Sorry. Mom. And I'm still not discussing this with you. Besides, there's nothing to discuss."

"Well, that's disappointing."

"You're disappointed I didn't sleep with Hank on the first date?"

"No, no, that's not what I mean. We're getting off track. I wasn't talking about sex. I was just hoping you'd tell me you had an amazing evening. Maybe thank me for inviting him to the pizza tasting and making sure you got together."

"Why do I feel like you already have a wedding venue in mind?"

"Considering your first one was at that awful hotel with all the modern decor, I think you should listen to my suggestions this time."

"There's no 'this time.' I went out on one date with a guy. Don't start dress shopping."

"Okay, but when the time comes, you'll of course take me with you."

"Mom," I groaned.

"When are you going out with Hank again?"

"I don't know. He hasn't called."

"What? Didn't you make plans last night?"

"No, and please stop trying to micromanage dating for me. He'll call."

I could practically hear her pouting. "He better."

"He will. We had a good time, and he said he would. He doesn't strike me as the type of guy who plays games. If he said he'll call, he'll call."

"I'm sure you're right. He does seem emotionally mature. And so handsome."

"Seems like you should date him," I said with a laugh.

"In another life, maybe. You know I only have eyes for your father."

"And I love that about you."

"All right, I'll let you get back to work. But tell me when Hank calls."

"I'm not telling you when he calls. You need to stay out of it."

"I just want to know."

"Look, as soon as I decide to let him bang me senseless, you'll be the first to know. How's that?"

Mom laughed.

Patrick stopped on his way past the front desk and gave me a look. I hadn't even realized he'd come into the lobby.

I rolled my eyes. "Mom, I gotta go."

Patrick shook his head and left.

We said goodbye, and I ended the call. Of course one of the guys would walk by right as I said that.

At least it hadn't been Luke.

I paused for a second, trying to imagine letting Hank bang me senseless. Not that I was in a rush to jump in bed with him—or any guy. But could I picture it? It seemed like I ought to be able to at least imagine it as a possibility to look forward to.

But I had nothing. No little bursts of heat between my legs. No dirty fantasy flitting through my mind, hinting at where I hoped things would go with him when the time was right.

Oh well. We'd been on one date, and it had ended with a rather friendly kiss on the cheek. He hadn't exactly given me any daydream material. Maybe we just needed another date for my hormones to wake up and take notice.

The door opened, and I glanced up. Luke walked in, sunglasses on his face, dressed in a gray T-shirt and faded jeans.

A flush crept across my cheeks, and warmth stirred in my core. The fireworks I'd been lacking with Hank absolutely did not begin to explode when Luke came in. Of course every cell in my body wasn't drawn to him. It had to be something else. Anger, maybe. I was mad, not aroused.

"Morning," I said with exaggerated cheerfulness. "Oh wait, it's afternoon."

He took off his sunglasses with a glare, and his tongue brushed his teeth. "I've been working. Just not here."

"I was just…" Something about his expression took the wind out of my sails. "Fine, I was being snarky. I'm sorry."

My apology seemed to catch him off guard. His glare melted, but he still eyed me with suspicion like he was waiting for my mood to flip.

"It's fine."

He hesitated, and the awkwardness I'd been dreading permeated the air. Should I say something about seeing him at the Zany Zebra? About Hank?

"I didn't sleep with him last night," I blurted out.

His eyebrows drew in.

Why couldn't I have a filter like normal people? "All I

mean is that I barely know him and we just had dinner. My mom introduced us. We were there for milkshakes and I went home after. Alone."

He moved closer to the front desk, his expression serious. My insides swirled. Why did he have to smell so good?

"Mel, it's fine. I don't need to know."

"Right, of course. You probably don't want to know. If it were you, I wouldn't want to know."

Something almost like alarm flashed across his expression. The tantalizing swirl was replaced by a mildly sick sensation. He had a date. He hadn't said a word, and the look was gone almost as quickly as it had come. But I knew.

Words started tumbling out of my mouth in a rush, and my hands were all over the place, gesturing wildly. "Maybe we should consider sharing our calendars so we know what places to avoid. In case of, you know, dates or whatever. That might be helpful. Although I'm not sure if it would have helped last night. I have a feeling we both wound up at the Zany Zebra on a whim. That's not the kind of place you plan for."

The corner of his mouth lifted.

"Are you laughing at me?" I asked, indignant.

His smile grew. "I'm not laughing."

"Okay, but you're smirking."

"I'm not smirking."

"You're absolutely smirking. You're making fun of me."

"I'm not. It's just…"

"What?"

He casually rested a forearm on the counter. My swirling insides were back, as was the warmth in my cheeks.

And elsewhere.

"I just never know what I'm going to get with you." He sounded mildly amused. "Sometimes you're completely self-assured, like you have no doubt you're going to get exactly what you want. And other times, you're a hot mess."

"I'm not a hot mess," I said with a pout.

He raised his eyebrows. "It's a miracle you didn't knock over your water bottle just now."

"I was talking with my hands, wasn't I?"

"A lot."

I tucked both hands under my thighs. "There."

He grinned again. "Look, let's just… be at work today. And not worry about the rest of it."

Still pouting slightly, I nodded.

With a soft laugh, he shook his head a little and turned to go to his office. I felt a hint of disappointment, as if I didn't want him to leave.

He paused and turned back to me. "Can I just ask you one thing?"

"Yeah."

"Him? Are you sure?"

It was my turn to smirk. "You said we were going to just be at work today and not worry about the rest of it."

"I know, I know. It's not my business. But really?"

"What's wrong with Hank?"

"That dude's name is Hank?"

I pressed my lips together to suppress a laugh. "Yes. And of course I'm not sure. I went out with him one time. And since apparently we are going to talk about this, if he asks, I'll see him again. I'm open to the possibilities."

"You're really ready, though?" His gentle concern was disarming. "For dating again?"

The way he said that softened me, and instead of being flippant, I answered honestly. "Yeah, I am. I know it seems like my divorce just happened, but we actually split up over a year ago."

"All right. Just making sure."

I pulled my hands out from beneath my thighs, pretty sure I wasn't going to knock anything over. "Thanks. You should probably go fix a car or something."

His half grin was back. "Yeah, I'll do that."

I scowled at the door as he left the lobby. But for once, Luke wasn't making me angry. It was the unfairness of it all. The fact that the last man on earth who ought to be giving me tingly feelings was the one who did.

My phone buzzed with a text. It was Hank. I blew out a breath, hoping to rid myself of all vestiges of Luke-induced sensations.

It didn't really work.

Hank: *Thanks again for last night. Had a great time. Are you free Friday?*

I hesitated. I was free on Friday. My eyes flicked between my phone and the door Luke had just gone through.

What did he have to do with it? I had a very strong feeling he was dating someone. And even if he wasn't, I could date Hank if I wanted to. It wasn't about Luke. It was about me, starting a new life. Moving on.

All those tingly feelings were just echoes—memories of something that had ended a long time ago.

Me: *Yes, I'm free.*

Hank: *How about I pick you up at 6?*

Me: *Perfect.*

Hank: *Great, it's a date.*

I set my phone down. Yes, it was a date. And it was fine. I'd go out with him again, and damn it, there would be sparks. There had to be.

And if not, it was probably Luke's fault. Somehow.

CHAPTER 16

Luke

NO WOMAN in the history of the world had ever been more confusing—or exasperating—than Melanie Andolini.

Instead of heading to my office, I went into the garage. Patrick and Ollie were working on restorations, and I had another project I was seeing to personally—a black 1968 Dodge Charger. But mostly, I wanted to keep my hands busy. Sitting at a desk would lead to brooding—over a girl I should not have been brooding over.

I got started on the Charger, determined to put Melanie out of my mind.

It didn't work.

Because, seriously. Hank? All right, it was a cool name, but why was she dating him? And did he have any idea what he was getting into?

I hoped he was ready for it.

Or maybe I hoped he wasn't.

Either way, that woman was a wildfire. I needed to keep my distance, or I was going to keep getting scorched.

My phone buzzed with a text, so I slipped it out of the back pocket of my jeans to check. It was Kyle. I didn't have to read it to know what it said. A race was on.

It was tempting. But the strange thing was, I wasn't craving speed. Not for the rush of adrenaline, at least. I was restless and frustrated—amped up with too much energy. It was hard to keep still, but I didn't know what I wanted.

What was wrong with me? Was it Melanie? Was I that pissed off that she'd gone out with another guy? Maybe, although I probably needed to stop blaming all my bad moods on her.

And there was the fact that I had no right to be mad. She went on a date, so what? I had a date on Friday. Would she be angry with me over it? I doubted it.

That kind of pissed me off, too.

Too many feelings. I didn't like it. But I said no to the race.

Time went by in a blur as I worked on the car. It was good to have something else to focus on. No dates or ex-girlfriends or frustrating emotions. Just the work I'd always loved.

I don't know what made me glance up. It was too loud to have heard her come in. I wiped my hands on a shop towel as I watched her walk to the parts area with a printout in her hand, my eyes drifting over the curves of her body. A heady rush of adrenaline surged through me, making my heart beat harder.

My gaze locked on her. I couldn't stop staring. She started to look for something on the shelf, referencing the sheet she held in her hand. Whatever she was after, she clearly couldn't find it.

She rose on her tiptoes to look on the top shelf but wasn't tall enough.

I put the shop towel down. "Hey, Mel."

She didn't answer. Too much noise.

I walked across the garage to see what she was trying to find. She moved farther down the wall of shelves and popped up on her toes again.

"Mel."

When she didn't turn, I reached out to tap her on the shoulder. "Do you nee—"

As soon as my hand touched her, and before I could finish the word, she whirled around, eyes wild with terror, and punched me right in the nose.

Pain made me stagger back, and my eyes immediately started to water. I covered my nose with my hand.

"What the fuck?"

Her eyes widened, and she clapped a hand over her mouth.

I lowered my hand to see if my nose was bleeding. It wasn't, but I had to keep blinking to get my eyes to stop watering.

"I'm so sorry," she said.

Gingerly, I touched the bridge of my nose. "Holy shit, Mel. What the fuck did you do that for?"

"You scared me."

"I tapped you on the shoulder. I don't think that warrants a fist to the face."

"I didn't mean to. I didn't even know you were there. You can't hear a thing in here."

Pain throbbed, radiating across my cheekbones. "I wasn't trying to scare you."

"But you did. Warn a girl before you touch her from behind."

I was about to snap at her, but the look in her eyes stopped me. There was still a wildness in her expression. And it wasn't anger. It was fear.

She looked terrified.

"Hey." I tried to soften my voice, although it was difficult with all the noise. "Are you okay?"

"Um, Luke?"

"What?"

She pointed at my face. "You're bleeding."

I felt the warm drip and cupped my hand under my nose to catch it as I ran for the bathroom. Melanie followed me in.

I unrolled a handful of toilet paper and tried to mop up the mess before I got blood on my shirt.

"Are you all right?" she asked. "Do you need more toilet paper?"

"I got it." I leaned over the sink and pinched the bridge of my nose, hoping to make it stop faster. "And no, I'm not all right. You punched me in the face."

"I'm sorry. You startled me."

"Most people get startled and gasp or scream or something. They don't turn around throwing punches."

"Well… I'm not most people."

I glanced at her. "No, Melanie, you are definitely not."

"I said I was sorry."

"It's fine. I'm not mad. I just don't want to bleed all over everything."

She grabbed another wad of toilet paper and held it out to me. "Here."

I hesitated. I didn't want her help. She'd just hit me. But obviously, she hadn't meant to. She was just being Melanie —overreacting.

Or was she? That look in her eyes. She'd been terrified. What was she so afraid of?

I took the toilet paper and replaced the blood-soaked wad I'd been holding. "Thanks."

"It should stop soon. Noses bleed a lot. I didn't break it, did I?"

"I don't think so." I scrunched my nose. The pain was dulling. Probably not broken. "I'm okay."

The bleeding was already slowing down. I mopped it up as best I could. I'd shove some more toilet paper in my nostrils if I needed to.

Melanie still stood there, watching me with concern. The fear was gone from her expression, but the memory of it was burned into my mind. I thought about asking her why that had freaked her out so badly, until I caught sight of the way she was holding her right hand—sort of tucked against her body.

"Did you hurt yourself?" I asked, shifting to face her.

"No."

I reached for her hand. "Let me see."

She put it behind her back. "It's fine."

"Then let me see it."

After hesitating for another second, she held her hand out toward me. I took it in mine and gently lifted it for a closer look. Her knuckles were red and starting to swell.

"Can you make a fist?" I asked.

She did, opening and closing her hand a few times.

I took her hand again and had the strangest urge to kiss the backs of her fingers. Lifting my eyes, my gaze met hers. A wave of heat swept through me, like fire in my veins, and the sudden pressure in my groin almost made my head spin.

A flush hit her cheeks and her lips parted. I wanted to taste that mouth. Kiss her so hard and so good that she forgot any other man had ever kissed her.

I dropped her hand like a hot rock and stepped back. Unfortunately, we were still in the tiny bathroom, and the sink was right behind me. I bumped into it hard enough that I couldn't play it off like nothing had happened.

"You're bleeding again." She scrambled for another wad of toilet paper, then moved closer and held it up to my nose.

Her proximity was somehow both unnerving and intoxicating. The heat of desire still flowed through me, putting thoughts in my head I had no business thinking. Like yanking her pants off, bending her over, and burying myself in her—

"Did it stop?"

Her voice jolted me back to reality, although my heart beat so hard, I wondered if she could hear it.

I took the wad of toilet paper from her and checked. There

wasn't much blood on it. After folding it, I pressed it against each nostril. Only a bit of red. Hopefully, it was done.

"I think so. Come on, let's get you some ice."

She went back into the garage, and I blew out a breath, trying to clear my head. What the hell was wrong with me? She was the last woman I should have been fantasizing about, especially when she was mere inches away. I didn't want her. I didn't even like her.

Except…

No.

I followed her out of the restroom. "I have a first-aid kit in my office. It should have a few ice packs."

"Maybe you should use one on your nose."

"Probably, but let's take care of you first."

I led her through the garage to my office and took the first-aid kit off the shelf, setting it on my desk. I dug through the assortment of bandages, gauze, and other supplies in the red plastic box, finally finding several small ice packs that would get cold if you squeezed and shook them up.

Ignoring the ache in my nose, I got the ice pack ready for her. When it started feeling cold, I lifted her hand and placed the pack gently on her knuckles.

"Thanks," she said. "Sorry about your nose."

"I'm all right."

I could have let go. Made her hold the ice pack herself. I could have told her I had to get to work and sent her back to the front desk.

But I didn't. I couldn't seem to make myself stop touching her.

Memories flitted through my mind. It wasn't the first time I'd held an ice pack for Melanie.

"You're smirking again," she said.

"No, I'm not."

"You totally are. What are you thinking about?"

"I was just remembering that time you slipped off a log and fell in the lake."

"In my defense, that log was very slippery."

"Right. I'm sure it had nothing to do with you reciting some monologue and gesturing with basically your entire body."

"I was not. That doesn't sound anything like me."

I chuckled. "And then you flailed around so much on the way down, you smacked your elbow on the log."

"What was I supposed to do, swan dive?"

"That would have been more graceful."

She sighed. "There's a reason I was never good at musical theater. The whole coordination part. But I do remember that. You jumped in after me and carried me to shore."

"I think you hit me in the nose that time, too."

"No, I didn't," she said with a laugh. "Oh wait, maybe I did."

"You did. You were still flailing around in the water when I got to you, like you thought you were going to drown."

"I was just very surprised to suddenly be in the cold lake water. It's freezing."

The rest was vivid in my memory. She had hit me in the nose. Once she'd realized I was there and the water was shallow enough to stand in, she'd thrown her arms around me and peppered my face with kisses to apologize. Then I'd gathered her in my arms and carried her to shore. We'd made out on a towel for a while before realizing her elbow was starting to bruise. So we'd gone to my folks' place to get an ice pack and spent the rest of the night cuddling on the couch.

Despite the minor injury, it had been a good day.

The memory hurt.

I let go of her and stepped away. She moved her other hand to hold the ice pack in place. Clearing my throat, I grabbed another ice pack and shook it up, then held it to my nose. Not because I thought I needed it, but to pull myself from her orbit.

"I should get back to the front desk. Hardly any calls all morning and there were probably twenty since I got up."

"Yeah, that's how it goes sometimes."

"Thanks for the ice pack. And sorry for punching you in the face."

"Sorry for scaring you."

She hesitated, her mouth partially open, like she had something else to say. But after a few seconds, she closed it, as if she'd changed her mind. Without another word, she turned and walked away, leaving me with an empty ache in my chest.

On the road

ROSWELL MILLS

TAKING A LONG DRAG FROM A CIGARETTE, I peered into the circle of light next to the gas station across the street. One of the girls looked high. There were two of them, dressed mostly in black, showing a lot of skin. Not unusual for summer, but they weren't clad so scantily because of the weather. They were looking for business.

I didn't care whether or not they were high. Hookers usually were. But the one on the left could hardly stand. She wouldn't do. Too sloppy. Loathing made my upper lip curl in a sneer.

What a disgrace.

The other one, though. She had potential. Her hair was blond—wrong color—but that wasn't important. It was the shape that mattered. Height, weight, body type. She was close enough.

I took another drag and blew out the smoke, flicking the butt to the ground. I straightened my back and crossed the street.

The stumbling one leaned against the building for balance.

Her legs wobbled and she sank to the ground, her eyes half closed.

Ignoring her, I approached the other.

She gasped as if startled. "Where did you come from?"

I gestured with a nod. "Across the street."

"Oh my god, I didn't see you coming."

Of course she didn't. No one ever saw me. I wasn't worth seeing.

"My apologies if I frightened you."

The corners of her mouth turned up in a slight smile, and her eyes swept up and down as if she were taking me in. "You have very nice manners. Are you looking for some company tonight?"

I wasn't stupid enough to believe she saw anything in me she liked—other than cash. "How much?"

She told me her price. It was steeper than I remembered for a whore, but it had been a decade. Even hookers were victims of inflation.

Besides, I had plenty of money. I'd added to my stash before I left Tennessee. My mother didn't trust banks, and she'd been stupid enough to use her birthday as the code to her safe. I had no idea if she counted it regularly, but I doubted it. I'd left enough and arranged it in such a way that the next time she opened it, she wouldn't notice anything was gone.

I'd procured other things I was going to need. The sedatives had been harder to score than the cash, but I'd managed to buy a healthy supply. I had new clothes, and I'd bought a car. A cheap one, but it would serve my purposes.

I hesitated before agreeing to her price. I did have the cash, but I didn't want to seem too eager. "Fine."

"You have a car?"

I shook my head. "Hotel room."

"Ooh, fancy. You're a regular gentleman. What should I call you?"

"John."

She laughed. "Naturally. All right, John. Lead the way."

My gaze flicked to the other girl. Her head lolled to one side. My companion for the evening—I wasn't going to call her by name yet—glanced at her.

"Hey," she said, her voice sharp. "You okay?"

The other girl's eyes opened wide. "Yeah. I'm great."

"You're never going to get any business like that." She shook her head. "Don't say I didn't warn you."

My patience was wearing thin. "Let's go."

"I'm coming." She gave me what she probably thought was a sultry smile. It emphasized the harsh red of her lipstick and the thick makeup on her face. "And you will be soon."

I didn't bother replying. That wasn't the sort of role-play I needed. "Just be quiet."

"You're the boss."

With her walking next to me, my mind wandered to what it would be like to have her. Not this trash, the only *her* who mattered. What would it be like when I could take her out and walk with her. Would we ever reach that level of understanding and trust?

In the beginning, she'd need to be restrained. She was far too spirited to be trusted without chains.

That aroused me far more than the hooker walking through the dirty street toward my cheap motel.

To help set the stage—heighten the experience—I took her wrist in my hand. The hooker didn't protest.

"Good girl," I whispered.

She didn't seem to hear me.

When we got to my room, I kept my grip on her wrist while I unlocked the door, only releasing her so she could go inside. She went in and took a few slow steps, looking around as if she hadn't been to this same motel a thousand times with a thousand different men.

"Not bad," she said. "Been a while since I got to work in a room. It has a bed and everything."

I closed the door behind me and locked it.

My voice was monotone. "Clothes off."

"All of them? Some Johns like me to leave certain things on."

"All of them."

She shrugged. "Have it your way."

I watched while she stripped. She didn't try to make a show of it. I wasn't paying her for that. She peeled everything off and set it aside, then stood in front of me.

"Well? What can I do for you, John?"

My eyes swept up and down. She was almost too thin. Not enough in the hips. But no one was perfect.

No one else was *her*.

She'd do.

I pulled an elastic band out of my pocket and held it out to her. "Put your hair up. Ponytail."

She smiled like she thought I might be joking. "Really?"

"You're too blond, but I don't want to pay you to dye your hair. So put it up."

"Oh, I see." She started gathering her hair into a ponytail. "I'm standing in for someone, aren't I?"

I didn't answer.

She tied the elastic band around her hair and pulled the strands to tighten the ponytail. "I can do that. Who am I? Ex-wife? Forbidden coworker? What's my name?"

My voice came out in a whisper. "Melanie."

"Melanie? I like that. It's pretty. I can be Melanie for you tonight."

She started to come closer, but I held out a hand. I didn't want to look at her face. "On the bed, on your knees."

She climbed onto the bed and got on all fours. I squinted, making her image blur. Yes. That was good. It wasn't her, but it would do. Tide me over until I could have the real thing.

I unzipped and put on a condom. I had no intention of taking off more clothes than necessary. I didn't really want to touch her—this poor substitute—but I was going crazy. It had been so long. I needed this. Deserved this. I'd been so patient. Melanie would understand.

The hooker obliged, answering to Melanie while I fucked her. I said her name every time I thrust—a rhythmic chant. *Melanie, Melanie, Melanie*. With my eyes closed, I imagined it was her. I wasn't in a cheap motel room with a stupid whore. I was in our place, wherever that was going to be. And it was her. My Melanie. It was her stream of yeses, her eager and willing body.

I knew it wouldn't be like this right away. It would take time. Years, most likely. She wouldn't be so compliant. Not my Melanie.

Not the one who got away from me.

But I'd teach her. Slowly but surely, I'd show her that she wanted me as much as I'd always wanted her. And we'd be together forever.

I finished with a roar of her name. With my eyes still closed, I held her hips for a moment longer, still pretending. Still fantasizing. Wishing I could be lost there. That I'd open my eyes, and it would be her.

But it wasn't.

A wave of revulsion swept through me as I pulled out. I went straight to the bathroom, still breathing hard, where I threw away the condom and fastened my jeans. Closing my eyes again, I washed my hands, chasing the feeling of satisfaction. Of heat and desire and the burst of pleasure. Imagining what it would be like when it was real.

Not yet. But soon.

When I came out of the bathroom, the hooker was mostly dressed, sitting on the edge of the bed putting on her shoes. She gasped again, like I'd somehow startled her.

"You're so quiet," she said.

I didn't reply.

"Well, I guess you weren't quiet before." She stood with a smile and held out her hand. "I'll be on my way unless you want another. Half off the second round, but you have to finish in thirty minutes or less. And trust me, I can make you finish in time."

"No." I pulled cash out of my pocket and handed it to her. "Get out."

"You sure? I liked being Melanie. I think I'll start using that name with all my Johns."

White-hot rage hit me like a bolt of lightning. Gritting my teeth together, I lunged for her. "You're not Melanie!"

She was bruised and bloody by the time I was done. But alive. I hadn't heard her protests, her pleas. I'd muffled her attempts to scream.

No one would care anyway. Not in that place, and not about her.

Still, it meant I had to leave. Pity. I'd paid for the room. I glared at her as she whimpered on the floor. It was her fault. She shouldn't have said that—shouldn't have dared to claim that name.

I gathered my duffel bag and stepped over her on my way out the door. Without another look, I left.

CHAPTER 17
Melanie

SOMETHING WAS DEFINITELY wrong with me.

I was out on a date with a nice, attractive man—who, I might add, was exhibiting none of the red flags my ex had inadvertently taught me to watch out for. He was well-spoken and had good manners, and our conversation had been interesting enough. My lack of filter didn't seem to bother him, although I was trying to think before I spoke as much as possible. All in all, the date was going well.

Except I was bored.

It wasn't even Hank's fault. He wasn't boring. He was fine. I couldn't understand it. How could I feel… nothing?

The clink of dishes and low hum of conversation surrounded us. The restaurant he'd chosen was pleasant— probably one of the nicer places in town. It was small and intimate, with dark hardwood floors, black-and-white artwork adorning the walls, and candles flickering on tables draped in white linens. And although only a few open tables were left, it didn't feel crowded.

I drew my attention back to Hank. He'd been talking about how much he loved vacationing in Hawaii.

"The snorkeling was fantastic, but I think my favorite part was swimming with sharks," he said.

"Sharks? You swam with sharks. Actual predators that could eat you."

He laughed a little. "I did, and it was amazing. It's all very safe. Or as safe as they can make it."

I shook my head slowly. "No, thank you. Snorkeling with pretty fish is one thing, but I wouldn't get anywhere near a shark. Especially on purpose."

"Fair enough."

"I've never been to Hawaii. I'd love to go someday. Minus the shark swimming."

He didn't reply—just went back to his dinner. A hint of awkwardness crept over our table. I hadn't meant to insinuate that I hoped he'd take me to Hawaii, but maybe the way I'd said it had given him that impression.

I took a bite of my mushroom risotto, letting the silence linger. Did I want to go to Hawaii with Hank? A vacation in a beautiful place certainly had appeal, but I didn't have any particular desire to go there with him.

Before I could finish thinking about what that obviously meant, the door opened, and Luke Haven walked in.

The sight of him in a button-down shirt and slacks made my insides swirl. But the tingle in my stomach was quickly replaced by queasiness as I watched a beautiful blond woman come in with him.

She was the one he'd been talking to at the garage. Tearing my eyes away, I took another bite. He'd said nothing was going on with her. Liar, liar, pants on fire, Luke. Clearly nothing was something, considering they were on a date.

Of course they'd come to the same restaurant. For a small town, Tilikum had plenty of dining choices. How was it possible we'd both wind up here?

Whatever. I'd just ignore them.

"So," I said, hoping to reignite the conversation with Hank, "where else have you gone snorkeling?"

He started to answer, telling me about snorkeling in the Bahamas. I kept my eyes on him, trying to listen attentively, while my peripheral vision caught sight of Luke and his date being seated a few tables away.

Without really meaning to, I glanced over. For a second, my eyes met Luke's. His narrowed. Mine narrowed back, then I snatched my gaze away.

"That sounds amazing," I said. Fortunately, I'd been keeping up with most of what Hank had been saying. "I've never heard of a porcupinefish. Are they dangerous?"

"Not at all. Sometimes people confuse them with pufferfish, but they're not poisonous. They're quite laid-back, actually. Sometimes they're called the cows of the Caribbean."

I smiled. "That's cute."

"What about you? Do you like to travel?"

My gaze flicked to Luke, and our eyes met for half a second. Why was he looking at me? It was bad enough that he was there—with a stupid date. Couldn't he keep his eyes on her? Fine, I'd looked at him too, but only the teeniest glance.

"I do like to travel," I answered. "Although I haven't done as much of it as I'd like. I don't mean to make it weird or turn this into an ex-bashing session, but I was with a man who hated anything that took him away from work. That kind of limited my travel opportunities."

"That's too bad. It's important to have good work-life balance."

"I agree."

I glanced at Luke's table again. It was as if my eyes had a mind of their own. I didn't want to look at him, but I couldn't seem to help myself.

And why did he keep glancing in my direction at exactly

the same time? Our eyes met again, and I almost dropped my fork.

"Are you okay?" Hank's head tilted with concern.

"Fine, yes." My answer came out a little too quickly to sound believable. "Actually, my high school ex-boyfriend, who's now my boss, is here, and it's a little uncomfortable."

Hank's mouth opened, then closed again, like he wasn't sure how to reply.

I could hardly blame him.

"Small-town living, am I right?" I was vaguely aware that I'd started talking with my hands. "You think you're safe, and then in walks someone to make things awkward. Honestly? When I decided to move back here, I hardly thought about it. And then suddenly here I am, and there he is, and he's everywhere. It's like we're magnetic. Although that opposite poles idea is probably accurate. We were always like fire and ice."

"And you... work for him now?"

I kept gesturing as I talked. "I know! It sounds like a terrible idea, and I thought it would be, but actually it isn't that bad. And it's only temporary."

Hank nodded slowly, but his face was colored with skepticism—or maybe confusion.

I was about to launch into a lengthy dissertation about how I had absolutely no feelings for Luke Haven, but I stopped. Because that wasn't true, and I knew it. I had all kinds of feelings for him. Mostly loathing, although that didn't account for the queasy feeling in my stomach every time I caught sight of his date from the corner of my eye.

"Excuse me." I stood. "I need to use the restroom."

"Sure," Hank said, sounding slightly bewildered. "No problem."

Forcing myself not to look at Luke or his date, I grabbed my clutch. The restroom was in the back of the restaurant, down a little hallway that turned to the right. My heart was beating too hard, and the queasy feeling in my stomach wasn't going away.

Fortunately, the women's room was empty. After using the bathroom, I took a few deep breaths in front of the mirror while I washed my hands.

"You're fine, Mel," I said to my reflection. "This isn't a problem. It's a little awkward, but we're all adults here."

I took out my lip gloss and started to reapply when the door opened, and she walked in. Luke's date.

My mouth hung open as our eyes met in the mirror.

Look away, Mel! Look away!

Too late. She smiled, her eyes lighting up in recognition. "Hi. We met at Luke's garage. I'm Jenna."

Smoothing my expression, I turned to face her. "Yes, I remember. Nice to meet you. I'm Melanie."

"This restaurant is so nice, don't you think?"

I nodded. "Very nice."

She scrunched up her shoulders. "I'm on a first date, but you probably know that since you work with Luke. We just got here, but I think it's going well. I'm so excited to wear this dress. I bought it a while ago but haven't had a chance to wear it."

I glanced up and down, but if you'd asked me a minute later what she'd been wearing, I wouldn't have had a clue. My brain spun a million miles a second, and it was hard to focus on anything.

"It's very pretty," I managed, and it was a credit to my years spent acting that I sounded so calm.

"Sorry I'm babbling. I'm just a little nervous. Luke is so hot. He's like the hottest guy I've ever been out with."

What was I supposed to say to that? If you think he's hot now, wait until you see him naked?

No, Mel, don't say that.

Pressing my lips closed, I nodded. Keeping my mouth

shut was not my best skill, but at that moment, it was beyond necessary.

She moved in front of the sink next to me, took her lipstick out of her purse, and started reapplying. "Are you here with a date, too? The guy at your table is gorgeous."

"Yes, Hank's my date."

"That's so great. I hope you're having a good time." She rubbed her lips together and leaned closer to the mirror to check her reflection. "I just love girl time in the bathroom, don't you? It's so fun how we can be basically strangers, but bond when we're in here."

"Yeah, it's the best."

I kind of wanted to hate her, but she was too likable. And talking to her—seeing that she was not only pretty but also friendly—made the queasiness in my stomach build until it threatened to become full-blown nausea.

"I should get back to my... table," I said, slightly stuttering. "I mean, date. Get back to Hank. He's probably wondering if I fell in."

She smiled as she dabbed a finger beneath one eye, fixing what must have been a tiny smudge of mascara. "Have a great night."

"You too."

Don't have too great of a night, though.

I pushed open the restroom door, simmering with anger. Stupid Luke had to bring his stupid, nice, pretty date to this restaurant. I felt like puking up my dinner, and it was absolutely his fault.

Before I could stop, I slammed right into someone coming out of the men's room.

His scent made my eyes widen. That subtle cologne mixed with a hint of rubber and engine grease.

Luke Haven.

"Sor—" He cut off his apology as he stepped back and lowered his voice. "What are you doing here?"

I kept my voice to a whisper. "What am *I* doing here? I was here first. What are you doing here?"

"I'm…" He sputtered for a second, gesturing toward the restaurant. "I'm on a date."

"Me too."

"Yeah, I saw that."

"I saw you too."

He rested his hands on his hips and blew out a frustrated breath. "I don't know how this keeps happening."

"I told you we should keep a calendar. With locations, apparently."

"Yeah, maybe." He glanced away. "Shouldn't this be fine, though? Can't we just, I don't know…"

"Yeah, of course it's fine." I was such a liar. "We're both adults. We can handle it."

"Right. This is normal. You're here with a date; I'm here with a date. It's fine."

"Completely fine."

"So it doesn't bother you?"

Tremendously. And I might barf on your shoe. "Not at all." Apparently, I sounded convincing because he nodded. "And it doesn't bother you?"

He huffed. "No. Of course it doesn't bother me."

"Good."

"Good."

"Okay, then," I said. "I'll go back to my date, and you go back to yours."

"That's what I'm going to do."

"Good."

"Good."

"You have a nice evening," I said, not meaning it. At all.

"You too."

I could hear his footsteps behind me as I made my way back to my table. Hank smiled as I sat down. I had to dig deep to smile back, hoping it looked natural and not like a grimace.

"Is everything okay?" he asked. "Sorry if that's an awkward question."

"Oh no, I'm fine. I actually ran into a friend in the restroom, so we chatted for a minute. Sorry about that."

The concern on his face softened, and he smiled again. "Oh, good. That's very cool."

"Yeah. Girl time in the restroom. It's a thing."

"Totally. So, I paid the bill while you were in there, but if you want dessert, we can still order."

I didn't think I could force another bite of anything down my throat. "No, I'm too full. And thanks for dinner. That was really sweet of you."

"You're welcome. Ready to go?"

"Yes, absolutely."

I stood and forcibly kept my eyes away from Luke's table. I didn't want to see him or Jenna again. If I did, there was a very real possibility I might make a horror-movie-esque scene right in the middle of the restaurant. Minus my head spinning around backward. But still.

Hank led me outside, and the fresh air helped. As did the distance once we got in his car and drove away. The farther we got from the restaurant—and Luke and Jenna—the calmer I felt.

We were quiet on the drive to my house, which meant I couldn't ignore the truth. I wasn't going to see Hank again.

It wasn't about Luke. Seeing Luke with a date actually made me want to go out with Hank again, just so I wasn't the one not dating while he had someone.

But that wouldn't have been fair to Hank. He and I didn't have a future, and even after only two dates, I knew it.

He parked in front of my house. We both got out, and he walked me to the front door. I took a deep breath, steeling myself to disappoint him.

"Listen, Melanie, this has been fun." He glanced away for a second. "But I don't think we should keep seeing each other."

For a moment, I was frozen, staring at him with my mouth hanging open. I'd been about to say the same thing, but for some reason, it was still like getting punched in the stomach. He wasn't supposed to break up with me. I was supposed to break up with him. At least I could have maintained a little bit of my dignity that way while Luke was off doing who knows what with Jenna.

"Yeah," I said when I finally regained the use of words. But what else was I supposed to say? I agree? You're right, but for the record, it was my idea. You just spoke before me? "That's fine, I think you're right."

"Really?"

I nodded. "Yeah. It's okay."

"Good. That's a relief. I had a nice time with you. It's just…"

I had a feeling I didn't want to hear what he'd been about to say. But apparently, I was going to dive in and be a glutton for punishment. "It's just what?"

"You're great, so don't take this the wrong way, but you're… kind of a lot."

Icy-cold numbness swept through me, and when I spoke, my tone was almost robotic. "Yeah. I know I am."

"That's not a bad thing. You have a lot of spark. That's great. I just think it's more than I can handle."

"That's fair." My voice was still monotone. "I wouldn't want to get you into something that's more than you're up for."

"I'm sorry." He leaned in and brushed a quick kiss on my cheek. "Take care, Melanie."

"You too, Hank."

With unfocused eyes, I unlocked my door and went

inside. I barely heard his car door shut or the engine start again as I closed the door behind me.

You're kind of a lot.

A few tears broke free from the corners of my eyes. I swiped them away, kicked off my heels, and flopped onto the couch. It was a stupid thing to cry over. I didn't want to date Hank. He was fine, but was it so wrong to want more than that? More than fine?

I'd been married before, so I knew life wasn't all passion and drama and excitement. That wasn't what I needed—wasn't what I was really looking for.

As I lay there, my view of the ceiling blurred by tears, I realized what I was looking for. Someone who understood me. Who knew me, and loved me for who I was, messiness and all.

I'd never had that. Or if I had, I'd lost it a long time ago. And now it was gone.

So I let myself cry. Me, who wasn't much of a crier. I curled up in a ball and sobbed until my stomach clenched in a knot and my shoulders ached with unreleased tension.

After a while, the torrent of emotion slowed to a trickle. Still curled up on the couch, I tucked my hands under my cheek and caught my breath.

Normally, I would have sat up and cursed Hank—and probably Luke—in Queen Ione's voice. Said something amusing, in character, in order to push away my feelings. But I hardly had the energy. I felt sapped and empty.

So I got up, and, not letting myself think about what had really made me cry so hard, I went to bed.

CHAPTER 18

Luke

THERE WAS REALLY something wrong with me.

I walked Jenna up to her front door with a sense of dread in the pit of my stomach. She was going to invite me in. I could feel it. The drive from the restaurant had been filled with tension, and usually I'd have considered that a good thing.

What guy wouldn't? Jenna was hot. Plus, she was sweet and we'd had a nice time. So why did the thought of going in with her make me want to crawl out of my own skin?

We approached her door, but she didn't make a move to unlock it. She faced me and bit her bottom lip with a suggestive hint of a smile.

"I had a really good time tonight." She moved a step closer, clearly expecting me to lean in and kiss her.

I absently wiped my hands on my pants. Were my palms sweating? "Yeah, me too."

"So…" She tilted her chin up. "Would you like to come in?"

It took me a second before I could get an answer out. "I don't think I should. Not tonight."

"Oh." She sounded surprised, but not upset. "Are you sure? I don't ask unless I mean it."

"I appreciate that. But not tonight."

"All right. If you need to take things slow, I totally respect that."

"Yeah, I do. Thanks."

Her eyebrows lifted. She wanted me to kiss her. I didn't want to kiss her, but I knew I'd feel bad if I didn't. I leaned in and, at the last second, moved to give her a quick kiss on the cheek.

"Night, Jenna. I'll talk to you soon."

"Okay. Goodnight, Luke."

Walking back to my car, I let out a long breath. I was ready to kick myself. What the hell, Luke? Why had I walked away from that? Why wasn't I in there ripping her clothes off instead of slamming my car door and driving away?

Because I didn't want to rip Jenna's clothes off.

But why?

It was not because of—

No, I wasn't even going to think her name. This was not about her.

Brooding and frustrated, I headed toward my place. Part of me wanted to detour through the Timberbeast to have a drink or two. But I was too likely to run into one of my brothers. That was the last thing I needed. I didn't want to admit that I'd turned down a perfectly good "come inside" offer. A couple of drinks, and I might even admit why.

Even worse, if they'd decided to stop for a drink after dinner, I might run into Melanie with that dumbass.

Damn it, Melanie.

Right as I pulled into my driveway, my phone buzzed with a text. I glanced at the notification.

Kyle: *We're on tonight. You in?*

Fuck yes, I was in. Speed was exactly what I needed. If I

drove fast and hard enough, maybe I could outrun the shitty feeling brewing inside me.

I sent a quick reply, then went inside to change.

————

The night air sparked with tension and adrenaline ran hot in my veins. The track was packed with people and cars—some there to race, others to show off their rides. Bets were placed, money seemed to be everywhere, and with the summer weather lingering, everyone was dressed like we were enjoying an afternoon at the beach.

I didn't care about any of it. I just wanted to drive.

Usually, I went into a race night ready for the wave of speed and adrenaline to make me feel alive again—chase away the emptiness that threatened to consume me.

But that night was different. I was amped up, seething with frustration. I didn't want to race to feel something more, I needed an outlet for my anger.

What was I even mad at?

Myself, for turning down Jenna? Or maybe for taking her on a date in the first place?

And Melanie. Fucking Melanie Andolini looking like a goddess with her dark hair spilling over her shoulders and that dress accentuating every curve. With her angry eyes and shiny lips.

I'd hated it. Hated seeing her dressed up for another man. Hated seeing her sitting with him, chatting with him, smiling at him. It had been all I could do to keep my eyes on my actual date, and not on her. I didn't know how Jenna hadn't noticed, but she'd seemed oblivious to my distraction.

And my anger.

But out on the track, in the middle of the night, with the smell of dust and gasoline in the air, I couldn't stop thinking about how pissed I was at Melanie.

"You okay, man?" Kyle asked, a look of concern on his face.

"Fine."

"How you feeling tonight?"

My eyes moved to meet his. "Fast."

A grin spread across his face. "That's what I love to hear. Make me some money tonight, buddy."

I looked away without answering, got in my car, and shoved on my helmet.

It wasn't long before they'd cleared the track. Cars were in place, drivers ready, engines revving. I curled my hands around the steering wheel, my jaw clenched, eyes on the road. My heart thumped hard in my chest, but instead of the beginnings of an adrenaline high, I just felt rage.

The gun went off and I slammed my foot on the gas. Tension rippled through my body as I pulled out ahead of the pack, heedless of how hard it would be to hold the lead. I didn't give a shit. I was still going to win.

I sailed around the first turns, hugging the S-curves. But I wasn't smooth about it. I wrenched the steering wheel, forcing my car to obey. Another car pulled ahead, but I floored it on the end of the last turn and took back the lead.

If the crowd cheered as I completed the first lap, I didn't care. I flew by, my focus intense, hints of red at the corners of my vision. Dust hung heavy in the air and my engine roared as I gunned it along the straightaway.

I kept the lead through the S-curves on the second pass. Sweat dripped down my temples and my jaw started to ache from clenching my teeth. I wasn't racing the other drivers. I was racing Melanie. And that fucking Hank guy. What a dick. Why would she go out with a guy like that? What the hell did she even see in him?

And why did I care?

So much dust was in the air, it was hard to see. We hadn't had rain in ages. I lost the lead for most of the third lap and pushed hard to get it back. Fuck those guys. Fuck it all. I hit the gas on the next turn, determined to overtake them.

My control was slipping. The tires felt like they weren't gripping the track, and my usual sense of elation was nowhere to be found. My muscles were tense, my hands sweating, and my heart beat fast. With a roar in my throat, I started to surge ahead. Two more laps. I could make it.

Without warning, the world went crazy. The back end of my car jerked to the right, and I lost all sense of direction. Everything spun as my body slammed around the cab. Pain exploded across my chest, and I couldn't get any air.

Just as fast, everything stopped.

For a second, I couldn't move—couldn't even breathe. In a panic, I threw off my helmet and tried to suck in air. It felt like my chest had caved in.

My car door opened and dusty air billowed in. That didn't help the breathing situation, but I could tell I wasn't choking. I'd just had the wind knocked out of me. Logically, I knew my diaphragm would stop spasming and I'd be able to breathe. But the seconds felt like minutes as I struggled for air.

"Get him out! Get him out!"

Someone reached over me and unfastened the seat belt. Voices came out of the darkness, shouting questions. My body finally let me take a breath and I held up a hand for them to give me a second.

"Get him out of there," someone said again.

Arms reached in to pull me out, but I waved them off. My brain registered pain, but I was still too busy trying to breathe to recognize where it was coming from. I got out and stood. Legs worked. That was good.

I took a few more labored breaths before I could speak, and when I did, my voice was a low croak. "I'm okay. I'm okay."

My head spun. I'd crashed. I'd fucking crashed my car.

"Luke!" Kyle ran up to me. "Holy shit. Are you okay?"

"Of course he's not okay, genius," someone snapped. "He just wrecked."

"I'm fine." I was vaguely aware of a guy with a fire extinguisher. "Is the car on fire?"

"No, man, no fire," someone said.

I nodded. That made sense, considering I was still standing right next to it.

"Did you have your helmet on?" he asked.

Still trying to catch my breath, I nodded again. "Took it off after."

A flurry of activity surrounded me, but it was hard to focus. Something hurt. A lot. What was it? My diaphragm was starting to work again, so I could breathe. I was standing, so it wasn't my legs. I fisted my hands a few times, opening and closing them, then extended my arms.

Probably just bruises from being knocked around in the cab.

"They're going to get your car out of the way," Kyle said. "You sure you're okay? Maybe you should get checked out."

"No." I put up a hand and took a step. "I'm—"

A wave of pain across my midsection made me gasp. I'd been about to say I was fine, but I was not fine. Clutching my ribs, I doubled over, groaning.

"Is Mike here? He's a nurse, isn't he?" someone asked.

"Don't take him to the hospital," someone else said. "He'll rat us out."

"He won't rat us out, you idiot."

"Someone should take him. He could have internal bleeding."

"I got it," Kyle said. "I'll go get my car. Wait here."

People around me kept arguing about what to do with me. A few discussed how to get my car out of the way so they could keep racing. But that was how it worked. I'd seen crashes happen. We stopped long enough to make sure no one needed medical attention, got their cars out of the way, and the race was back on.

It was fucked up, when I thought about it.

Still clutching my ribs, I leaned against my car and waited for Kyle. What a mess. I didn't even want to turn around and survey the damage to my car. Didn't want to know. The pain in my side was blinding, making sweat drip down my back and nausea roil through my stomach. Idly, I wondered if I had broken ribs.

Someone had said the words internal bleeding. That wasn't good.

It served me right. I shouldn't have been driving angry. I was just glad I hadn't done worse. Glad I was still alive.

Kyle pulled up, and someone I didn't know helped me into the passenger side of his old Dodge Challenger. Grimacing, I tried not to groan as I got in. Fuck, it hurt. And all I could think about as he started down the track to the bumpy dirt road that would lead out of there was how much I wanted to call Melanie.

CHAPTER 19

Luke

THE DRIVE to the hospital was torture.

We were out in the middle of nowhere, so the closest facility was in Echo Creek, about half an hour from home. I was glad Kyle didn't have to take me straight to Tilikum. There was a hospital there, too, but if I rolled in with broken ribs in the middle of the night, the gossip line would go nuts.

And they'd probably call Garrett. That was the last thing I needed.

As it was, I didn't think about how I was getting home. The words internal bleeding kept echoing through my mind. I didn't want to bleed out in the passenger seat of Kyle's car. That would be a shitty way to go.

I was such an idiot.

"Hang on," Kyle said.

"What?"

The car started bumping up and down, over and over. It wasn't the feel of a dirt road, even one that was pitted with potholes. It was steadier, but also worse, like we were driving on a railroad track.

Wait. I glanced out the window. Were we driving on a railroad track?

Clutching my midsection and gritting my teeth against the pain, I looked at Kyle. "Where the fuck are we?"

"It's an old railroad bridge. Not in use anymore. It's faster. I don't want you bleeding out before I get you to the hospital."

Faster? Kyle's so-called shortcut was going to kill me. I looked out the window again, squinting my eyes against the darkness. From what I could see, Kyle's shortcut didn't have a wall or guardrail. We were crossing a ravine.

Fuck.

Finally, we made it across the bridge. The dirt road was still uneven, but nothing like the bridge had been. We got to the highway, and I leaned my head back, trying to breathe through the pain.

After what felt like an eternity, Kyle pulled up in front of the emergency entrance to the Echo Creek hospital.

"You can walk, right?" he asked. "You'll make it inside?"

I glanced at him out of the corner of my eye. He fidgeted, his nervousness clear. He didn't want to have to answer questions about how I got injured.

It wasn't like I thought this guy was actually my friend, but damn. He wasn't even going to park and make sure I got all the way inside. Brutal.

"I got it."

Wincing, I unfastened the seat belt, opened the door, and eased my way out. I had to stop and take a few breaths before I could straighten enough to walk.

Kyle was already driving away before I made it through the automatic doors. At least someone had been willing to get me to a hospital. I figured I should be grateful for that much.

I staggered to the front desk, and the receptionist raised her eyebrows.

"You need to be seen," she said. It wasn't a question.

"Yeah. I wrecked my car."

To the hospital's credit, they didn't make me stand there

to check in or sit in the lobby for an eternity. A nurse brought out a wheelchair and took me back to a curtained-off room. Someone else came in and got my information while the nurse took my vitals.

I didn't lie, exactly. But I didn't tell them the truth about the race, either. Just that I'd been driving too fast on some backroads and wrecked. A friend had dropped me off.

Since there was concern about internal bleeding, everyone worked fast. I was in too much pain to track what was going on. Medical staff swarmed around me, and as I lay there, a horrifying thought took root in my mind.

What if I didn't make it?

I squinted at the harsh lights above me. This wasn't how I wanted to go. I hadn't done half the things I'd wanted to do with my life. Sure, I'd built a successful business, and that was great. But lying there, contemplating my own mortality, that sort of thing didn't seem to matter. Not the money, the stability, the accomplishments, the awards I'd won. Who cared if I could restore an old car?

Instead, I thought about the people in my life—the people I might be about to leave behind. My parents. My brothers. My nieces and nephews. I wanted to watch them grow up.

They were what mattered.

And I thought about Melanie. As they wheeled in an ultrasound machine and discussed whether I needed emergency surgery, I thought about her.

Why? I had no idea, any more than I knew why I'd thought about calling her on the way to the hospital.

But she was there, at the forefront of my mind. What if I died and she married Hank? I couldn't let that happen. Urgency gripped me. I wanted to jump out of bed and find my phone. Call her and tell her to break up with him. Whatever else she did, she couldn't stay with Hank.

I'd been wearing my helmet, but I kind of wondered if I

had a head injury. Why did I care so much about who Melanie dated?

It's hard to keep deluding yourself when you think you might be dying. I knew exactly why I cared so much. Because I cared about her.

I always had.

Finally, the flurry of activity around me slowed. One nurse and the doctor remained. I blinked, my attention coming back to the room.

"I have good news and not-so-good news," the doctor said. "The good news is, there's no evidence of internal bleeding."

"What's the not-so-good news?"

"You probably have bruised ribs. There might be a small fracture or two, but the treatment is the same. Which is to say, you mostly have to wait for them to heal."

"So I'm not dying?"

"No, you're not dying. But you're going to be in a fair amount of pain for a while."

I closed my eyes in relief. I wasn't going to die. That was good news.

But it also meant I would have to face the truth about Melanie. I kept trying to hate her, but I didn't. Not at all.

In fact, it might have been the opposite.

The doctor had more to say, but it was hard to focus. They wanted to keep me there for a few hours for observation. Then they'd release me to go home.

The nurse gave me something for the pain and helped get me into a position that was relatively comfortable. I spent the next several hours in and out of sleep, dimly aware of the nurses coming in to check on me. Eventually, they decided I could be released.

Which brought up another problem. How was I going to get home?

It was five in the morning, and whoever I called, I was going to have to tell them the truth.

The stupid thing was, I wanted to call Mel. She'd hate me for it. I'd probably never hear the end of it if I woke her up at the ass crack of dawn to come get me after I wrecked my car in an illegal race. She'd be worse than my dad. Or Garrett.

Besides, I couldn't call her. What if she wasn't alone?

I didn't want to think about that, so I made a snap decision. I'd call Theo. He wasn't going to be happy with me either, but at least he didn't have a wife I'd wake up.

He picked up on the third ring, his voice gravelly with sleep. "Yeah?"

"It's Luke. I'm okay, but I'm at the hospital down in Echo Creek."

"What?" He sounded much more awake. "What happened?"

"I wrecked my car."

"Holy shit. Are you hurt?"

"Nothing serious. I'm banged up, and I have bruised ribs. They're releasing me, and I know it's early as fuck, so I'm sorry about that. But I need a ride."

"What the hell happened?" he asked, and it sounded like he was up and moving around. "Never mind, you can tell me when I get there. The hospital in Echo Creek?"

"Yeah, do you know where it is?"

"I think so. I'll find it."

"Thanks, man."

"I'll be there in about thirty."

"Thank you." I let out a relieved breath. "Seriously, thank you."

"Yeah. I got you."

I really didn't deserve my family.

The nurse came back and helped me get dressed. Even with the pain meds, it hurt like hell. I was starting to feel other bruises as well, pretty much everywhere. Still, I'd gotten lucky. It could have been a lot worse.

Before Theo arrived, I was released with a bunch of paperwork telling me what to expect and when to see my regular doctor. I didn't remember all the instructions the nurse had given me, but one thing stood out. I couldn't drive for two weeks.

No driving. How the hell was I going to get around? And I didn't want to think about what I was going to do about my wrecked car at the track.

Problems for later. I just wanted to get home so I could get a few hours of sleep.

Theo showed up, and I'd never been so happy to see him. He had a serious case of bedhead, and his eyes still looked tired.

"Thank you," I said as soon as he walked in. Clutching my ribs, I groaned as I eased myself off the bed.

"Do you need help?"

I slowly straightened. "I got it. Just hurts."

He didn't ask me any questions as we left. I waited by the doors while he brought his truck around. He got out and opened the passenger door, and I wasn't too proud to take the hand he offered to help me get in. Putting on the seat belt took several deep breaths and gritted teeth, but I managed.

When I was finally settled, Theo pulled out of the hospital parking lot and headed toward Tilikum.

"So what happened?" he asked. "Where's your car?"

"You know the old racetrack?"

"Yeah."

"It's there."

He shot a glance at me. "You were racing?"

"Yeah."

"What the fuck?" There was no missing the surprise and frustration in his voice. "I thought you quit doing that years ago."

"I did. For a while."

He just shook his head.

I waited, but he didn't say anything else. "What, no lecture about how dangerous it is? How I should know better?"

"Sounds like you already gave yourself the lecture. You just need to start listening."

"True."

"Besides, if this doesn't convince you to quit, nothing I say is going to make a difference."

I shifted slightly, trying to ease the feeling of pressure in my chest. It didn't help. "Good point."

We lapsed into silence as we drove. I was still drowsy, and it was hard to keep my eyes open. I kept almost drifting off then jerking awake with a jolt of pain.

Finally, we got to my house. I lived in what was essentially a big garage with an apartment above, and I struggled to walk up the stairs. Theo followed and went in with me. He looked over my discharge paperwork while I eased myself onto the couch with a groan.

"Ice packs?" he asked.

"Freezer. Hopefully."

Thankfully, I had one shoved in the back. It was bunched up, and he had to massage it a bit to get it to flatten, but at least it was cold. I put it where the worst of the pain was and let my eyes close.

"I have a ton of those," Theo said. "I'll bring more so you can rotate them."

"Thanks."

"Need anything else?"

"I don't think so." I opened my eyes. "Thank you. Really."

He nodded. "Of course. You know I've always got your back. Even when you're being stupid."

"So stupid."

"You have your phone?" he asked.

"It's in my pocket."

"Okay. Rest up."

I nodded, my eyes drifting closed again.

Theo left, and I settled into a restless sleep, filled with dreams of car wrecks and Melanie's voice asking me if I was okay.

CHAPTER 20

Melanie

THE SHRIEKS of child happiness on a sunny day were soothing to my soul. And the crunchy dill pickle, while not exactly healing the previous night's wounds, was delicious. There were worse ways to spend a Saturday.

I'd met Nathan, Sharla, and the kids at Lumberjack Park so the small humans could run around and play. Sharla had packed a picnic, complete with a red-and-white-checked tablecloth that we'd spread out on one of the tables near the play equipment. The pickles were my contribution, although I was probably the only one who'd eat them.

A group of squirrels ran by, their bushy tails streaming behind them. One stopped and looked at me.

"Don't even think about it, tiny mammal," I said. "You're not getting my pickles."

The squirrel scampered off, following its friends. A second later, a man with a wide-brimmed brown hat and shaggy beard wandered by, looking as if he'd lost something.

"Hi, Harvey," Sharla said. "Is everything all right?"

He turned around, blinking. "Have you seen them?"

"Seen who?" she asked.

"My friends."

"Um… are your friends squirrels?"

He grinned at her. "That's them!"

She pointed. "They went that way."

Tipping his hat, he gave her an awkward bow. "Thank you, kindly."

He kept walking, still looking lost.

"Was that Harvey Johnston?" I asked. "He's still around?"

"Where else would he be?" Sharla asked.

"Tilikum is so charming," I said, and I meant it. "Why did I ever leave?"

"College. Dreams of stardom."

"I didn't really want stardom. I know, that's surprising. A drama queen like me obviously wanted to be famous. But I didn't."

"Then why did you leave?" Sharla asked, her voice gentle.

I didn't really want to answer that question because I had a feeling it had a lot to do with running. Glancing away, I adjusted my sunglasses against the brightness of the sun and took a bite of my pickle.

"That's disgusting." Nathan sat across the table from me.

"Don't mess with me. This is my emotional support pickle."

Sharla laughed. "Why do you need an emotional support pickle?"

"I got dumped last night. To be fair, I was going to dump him anyway. And I mean that. I'm not just trying to save face."

"Sure," Nathan said.

Sharla nudged him with her elbow. "Be nice."

"Sorry. I have years of sibling trash talk to make up for."

"It's only fair," I agreed, gesturing with my half-eaten pickle. "I'm the one who was gone so much."

"You two are so weird," Sharla said. "Anyway, you were going to dump him, but he dumped you first. Wait, who is this guy?"

"Hank. Mom introduced us at the pizza tasting. Which is to say, she invited him with the express purpose of shoving us together and probably already has a mother-of-the-bride dress picked out."

"Sounds about right," Sharla said.

"Anyway," I said, still gesturing with my pickle. "Hank was fine. Nice guy and everything. But he obviously couldn't handle all this."

"Takes a brave man," Nathan said.

Sharla and I ignored him. Lucia ran up to her mom with a juice box and Sharla helped her with the straw.

"So that didn't work out," I said. "Which is fine. I'm not desperate."

"Of course you're not," Sharla said. "And I'm proud of you for giving it a shot, even though it didn't turn into anything."

"Thanks. It would have been nice if I'd been the one giving the *it's not you, it's me* speech. Especially because he gave me the, *it's definitely you* speech."

"Ouch." Sharla's tone was sympathetic. Zola came over with her juice box and flushed cheeks. Without missing a beat, Sharla helped her with her straw. "What a jerk. Can I hate him? I think I want to hate him."

"How about we disdain him," I said. "Hate seems a bit dramatic, even for me."

"I can live with disdain."

A few more kids ran to the playground—a little boy of about four, two girls, and a bigger boy who was clearly the older brother.

"Will, don't run up the slide when other kids are going down," the older boy said. "Emma and Juliet, you have to stay on the playground."

Sharla waved. "Hi, Thomas."

The kid waved back. "Hi, Mrs. Andolini."

"Are your mom and dad here?"

"Yeah, they're bringing our lunch from the car."

A moment later, Annika and her husband, Levi, walked across the grass. Levi pulled a wagon with a cooler, and they stopped at the picnic table next to ours. The kids were already running around the playground together.

We all said our hellos while Annika and Levi unpacked their lunch. Annika kept a close eye on the kids, especially her youngest.

"Are you going to the bachelor auction?" Sharla asked.

I looked at her over the top of my sunglasses. "Are you asking me?"

"Yes, you. Nathan and I are going to show our support, but obviously not to bid in the man auction."

"Why would I go to a man auction?"

She shrugged. "For fun."

"It's for a good cause," Annika said. "The SPS is building their headquarters."

"What's the SPS?" I asked.

"The Squirrel Protection Squad," Sharla said, her forehead creasing as if I'd asked a dumb question.

"What is the Squirrel Protection Squad?" I asked. "Never mind. I didn't think Tilikum could get weirder, but there you have it. But why do the squirrels need protecting?"

"They're really more of a grassroots civilian security team," Sharla said. "They've done a lot of good for the community."

"And they're going to auction off single men to raise money? How is that legal?"

Sharla laughed. "It's not like that. You know how these things are. Just all in good fun. You get an evening with a bachelor. It's not a romantic thing. Most people will probably have them do yard work or chop wood and stuff."

"Well, that's good at least. But no. After getting dumped, the last thing I need is to be seen paying a guy to go out with me. Even if it is for a good cause. And I don't need anyone to chop wood."

"A bunch of the single guys from the firehouse will be up for grabs," Annika said. "A couple of the newer deputies who work with my brother, Garrett, too."

"Men in uniform will go for a premium," I said. "The SPS will be building their headquarters in no time."

Annika pulled her phone out of her purse. "Hey, Theo."

The look of surprise that immediately crossed her features got my attention. Something seemed wrong.

"Oh my god, is he okay?" she asked.

My eyes widened. They were talking about Luke. I didn't know how I knew, but I did. A sick feeling spread through my stomach.

"Are you sure?" Annika asked. "That's so scary. I'm glad he was able to reach you." She paused again, listening. "Okay. I'll do that. Thanks for letting me know."

My heart started to race, and she'd barely ended the call before I blurted out, "What happened?"

"Luke was in an accident last night."

I stood, my pickle falling to the ground, forgotten. "What? Where? Is he okay?"

"He's hurt, but nothing life threatening. It sounds like bruised ribs is the worst of it. Theo picked him up from the hospital and took him home early this morning."

Without thinking about what I was doing, I grabbed my purse. "I have to go."

"Where?" Sharla asked.

"Luke's."

Sharla glanced at Annika, then back at me.

"I just need to make sure he's all right," I said, trying to hide the worry in my voice. "See if he needs anything. Don't look at me like that. It's a totally normal thing to do."

"I wasn't looking at you like anything," Sharla said.

"Good." I started toward the street where I'd parked, but

stopped in my tracks and turned around. "I don't know where he lives."

Annika was watching me with raised eyebrows, as if she had no idea what to think. I didn't blame her. I didn't know what I was doing either.

"I'll text you his address," she said.

"Perfect." I spun around and resisted the urge to run to my car.

What was I doing? I didn't need to rush to Luke's house just because he got hurt. If it were serious, he had his whole big family to help. He didn't need me.

But the words *Luke was in an accident last night* reverberated through my mind, bringing with them a sick terror. The urgency to see him with my own eyes—make sure he was really okay—was impossible to resist.

And if he really was all right? I was going to throttle him.

By the time I got in my car, Annika had texted me his address. It was only about ten minutes from the park. With a lump of worry in my throat, I drove to his house and parked.

Luke's house was exactly what I would have imagined if I'd been thinking clearly on the drive over. It was set back from the road, down a gravel driveway, and surrounded by pine trees. In the clearing was a two-story building, and it looked like the bottom was nothing but a four-car garage. Windows upstairs indicated an apartment or living space, and a stairway on one side led up to a door.

Of course Luke's house was more garage than home. That totally fit.

There weren't any cars parked out front, but that didn't surprise me either. He was pretty meticulous about his vehicles. And the garage was huge.

Without pausing to ask myself what on earth I was doing there, I went up the stairs. The landing extended across the entire side of the building and wrapped around to a deck on the back. I took a quick breath and knocked.

"Luke, it's me," I said through the door. "Don't get up. I'm just going to see if it's unlocked and poke my head in to make sure you're all right."

I tried the knob. It turned, and I eased it open a few inches.

"Luke? Are you okay?"

"What are you doing here?"

Worry burst through me like a firecracker at the hoarse sound of his voice. I flung the door the rest of the way open. "What happened? How bad is it?"

He lay on the couch, covered with a blanket, except for one leg sticking out. His face was pale, and he had dark circles under his eyes.

"I'm fine. Why are you here?"

That was an excellent question. Why was I there? "I heard you were in an accident."

"Heard from who?"

"Annika. We were at the park, and she got a call from Theo, and he said you were in an accident last night and are mostly okay except bruised ribs and I'm realizing as I say that I didn't need to rush over here and I look like an idiot right now."

He chuckled a little, then clutched his side. "Ow. Don't make me laugh. It hurts."

"I wasn't trying to make you laugh."

"I know. Can you just shut the door?"

Instead of stepping through it, saying goodbye, and closing it on my way out—which would have been the reasonable thing to do—I stayed inside and shut it.

The living area was bare—total bachelor pad. He had a couch and an armchair facing a TV on the wall. The coffee table had a water bottle sitting on it and not much else. At the back was a kitchen, and at a glance, it looked clean. A large sliding glass door led to the deck I'd seen on my way in, and the view of the forest with the mountains rising in the background was gorgeous.

"Since I'm here, do you need anything?" I asked.

"No. I should probably eat something eventually, but the thought of food makes me want to puke right now."

I walked over to the armchair and lowered myself down. "What happened?"

"I wrecked my car."

"The Chevelle?"

"No, one of my other ones."

"Dare I ask how?"

He closed his eyes for a second. "Racing."

"Racing, where? Out at that track that closed? They still do that?"

"Yeah."

My lips parted, and for a second, I wasn't sure what to say. He'd started racing when we were in high school, and it had always been a sore spot for us. We'd had more fights about it than I could count.

But strangely—especially for me, because I was rarely one to shy away from an argument—my gut reaction wasn't anger. I had no desire to tell him how stupid it was or give him an I-always-told-you-so speech.

Only one question came to mind. "Why?"

He seemed as surprised as I was. His eyes cracked open, and he moved his head to look at me. "Why?"

I nodded, and my voice was uncharacteristically soft. "Why would you be out there racing?"

He blew out a long breath. "I don't know."

"And why didn't you call me?"

"Why would I call you?"

I huffed. "I don't know. But you should have called me. I could have picked you up or brought you soup or gotten you ice packs or something."

One corner of his mouth lifted in a grin. "Melanie Andolini, were you worried about me?"

I huffed again. "No."

"Yes, you were."

"Fine. There was a modicum of concern."

"You drove over here out of a modicum of concern?"

I started gesturing with my hands. "Well, can you blame me? You're my boss, and I need the job and if something happens to you, do I go to work on Monday? And if I don't go to work, will I be able to pay my rent? What else was I supposed to do?"

He kept grinning. "You care about me."

"No, I don't."

"Yes, you do." The hint of amusement in his voice made me want to throw something at him. Something soft, but still.

Standing, I decided to ignore his teasing. "Are you supposed to be icing your ribs?" Before he could answer, I pulled back the blanket to check. Swallowing hard, I tried to ignore his bare chest, covered in a dusting of chest hair.

A dark blue ice pack covered part of his rib cage. I gently touched it. Hardly even cold.

"Mel, it's fine. I can get it later."

"This isn't doing anything." I picked it up and took it to the kitchen. "I hope you have more than one of these so you can rotate."

"Yeah, Theo brought them over."

"Good." I grabbed a cold ice pack out of the freezer and put the warm one in to re-freeze. "What else do you need? More water? You need to stay hydrated."

"I'm fine. I have water."

I brought the ice pack and laid it across his ribs, then pulled the blanket up to his chin. Our eyes met, and for a second, I had the craziest urge to run my fingers through his messy hair. To lean down and gently press my lips to his.

Jenna.

His date from the previous night popped into my head like a jack-in-the-box from hell. I could almost imagine her with clown makeup and a little jester's hat, bouncing around like she was on a spring, laughing at me.

Straightening, I took a step back. "Sorry. I shouldn't have come over. I'm totally making it weird."

"It's okay, you're not making anything weird. Or maybe you're always weird, and I'm used to it."

I needed to get out of there before Jenna came over to take care of him. Surely, she would, wouldn't she? He must have called her to tell her he was hurt. She was probably on her way. Why hadn't I thought of that before?

I picked up my purse. "I'm glad you're okay enough to be home. If you need help with anything, let me know. I'll be around. And if you don't, that's fine too. I don't have any emotional attachment to being the one to help take care of you."

"Are you sure?"

"Of course I'm sure."

He cracked a smile again. I didn't understand why he kept looking at me like that, but it made my insides swirl in decidedly uncomfortable ways.

Tantalizing, but so uncomfortable.

"Thanks for checking up on me," he said.

"You're welcome. I'm sure you'll have plenty of people taking care of you, so you don't need me."

He opened his mouth like he was going to reply but hesitated. He closed it again, and I decided I probably didn't want to hear what he'd been about to say.

Without another word, I was out the door.

Our place

ROSWELL MILLS

I STOOD outside my car and breathed in the dry mountain air. The heat pressed at me from all sides, making a bead of sweat drip down my spine, and a sheen of dust from the gravel road settled on everything.

But none of that bothered me. I was near Tilikum. And that was where she was.

I hadn't seen her yet. When I'd arrived in town, it had been tempting to drive around, circling the main roads on the off chance I might run into her. Even just a glimpse would help sate my growing hunger.

But I couldn't let my passions get away from me. There was too much to do, too many ways this could all go wrong. I only had one shot to get it right. Everything had to be in place —everything perfect—before I made my move.

The first thing I needed was a place to bring her.

It would be our place, for a time at least. I couldn't expect to keep her near her hometown for long. But there would be a time of acclimation, of teaching. She'd need to get used to the way things were going to be.

Eventually, we'd go somewhere else. Where, I hadn't decided yet. Out of the country would be ideal. Somewhere tropical, maybe. I wondered if she'd like that—living where it was warm all the time.

It didn't really matter. Wherever I took her, she'd learn to like it.

I eyed the cabin where I'd stopped. It looked small from the outside, but I wasn't worried about that. It had the two most important things I was looking for—isolation and a basement.

Beyond the clearing that passed for a small yard, pine forest stretched out in every direction. I'd driven down a long dirt road to get there, and there wasn't a neighbor in sight.

So far, it looked perfect.

The owner hadn't asked many questions, either. That had been another plus. I had a new identity, so I wasn't concerned about anyone finding out who I was, or that I'd just been released from prison. People had no idea how easy it was to fake your identity, if you knew the right sources.

I did. Prison had taken care of that for me.

So I was no longer Roswell Mills from Tennessee. I'd become Colton Broward from Colorado without a hitch.

The cabin was an hour or so from Tilikum, closer to the neighboring town of Echo Creek. The owner had said it was usually rented by hunters. It had plumbing, and a generator supplied electricity.

I'd concocted a story about being a writer on a deadline who needed quiet and privacy to finish my book. He hadn't seemed to care, just wanted the cash payment up front.

Jingling the key he'd given me, I went up to the front door, unlocked it, and stepped inside.

The air was musty, and the furniture was old and worn. The walls were decorated with mounted antlers and a large, faded map of the Cascades. It had a small kitchen with ancient, olive-green appliances, and an old wood stove with a cooktop.

The single bedroom had two sets of bunk beds, and there was a small bathroom with a cracked mirror. Not exactly luxury accommodations, but that didn't matter. I'd lived in much worse. And this was only temporary.

My body trembled with anticipation as I went back to the kitchen and opened the door to the basement. A bare light bulb hung from the ceiling. Flipping a switch, I walked down the basic open wooden stairs.

The musty scent grew stronger. The walls were bare plywood, but the floor was finished with some sort of vinyl. An egress window set high in one wall let in a bit of daylight and a door stood ajar in a corner, leading to a small bathroom. That was good. I'd just have to take the door off and make sure there was nothing she could try to use as a weapon.

I walked into the center of the room and turned slowly, creating a mental inventory of what I'd need to make things ready for her. I'd bring down one of the mattresses from the bunk bed upstairs. Bedding too, although that could be something to offer her as a reward for good behavior.

Restraints, though. I'd have to install something. I went over to a wall and tapped in a line, listening for the sound of studs behind the plywood. I'd make it work. And there would come a time when I'd no longer need to chain her to a wall to keep her with me.

She'd learn.

I went back upstairs to bring in the rest of my things. There were preparations to be made, and I wasn't going to take her until I was sure everything was ready.

A haunting memory swept through me. Closing my eyes, I tried to push it away, but it ate at me, relentless in its judgment. I'd failed once. She'd gotten away. I'd never had a chance to explain. To tell her what I was really trying to do.

Suddenly, a new realization swept in on the tide of that

awful recollection. I'd failed because I'd underestimated her, yes. But knowing she'd be difficult to subdue wasn't enough. I had to be ready for things to go wrong—be prepared for every scenario.

I needed to practice.

A smile crossed my face again. Of course. Why hadn't I thought of that before? If I tried to take my Melanie without rehearsing beforehand, too many things could go wrong. But if I practiced on a few others, especially if they reminded me of her, I could work out the kinks. Be ready for the big show.

It was a risk. A big one. I couldn't deny that. If I got caught, I'd be throwing it all away. All the pining, all the preparing, for nothing.

But I wouldn't get caught. I'd learned too much.

And for Melanie, any risk was worth taking. Soon, she'd be mine.

CHAPTER 21

Luke

BRUISED RIBS WERE A BITCH.

I stood in my kitchen, fresh out of the shower, my hair still damp, and a towel wrapped around my waist. Leaning back against the counter, I sipped a cup of coffee, then rubbed the stubble on my jaw.

My midsection looked about as bad as it felt. I was black and blue, and basically everything hurt. It was hard to move, hard to sleep, hard to breathe. I was supposed to be careful, but I'd spent the weekend lying around, and I was ready to crawl out of my skin. It was Monday morning, and I needed to go to work.

It wasn't like the garage would fall apart without me. But if I had to spend one more day cooped up in my house with nothing to do, I was going to lose it.

The problem was, I wasn't supposed to drive. Despite what the doctor had said—no driving for at least a couple of weeks—I'd assumed it would only take a day or two to feel well enough to get behind the wheel. But every time I moved wrong, sharp pain exploded across my midsection. All it would take was swerving to avoid a squirrel in the road, and I'd probably hit a tree.

Which meant I needed a ride. And for some reason, that had left me paralyzed with indecision.

My family all knew I was hurt. Theo had spread the word. Dad had bellowed at me a bit, then helped Mom stock my fridge with food. Everyone else had stopped by throughout the weekend, adding more ice packs, electrolyte drinks, snacks, and cookies from my sister-in-law, Harper.

I could have asked any of them for a ride. But when they'd asked how I was going to get around, I'd told each of them I had it covered.

You should have called me.

It was so weird that Melanie had said that. Because I *had* been thinking about calling her. Which made no sense. Why would I have called her? And why would I call her to drive me to work?

But damn it, the way she'd burst in on Saturday had done something to me. I'd spent the rest of the weekend thinking about her. About the worry in her voice and the look in her eyes when she'd replaced my ice pack.

You should have called me.

I wanted to be mad at her for getting in my head. But she'd *been* in my head since the day she'd almost run me off the road.

Actually, she'd been in my head a lot longer than that. She'd never really left.

With a groan of frustration, I set my coffee down and grabbed my phone. "Fine, Mel. I'll fucking call you."

It was a mistake. All she was going to do was piss me off. I hit send anyway.

"Are you okay?" she answered, urgency in her voice.

"Yeah, fine. I just…"

"What? What's wrong? You're not at work, which makes sense because you're injured, but I've also been trying not to call you all morning."

My lips twitched in a grin. "Why were you thinking about calling me, Mel?"

"You know, because you're usually here and you're not. Except you're not always here, sometimes you're off site. I don't know. I'm worried about you, okay? That's not illegal. It doesn't mean anything."

"So there's a modicum of concern again?"

"Yes. Just a small amount."

I could picture her gesturing with her thumb and forefinger to show me just how little concern she had.

She was such a liar.

"So, as part of your job, I need you to run an errand for me."

"Oh. That's why you're calling? Of course it is, it's a workday and I'm here... working. That's what I do. I work for you. What errand?"

"I need you to come get me."

"Come get you?"

"I can't drive because of my ribs, so I need a ride to work. I figured if I didn't call you, you'd probably complain about it, so I'm just avoiding an argument."

"Oh." She was quiet for a second. "I'm glad you called."

Why did she keep doing that? Going all soft when I expected her to snap at me. The woman made my head spin. "Yeah, well, you said I should have before. So I am now."

"I did say that." Her gentle voice was disarming. "Sure, I'll be right there."

"Thanks."

I ended the call and set my phone down.

Okay, so I'd called her. And it was fine. I needed a ride, she was coming to get me. It made sense. It wouldn't have been weird if I'd have called Andrea when she was working. Just part of the job.

Except I hadn't called Melanie because it was her job.

My phone buzzed. It was my aunt Louise.

"Hi, Aunt Louise," I answered.

"Luke, I've been worried sick. Your mom told me you were in an accident. How are you? Are you all right?"

"I'm a little banged up, but otherwise I'm fine."

"Are you sure?"

"Yeah, I'm sure. Thanks for checking up on me."

"Of course, dear, of course. I'll be by later with soup, and I'd bring cookies, but I suppose Harper already beat me to it."

"She did, yeah. And thank you for the soup, but I'm all stocked up. I don't think there's room in the fridge."

"That's fine, you can freeze it."

I shook my head. Sometimes it was easier not to argue with her.

"And one more thing," she said. "Do you think you'll be feeling up to the bachelor auction this weekend? There's absolutely no pressure if you're too injured. I just need to know since we're printing the programs."

I stifled a groan. I'd completely forgotten about the bachelor auction. "I don't think—"

"You know what? I'll leave your name in, and we can just cross it out if you decide not to come. But I bet you'll be fit as a fiddle by Saturday. That's almost a whole week."

I wanted to tell her no. But then again, the SPS had actually done a lot for my family. The least I could do would be to stand on stage and let them auction me off for an evening. I'd just have to let the winner know I wasn't up for any strenuous manual labor.

"You know what, Aunt Louise, I'll be there."

"Oh, that's wonderful. I just know you're going to bring in a hefty sum. I can feel it."

"Just make sure people know I'm hurt. I wouldn't want anyone to bid on me with the expectation that I can build a fence or something."

"I'll spread the word. Thank you, dear, I'll see you soon."

"Bye, Aunt Louise."

With a slight shake of my head, I ended the call and set my phone down. This bachelor auction was going to be interesting.

In the meantime, I needed to get dressed. I went to my bedroom to throw on some clothes. I had to clench my teeth against the pain while I pulled on a pair of jeans. The T-shirt wasn't as bad. I tugged it down gingerly and took a few deep breaths. It hurt, but I'd live.

Shoes, though. Those were going to be an issue. I had a pair that slipped on my feet easily enough, but tying them was going to be a special kind of torture.

I got them on, leaving them loose, and went to the living room to figure out how to tie the laces. I tried putting one foot on the coffee table to make it easier to reach, but I only bent over about three inches before I had to stop.

Maybe I needed to sit. I lowered myself onto the edge of the couch, took a breath, and tried to reach my shoe.

Pain wrapped around my midsection, making me feel like I couldn't breathe. Groaning, I leaned back.

There was a knock on my door.

"Yeah, gimme a second," I called out.

Melanie waltzed right in like she owned the place and shut the door behind her. "Ready?"

"I said give me a second. That means wait, not walk right in."

"It was unlocked."

"I could have been naked."

She shrugged. "Nothing I haven't seen before."

She wasn't wrong, but hearing her flippant reference to a time when we'd been getting naked together was both arousing and mildly infuriating.

I ran my tongue along my top teeth. "No, I'm not ready. I need a minute."

"Okay." She crossed her arms and glanced around.

Steeling myself to endure the agony, I sat up and started to bend forward so I could tie my shoes. The groan that crawled out of my throat was completely involuntary.

"Don't hurt yourself." She came over and got on her knees in front of me. "Here, let me."

There was a hell of a lot of pride swallowing in letting Melanie tie my shoes for me. She was matter-of-fact about it. Didn't make fun of me for not being able to do it myself, or drop a snide comment about deserving it because I'd done something stupid.

In fact, she hadn't lectured me about the accident at all.

A feeling spread through my chest, and it wasn't pain. It was warm and pleasant, a deep sense of gratitude. I wanted to reach out and run my fingers through her hair. Touch her face and bring her close. Kiss her soft lips.

Damn it, no. I didn't want Melanie like that. I couldn't. I couldn't take that risk again.

"So when am I going to hear about it?" I snapped.

Her gaze lifted to meet mine as she finished tying my second shoe. "Hear about what?"

"My accident. Racing. Me being an idiot."

"Am I supposed to say something about it?"

"Figured you would."

"Why, because I used to hate it when you raced back in high school? That was a long time ago."

My jaw hitched. This turn of subject was my doing. I wanted to antagonize her. Get her arguing with me so I could go back to being mad at her for existing, instead of whatever else it was that kept happening to me when she was around.

But she wasn't taking the bait.

"We used to fight about it then. Why not now?"

She paused, her brown eyes fixed on mine. No flash of anger lit up her features. I didn't sense her gearing up to fire back at me.

"Honestly?" Her voice was soft. "You're not stupid. You know when something is dangerous. And I think you're old enough to have outgrown your teenage immortality delusion. So you must have a reason for doing it. And until the reasons not to outweigh the reason you do it, you're going to do what you want. This isn't my problem to fix."

I watched her as she stood, at a loss for words. What was I supposed to say to that? She was absolutely right.

"I wasn't expecting you to be the calm and reasonable one," I said.

"Weird, isn't it?" She smiled. "It happens more than you'd think. I'm a hot mess, but I'm not as high strung as I used to be."

One corner of my mouth lifted in a grin. "You sure about that?"

"I didn't say I wasn't high strung at all. Just that I've mellowed out a little."

"All right, I'll buy that."

"Can you stand by yourself, or do you need help?"

"I got it." Gritting my teeth, I stood. "Thanks for the help with my shoes."

"Of course. Ready?"

"Yeah, let's go."

I followed her outside to her car. The weather was hot with a slight haze of brown in the sky. Must have been a wildfire somewhere, hopefully not too close to town. I didn't smell smoke, so that was a good sign.

We got in, and putting on the seat belt wasn't as agonizing as I'd feared. She pulled out of the driveway and onto the road, but hardly sped up.

I leaned over to look at the speedometer. "Why are you going twenty-five?"

"I'm being careful."

"You're not even going the speed limit."

"You ask for a ride to work, and now you're going to complain about how I drive?"

"Thirty, Mel. You can at least go thirty on this road."

"You're just so used to driving too fast, you don't know what safety feels like."

"Right, because you're the epitome of a safe driver."

She glanced at me, pressing her lips together like she was trying not to smile. "I'm not the one with a wrecked car and bruised ribs. What happened to the car, by the way?"

"Evan Bailey went out there and loaded it on his trailer yesterday. Saved my ass."

"That was nice of him."

"Yeah, I owe him."

"How bad is the damage?"

I shifted in my seat, trying not to visibly wince. "Pretty bad. I can fix it, but... yeah."

My eyes flicked to the speedometer again. She'd finally gotten up to the speed limit. It almost made me chuckle. She was such a fireball, but she was right, I was the one who'd wrecked a car racing illegally.

It was too bad she was dating someone.

But why? Why did I care? Maybe racing—and crashing—made it look like I had a death wish, but I didn't want to get hurt. And Melanie and I together? There was only one way that ended, and it would be worse than my bruised ribs.

The truth was, it had taken me years to get over her the first time. Why would I do that to myself again? Why even think about it?

Because there was something about her. A warmth that drew me in, like a fire on a cold night. I glanced at her from the corner of my eye. Could I bask in her heat without getting burned? Could any man?

It didn't matter anyway. Whatever she was doing to me—stirring up all these very inconvenient feelings—she was dating someone else. I wasn't going to get in the way of that. Granted, the guy looked like a douche, and I didn't know what she saw in him, but who was I to tell her who to be with? My opinion didn't count for shit.

After the slowest drive in the history of ever, we finally arrived at my garage. I managed to get out of the car without audibly groaning, which was a small miracle. Wordlessly, we went in together.

She went to the front desk and set her purse down. I hesitated by the door to the garage, the ache in my chest not a result of my injuries.

It was her. Damn it. She'd left that empty space behind, and I'd spent years trying to fill it. But nothing worked. And I hated it.

I took a breath and almost said something, but stopped. I didn't know what to say. She'd always been the one who got away, the girl who broke my heart. I'd been in denial about that for years, but it was the truth.

Didn't matter. We'd had our chance and that was over. Without looking back, I went through the door into the noise of the garage.

CHAPTER 22

Melanie

THE BALLROOM of the Grand Peak Hotel was a sight to behold.

A huge SPS sign hung from the ceiling, and a collection of plush squirrels was spread out across the check-in table. The volunteers all wore SPS buttons on their suits and gowns. Green plaid tablecloths adorned the tables, and the centerpieces were made of pine cones and greenery. The silent auction tables were all made of logs and raw edged wood, and their surfaces were similarly decorated—greenery and pine cones tucked in among the items available for bidding.

But it was the giant inflatable squirrel on the stage that really set the mood. It must have been at least twelve feet tall, complete with a huge tail and an acorn grasped in its front paws.

I took a sip of champagne and leaned closer to Sharla. "That's not something you see every day."

"Isn't it so cute? Oh my gosh, the kids would love it. Hopefully, they'll set it up in the park sometime."

"I feel like Nico would try to climb it."

"Probably."

Although everyone was dressed up, it felt a little strange

to be wandering around in a black evening gown among pine cones and plaid. But that was Tilikum for you. It certainly didn't lack charm.

"Where did Nathan go?" I asked.

Sharla glanced around. "He's standing in front of something he wants over in the silent auction so no one else will bid on it."

"That's one way to win. What is he bidding on?"

"A Blackstone grill."

"Don't you already have a grill?"

"We have two. And a smoker. But this one is bigger than the one we have, so obviously that means he needs it." She shook her head.

"Men and their meat," I said with a slight laugh.

"I swear, he's going to get kicked out. I'm going to go make him move."

Sharla stalked off toward the silent auction area. I took another sip of champagne, wondering if I could sneak out early. I'd put a small donation in the basket when I'd checked in. It wasn't much, but I wasn't exactly swimming in cash. Every little bit would help. There wasn't anything in the silent auction that I wanted, and I certainly wasn't going to bid on any bachelors. I'd made my appearance. I could probably just leave.

Then again, dinner was provided. Maybe I'd stay for the meal.

Mom sidled up next to me. To the surprise of no one, she wore the loudest dress in the room—a floor-length gown with bright pink sequins.

"Have you perused the bachelor photos yet?" She nudged me with her elbow.

"No. That's weird."

"Why is it weird?"

"I'm not going to go over there and ogle a bunch of guys, most of whom are probably ten years younger than me."

"Who said anything about ogling? Aren't you going to bid on anyone?"

"No. Absolutely not."

"There are some cute ones."

"Do you really think I'm so desperate for a date that I have to buy one at an auction?"

"There are worse ways to meet someone."

I rolled my eyes. "Mom. You're killing me."

"It's just for fun. He doesn't even have to take you out on a date. He could come over and help you set up your recording booth."

"My recording booth is all set up."

"Then why aren't you working?"

"I don't have a script."

"Then why not get another voice acting job until you do?"

"I'm stuck with a noncompete," I said. "I can't do anything else until my contract for *Enchanted Hollow* is over."

"Well, that seems silly. Do you want me to call them?"

I almost burst out laughing. "No, I do not want you to call the studio and tell them how you feel about noncompete clauses."

"I'm just saying, I will."

"I have no doubt." It was time to change the subject. "So, which new pizza flavor is doing the best these days? It's the pickle pizza, isn't it? It has to be pickle."

"Actually, the pickle pizza is selling enough to stay on the menu."

"Why do you sound surprised by that? It's amazing."

"Not everyone loves pickles as much as you, lovey."

I shrugged. "Not everyone has good taste."

"People seem to be enjoying the loaded baked potato. We'll probably make that a seasonal flavor."

"That one wasn't bad." I glanced at the silent auction tables. Nathan had moved a few feet from his intended prize, but it looked like he was lingering close enough to outbid anyone else who tried. Sharla stood next to him, double-fisting wine and champagne. Seemed like a good choice.

"Good evening, friends and neighbors." Mayor Bill Surrey stood center stage in a brown suit with a green plaid tie and spoke into the microphone. "Can you hear me all right?"

A murmur of assent rose from the crowd.

"Wonderful. If everyone could take your seats, dinner will be served, and we'll begin our program. Thank you."

I followed Mom to our table. Dad was already seated, and next to him were spots for Nathan and Sharla. I had a feeling Nathan wouldn't be using his place. He looked fairly well encamped next to the coveted grill.

Rounding out our table were Doris Tilburn—Harper's aunt—along with Louise Haven and her husband, George. Doris looked lovely in a simple black gown, proudly displaying her SPS button near her left shoulder.

Shockingly, Louise wasn't in a tracksuit. She stood behind her husband's chair, rocking a floor-length turquoise velour gown with a mermaid silhouette.

I hoped my butt looked that good when I was her age. Damn.

Mom kissed Dad on the cheek before taking her seat. "Hi, everyone. I'm so excited for this."

Louise turned toward us and smiled. "Ah, Andolini family. I'm so glad you could join us at our table."

I took my seat next to my mom and leaned closer. "I thought this was your table?"

"No, Louise invited us to sit with her. Isn't that sweet?"

Louise winked at me. Not a quick, subtle wink. She scrunched up her entire face with a too-long, very obvious wink.

That was a woman who was up to something.

"Very sweet," I said, still keeping my voice low. "Or suspicious."

"Suspicious? What are you talking about?"

"Look at her."

Louise lowered herself into the seat next to her husband. She smiled at me again, batting her eyelashes as if to maintain her innocence.

Mom touched my hand. "Don't worry about it. Just have fun."

I picked up the bidding paddle off my plate and tucked it beneath my chair. "Won't be needing that."

Mom moved hers and set it on the table next to her silverware. "I should bid on someone just to get a rise out of your father."

I laughed. "That's terrible. Don't do that to poor Dad."

"Why not? He might make me pay for it later."

"Okay, that's disgusting and also adorable. You two set such a good example. How did I end up divorced?"

"That's a great question, but it definitely wasn't me," she said.

I laughed again. "No, Mom. Definitely not your fault."

Servers started bringing out dinner while Mayor Bill took the mic again. He gave a short speech about the importance of the SPS to the Tilikum community and thanked several of its members. Then he shared a few SPS success stories. Only one involved an actual squirrel. The others were locals who'd been facing difficult circumstances, including a young woman leaving a toxic relationship, and a family undergoing a contentious custody dispute that had led to kidnapping concerns. In each case, the SPS had provided security and support.

It was heartwarming. They really were doing a lot of good in the community.

Finally, he introduced the auctioneer. The room suddenly sparkled with excitement as people—mostly ladies—grabbed their bidding paddles and sat forward in their seats.

The first bachelor to take the stage was probably in his mid-twenties, dressed in a suit and tie. He played to the crowd as the auctioneer introduced him, spreading his arms wide as if to say *go ahead, ladies, bid for me.*

Bidding began, and paddles were thrust into the air. Mom and I laughed as we watched the commotion. The crowd clapped and cheered as the price climbed. Finally, the bidding reached a crescendo and there was a winner—a woman two tables away from us.

Next up was a firefighter who clearly understood the assignment. The crowd erupted in cheers as he took the stage shirtless, wearing only his turnouts and suspenders. All he needed was a kitten, and half the room would have swooned out of their seats.

The bidding for him was bonkers. My mom even raised her paddle a few times. Dad just eyed her with a slight grin every time her arm went up. Finally, someone was declared the winner. He ran down the steps from the stage to give her a shirtless hug. I had a feeling she already considered it worth the money.

A guy in a sheriff's deputy uniform took the stage next. Although he was dressed, his muscular arms and aviator sunglasses were too much for the crowd to resist. Everyone went wild. Mom bid on him too, although I could tell she wasn't serious. Eventually, after an intense bidding war between two women at the same table, there was a winner.

The auctioneer announced the next bachelor—Theo Haven. I clapped for him as he sauntered onto the stage, dressed in a blue flannel and jeans. He tucked his thumbs into his pockets, and one corner of his mouth lifted in a grin. That was all it took to get the crowd going—no bare chest or cool sunglasses necessary. Even I found myself gazing at him appreciatively. There was just something about those Havens.

After a frenzy of bidding, Theo was auctioned off. I was about to take another bite of my dinner when the next bachelor took the stage. My mouth hung open, and I dropped my fork with a clatter.

Luke Haven.

I didn't know why I was so surprised to see him. Maybe because he was injured. Or because he hadn't said a word about the auction all week. Of course, why would he? Our weekend plans hadn't come up. Still, I found myself feeling slightly pouty that I hadn't known he'd be there.

"My nephew," Louise said, pointing at the stage. As if we all didn't know they were related. "He's such a catch." She turned and made eye contact with me, eyebrows raised.

That was weird.

I looked away as the bidding began.

Paddles flew into the air while the crowd cheered them on. Luke ran a hand through his thick hair, a sheepish grin on his face.

Why did he have to be so freaking gorgeous? He wasn't even dressed up, but the faded Haven Auto T-shirt and perfectly fitting jeans were so… him. Understated but sexy. I watched as he squinted into the crowd. It was probably hard to see from up there with all the lights. People kept bidding, and the auctioneer kept calling out numbers.

I glanced around as people dropped out, the bids getting too high for their taste. Someone across the room seemed very determined to get him. Her paddle went up instantly every time someone outbid her.

Wait. I leaned over, trying to see her through the throng of people. It wasn't… It couldn't be…

It was. It was Jenna.

I huffed in disgust. Jenna? Why was she bidding on Luke? Who bid on the guy they were dating?

Were they dating?

They'd been on a date, but I actually had no idea if they'd seen each other again. Was she just bidding him up, trying to raise more money for the SPS? Or did she actually want to win?

Without thinking it through—at all—I grabbed my mom's paddle and thrust my arm into the air.

The auctioneer pointed at me. "Bidder 131 has entered the fray."

"What are you doing?" Mom asked.

Jenna outbid me. I raised the paddle. "I'll pay you back when I have a real job again."

"Are you sure you know what you're doing?"

Jenna bid, so I bid again. "Of course not. I'm being completely irrational."

"Okay, as long as you know."

After I outbid Jenna one more time, she twisted in her seat to see who was giving her a run for her money. Our eyes met, and her mouth dropped open.

My eyes narrowed. So did hers.

"Bring it, honey," I muttered. "I'll do this all night."

"Just know this is coming out of your inheritance," Mom said.

"That's fair."

Jenna and I went back and forth, bid for bid, at least half a dozen times. How did she have so much money? Maybe she was doing what I was doing—bidding with someone else's bank account.

At first, my hand flew up as soon as the auctioneer acknowledged her bid. But after a while, I decided I needed to slow this down. Jenna bid, and I waited, pretending like I had to think about it. The auctioneer was good. He coaxed and cajoled, encouraging me to raise my paddle again.

I did and the crowd cheered. Jenna did the same, hesitating, like she needed to think about it. When the auctioneer was about to declare me the winner, she raised her paddle again to more applause from the other guests.

My eyes flicked to Luke. He stood with his hands resting on his hips, a slight grin on his face, his gaze on me. I could see the challenge in his face. The dare.

There was no way I was losing.

Without looking at Jenna, I lifted my paddle again. Luke's expression didn't change. Apparently Jenna bid, but I ignored her. Just kept my eyes on Luke and listened to the cues from the auctioneer.

The crowd cheered encouragement, egging us on to bid more money. Every time I lifted my paddle, my whole table erupted with shouts. Even Nathan had joined us, and he clapped and whistled along with the rest of them.

Turning to me, the auctioneer asked if I wanted to bid again. I waited a few seconds, then raised my paddle. He turned to Jenna. She hesitated.

My heart thumped hard, and my stomach tingled with excitement. Luke's eyes weren't on the auctioneer or on Jenna. They were on me, his gaze intense. I waited for Jenna to bid again. For the auctioneer to point at me, asking for an even higher number.

Jenna didn't. From the corner of my eye, I could see her shake her head and set her paddle on the table.

With a dramatic gesture, the auctioneer pointed at me. "Sold, to bidder 131."

The room erupted with cheers and applause. Louise stood, clapping vigorously while her husband whistled.

Laughing, I stood and bowed, then waved to the crowd. When I took my seat again, I glanced up at Luke. He shook his head a little with that same subtle grin, then walked off stage.

"Well, that was exciting," Mom said.

I brushed my hair back from my face. "It's possible I got a little carried away."

Sharla raised her eyebrows and gave me a knowing smile.

"Hush, you." I pointed at her. "It's for a good cause. I don't want to hear it."

"I wasn't going to say a word."

Nathan shook his head. "I don't even want to know."

Louise clasped her hands to her chest as she sat back down. "That was thrilling. Absolutely thrilling. I knew you'd get him in the end." She winked at me again.

I let out a slow breath. What on earth had I just done? Outbid the girl Luke was probably dating for an evening with him? It was arguably the stupidest thing I'd ever done in my life.

Actually, no. I'd done much stupider things.

But still. I was already seized with pangs of regret. What were we going to do? Did I actually have to spend an evening with him? Did I want to?

And there was the problem. I did want to. And I shouldn't.

It was such a disaster.

Mom nudged me and nodded toward the stage. The auction continued, but I hadn't seen who was next.

Hank. Of course it was Hank.

I watched as people bid. The energy wasn't as frenzied as when Jenna and I had been battling it out for Luke, but that wasn't Hank's fault. Bidding wars tended to do that at these events. I glanced toward Jenna's table and realized she was one of the bidders.

Huh. That was interesting.

It came down to Jenna and a woman in the back. I had a feeling Jenna was not going to lose another one. Maybe that was why she was bidding so furiously on Hank. She was annoyed at me for costing her Luke.

The two women bid back and forth a few more times before the one in the back finally gave up. She set her paddle down, and the auctioneer declared Jenna the winner. The guests applauded, and she waved, smiling like she'd just won a big teddy bear at a carnival.

My cheeks felt flushed, and the swirl of emotion was dizzying. I fanned myself and stood. "I need to use the ladies' room."

The closest restrooms were just outside the ballroom. I ducked inside, grateful for the cooler air and relative quiet. And the lack of Jenna. The last thing I needed was another run-in with Miss Bathroom-Bonding-Is-Fun.

I used the bathroom, double-checked to make sure my dress was all the way down and not tucked into my underwear, and washed my hands. My cheeks were still a bit flushed, and I fanned myself again, wishing I could get it together and calm down.

This didn't have to be a big deal. It was funny when I thought about it. Me, bidding like a rich heiress with Daddy's credit card on one of Tilikum's most eligible bachelors. He was my ex-boyfriend. So what? That had been a million years ago, almost in another life.

We'd have a good laugh about it and then move on.

Feeling a little less like I was about to have an early hot flash, I reapplied my lipstick, tucked it back in my clutch, and walked out of the restroom.

Right into Luke.

This time, we didn't collide. But there he was, coming through the men's room door. I lifted my eyes to the ceiling. *Really, universe?*

Before I could slip by him unnoticed, he caught sight of me, and his lips curled in that subtle grin.

I put my hand up, palm out. "Don't."

"Don't what?"

"Don't say anything."

His grin spread. "I wasn't going to say a word."

"Yes, you were, but don't bother. I wasn't bidding for me. I was bidding for someone else."

"Oh yeah? Who?"

"My mom. It was her paddle."

"And what does your mom want with me?"

"You know," I said, idly gesturing with one hand, "help

around the house. Handyman-type stuff. Or maybe something with her car. I don't know. She probably has a list."

Still smiling, he stepped closer. "I can't do any of that stuff. Bruised ribs, remember? I can't even drive."

"Of course I remember. I've been taking you to work every day. How could I forget?"

"Which means your mom must know I'm injured and can't help around the house. Or fix her car." He moved closer still.

I took a step back only to find my back against the wall. "I'm sure she'll find something for you to do."

His nearness made my heart race and my cheeks flush all over again. Why did he have to smell so good? His raw masculinity washed over me, turning my stomach into a whirlpool.

"What time?" he asked.

My voice was embarrassingly breathy. "What time for what?"

"Your winnings. According to the auction rules, you get me all to yourself tomorrow. Any time after noon, and no later than ten. Unless otherwise agreed upon."

I pressed my back into the wall, trying to keep space between us. "Okay, noon, then."

He lifted his eyebrows. "You want the whole ten hours?"

"No," I said quickly. "I don't know. You said noon, so I said noon. I see you all day at work. You don't have to come over that early."

He placed his hand on the wall and leaned in, lowering his voice. "How about this? I'll be at your place at six. With dinner."

My entire body was on fire. It was hard to think. Everything was swirling out of control. His face was so close, all I'd have to do is lift my chin and our lips would touch.

"Dinner is good. But how? You can't drive."

"I'll get a ride."

"Well, that's good at least. I paid good money for you. I shouldn't have to pick you up too."

He grinned again, his nose almost brushing against mine. "Great. It's a date."

My breath caught as he hesitated—not moving away but not moving in either. A second later, he stepped back, still looking at me like he knew all my secrets.

"It's not a date," I said. "I bought you."

"All right, Mel. Not a date. I'll see you tomorrow."

It felt like I couldn't quite catch my breath as I watched him walk away. Why had I let him fluster me like that? It was just Luke. I didn't have feelings for—

And for the first time, I couldn't finish my own lie.

CHAPTER 23

Luke

DARK CLOUDS HAD ROLLED IN OVERNIGHT, BRINGING humidity but not a drop of rain. The gloomy sky added to the ominous sense of foreboding in my gut as Theo drove me to Melanie's house. His auction "date" was already over. The woman who'd won him had wanted him to play football with her four sons. He'd had a great day.

As for me, how would this go down? Would Melanie and I spend the evening fighting? Or maybe find some common ground? Hard to say. When it came to Melanie Andolini, you could never be quite sure what you were going to get.

There was excitement in that, though. I could feel the tingle of adrenaline flowing through me. I didn't know why she did that to me, how the anticipation of seeing her lit me up more than a race ever could. But it happened all the time.

I liked it.

It was dangerous. She was dangerous, and I knew it. We'd crashed and burned once, and the fallout had been worse than bruised ribs and a wrecked car. It had taken me years to get over her.

Maybe I never really had.

"How are you feeling?" Theo asked.

The pain from my injuries had mostly receded to a dull ache as long as I didn't make any sudden movements. "Not too bad. Thanks again for the ride. I could probably drive, but—"

"Don't," he said, cutting me off. "You start driving before you're healed enough, and you'll just do more damage."

"Fair enough."

He hesitated for a moment. "We're not going to talk about it, are we?"

I knew what he meant. Melanie. "Nope."

"Okay. But…"

"But what?"

He glanced at me as we pulled into her driveway. "Are you sure you know what you're doing?"

"Not at all." I unfastened the seat belt, grabbed the takeout we'd picked up from Copper Kettle Diner, and opened the door.

"Need a ride home?"

"Maybe. I'll text you if I do."

"All right, man. Make good choices."

I chuckled. "Thanks, Mom."

He grinned as I got out and shut the door.

With a deep breath, I watched him back out of the driveway, then I walked up to her front door. *Here goes nothing.*

I knocked and waited. No answer. I knocked again, louder this time. Maybe she hadn't heard me. I waited. Still nothing.

Where was she? I pulled my phone out of my pocket, but she hadn't messaged me. We'd said six, and it was a few minutes past. Was she home? Was she all right?

I knocked again, hard. "Melanie? You okay?"

No answer.

That was alarming. Had the sense of foreboding actually meant something was wrong? I tried the doorknob, and it opened.

"Mel?" I called, poking my head in. "Are you there?"

She didn't answer. She'd probably chew me out for going in, especially if she was just in the bathroom or something. But we had plans. I wasn't too proud to admit this was making me worry about her.

I stepped inside and shut the door behind me. The entryway led to a living area with a couch and coffee table. The dining room had no table, and the kitchen counters were almost bare.

Hesitating, I listened. No noise. Was she home? Was I an idiot for being there?

Probably. But I walked farther into the house anyway. A short hallway led to the bedrooms. I moved quietly, ready to duck if she jumped out and swung at me again. I had enough bruises. I didn't need another fist in the face.

"Mel?" I whispered.

One of the bedroom doors was slightly ajar. I moved close enough to see through the crack.

There she was, lying on the bed, asleep. She was fully dressed, and the bed was made, like she'd flopped down and fallen asleep without meaning to. Her arm draped over her forehead, some of her hair was stuck to her cheek, and one foot hung over the edge of the bed.

Such a beautiful mess.

For a second, I thought about taking a picture. Mostly because I knew she'd hate it. But I decided not to provoke her. She'd paid good money for me. The least I could do was be nice.

I took our dinner to the kitchen—sandwiches with extra pickles for Mel—and put them in the fridge. Then I eased myself onto the couch to wait for her to wake up.

It didn't take long. I grinned with amusement as I heard a commotion coming from her bedroom. It almost sounded like she'd fallen off the bed. She started muttering to herself, banging things around, and a moment later, she burst out of the bedroom.

"Where's my phone?"

She rushed past me into the kitchen and started digging through her purse.

"Why do you need your phone?"

"I need to call Lu—" Stopping abruptly, she turned. "You're here."

"We said six."

"Sorry, I didn't get much sleep last night. I didn't mean to take a nap. I was only going to rest my eyes for a few minutes. Wait, how did you get in?"

"The door was unlocked."

Her eyes widened. "What? Are you sure?"

"Positive."

"No, it wasn't. I never leave it unlocked." Sounding oddly panicked, she went over to the door and locked the deadbolt. "When did I unlock it? Must have been when I took the trash out. But I always lock it when I come in."

"It was the middle of the day. It's fine."

"But you walked right in." The pitch of her voice started to rise, and the words tumbled out of her mouth. "The door was open, and anyone could have come in. There you are, sitting on the couch because I left it unlocked and I don't know how I did that."

I stood and walked over to her, full of concern. "Why are you so upset?"

She was practically in tears. "I'm not."

"Yes, you are." I reached out and took her by the upper arms, gently so I didn't startle her. "Mel, it's okay. Nothing bad happened. You're safe."

She covered her face and collapsed against my chest. I winced a little, but ignored the pain and wrapped my arms around her. She shook with sobs as I held her tight. I wasn't sure what else to do. Melanie was not a crier, so seeing her reduced to tears was unsettling.

"It's okay," I murmured, rubbing slow circles across her back. "I've got you."

She felt dangerously good in my arms. Soft and familiar. Her lightly vanilla scent enveloped me, and I let my eyes close as I breathed her in.

After several long moments, she stopped crying. Her body stilled, and with her face still buried in my chest, she took a few deep breaths.

"Sorry." She moved back, and I reluctantly let her go. "I'm fine."

"Obviously, you're not. What's going on?"

Wiping her eyes, she shook her head. "Nothing."

"Mel, don't do that."

She stepped away, turning toward the kitchen. "I'm not doing anything."

"Yes, you are. Just tell me."

"There's nothing to tell. I'm sleep deprived." Her voice was returning to normal, and she waved me off as she opened the fridge. "You know how weird I get when I don't sleep."

Something was not adding up. "Why couldn't you sleep?"

She stood in front of the fridge, her back to me. "I don't know."

"Liar."

"I'm not lying."

"Yes, you are." I couldn't keep the frustration out of my voice as I followed her into the kitchen. "Why won't you just tell me what's wrong?"

"I did. I'm tired."

"You're not just tired. What's wrong?"

"Nothing."

"Will you stop shutting me out?" I snapped.

She whirled on me, slamming the fridge door. "I'm scared, okay? I'm fucking terrified."

"Of what?"

"Him. He's still out there."

"Who's him? What are you talking about?"

She was breathing hard, and the fear in her eyes almost broke me. I closed the distance between us, wrapped my arms around her, and hauled her against me, heedless of the ache in my ribs.

"What happened?" I asked, my voice soft. "Who hurt you?"

For a second, she was stiff, and I expected her to shove me away. But her body softened, relaxing as I gently rubbed her back.

"It's a long story," she whispered.

"We've got time." I squeezed her, then took her hands and led her to the couch. "Tell me."

She followed without protest and sat down next to me. I waited for a moment while she fiddled with her hands.

Finally, she spoke. "It was eleven years ago, when I lived in LA. I was abducted outside my apartment."

"Holy shit, Mel."

"He grabbed me from behind and choked me out. Then he injected me with something that kept me unconscious for a while. It was late, so no one saw anything. When I woke up, I was so out of it, it's hard to remember what actually happened. But I was tied up and in the trunk of a car."

She stopped talking, her eyes downcast. I took her hand, twining our fingers together, and waited for her to continue.

"Eventually, the car stopped, and someone opened the trunk. He started talking to me, telling me he was going to untie my feet so I could walk and how he wasn't going to hurt me. Then he asked if I'd be good if he untied me. I remember nodding that I would.

"He cut the tape from my ankles and helped me out of the trunk. He was wearing a mask so I couldn't see his face, but I'll never forget his voice. It was soft, like he was talking to a pet or a child. He took my hands and started to lead me away from the car. There was another one parked there. It was like he was going to switch vehicles."

She paused again, and I squeezed her hand. She squeezed back.

"Honestly, I don't remember a lot about what happened after that. It's all a blur. I just knew I couldn't let him take me anywhere else. So I started fighting. I kicked him and hit him even though my hands were still tied. I must have managed to kick him in the balls because he fell to the ground. So I kicked him again, hoping to knock him out. And then I ran."

I pulled her against me, and she settled her head on my chest. She took a deep breath, and her body seemed to relax. Anger simmered deep inside me. I wanted to find whoever had done that to her and rip him to pieces.

"Luckily, I ran in the right direction and got to a road. A car pulled over and of course they freaked out when they saw I was tied up. They called 911 and stayed with me until the police got there."

"I take it they didn't find the guy."

"No. Never. It all happened so fast, I didn't have a lot of details. I couldn't even remember the color of the car, and I didn't see what he looked like. There was some trace evidence, but it didn't lead them anywhere."

I kept my arms around her and let out a long breath. "So that's why you punched me in the face that day."

She nodded against my chest. "See? You can hardly blame me."

"Actually, I'm kinda proud of you."

Pulling away slightly, she looked up at me. "Why?"

"It was a badass move. If I'd been trying to grab you from behind, you probably would have stopped me."

Her mouth turned up in a smile. "Thanks."

I tucked a lock of hair behind her ear. "Is that why you couldn't sleep?"

She nodded again. "I have nightmares."

"I can't believe they didn't find him."

"I know. It was awful. It's also kind of why I moved in with Jared, my ex. We hadn't been dating very long, but it seemed like a good idea at the time."

"So you could say you got married under duress."

Her smile grew. "You could say that, yes."

I hugged her against me again. Mostly because I wanted to comfort her—make everything better somehow. But also because she felt so good, I couldn't resist.

"I'm so sorry that happened to you."

"Thanks. I've had a lot of therapy to deal with it, but nothing has ever helped with the nightmares. I don't have them every night or anything, but when I do, it's over. No more sleep."

"That's so shitty. It's bad enough you had to go through something like that. But to have to keep living with it."

"Definitely zero stars. Do not recommend."

I rested my cheek on the top of her head. We sat there for a while, just breathing.

"Luke?"

"Yeah?"

"Did you bring dinner?"

That made me laugh. The woman had just opened up to me, and the next thing she wanted was food. "Yes, I brought dinner. I put it in the fridge."

"Don't get up. I'll get it. But how did I not notice it in there?"

"I don't know. Your fridge is almost empty."

She eased herself off me and stood. "Don't judge me for being broke. My boss is a cheapskate."

I shook my head while she went to the kitchen and opened the fridge. "So, how mad is Hank that you bid on me instead of him at the auction?"

She turned toward me, her eyes flashing.

I was definitely getting too close to the fire.

"Not mad in the least, I suppose, considering he dumped me after our second date. However, I'd like to state for the record that I was going to dump him, he just said it first. It was a mutual dumping."

I couldn't help the slow grin that crept over my face. Not with Hank? That was interesting information.

"How mad is Jenna that I won instead of her?"

"Why would she be mad?"

"Maybe because you're dating," she said, like I'd just asked a stupid question.

"We're not dating."

Her voice went low and sultry. "Do not lie to me, Luke Haven."

"I'm not."

"Excuse me," she said, returning to her natural voice as she took the to-go boxes out of the fridge and set them on the counter. "I saw you on a date with her."

My brow furrowed. "Yeah, we went out that one time. That doesn't mean we're dating."

"Does she know that? Because she cost me a hell of a lot of money last night trying to outbid me for you."

"She knows. I texted her this morning. It felt weird to leave it unfinished. But if I recall, you jumped in to outbid her, not the other way around."

"Fine, aliens briefly took over my body and made me bid entirely too much money for an evening with you."

"Are you kidding? A guy with all this?" I gestured at myself. "You got me for a steal."

She grabbed the to-go boxes and brought them in, setting them on the coffee table. "You're basically useless. You can't even fix my car or chop wood for me or whatever the other bachelors are all doing tonight. I'll probably have to give you a ride home."

"Yeah, I definitely need a ride home. But I brought dinner."

Lowering herself onto the couch next to me, she sighed dramatically. "I suppose that is something. What are we having?"

"Sandwiches. I know it's not fancy, but you said it's not a date."

"I did say that." She opened her box and gasped. "Look at all those pickles!"

"There should be more on the sandwich."

She picked one up and took a crunchy bite. "So good."

I shook my head slightly. "See? I was worth every penny."

"I take back all the bad things I've said about you. At least in the last week."

"That's very generous of you."

Still eating, she nudged my arm with her elbow. The brush of her skin against mine sent a wave of heat surging through me. The urge to turn and kiss her was so strong, I almost lost my mind and did it.

But I didn't. I held back.

She glanced at me from the corner of her eye, and I didn't miss the flash of suspicion that crossed her face. I picked up my sandwich and took a bite.

Don't do it, Luke. Don't go there.

We ate our dinner and then she declared that my final duty as her bachelor of the evening was to make her popcorn and watch a movie with her. She picked some romantic period film, probably thinking I wasn't going to like it. Joke was on her, because I did.

The wet spot on my chest from her tears dried, but I couldn't stop thinking about it. The way she'd felt in my arms was burned into my memory. Soft, warm, familiar. And good. Way too good. But it wasn't just how she'd cried while I'd held her, it was everything she'd been through.

A streak of fierce protectiveness raged inside me. I wanted

to find the piece of shit who'd hurt her and make sure she never had to worry about him again. I wanted to keep her safe and secure, so she could sleep without fear. Be the wall that guarded her, no matter what it cost me.

Except I didn't know if I could. Because if I went down that road again, it was going to cost me everything.

Rehearsal

ROSWELL MILLS

SITTING IN A CORNER, unnoticed, I sipped my soda. The bar was busy. People chatted over their drinks, a group of guys played a game of darts, and every so often a pair of women would get up and dance next to their table.

I took it all in, looking for her. For the right one.

My instincts told me that was the place—the small-town bar in Echo Creek, a town not far from Tilikum. I'd find her.

The more I considered my plan to practice first, the more convinced I was that I was right. If I could successfully take, subdue, and keep a few substitutes, I'd know my technique and preparations were adequate.

Not just adequate. Perfect.

The risk would be worth the reward, especially once I had the one I really wanted.

These would be my rehearsals. My training.

Someday, I'd tell Melanie all about them. All the work I'd done to prepare for her. My lips curled in a smile, imagining how impressed she'd be with the lengths I'd gone to for her.

I took another sip of my drink, watching the scene before

me. No one was going to live up to my standards, be a true replacement. Like the whore in that forgotten town, she'd be a poor substitute. But I still wanted someone similar, so I could lay her on the mattress in the basement, chain her to the wall, and watch. Imagine that it was her.

A shudder of anticipation ran down my spine just thinking about it.

Glancing around the bar again, my gaze lingered on a woman sitting by herself, drinking heavily. She was about the right age with brown hair. Too thin, but I didn't plan on using her body to sate my lust, so what did it matter if her hips weren't right or her tits were too small? She could still be my first rehearsal.

I considered whether she was the one. Drunk would work to my advantage. I didn't expect Melanie to be intoxicated when I took her, but this was my first attempt. And the more I watched her, the more I wanted to take her. Prove to myself that I could.

She signaled the bartender. He came over, but from the look of it, he was refusing to serve her any more alcohol. I couldn't hear everything she was saying, but it was clear she was arguing. The bartender didn't seem swayed. He shook his head and walked away.

The woman got off her stool. She had to hold on to the bar for a few seconds to steady herself. I wondered if she'd fall over, but she kept her feet. A moment later, she headed for the door.

"You're walking home, right?" the bartender called out.

She waved her arm at him without turning around. "Yeah, yeah. Walking."

Excitement seized me, a rush of adrenaline flowing through my veins. It was time.

Casually, I left, confident no one noticed me. I was plain, invisible, not worth anyone's attention.

My heart beat faster as I emerged into the night air. The

woman stumbled and paused, as if she wasn't sure which direction was home.

I moved in behind her and gently touched her elbow. "Let me help."

She jerked her arm away. "I'm fine."

I didn't need to keep hold of her to guide her where I wanted her to go—closer to my car. Turning slightly, I angled her so she was walking into the parking lot instead of toward the sidewalk.

"It's okay, I'm a friend. Just trying to help."

"I don't need help."

"All right." We were close enough to my car and outside the glare of the streetlight. My heart pounded as I pressed the remote to pop the trunk and lowered my voice to a whisper. "Don't be scared. Everything is going to be okay."

"I'm not—"

Stepping behind her, I wound my arm around her neck, cutting off her words, and the blood to her brain. A blood choke only took about ten seconds if you knew what you were doing. And I did. She struggled a little, but she was too weak—and too drunk—to do anything to me. Her body went limp, and I carefully lowered her to the ground.

The advantage to a blood choke was speed. The disadvantage was duration. She'd only be out for ten or twenty seconds. Maybe longer because of the alcohol.

Reaching for the needle in my pocket, I paused for a second. The sedative would react with the alcohol in her system, but I didn't have time to figure out how to adjust the dosage. I jabbed the needle into her upper arm and injected some of it. I'd have half an hour, possibly more, before she woke up. Plenty of time.

I picked her up, eased her into the trunk, and shut it, then glanced around. No one was there. She hadn't seen my face. And she wouldn't. I wouldn't let her.

It was a shame. She'd never know who I was. I'd be invisible to her, like I was to everyone else.

A jolt of anger rippled through me as I got in my car. Invisible. Unnoticed. Unwanted. This one wouldn't see my face—wouldn't know who had control of her. As necessary as it was, I hated it.

It made me hate her, the second-rate substitute in my trunk. I hated everything about her. I'd use her for my rehearsal—practice would make perfect.

And she'd be good for me. I'd make her be good for me.

And if she didn't, I'd make her pay.

CHAPTER 24

Melanie

BEING at work on Monday wasn't the least bit disconcerting. I'd picked Luke up, since he still couldn't drive. We'd made small talk and gone our separate ways once we arrived. It was like nothing had happened over the weekend.

And really, nothing had.

Everything was fine.

Okay, so I'd opened up to Luke and told him my traumatic tale. It wasn't like it was a big secret. If it had happened locally—not several states away—the entire town would have known the story. I didn't keep it from people, necessarily. I just didn't like talking about it.

And fine, I'd cried. On his chest. I almost never cried, so I couldn't pretend that was nothing. But it didn't have to be something big or important. Sleep deprivation could heighten anyone's emotions. I wasn't immune to that.

I'd been upset, I'd freaked out over the unlocked door, and a few tears had been shed. It was all a big, fat nothing.

Or it was to him. That was clear. He'd barely looked at me all day.

Instead of getting worked up about it, I sat at the front desk, trying to focus on my job. Because I didn't know what there was to get worked up about. What did I want from him? It wasn't like he was ignoring or avoiding me. It was a normal day.

The problem was, I didn't feel normal. Not after the other night.

I'd gone to bed with the memory of his arms around me. His embrace had felt so good, I wasn't even embarrassed that I'd cried. I kind of wanted to do it again to see if he'd hug me the same way.

Which was ridiculous.

Wasn't it?

And he'd given me the look—a look I remembered all too well. One that sent shivers down my spine and made my lips tingle with anticipation.

He'd been thinking about kissing me.

To my relief—or disappointment, I was very confused—he hadn't. Not then, when we'd been sitting on the couch together. Not later, when we'd watched a movie. And not at the end of the night, when I'd dropped him off at his place.

No more heat in his eyes. No more longing glances.

I finished sorting a stack of invoices and tapped them to line up their edges. It was just as well. I didn't want Luke to kiss me. We'd been down that road and it hadn't ended well. If he wanted to move on like we hadn't shared a moment over the weekend, it was for the best.

But if that were true, why was I so furious?

He walked into the lobby, and with barely a glance at me, grabbed the invoices. Without a single word, he turned and left, disappearing through the door that led to his office.

My mouth dropped open. How dare he waltz over to my desk like I was just a random employee. Like I was nothing to him.

I closed my mouth and forced myself to take a deep breath

through my nose. I was getting carried away. He wasn't acting any different from how he always acted at work. He probably had a million things on his mind.

It was fine. I tucked my hair behind my ear. Completely fine.

But an angry blaze still burned hot in my chest.

I needed to get out for a few minutes, otherwise I was going to burst like a firecracker. I decided to take a quick walk to Nature's Basket Grocery. I knew myself—sometimes I wasn't angry, I just needed a snack. The weather was oppressively hot, but I didn't care. A little sweat down my back would be better than having a meltdown the next time Luke walked by my desk. I forwarded the phone to voicemail, grabbed my purse, and left.

A wave of heat hit me as soon as I walked out the door. Hoping I'd remembered to put on deodorant that morning, I headed up the sidewalk to the grocery store.

I was in a mood where nothing sounded good, so I wandered aimlessly up and down the aisles for a few minutes. Eventually, I picked up a bag of dried apple chips and a cup of cubed cheese from the deli.

There was only one cashier available, so I got in the short line. A moment or two later, it was my turn. I checked out, tucked my snack and receipt into my purse, and left.

I'd hardly been in the store for ten minutes, but it seemed hotter outside on the walk back to the garage. I pushed open the front door, eagerly anticipating the air-conditioning that awaited me inside.

Luke stood behind the front desk, an angry expression on his face. "Where were you?"

"I went to the store," I said, confused. "Why are you snapping at me? I was gone for like fifteen minutes and I forwarded the phone. Since when do I have to check in with you every time I move? Should I ask permission to go to the bathroom too?"

"No, I just… I didn't know where you were."

"I got a snack." I walked around the desk, but he was in my way. I couldn't sit down. "If you wanted to know where I was, you could have just called me."

"I did. You didn't answer."

"Oh. Sorry, I didn't hear my phone."

He raked his hands through his hair. "Damn it, Mel, you scared the crap out of me."

"Why? Because I walked to the store to get a snack? I know it's hot out there, but I drink plenty of water. It's not like I'm a heat stroke risk."

He let out an exasperated breath. "Never mind."

Not quite sure what had just happened, I watched him leave. The sound of power tools in the garage carried through the door until it swung shut behind him.

Wait.

He was upset because he didn't know where I'd gone, and that was all he was going to say about it? The big fat jerk was worried about me, and he wasn't even going to admit it?

Oh hell no.

I marched to his office and burst through the door. "Why don't you just say what you're thinking?"

He was standing next to his desk and whirled around to face me. "What?"

"You told me to stop shutting you out, so I did. And now you're doing the same thing to me. So just say it. Tell me why you were mad when you didn't know where I was."

"I wasn't mad. I was concerned."

"You looked mad."

"I wasn't."

"Damn it, Luke. Stop. What are we doing? Why don't you just tell me what's in your head?"

His expression changed, anger and frustration replaced with heat. His eyes narrowed and he stalked toward me.

Leaning close, he lowered his voice. "Do you really want to know what's in my head?"

He moved closer, so I stepped back. "Yes."

Another step put my back against the wall. He didn't give me an inch, caging me in with his arms, his palms pressed against the wall behind me.

"You're in my head, Mel. Every part of you. And you're driving me fucking insane."

"I—"

His lips crashed against mine in a hard kiss, but only for a second. He pulled away, leaving me gasping.

"Shut your mouth," he growled. "I wasn't supposed to care about you. Not like this."

"I'm sorry?"

He stopped me with another kiss, as brief and aggressive as the first. "I really wanted to keep hating you, but I just can't. Even though you drive me nuts. I can't get enough of you."

His nose brushed mine, his lips so close, and my breath hitched. A flush hit my cheeks and heat throbbed between my legs.

"I can't hate you either."

"This is a terrible idea," he said, his voice still growly and low.

"Absolutely awful."

"We were a mess together."

I nodded, tilting my chin up, my desperation for him growing. "A total mess."

He hesitated, his face so close, his eyes roving over me. For a second, I thought he was going to pull away, and I was going to lose my shit.

"Fuck it," he growled.

His kiss swept over me like a wave, deep and demanding. Still dimly aware of his injuries, I draped my hands over his shoulders as I opened for him, hungry for the feel of his tongue sliding against mine.

For a terrible idea, it sure felt amazing.

Gradually, he took the kiss from deep to shallow and pulled away.

"You're not going out with Hank again," he said.

That kiss had completely scrambled my brain. I blinked a few times. "What? I wasn't anyway."

"Then you're not going out with anyone else."

His sudden possessiveness left me breathless. The instinct to snap at him—tell him he couldn't tell me what to do—was there. But I ignored it. I loved Luke's demanding side.

Still, I couldn't resist a demand of my own. "Fine, then neither are you."

"I wasn't going to."

"Good."

Surging in, he kissed me again. It was somehow both exhilarating and calming all at once. A flash of heat and a cool breeze. I relaxed into him, enjoying the feel of his mouth on mine, and ran my fingers through his hair. His hands slid around my waist, and he pulled me tight against his body.

We fit so well. How could I have forgotten?

Suddenly, the tension between us intensified, the mood shifting, and the low growl in his throat lit my body on fire. Without quite meaning to, I whimpered into his mouth and rubbed against him as pulses of pressure in my core begged to be sated.

He shifted his leg, pressing it between mine, and I just about lost my mind. I straddled his thigh as he gripped my backside and rocked me against him in a steady rhythm. I felt his lips curl in a smile as I clutched onto him for dear life, my breath coming in quick gasps.

There was no way... He couldn't... With his...?

Oh, yes he could.

The pressure built so fast, my mind went blank, and my

entire body thrummed with intensity. His fingers dug into my ass as he ground his thigh between my legs. A few more strokes and I burst, spiraling as heat exploded through me.

His hand clamped over my mouth, and he watched me come with triumph in his eyes.

My face flushed as he let go, his hand slipping from my mouth to gently grip my neck. He shifted his leg, and miracle of miracles, mine didn't buckle beneath me.

"What just happened?" I whispered.

He didn't answer. Just smiled and brought my mouth to his for a soft kiss.

When he pulled back, my eyes fluttered open. My body felt languid, and the fact that he'd just given me a spontaneous orgasm in his office—with his thigh—seemed somehow inevitable. Or maybe that was all the happy chemicals in my brain.

"How do you feel?" he asked, his voice low but surprisingly even.

"Okay, I guess. If you're into that sort of thing." My lips turned up in a smile. "What about you? Are you...?" I glanced down at the bulge in his pants.

"Fine," he said. "That was just for you."

For a second, his casual generosity made me want to run. It was too much—too intense. A voice in the back of my mind kept trying to get my attention, telling me to slow down and think about what I was doing. This was Luke. Luke Haven. We'd tried this before and failed. Spectacularly.

But that had been so long ago. Almost another life.

Could we try again?

Instead of bolting out the door, I leaned in and kissed him. "So, where are you taking me?"

"What do you mean?"

"On our first date."

"Who said I'm taking you on a date?"

"You did."

The corners of his mouth lifted in a subtle grin. "When did I say that?"

I planted my hands on his chest. "You said I'm not going out with anyone else. Someone needs to take me out. If it can't be anyone else, that leaves you."

His fierce gaze locked with mine. "Only me."

My heart fluttered. I'd expected him to fire back with something snarky, not scorch me with a look. I nodded.

"An orgasm wasn't enough?" He grinned again. "You need a date too?"

"I admit, that was both unexpected and spectacular."

"Good." He took my chin in his hand and tilted my face up. "All right, a date. How about now?"

"Now? It's the middle of the day."

"I'm pretty sure the boss won't mind."

"Okay." I hesitated. "Should I change?"

He grinned again and pressed his lips to mine. "No. You're perfect just the way you are."

I knew he meant what I was wearing, but the comment almost brought me to tears. I side stepped and he let go of my chin. "You figure out where we're going, but I'll drive. Since you can't."

"Thank you."

"You're welcome." I moved closer to the door. I needed a minute so my head would stop spinning. "I'll be ready in a few."

He nodded and his smile sent a pleasant shiver down my spine. Still slightly breathless, I left his office, stopped in the restroom, then went back to the lobby.

I plopped onto the chair and, for a moment, stared into space. The phone lit up, but it was still on break mode, so I ignored it.

My entire body tingled with the memory of Luke. His hands. His kiss. His strong grip. The way he'd taken control of my body and given me pleasure without a single thought for his own.

But as the heady rush of climax continued to subside, doubt crept in. Or maybe it was fear.

Was it all a big mistake? Would we crash and burn a second time?

And if we did, would either of us survive the fallout?

CHAPTER 25

Melanie

LUKE CAME out to the lobby wearing a fresh T-shirt, although his hair was still a little disheveled from my fingers running through it. I liked the contrast.

I still felt euphoric from the unexpectedly hot encounter in his office. And more than slightly amazed that he'd calmly gone from making me climax to planning a date.

His self-control was incredibly sexy.

"Where'd you get a clean shirt?" I asked.

"How did you even notice?"

"Women notice these things." I stood and looked down at what I was wearing. The sleeveless blouse and slacks were great for work, but I wouldn't have picked it for date attire. "Are you sure I shouldn't change first?"

"No, you look great."

I shouldered my purse. "All right. Where are we going?"

"Wine tasting."

I blinked in surprise. "Oh. That sounds lovely."

"Why are you so shocked? Didn't think I could come up with a good first date idea?"

"No, that was just very fast." I narrowed my eyes. "Wait.

Is this your standard first date? How many women have you taken wine tasting?"

"None."

"Are you sure?"

"I think I'd remember."

"Okay, then," I said with a smile and came around the front counter. "Lead the way. Actually, I'll lead the way since I'm driving. Where's the winery?"

"Echo Creek. It's called Salishan Cellars. You've never been there?"

"I don't think so."

"Even better. It's beautiful." He walked to the front door and held it open for me.

I stepped out into the heat. "I thought you said you haven't been there."

"I've been there, just not with a date. Weddings, mostly."

We got in my car, and I brought up the location on my GPS. It wouldn't be hard to find, and Echo Creek was a pretty town.

Despite a haze in the air, the drive was beautiful. The highway followed the river as it curved and the mountain slopes rose on either side, rocky and gray.

We didn't talk much on the way. Luke turned on a classic rock playlist that made me smile. It reminded me of summer days cruising along that very highway, windows rolled down, music blasting. Me in the passenger seat with Luke's hand on my thigh.

The entrance to the winery was right off the highway. I turned up a long driveway lined with vineyards and a big sign that read, Salishan Cellars.

There was parking outside a large building surrounded by gardens. Flowers bloomed in beds and hanging baskets, and the green lawn was pristine.

Inside, the cool air was refreshing. The lobby was decorated with rich wood, greenery, and wine bottles. There were photos on one wall—some old and faded, others new.

"You know, I'm almost related to the family who owns this place," Luke said, gesturing to a wedding photo on the wall.

"How can you be almost related to someone?"

"You know Annika's husband, Levi Bailey?"

"Yeah."

"His oldest brother, Asher, is married to Grace. She's a Miles—related to the Miles family who owns Salishan."

"So your sister's sister-in-law is related to the family who owns this winery?"

"Exactly."

I paused to let that process. "Okay, I suppose that qualifies as almost related."

A young woman dressed in a black blouse and skirt came out from another room with a friendly smile. "Hi, can I help you?"

"We're here for a wine tasting," Luke answered.

"Great," she said. "I'll take you back to the tasting room."

We followed her into a room with a bar fronted by cushioned stools. Low light, dark wood, and more greenery created a comfortable ambiance. A group sat at a long table with bench seats, but the others were empty. The woman gestured to a small table with two chairs, and we took a seat.

"Brynn will be right with you," she said.

Another woman came out, also dressed in black. Her dark hair was pulled back and she smiled as she handed us menus. "Welcome to Salishan. Have you visited us before?"

"I have, she hasn't," Luke said.

"Wonderful. Are you from out of town or nearby?"

"Tilikum," he said. "And I've been here for a few weddings."

"I love Tilikum. My sister and her family live there."

"Grace Bailey?" Luke asked.

She smiled. "Yes! Do you know her?"

"A little bit. My sister is married to Levi Bailey."

"Oh my gosh, we're practically related."

Luke grinned and winked at me. "See?"

"I'm Brynn, by the way. Brynn Reilly, although my maiden name is Miles."

"Luke Haven. And this is my beautiful date, Melanie Andolini."

I smiled. "Nice to meet you. So this is a family business? You're very brave. My parents own Home Slice Pizza in Tilikum and I shudder to think of what would happen if I worked there."

"Home Slice is my favorite," Brynn said, her voice enthusiastic. "My husband drove out to Tilikum just the other day because I mentioned pizza sounded good."

"Sounds like you married the right man," I said.

"He's the best. Anyway, if you'd like to take a minute with the menu, that's fine. We have several different wine flights and a selection of hors d'oeuvres. Or I can treat you to the family special."

Luke raised his eyebrows at me. "Family special?"

"I don't think we can pass that up," I said.

"Good choice," Brynn said and took our menus. "I'll be right back."

A few minutes later, she brought our first wine and poured—a sparkling white.

I picked up the glass and took a sip. "What was our first date? Do you remember?"

"Homecoming."

"Was it?" I thought back. "You're right, it was. I wore that pink and black dress."

"That was hot."

I laughed. "I doubt it. But we had fun, didn't we?"

"The dance was okay." One corner of his mouth lifted in a grin. "Afterward was better."

My stomach tingled at the memory. "We parked somewhere and made out in your car, didn't we?"

His grin grew. "Oh yeah, we did."

"You know, you were the first boy I ever kissed."

"Was I really? I thought you went out with Johnny Montgomery freshman year."

"I did. For about two weeks. And all we did was talk on the phone. He wouldn't even hold my hand at school." I took another sip. "Don't worry, I know I'm not the first girl you kissed."

"Actually, you are."

My mouth dropped open, and I set my wineglass down. "I don't believe that for a second."

"It's true."

"I thought you and Brittany Delaney used to sneak away to make out under the bleachers sophomore year."

"That was just a rumor. Never happened."

"Seriously?"

"Okay, I didn't deny the rumor, because at the time, I wished I would have been able to make out with Brittany Delaney under the bleachers. But no. I never did."

"Are you telling me making out in your car after homecoming was your actual first kiss?"

"Yeah. You were my first everything."

I gazed at him for a long moment. It wouldn't have bothered me to know I hadn't been his first kiss. But discovering I was? It made my heart want to burst right out of my chest.

"I guess we were each other's first everything," I said softly.

"Kinda cool."

"Yeah. It is."

Brynn brought a charcuterie board with several types of cheese, olives, salami, fancy crackers, and to my endless delight, several mini pickles. We thanked her and continued sipping our bubbly while we sampled the snacks. Once we were done with the first glass of wine, she came out with another—a dry white Pino Grigio. I liked it even better than the sparkling white.

"Look, I know this is really personal, and it doesn't have anything to do with me," Luke said, "but can I ask what actually happened with your ex?"

I shrugged one shoulder. "Sure. I told you I moved in with him after the abduction. I didn't feel safe living alone. After that, we realized it would work better financially, in terms of health insurance and everything, if we got married. To be fair, I thought I wanted to marry him anyway. But looking back, I don't think I would have if I'd given it more time."

"So, you basically broke up because you shouldn't have been together in the first place?"

"More or less." I paused. I could leave it at that and not tell him the whole story, but something compelled me to keep talking. "He had some specific grievances with me, though."

"Grievances? What do you mean?"

"One, in particular. I can't have kids."

The confession seemed to hang in the air for a long moment. I watched Luke's face while he processed what I'd just said, ready for him to pull away. To realize what I was saying.

I was broken. He wasn't going to want me.

Anger crossed his features like a storm cloud. "Are you telling me he left you because of that?"

"It wasn't only that. Like I said, our relationship wasn't exactly sunshine and roses. But that was definitely his last straw. He decided it was a deal breaker."

He leaned forward, and when he spoke, his voice was a low growl. "That piece of shit. How fucking dare he?"

His reaction made a lump of emotion rise from deep inside, lodging in my throat, and tears threatened to gather in my eyes.

"It wasn't the end of the world," I said, trying very hard to hide behind a mask of flippancy. "Our relationship would have ended regardless."

"Still. Melanie, that's awful. He was wrong to do that to you."

I swallowed hard. "I know."

"Do you?"

It was hard to look him in the eyes, so I glanced away. "Of course. I don't know why he was so obsessed with perpetuating his genes. It's not like he would have made a good father. Or will make, since I'm sure his new girlfriend is long since knocked up by now. You know he wouldn't even consider adoption?" I was talking too fast, and too much, but I couldn't seem to stop. "I did all the research, and goodness knows he made plenty of money. As soon as I brought it up, he completely shut it down. Said I was giving up."

Luke reached across the table and took my hand. But apparently, I wasn't done.

"It's like he thought I wasn't trying hard enough to get pregnant. Like I was in control of my messed-up reproductive system. It wasn't my fault."

"No, it wasn't."

"I went through all the tests, and do you know how invasive it all is? Having a freaking fertility doctor up in your lady parts all the time? And his tests, of course they came out just perfect. All those sperm, just going to waste in my barren, broken body."

Luke took my other hand. "Mel."

I kept my eyes on the table. "What?"

"Look at me."

Reluctantly, I lifted my gaze to meet his.

"It's not your fault." His voice was soft, but decisive. "And I'm glad it happened."

I tried to snatch my hand away, but he held it. "Why?"

"Because if you'd had kids with him, you might not be here with me. And I know a date with your high school ex-boyfriend isn't exactly a worthy consolation prize if you wanted to have kids and couldn't. That's not what I mean. I just mean that you weren't meant to be with him."

"And I'm meant to be with you?" I asked, my tone skeptical.

"Yeah, maybe. We're here, aren't we? Giving it a shot."

"Luke, it's our first date."

"Not really. We've been on lots of dates."

"Yeah, and we both know how that turned out."

"We were stupid kids. We're not anymore. Life has kicked us around, made us smarter. Maybe even wiser. I certainly know a lot more about what I want. I'm sure you do too."

I hesitated again, afraid to say it, but knowing I had to. I had to ask the question—had to know. "Since you seem to have a talent for getting me to open up about things I don't like to talk about, and I keep telling you all my awful secrets, I need to know something. And it's probably best that it comes out now, instead of kicking me in the stomach later."

"What?"

"I can't have babies, Luke. It's not going to happen. I have a wicked combination of messed-up hormones and messed-up anatomy." I paused, my stomach suddenly churning with dread. "Is that a deal breaker for you? Because if it is, I need to know now."

"No."

My shoulders slumped, and I tilted my head. "You answered too fast."

"Because it's not a hard question. That's absolutely not a deal breaker."

"You don't want kids?"

He hesitated, and I appreciated that he actually considered the question.

"Kids would be great. But if it's not going to happen, that's okay too."

Until that moment, I hadn't fully realized how heavy a

burden I'd been carrying. Was it worse than the trauma of my abduction experience? They were such different things, it was hard to compare. But deep down, I'd assumed no man would ever love me unless I could have his babies. Or at least, no man would ever love me enough to keep me.

The one who'd made that promise certainly hadn't.

I let out a long breath, grateful my eyes hadn't betrayed me and started leaking. "That's good to know."

"Do you want kids?" he asked.

I blinked. "I just told you I can't have any."

"I know. But you said you looked into adoption. Was that just for your ex, or was it for you?"

"That's actually a good question. I love the idea of having kids, but going through years of infertility was rough. And when my ex left, I sort of figured that was it. I wasn't meant to be a mom. But I guess, when I think about it, I'd be open to it, at least as a possibility. You know, if I ever got married again, which I probably won't."

He chuckled. "You don't think so?"

"It would take quite the man to convince me it was worth taking that risk again." I smiled. "I don't think he exists."

"I bet he does. In fact, I'll bet you a hundred dollars you get married again."

"To someone specific, or just anyone?"

He didn't answer. Just grinned at me.

"That's not a fair wager. How do I win? Die single? Then I can't even collect."

"All right, how about this? I bet you a hundred dollars you get married again in less than a year."

"Less than a year?" I reached across the table to shake his hand. "I'll take that bet."

He took my hand, and we shook on it.

"You might as well give me the money now. There's no way I'm getting married in less than a year."

"We'll see."

Brynn came back with another wine—a delicious Cabernet. We chatted, ate, and sipped, finishing our flight with a sweet Moscato alongside a rich chocolate torte.

I was relaxed, and not from the wine. Something had changed between us. Over the past few days, I'd told Luke some of my worst memories and darkest secrets, and he hadn't shied away. Instead, it had drawn us closer.

Tension still pulsed between us, but it was different—no longer anger. My instinct to snap at him was melting in the heat of his gaze into something much deeper. A swirl of desire that pooled in my core.

The attraction had always been there, but as we let go of the layers of sarcasm and ire, it moved to the surface, hot and demanding. What he'd done to me in his office had been only the beginning.

I wanted him.

Brynn gifted us a bottle of the Cabernet—after all, we were practically family. We left, and the hand he placed on the small of my back as we walked to my car lit my body on fire.

He felt it too. I watched him from the corner of my eye as I drove back to Tilikum, and I could see it in the set of his jaw and the way he flexed his hands.

When I parked in front of his house, he glanced at me, and I could see the question in his eyes.

Ask me, Luke. Ask me to come in.

"Do you maybe—"

"Yes."

He smiled. "How do you know what I was going to say?"

"You were going to invite me in."

"I want to lean over and kiss you right now, but I don't think I can."

"How about we go inside?" I bit my lower lip. "I'll be gentle."

"I won't."

I made a little noise in my throat as I unfastened the seat belt and lurched over the center console to kiss him. I probably should have pretended to be less eager—play at least a little bit hard to get. But I was over playing games. I wanted him. He wanted me. That was all we needed.

We got out of the car, and he took my hand as we walked up the steps on the side of the building. My heart started to race, and heat was already building in my core. He unlocked the door, and we went inside.

The door had hardly finished closing before he hauled me against him. His mouth devoured mine, his kiss hard and aggressive.

"Bedroom," he growled into my mouth. "Clothes off. Now."

"You think you can boss me around?" I asked between frantic kisses.

He pulled my shirt off as he backed me toward the bedroom. "Yes."

"Fine, you can. But only in here."

The rest of our clothes came off and my eyes widened when I saw his bruises. A large part of his torso was black and blue.

Gently, I reached out to touch him. "This looks terrible. Are you sure you can…?"

"It'll hurt, but it'll be worth it." His eyes roved up and down. "Holy shit, Mel. Look at you. You're fucking gorgeous."

He pulled me against him, kissing me deeply, and the feel of his skin on mine was electric. My body ached, desperate for him.

We got on the bed, and he put on a condom. Despite his assurances that he'd be fine, I didn't want to hurt him. I nudged him onto his back and climbed on top.

"Will this work?" I asked.

"Baby, this is amazing."

I loved the way his voice was awed, almost breathless.

He groaned as we came together and started to move. I draped myself over him, brushing skin against skin, our mouths tangling. My body came alive, the heat intensifying.

He squeezed my hips, moving me the way he wanted, and I relented to his commanding touch. Pressure built fast, and I realized with a heady sense of euphoria that he was going to finish me. Again.

"Yes, Luke. Yes."

"Fuck I love hearing you say my name. Say it again."

"Luke. Yes, Luke."

I kept it up until my voice was nothing but a rhythmic whimper. I felt the beginnings of his climax right before he gave me a warning. I was already there, swirling and spiraling out of control, pleasure bursting through me. He clasped my hands so I could brace myself and I threw my head back, inhibitions gone, riding the waves of ecstasy.

Breathing hard, my hair fell around my face. He let go of my hands and reached for me, bringing my mouth to his for a kiss. I lingered there, my tongue dancing with his, savoring the moment.

Eventually, I got off him and we took turns cleaning up in the bathroom. When I came back, I slid into bed, and he drew me against him.

"Are your ribs okay?"

"Don't even feel them," he said, his voice dreamy. "Might be sore later, but I do not care."

I nestled my head against his chest, and he drew lazy circles on my shoulder. His familiar scent surrounded me and I took a deep breath.

"So, I'm not allowed to date anyone else," I said.

"No."

"And you're not allowed to date anyone else."

"Nope."

"And we just went on a date, and now we're… here."

"Are you asking what it all means?"

"I think it's a fair question."

"Look at me."

I propped myself up on one elbow. He reached out and touched my face.

"You're mine now," he said, his voice low.

"Just like that?"

"I'm not interested in anything less. Either you're mine, or this is the last time this happens. There's no in-between for me."

I pressed my lips together, trying not to smile. "I guess I can live with that. If you insist."

His lips twitched in a grin. "I do insist."

The fear was back, sweeping through me. "But what if…"

"What if it doesn't work?"

"Yeah. We can't pretend we didn't break up once already."

"I know we were a mess back then, but shouldn't we at least try?"

I gazed at him for a moment. "You really want to try, don't you?"

"I do." He caressed my cheek with his thumb. "Maybe I'm crazy, but there's no one like you. And let's be honest, we can't seem to avoid each other. This was probably inevitable."

"Probably. All right, Luke Haven. Let's give this a real try."

I settled against him, and he tightened his arm around me. And for the second time since I'd moved back to Tilikum, it felt like I was home.

CHAPTER 26

Luke

OPENING the door to the Timberbeast, I gestured for Melanie to go ahead of me. With a little twitch of her lips, she stepped inside. I walked in behind her and immediately touched her lower back as my eyes swept the bar, ready to level every guy in there with a hard glare.

Don't even think about it, assholes. She's mine.

Rock music played in the background, Rocco was tending bar, and the place was busy, especially for a weeknight. It seemed like the heat was getting to everybody. Looked like we weren't the only ones who thought a cold drink sounded good.

Garrett and Harper were at a table together, sitting on one side rather than across from each other. Harper waved, so we veered in their direction.

"I don't want to alarm anyone, but you seem to be missing a baby," I said.

"I know, I feel so naked without her," Harper said.

Garrett put his arm around Harper's shoulders. "Mom's at our place watching her for a couple hours."

"And Owen is home too, so I know everything is fine,"

Harper said, like she was trying to convince herself. "Do you want to sit down?"

"We don't want to interrupt your date night," Melanie said.

"I don't mind." Harper glanced up at Garrett. "Do you mind?"

He shook his head. "No. We have to head home soon anyway. Have a seat."

The fact that I was there with Melanie—and obviously *with* Melanie—didn't faze them. Since our second first date, word had spread through my family that Melanie and I were together. I'd expected some degree of concern, but no one seemed to think it was weird. My brothers had given me crap, of course. But that was their job.

Melanie took a seat, and I went to the bar to get us drinks. I brought them to the table and sat next to her, then scooted her closer and draped my arm over the back of her chair.

"How is the little one?" Melanie asked. "I'm sorry I can't remember her name, but your family has a lot of baby girls."

"Isla," Harper said with a smile. "Don't worry about it. She's fine. She had a bit of a cold, but she got over it, and she's been sleeping a lot better. Which is good for everyone."

"Especially you." Garrett leaned over and kissed her temple.

"So have you started working on the cartoon again?" Harper asked. "It was a cartoon series you were waiting on, right? The one with the evil queen?"

"Wait, what?" I asked. "What cartoon?"

"It's called *Enchanted Hollow*," Melanie said.

"That's the job you've been waiting for?" No way. "The cartoon with the evil queen? The one with the voice?"

She hesitated, like she wasn't sure what I was getting at. "What voice? Do you mean my voice? Because if so, yes, it's my voice. Have you seen it?"

"Yeah, my nieces and nephews were watching it one time

when I was over there," Luke said. "I heard the voice, and… that was you?"

"If it was Queen Ione you heard, yes, it was me."

I shook my head slowly. "That's so wild."

"Can you do the voice?" Harper asked. "Sorry if that's weird. I just realized I probably shouldn't have asked that out loud. But I'm so curious."

"No, it's fine. I don't mind." Melanie's voice changed, her tone low and sultry. "Foolish princess. You think you can defy me?" She held up a fist. "I am queen of these lands, and you will learn your place or face my wrath."

"That was so good," Harper exclaimed. "Oh my gosh, I have tingles."

"She's a lot of fun to portray," she said, returning to her natural tone. "Especially when she's threatening to destroy people. And no, we haven't started recording yet. I'm hoping they'll send the script soon, though."

I gazed at her, a little bit in awe.

"What?" she asked. "Why are you looking at me like that?"

"I basically had a crush on your character and didn't know it was you."

"You did not."

"I did. She's an evil queen, but she's hot."

She laughed. "I don't know what that says about you, but okay."

I smiled and leaned in for a quick kiss.

Garrett took his phone out of his pocket, and his brow furrowed. "Sorry, love. I should take this."

"That's okay," Harper said. "Go ahead."

Garrett got up and stepped outside to take his call.

I put my arm around Melanie again and took a drink of my beer. No wonder that voice had captivated me. It had been her.

Granted, if I'd known at the time, I would have found a

reason to hate it. But it said something that her voice—even in character—had penetrated my defenses.

A few minutes later, Garrett came back and took his seat next to Harper.

"Is everything okay?" she asked.

"Yeah, just a buddy of mine from the Echo Creek PD."

"You're not working another cold case, are you?" I asked.

"No, but we've got two cases of women being abducted. One was down in Echo Creek, the other here. We've been pooling our resources since the details match. It's gotta be the same guy."

"Abducted?" Melanie asked. "What happened? Were they found?"

"Both found after a few days," Garrett said. "But neither were in great shape. They'd been assaulted pretty brutally. And that's after being drugged and coming to, chained to a wall."

"What the fuck?" I asked. "Chained to a wall?"

"Sugar cookies," Harper breathed, like it was a curse word. "You didn't tell me they'd been chained up."

Garrett nodded. "It's kind of perplexing, to be honest. No evidence of sexual assault. Which is good, obviously, but odd. Usually when a guy shoves a woman in the trunk of his car, that's what he's planning."

Melanie stiffened in her seat.

"So what's this guy doing?" I asked. "Abducting women just to chain them up?"

"We don't know. We don't know why he's assaulting them but leaving them alive, or why he's letting them go. It's not a typical pattern."

"That's so awful," Harper said. "Do you know where the Tilikum victim is now?"

Garrett's mouth lifted in a slight grin. "You want to send her cookies, don't you?"

"I know cookies won't fix anything, but it might help her feel better to know people care."

He leaned over and kissed her cheek. "I'll see if I can arrange something."

Melanie shifted closer to me and I tightened my arm around her. It had to be hard for her to hear about an abduction after what she'd been through.

"It's been nice to get out, but we should probably head home," Harper said.

Garrett checked his phone. "Yeah, it's about that time."

"Thanks for letting us join you," Melanie said as they got up from their seats.

"Yeah, it was great to see you," Harper said with a smile.

"Night," I said, tipping my chin to my brother.

He tipped his. "Night."

Garrett and Harper left, and I started idly fingering Melanie's hair as I took a drink of my beer.

"Are you okay?" I asked.

"I'm fine." She let out a breath. "Actually, no, I'm a little shaky."

I set down my beer and gently touched her chin, bringing her gaze to mine. "Of course you are. It can't be easy to hear about something like that."

"The part about putting her in the trunk made me sick to my stomach. All of a sudden, I remembered what it was like to wake up and realize I was in the trunk of a car."

The need to protect her swept through me. She didn't resist as I drew her against me, letting her cheek rest on my chest. With her deep breath, her body seemed to relax. I cast another glare around the bar as if the perpetrator was there, eyeing my woman.

Fuck that guy. Hopefully, he'd be caught soon.

Pulling back, I brushed her hair off her face. "Do you want another drink? Or are you ready to get out of here?"

"I'm ready to go."

I leaned in and kissed her forehead, then moved so my mouth was near her ear. I spoke in a low growl. "How about I take you home and fuck you senseless?"

The way her body trembled set my blood on fire.

"Yes," she whispered. "Now."

Taking her hand, I helped her to her feet and led her out to my car.

Her wish was my command.

CHAPTER 27
Melanie

THE DULL ACHE behind my eyes made it hard to focus. Fortunately, it had been a quiet day. The guys were all busy in the garage, the parts we were expecting had arrived, and no grumpy customers had waltzed in to give anyone a piece of their mind.

That last one was particularly fortunate. I probably didn't have the patience to be diplomatic if someone was being an idiot. Even if they were a customer.

My real career didn't involve customer service for a reason.

I rubbed my temples, hoping to ease some of the tension. Sleep had been hard to come by the past couple nights. As if nightmares weren't bad enough, I'd been hit with a bout of insomnia. It was a special kind of torture to lie in bed, unable to fall asleep, only to be jolted awake by a nightmare hours later.

Not fun.

Ollie walked into the lobby from the garage and handed me an order form. His eyebrows drew in. "You all right?"

"Fine." I tucked my hair behind my ear. "Why?"

"No reason. You look fine." He turned and walked out, like he was suddenly in a hurry to get back to work.

I scowled at the door, but I wasn't really offended. Concealer wasn't enough to hide the dark circles under my eyes. Fortunately, it was Friday, and almost time for me to go home.

The door to the garage opened again, and Luke walked in. I couldn't help the smile that crossed my face. He looked delicious in his T-shirt and jeans, and the way his eyes roved over me made my stomach tingle.

He leaned down to place a soft kiss on my lips. "Heading home soon?"

I nodded. "It's about that time."

"I was hoping to hang out tonight, but my dad needs help with something up at the house."

"That's fine."

"Are you sure?" He trailed a finger down my cheek. "Won't you miss me?"

I would, but I wasn't about to admit it too easily. "Why do you think I'd miss you?"

"Because you can't get enough of me."

"Way to be full of yourself."

He leaned down so his lips brushed my ear as he spoke in a growly whisper. "I think you want to be full of me."

Scrunching my shoulders, I giggled. The man actually made me giggle. It was an outrage. Playfully, I pushed him away. "Get out of here. I don't even like you."

He grinned.

"Are you sure your ribs are okay?"

"You're cute when you admit you care about me."

I scoffed. "I just don't want you to re-injure yourself. Then I'll be stuck driving you around for the next month."

"I've been following doctor's orders."

I stood and gently ran my fingers across his ribs. "How are they feeling today?"

"Better."

"Good."

He leaned in and kissed me again. "If I'm done early enough, I'll call you."

"That's okay. I'm probably going to bed early."

His brow furrowed with concern, and he tucked a lock of hair behind my ear. "Are you okay?"

"Yeah, fine."

"Are you sure? You look tired."

I leaned away. "I don't think we've progressed to that level of honesty. Compliments only."

"I didn't say you looked bad."

"Tired is code for awful."

With a slight shake of his head, he rolled his eyes. "Tired or not, you're beautiful."

"That's better." I tilted my chin up, and he kissed me again. "Fine, I'll miss you tonight."

The corners of his lips turned up as he took a step toward the door. "I know."

He left, and after forwarding the phone to voicemail, I gathered up my things and headed home.

I spent the afternoon too tired and headachy to do much. Taking a nap was an option, but a risky one. It might make my insomnia worse. The last thing I needed was to sleep too hard and wake up dehydrated with no idea what day it was, only to stare at the ceiling all night.

Been there.

But it wasn't just fatigue that was bothering me. I had a hard time sitting still and found myself wandering around the house, peeking out the windows. My shoulders were tense, and no matter how many deep breaths I took, my heart kept beating too fast.

As much as I didn't want to admit it, I was scared. I'd been scared since we heard about the abductions.

It made me angry. I didn't want to be afraid again. I hated

feeling weak and helpless. What had happened to me had been traumatic. I'd come to terms with that. It was okay to experience alarm when I heard about a similar incident or when something reminded me of my abduction. But it had been two days, and I was still so jumpy. Every little noise set me on edge, especially when I was alone.

I glanced at the clock. A little after seven. I'd been driving myself crazy for hours. What I really wanted was Luke, but he was busy. I didn't want to lean on him too much anyway. We were giving things a real try, but we'd only just begun. I didn't want to be the needy girlfriend who couldn't be alone.

Instead, I called Sharla to see what she and Nathan were up to.

"Hey," she answered. "What's going on?"

I could hear background noise, like she was in a car. "Nothing much. Just wondering what you guys are doing. Hot date tonight?"

"Actually, yes." Her voice sounded almost giddy. "Your parents took the kids for the weekend. Nathan surprised me with a trip to the coast. We're on our way to a cabin in Jetty Beach."

"Aw, how sweet is that?"

"I know, I'm so excited. I haven't been to the beach in so long. Plus, the forecast is amazing. Low seventies and breezy all weekend."

"That sounds like heaven."

"It will be. How are you? Are you doing all right?"

"Why does everyone keep asking me that? You can't even see the dark circles under my eyes."

"Dark circles are the worst. I have a great concealer if you want to try it."

"Send me a link."

"I will. But… are you?"

"I'm fine. Why wouldn't I be? Are you worried about the Luke thing? I know you weren't around when Luke and I dated, but I can assure you it was an absolute train wreck. I'm surprised no one is staging an intervention now that people know we're dating again."

"That's just you being dramatic, right?"

"More or less."

"Thought so. No, haven't you heard about the women who were abducted? It's all over town."

"Oh, that. Yes, I heard."

"I just wondered if it might be bothering you. You know, since it was so close."

Pinching the bridge of my nose, I closed my eyes for a moment. "It's not bothering me."

"Are you sure?"

"Positive." I didn't know why I was lying to her. "I feel awful for the victims, of course. But it doesn't have anything to do with me."

"Okay," she said, but I couldn't tell if she believed me. "Listen, I know we're out of town, but if you need to talk or anything, don't hesitate."

"No," Nathan said in the background. "Hesitate. Call Mom first."

"Nathan, stop," she said.

I laughed. "Tell your husband not to worry. I won't interrupt your sex-cation."

She laughed. "You should go hang out with your mom and dad and the kids, though. They'd love that. Although I think they're going to the drive-in tonight."

"I might do that tomorrow. Have a great weekend."

"Thanks, Mel. You too."

I ended the call and put my phone down with a sigh. Good for Nathan. I'd always been proud of him for being such a good husband and father. I hoped they had a nice time at the beach.

As for me, I'd be fine. I didn't need anyone's help.

―――――

The slight texture in the ceiling above my bed was starting to look like constellations. I picked out dots and connected them, trying to create designs. And what was up with constellations, anyway? Some were clearly shapes, but others? I didn't understand how ancient people could see giant animals in the night sky based on a few points of light.

My mind had been wandering like that for hours as sleep eluded me. Again.

I checked the time. After midnight. Letting out a long breath, I pressed my fingers against my temples and rubbed my eyes. What was it going to take to get my brain to shut off and my body to finally sleep?

My phone buzzed. That was odd. Who would be texting me in the middle of the night?

Luke: *Are you awake?*

Me: *Unfortunately.*

Luke: *Answer your door.*

A second later, I heard a knock.

I got up and walked through the dark house to open the front door. Luke stood there, illuminated by the porch light.

"Can I come in?" he asked, his voice soft.

"Sure."

I stepped aside, then shut and locked the door behind him.

He slipped a hand around my waist and drew me against him. His mouth came to mine in a gentle kiss.

"What are you doing here so late?" I asked.

"Sorry about that. Helping my dad turned into dinner and board games."

"It's fine. We didn't have plans."

"I know." He brushed my hair back from my face and lifted my chin. "You haven't been sleeping, have you?"

"We've been over this. You're supposed to tell me I'm a beautiful mess, not that I need sleep."

"I'm not talking about how you look. And you are a beautiful mess, whether you've been sleeping or not."

"I'm fine. You don't need to worry about me."

"You don't get it, do you?"

"Get what? That—"

He placed a fingertip on my lips, cutting me off. "You're mine, which means I take care of you." He clasped my hand and tugged me toward the bedroom. "Let's go. Bedtime, princess."

"Believe it or not, sex doesn't solve all of a woman's problems."

"That's not why I'm here." He paused and glanced at me. "Although if you start something, I'm certainly not saying no."

"It's the middle of the night. If you're not here for sex, why are you here?"

He led me into my bedroom and shut the door. "To help you sleep. I figured it might be easier if you're not alone."

I stared at him for a moment, dumbfounded. He was serious. I hadn't even told him I was having trouble sleeping. He just knew. And he was going to do what he could to fix it.

"Really?" I asked, my voice quiet.

"Of course. Look, I know you don't like to admit when something is hard, so you don't have to. And if you want to kick me out, I'll go."

"No, don't go."

He smiled and stripped down to his boxer briefs. We got into bed, and he slipped an arm around my waist, drawing my back to his front.

The warmth of his embrace and feel of his slow breathing were like magic, unraveling the tension in my body. My eyes were heavy, so I let them close.

And for the first time in days, I felt safe.

Soon

ROSWELL MILLS

THE ACRID SCENT of bleach permeated the air in the basement as I walked down the steps. The mattress was empty, the chains I'd attached to the wall hanging loose. I paused, holding the freshly washed fitted sheet, and remembered.

She'd looked good, lying there with her wrists chained to the wall. Not as good as Melanie was going to, but I'd enjoyed it more than I'd thought I would.

Unfortunately, she hadn't behaved.

Neither had the first.

The drunk one had been a disaster, vomiting all over the place when she finally woke up. I'd been angry with her from the beginning. Despite my attempts to coax her into calming down and sipping water, she'd done nothing but sob and complain.

I'd hated her. The bruises I'd given her were her fault. If she'd done what I said and calmed down, I wouldn't have had to lay a hand on her.

Still, she hadn't been a total waste of time. Taking her had given me what I'd been after in the first place—a practice run.

I'd learned that I needed to keep cleaning supplies on hand. I didn't want it to stink down there. More importantly, I'd learned the basement was quite soundproof. I'd left the first one to scream, and with the door shut, the noise was muffled upstairs. Nothing could be heard outside unless you went to the back of the cabin.

Pleased with my first rehearsal, I'd drugged her again and dumped her in the woods, far from my hideaway.

I was confident no one would find me. She never saw my face, and she'd been drugged when I brought her into the cabin and when I took her out. As hysterical as she'd been, I doubted her story would be coherent enough to give them anything.

The second one had been better. She looked more like Melanie, which I'd liked. I'd been able to watch her and imagine it was real. I'd enjoyed the way she looked so much, unconscious and chained to the wall, that I'd gotten off on it.

That added layer of pleasure had been surprisingly intoxicating without the guilt I felt when I'd been with the whore. Melanie wouldn't mind, and it didn't require me to touch an unworthy substitute.

She'd even answered to Melanie when I'd told her to. I'd liked that too, although her voice had been a weak whimper. She'd been sniveling and afraid.

Eventually, she'd angered me too. Was it too much to ask that they play their part? I'd told her exactly what I wanted her to do—how I wanted her to behave. I'd explained that I wouldn't hurt her if she'd be a good girl and do what I said.

It was her fault that she hadn't. I'd snapped. Maybe gone a little too far.

But she'd live. They both would. I wasn't a murderer.

Although I'd found myself thinking about it. Wondering if I could.

Wondering what it would feel like to take her life.

I hadn't. And was anyone going to appreciate my self-control? Of course not. They wouldn't know anything about me.

I was invisible. Not worth noticing.

But I'd heard the murmurs when I'd been in town. Word was spreading. People were scared.

That was an unexpected benefit. I couldn't get caught—that was imperative—but a reputation that spread? My lips curled in a smile. I could walk through their towns unnoticed, unremarkable. But I'd know they were talking about me. I was the one making them afraid.

I couldn't wait to tell Melanie all about it.

After putting the sheet back on the mattress, I went upstairs. I was getting anxious for the real thing—to have my Melanie there, with me.

But I needed patience above all. Soon, I'd start following her, learning her routine. I'd have to be ready at a moment's notice. The circumstances were unlikely to be perfect. I doubted I'd catch her coming out of a bar alone, tipsy or otherwise.

Which meant I needed to take on a bigger challenge first. A woman in an empty parking lot in the dark was an easy mark. I had to prove to myself I could do it during the day.

Wandering over to the wall near the kitchen, I looked at my photos. I'd framed them, the photos I had of her, and hung them on the wall. A gallery of my passion. My preoccupation.

My obsession.

Who wouldn't be flattered by such attention? By such wanting?

Such need.

"Soon." I touched the photo I'd taken of her in my trunk all those years ago. "Soon, I'll bring you home."

CHAPTER 28

Luke

I WOKE to the sudden feeling that I was about to fall off the bed.

My back was right up against the edge, and one foot dangled off the side. Blinking my eyes, I started scooting closer to the middle when I realized why I was about to roll off. Melanie took up most of the bed.

She was on her back, her hair a mess all over the pillow. One leg was jutted out toward me, and I worried that if I startled her awake, she'd punch me in the face again.

She was out—sound asleep—and I was pretty sure she'd slept all night. I'd woken up a few times when she moved, and she'd definitely been asleep. She hadn't even stirred when I'd softly kissed her temple.

I gazed at her for a long moment. Waking up with her felt good. Really good. She knew how to drive me crazy, but there was so much more than that. She was like the high of a race, without the crash.

I was falling hard and fast for Melanie Andolini. Again. I'd been a goner for her the first time around and it hadn't ended well. But this time would be different. I was all in. I didn't know how else to be. I wasn't a guy who did things halfway, so like I'd told her, she was mine.

It was possible I was making a huge mistake. But I had to take the risk.

She was worth it.

I decided to let her sleep. She needed it. Besides, I didn't want to risk another face punch.

Carefully, I rolled out of bed. With a soft noise in her throat, she turned onto her side, squishing her cheek against the pillow. I couldn't help but smile. Such a beautiful mess.

She didn't stir as I tugged my T-shirt and jeans back on. I slipped out and shut the door softly behind me.

It was a Saturday, and I didn't have anywhere to be, so I went to her kitchen and made some coffee. I hung out for a while, scrolling through random stuff on my phone, until I heard her stirring in her bedroom.

A few minutes later, she came out, still blinking sleep from her eyes. She'd pulled her hair up into a loose ponytail and still had on the tank top and pajama pants she'd slept in.

"Sorry," she said. "Have you been up for a long time?"

"Not long. Did you get some rest?"

Reaching out, I took her hand and drew her onto my lap, straddling me.

"Mm hmm. Best night's sleep I've had in a long time."

That made me smile. I rubbed her thighs. "Good."

She hesitated for a moment and when she spoke, her voice was quiet. "Thank you."

"You're welcome."

"How's your dad?"

"He's good. He's been working on redoing the pantry for my mom."

"Are your ribs okay?" She ran a hand along my midsection.

"Yeah. There wasn't much lifting involved. He mostly just needed an extra set of hands."

"That's good. I'm glad you're healing."

"Me too. Pain sucks."

"Do you need to go back up there to help again today?"

"Nope. We got him all taken care of. What about you? Any plans?"

"Not a one."

"That's good news for me."

"Why? Do you think I want to hang out with you all day?"

"I think that's exactly what you want," I said. "And then you want me to sleep over again so you can almost push me off the bed."

"I didn't almost push you off the bed."

"Yes, you did," I said with a soft laugh. "I woke up on the verge of rolling off."

"Sorry about that."

"It's all right."

"Fine, you're right. I want you to myself all day."

"Done. You know what we should do?"

"What?"

"Go to the lake."

"That does sound fun. Especially if it's going to be hot again."

Her lips were irresistible. With a gentle hand on her chin, I pulled her in for a kiss, enjoying the warm softness of her mouth and the velvety brush of her tongue.

"You should come back to bed first," she said between kisses and rolled her hips against me. "So I can thank you properly."

"You don't owe me anything."

"I know. But I want to. I want you." She pushed herself off my lap and stood.

With a grin—I definitely wasn't saying no—I got up and followed her to the bedroom.

And it was everything.

———

Melanie Andolini dressed in nothing but a pair of denim shorts over her bright red bikini, sitting in the passenger side of my Chevelle, was seriously hot.

Hot girl. Hot car. In that moment, I had it all.

I pulled out a cassette tape and pushed it into the player.

"You still have cassettes?" she asked.

"Hell yeah, I still have cassettes. Best way to make a mixtape."

"What one is this?"

I hit play, and classic rock filled the car. "Luke Haven's make-out mixtape."

She turned to look at me, her lips parted in surprise. "Did you have this... back then?"

I gave her a crooked grin. "Haven't listened to it since. This one was all yours."

With a slight shake of her head, she smiled.

We grooved to the music as we drove out to a spot on my family's land, near a trail that led to the lake. The sun was out, not a cloud in the sky, and there wouldn't be a bunch of out-of-towners to get in the way. We'd brought drinks and a few snacks, along with towels and a blanket. I grabbed most of it, she took the rest, and we made our way down the trail.

The roar of a waterfall grew as we got closer. We emerged from the trees on a secluded beach not far from the falls. The water sparkled in the sun, and the mountains surrounded us.

"I haven't been out here in so long," Melanie said as we set our things down on a flat spot near the water's edge. "It's so pretty."

We laid the blanket on the ground and put our towels aside. I peeled off my shirt and Melanie slid her shorts down her toned legs and kicked them off. The air was still, the temperature rising, and the sun baked down on us. The cold water was going to feel great.

I eyed my girl. She was going to feel great, too.

"Ready to get in?" she asked.

"Let's do it."

She took a few slow steps into the icy water, gasping at the cold.

"You gotta jump in and get it over with," I said.

"I can't. It's freezing."

I grinned at her, then jogged a few steps into the water, and dove in.

She was right, it was freezing. The cold hit me like a truck as I glided beneath the surface. But the rush felt good. Letting my feet drop, I found the bottom and stood. Taking a big breath, I shook the water off my face and ran my hands over my hair.

Melanie was still only ankle deep.

"Come on, beautiful. You'll feel better once you're in."

She took a tiny step.

"You big baby."

Pushing my body through the water, I marched up the bank, dripping wet, and picked her up. She shrieked for me to put her down, but there was laughter behind it. I walked her into the deeper water and paused.

"Ready?"

"No!"

She kept one arm around my shoulders and plugged her nose. Bending my knees, I dunked us both, then came up. She gasped as we broke the surface.

"So cold!"

I let go of her legs so she could stand. "Feels good, doesn't it?"

She wiped her face. "Only because it's probably a hundred degrees out here."

"Exactly."

We swam around a bit, enjoying the water, but staying close to the shore. Surrounded by mountains, with the blue sky stretched above us, the lake felt secluded, like the cares of the world couldn't reach us.

After a while, we moved into waist-deep water to let the sun warm us.

She traced her fingers across my ribs. "It's still so bruised."

"It looks worse than it feels."

"That's good at least." She paused. "Do you think you'll race again?"

"No." I was surprised at how easily the answer came. But it was true. "I'd say the wreck knocked some sense into me, but it's more than that. I don't need it anymore."

"Why did you need it before?"

I hesitated, considering. "It was like the only time I felt alive was when I was driving fast. I was always chasing something—chasing the high, I guess—only to crash soon after. Being with you is like that, only without the crash. And without the likelihood of dying. Although you do have a mean right hook, so I won't let my guard down too much."

"Being with me is like driving a race car?"

I pulled her against me. "Being with you is being alive. Whatever I was chasing, it wasn't what I needed. You are."

Our lips met in a soft kiss, and she wound her arms around my neck.

"I only raced that night because I was mad at you," I said, my mouth turning up in a grin.

"Mad at me for what? Oh. Never mind. That was the night we ran into each other at the restaurant, wasn't it?"

"It was."

"That's okay. I was mad at you too."

I touched my forehead to hers while the water lapped around our waists. "I hated seeing you with someone else. So much."

"I hated it too. She seemed really nice, which made it so much worse."

"She might have been nice, but she wasn't you. No one is."

"And the rest of the world is relieved about that. What would life be like if there were two of me?"

"That is a scary thought."

She laughed. "Hey."

"You're a handful, Melanie Andolini. But it's possible I'm a little bit crazy about you."

"It's possible I'm a little bit crazy about you, too. This wasn't what I expected when I moved back to Tilikum. I was just trying to pick up the pieces. I didn't think you'd be there to help."

"We don't even need to pick up the pieces of your old life. We can just sweep them into a corner and be done with them. Start fresh."

She smiled. "I'd like that."

"Me too."

I kissed her again, intoxicated by the feel of her mouth on mine. We enjoyed the cool water for a while, then made our way back to our towels to dry off in the sun.

Eventually, we ran out of snacks. That meant it was time to head back to town. Spending half the day swimming in the sun had left us both hungry, so we stopped at the Zany Zebra for an early dinner.

I held the door open for her, and the scent of fries spilled out into the evening air. Melanie started toward the counter but abruptly stopped in her tracks and spun around.

"Oh my gosh," she whispered. "Is that who I think it is?"

There were people at most of the tables, but it only took me a second to see who she was talking about. Hank. "Yep, that's him."

"Him?" Her forehead creased in confusion. "I was talking about Jenna."

I looked again. "Holy shit, that is Jenna. She's here with Hank."

Melanie's eyes widened, and she grabbed my arm. "I want to look. Can I look?"

Hank and Jenna were sitting across from each other, sharing a milkshake. Neither of them cast even the slightest glance in our direction. They were too busy staring into each other's eyes.

"You can look."

She slowly spun around to look then turned back to me.

"Oh my gosh," she whispered again, her eyes still wide. "They're so cute together."

"Your whisper is louder than you think, secret agent Mel. Let's go order some food. Everyone else in the restaurant is starting to look concerned."

"Sorry, my mind is just a little bit blown right now."

I took her arm and led her to the front counter to order. Hank and Jenna still didn't seem to notice us despite the way Melanie was openly staring. She was many things, but subtle was not one of them.

The cashier came over and I ordered our dinner. Right as I was paying, Melanie grabbed my arm again.

"They just kissed over the table."

"Good for them," I said, my voice low. "Will you be quiet about it?"

"Sorry."

Once our order was in, I moved her down the counter to wait—away from Hank and Jenna. I tried to block Melanie's view of them, but she kept leaning over to look.

It was hard not to laugh.

Finally, our food came out. I grabbed the bags and dragged her out of there. We got in the car and my stomach rumbled at the smell of burgers and fries.

"That was crazy," she said as she fastened her seat belt. "Who would have thought?"

"The only crazy thing in there was you."

"I wasn't being crazy."

"You were being obvious. They must have been very wrapped up in each other not to notice you staring at them."

"You know what this means?"

"No, what?"

"I'm basically a matchmaker."

"How does that make you a matchmaker?"

"If I hadn't outbid her for you," she said, gesturing with her hands, "she wouldn't have bid on Hank."

I grinned at her. She was so ridiculous. "I don't think that makes you a matchmaker."

"Fine, matchmaker isn't the right word. But it does mean I'm responsible for getting them together. If they get married, they better invite me to the wedding. I wonder if Jenna has any sisters. She might need a bridesmaid."

"Somehow I don't think you're going to be in the wedding."

"She and I bonded in the bathroom. We're basically besties now."

I laughed. "Okay, Mel. Bridesmaid it is. But that's not the real question."

"What is the real question?"

"Is she going to be a bridesmaid in yours?"

Her head whipped around to look at me. "I'm not getting married, so I don't need a bridesmaid."

I grinned again. "Of course not. Gotta win that bet."

Pressing her lips in a smile, she narrowed her eyes but didn't say anything.

Maybe I was the one who was being crazy, but I was going to win that bet. She was going to get married in less than a year.

And it was going to be to me.

She just didn't know it yet.

CHAPTER 29

Melanie

LUKE SET my iced coffee on the table and took the seat next to me. He scooted my chair closer so our legs were touching, and put his hand on my thigh.

I'd forgotten how much I loved the way he used physical touch. It wasn't always sexual—although he was excellent in that department as well. Sometimes it was a mix of affectionate and possessive. A way of showing me, and everyone else in the room, that I belonged to him.

I was Luke Haven's girl.

The Steaming Mug was about half full, with a short line at the counter and a few of the tables filled with chatting customers. It was midmorning on Thursday, and Luke had suggested we slip out for coffee. One of the perks of dating my boss, even if that part was temporary.

He leaned close and pressed a kiss to my temple. "How's your coffee?"

I took a sip. "Perfect. Although I'm kind of looking forward to cooler weather and cozy cups of hot coffee. Maybe in front of a fire."

"That does sound good."

It was sweltering outside, the air hazy brown with wildfire smoke. It was too deep in the mountains to pose a danger to anyone, as far as I knew, but the air quality wasn't great.

"I finally heard from the *Enchanted Hollow* people," I said. "They're still revising the script, but they don't expect any more delays. Which probably means minor delays, just not major ones."

"Does this mean you're going to start walking around talking like Queen Ione?"

"Foolish mortal," I said in my queen voice. "You think you can mock me? Watch your tongue before I banish you from my presence."

He kissed my temple again. "That's what I thought."

Louise Haven walked in, dressed in a bright orange velour tracksuit with a large yellow handbag dangling from her arm. She was followed by her friend Doris and several other white-haired ladies, all engaged in hushed conversation. Before she got to the counter, Louise spotted us. Her face lit up with a smile as she veered to our table.

"Look at you two all cozied up like a proper couple."

"Hi, Aunt Louise," Luke said.

She pulled a small notebook and a pen out of her bag, then started thumbing through the pages. "I'm glad you're here. This confirms what I already knew, but it's nice to see for myself."

"What's that?" he asked.

"That I need to take you off the bachelor hierarchy. Well, to be precise, I'm moving you into the taken-but-not-yet-married subcategory."

"Bachelor hierarchy?" I asked. "Tell me more, Louise. I have a feeling this is gonna be good."

"Oh, you know, it's just a little thing we do," she said with a wave of her hand. "There's a ranking system for the most eligible Tilikum bachelors, and now and then we might make a friendly wager on who'll be the next to graduate off the list. Nothing but an amusement, really."

"You were betting on Luke to drop off the list next, weren't you?"

"It's all confidential, dear. I'm afraid I couldn't say."

My lips turned up in a smile. "That's why you invited my family to sit with you at the bachelor auction. You paid for an entire table just to get me there, didn't you?"

She pressed her lips together, as if trying not to smile. "The auction had nothing to do with it. That was all for the SPS."

I laughed. "I don't believe that for a second, you sneaky little minx."

Her eyebrows lifted. "I don't see you complaining about the results."

"Fair enough. Did you win some good money? I hope so. Your little auction stunt certainly cost me a pretty penny. Or cost my mom a pretty penny, to be precise."

"I had nothing to do with that part. I simply made sure the pieces were all in place. What happened with the bidding was out of my hands."

I gasped. "You made sure Jenna was there, too, didn't you? Did you pay for her ticket?"

Louise fidgeted, looking up and around—anywhere but at me. "I don't know what you're talking about."

I shook my head. "You're a little bit extra, Louise. I love that about you."

"It all worked out in the end, didn't it? And word on the street is, what Jenna thought was her second choice turned out to be anything but." She leaned closer and lowered her voice, like she was letting us in on a big secret. "I heard she and that Hank fellow have been seen around town together on several occasions."

"We saw them at the Zany Zebra," I said.

"Well, that's an interesting tidbit, isn't it?" She glanced at her knot of friends making their way through the line to order. "If you'll excuse me."

"Can't wait to share the gossip, can she?" I asked, watching her join the group.

"She wouldn't be Louise Haven if she could."

I shook my head again. "I should have known she was up to something. I thought it was odd that she invited my family to sit at her table."

He squeezed my thigh. "For once in my life, I'm glad she meddled."

We kept sipping our coffee and idly chatting while people came and went. A group of firefighters arrived while Louise and her friends moved several tables together next to us and started taking their seats. They immediately huddled and started whispering fiercely. I wondered how many of the firefighters were on their bachelor hierarchy.

Probably all of them, if they weren't married.

As the firefighters left with their drinks, another silver-haired lady burst in—Suzanne Montgomery. I'd met her at Luke's shop. She darted to Louise's table and started talking frantically.

"What's that about?" I asked.

"We probably don't want to know." Luke took a sip of his coffee. "Some kind of matchmaking, meddling-aunt emergency."

"Found dead?!" Louise exclaimed. "Oh no."

That got my attention. I didn't bother to wait for a break in their conversation. "Who was found dead?"

"The latest missing woman." Louise put a hand to her chest. "We were hoping she'd be found like the others."

I glanced at Luke in alarm. The others must have been the women Garrett had been telling us about. Apparently, the woman in Echo Creek had been released from the hospital and was expected to recover from her injuries. The victim from Tilikum—her name was Bella Lewis—had also gone home. I'd heard from Harper that she was doing well, all things considered. She had a lot of bruises, and he'd broken her arm, but she'd be okay.

"Since when was there another missing woman?" Luke asked.

"You didn't hear?" Louise asked. "She went out for a jog and never made it home."

"How do they know it's the same guy?" he asked.

Suzanne chimed in. "My nephew works for the sheriff's department, and he was first on the scene. He says they can't say definitively yet, but the signs were there."

"I don't know what's worse," Doris said. "The same man responsible for all three, or more than one perpetrator to worry about."

"Four," Louise said. "Isn't that right, Suzanne?"

I sat forward. "Four? There have been four victims?"

Doris fanned herself. "Oh my, I had no idea."

"One was from Pinecrest," Suzanne said. "She was found like the others. Hurt, but alive. This one, though." She shook her head sadly.

"I'd get some pepper spray if I were you, dear," Louise said, meeting my eyes.

"I already have some." A sick feeling spread through my stomach. Four victims. What was even happening?

"Although I'm not sure how much good it would do if you don't see him coming," she said.

I stiffened in my seat. Luke stood and offered me his hand. "We should get going."

Vaguely, I nodded. Ignoring the continuing chatter from Louise and her friends, I got up and we cleared our table. I didn't want to hear more of their conversation.

Luke took my hand, and I held it gratefully as we left the coffee shop and started up the sidewalk. I knew the abductions didn't have anything to do with me, but four? And the latest wasn't just an abduction, it was a murder.

But I didn't want to let something I had no control over get to me. I didn't want to live in fear.

"Are you okay?" he asked as we walked. "Maybe that's a stupid question."

"I'm fine." It came out like a reflex. "Actually, I feel a little sick."

He stopped, and we moved aside as a group walked past us. Meeting my eyes, he pressed his palm to my cheek. "I'm not going to let anything happen to you."

I stepped in, and he wound his arms around me as I rested my head on his chest. I believed him. Or I believed he meant what he said.

But he couldn't always be there.

Taking a deep breath, I moved back. "I don't know why I'm letting this get to me."

"Because you've been through something similar. Of course it's going to bother you."

"Yeah, but whoever this guy is, he doesn't have anything to do with me."

"Still. We'll be careful." He kissed my forehead.

I loved it when he did that.

We walked back to his garage, and as we went inside, the rush of cool air washed over me, making my skin prickle. It helped, as if the chill grounded me in reality. This wasn't LA eleven years ago. It was Tilikum. And whatever was happening out there wasn't going to touch me.

Still, I dug through my purse, making sure I did have my pepper spray. Maybe I'd get a few more. I wasn't going to take any chances.

CHAPTER 30

Luke

A FEW DAYS after the murder victim was found, it was confirmed that law enforcement believed the perpetrator was the same. Garrett said it looked like he was escalating.

Without much of a description, and very few clues, I had no idea how they were going to find the guy. He'd attacked women across three towns, leaving them in different places each time. Two had been taken at night, two in broad daylight. No one knew how he was doing it without being seen.

It made me want to stick to Melanie like glue.

She'd be going back to her regular job sooner rather than later, and I was dreading it. I wanted her with me, where I could protect her.

I walked up the sidewalk in the heat, on my way to the Copper Kettle. I'd decided to run out and grab lunch for me and Mel. I went inside and the diner was packed. There seemed to be more than the normal bustle of staff and customers. Some people were eating at booths or tables, but the entire lunch counter was dominated by a knot of people, some sitting, others standing. It looked more like they were having a meeting than eating a meal.

Absently, I rubbed my midsection. My ribs were healing well, but I could tell when I'd overdone it or slept wrong. They'd been aching all morning.

Heidi, the hostess, came to the front. She was young with a bouncy dark blond ponytail and a Copper Kettle name tag pinned to her shirt.

"Are you with them?" She gestured to the men and women buzzing around the counter.

"No, I was just going to grab a to-go order. Who are they?"

"The SPS." She didn't elaborate, as if that were self-explanatory.

"What are they doing?"

Her eyes widened. "Don't you know about The Whisper?"

"The what?"

"Not a what, a who. The man attacking women. There was another one, you know."

"Please tell me you don't mean there have been five."

"No, four. But the last one…" She winced.

"Yeah, I heard. I think everyone's heard by now." My brow furrowed. "What did you call him? The Whisper?"

"Yeah, that's what everyone is calling him. It's because he whispers in your ear when he gets you."

"What are the SPS doing?"

"A whole bunch of stuff. You should go talk to them. I bet they could use your help. Oh, do you still want to order?"

"Yeah." I put in my order, then went over to see what the SPS members were up to.

The owner of the Copper Kettle, Rob Landon, was dressed in his SPS T-shirt and carrying a clipboard. He nodded along as he conferred with several other similarly clad SPS members, and wrote something.

"Hey Rob," I said. "What's going on?"

"We're responding to the crisis." He gestured to the other SPS members. "Obviously, we can't sit around and do nothing. This is our town, damn it, and we're not letting this happen again. We're setting up a booth in Lumberjack Park to hand out whistles and pepper spray to anyone who wants them. We've got sign-ups going for a buddy system, so women don't have to be out and about alone. And volunteers are on hand to walk women to their cars after work and so forth, especially if it's after dark."

I had to admit, I was impressed. "That's great stuff. I'm sure everybody appreciates it."

"We've got the sign-up sheet over there if you want to take a shift."

"I've already been assigned a special detail. It's kind of a twenty-four seven thing."

"Understood. You need any help, just let us know."

"I will. Thanks, Rob."

"Does your girlfriend want a whistle?" He grabbed one, dangling from a bright red lanyard, from the counter. "We're out of pepper spray, but Mayor Bill is working on getting more as soon as possible."

I took the whistle. "I'll give it to her."

"You can have one too, if you'd like. So far, the victims have been women, but we're not ruling out anything."

"I'm good, but thanks."

"Stay safe out there," Rob said.

"You too."

I went back to the front of the restaurant to wait for my lunch order. It wasn't long before Heidi brought it in a to-go bag. I paid, thanked her, and headed back to work.

What was going on? Tilikum wasn't immune to crime, even violent crime. But incidents were usually few and far between. This guy had taken four women in a matter of weeks. Granted, they hadn't all been from Tilikum, but the fact remained that a potential serial killer was on the loose.

The heat pressed at me as I walked. I noticed a squirrel splayed out on the sidewalk, flat on its belly, legs sticking out.

"Are you hot, little guy?"

I took one of the bottled waters out of the bag and opened it. Crouching down, I trickled some water near its face and sprinkled more on its back. It perked up, lifting its head to drink, so I gave it a bit more.

It popped up onto its back legs, bushy tail twitching. I gave it another drink, trying not to douse it. It wiped its face with its front paws and scampered away between two buildings.

"You're welcome."

Closing the water bottle, I stood and walked the last block to my shop. I rolled my eyes as I walked in the lobby door, thinking about The Whisper. They shouldn't have given him a nickname. He was probably getting off on it.

Melanie looked up from the front desk and a smile lit up her face.

"There's my girl," I said as the door shut behind me. "Hungry?"

"Starving. I didn't know you were surprising me with lunch."

"It's for my own good. No one's safe if you're hangry."

She stood. "I'd be offended, but you're not wrong. Did you get pickles?"

"All the pickles, my beautiful weirdo."

We went into my office and got our lunch out, using my desk as a table. The hot weather was dragging on, so nothing had sounded good except cold sandwiches. And pickles for Mel, of course.

I pulled out the whistle Rob had given me and handed it to her. "The SPS is over at the Copper Kettle. They're handing out whistles for safety. This one's for you."

She held it up. "That was nice of them."

"They're also organizing sign-ups for a buddy system, so women don't have to be out and about alone."

"I guess I'm glad I spent so much of my mom's money on

you at that auction. It was for a good cause." She took a bite of her pickle.

"People are calling the perpetrator 'The Whisper.' It seems like a bad idea to give him a nickname. It's just giving him attention."

"Why do they call him 'The Whisper?'"

"Apparently, he whispers in the victim's ear when he first attacks them."

The color drained from her face. "He does?"

"It's just what I heard." I hesitated. I had a bad feeling I knew why she looked so shaken. "Is that what happened to you?"

She nodded. "Just as I was starting to black out, I heard him say, 'Don't be scared, it's going to be okay.'"

"Well, that was a fucking lie."

"I know, right?" The fire returned to her voice. "If you're going to whisper something creepy in your victim's ear, at least be honest. Everything was not going to be okay."

"Not for him, either, as it turned out. He picked the wrong woman."

She picked up another pickle. "I think I just got lucky."

"I think you're a badass and should give yourself some credit. Also, fuck that guy."

"Indeed," she said, gesturing with her pickle, then took a crunchy bite. "I keep wanting not to think about this, because despite my tendency to be dramatic, I actually don't want to make everything about me. And I really don't want this to be about me. But…"

I knew what she was getting at. "The similarities."

"Yeah. Garrett said the first victims had been drugged and put in the trunk of a car. And now whispering in their ear? That has to be a coincidence, right? It couldn't be the same guy."

I met her eyes. I didn't know the answers, but I was

wondering the same thing. Could it be him? Was that even possible? The chances had to be astronomical.

"I wonder what he whispered," she asked.

"Garrett might know. Do you want me to call him and ask?"

Thoughtfully, she took a bite of her pickle and chewed slowly. "Yes, but also no. I'm a little bit afraid of what he'll say. But not knowing isn't going to help. And it's not going to change anything." She met my eyes again. "You don't think I'm overreacting to at least wonder?"

"No, you're not overreacting. And I think Garrett needs to know what happened to you."

"Okay. Call him."

I pulled out my phone and called, putting it on speaker so Melanie could hear.

"Yeah," he answered.

"Sorry to bug you if you're working, but I have a good reason."

"Go ahead."

"Is it true that the guy who's been abducting women whispers in their ear when he takes them?"

"Yeah, it's true."

"Do you know what he said to them?"

"Why?"

"I just need to know. Was it something like, 'Don't be scared, it's going to be okay?'"

"Hang on." He paused for a moment. "That's exactly what all three victims reported him saying. How did you know?"

Melanie buried her face in her hands. A hit of anger rippled through me. I wanted to rip this guy to pieces.

"Fuck," I breathed. "Eleven years ago, Melanie was abducted outside her apartment. It happened in LA, but there are some weird similarities, including that one."

"What else?"

I met her eyes, and she nodded. I could tell him what I knew.

"She was alone at night in a parking lot. He grabbed her from behind and choked her until she blacked out. He whispered the same thing in her ear when he did it. He drugged her, and she woke up in the trunk of a car. She got away before he could do anything else. She didn't see his face, and they never found him."

"You said LA?"

"Yeah."

"Okay. I want to get in touch with the agency down there who worked that case."

"It couldn't be him, could it? Here? What are the chances?"

"I don't know what the chances are, but it's worth investigating. We need every bit of information we can find. Where's Melanie staying?"

I met her eyes. "With me."

She didn't protest. Just pressed her lips together and nodded.

"Good," Garrett said. "We don't know what this guy's game is or where he might strike again. Pinecrest and Echo Creek are watching out for him as much as we are. They've got neighborhood patrols and retired cops keeping watch, especially after dark."

"The SPS is handing out whistles and set up a buddy system."

"Yeah, we're aware. It should help. I don't want the whole town freaking out, thinking they can't leave their homes. But be cautious. You especially. Don't leave Melanie alone until we catch this guy."

"I won't. Keep me posted if there's anything else we should know."

"I will."

"Thanks." I ended the call.

A second later, I was out of my chair, scooping Melanie into my arms. We settled on the couch, and I held her tight.

"What if it's him?" she whispered. "What if he's here? How could he be here?"

"I don't know. But he's not getting anywhere near you."

She took a deep breath. "It might be someone else. This could be a big, unfortunate coincidence."

"It could be. But I'm not taking any chances. Come stay with me."

"Honestly, I don't think I'd be able to sleep by myself right now." She nestled her head against my chest.

"We'll stop by your place this afternoon and grab whatever you need."

She nodded.

Keeping my arms around her, I took a few breaths. Anger burned hot in my veins, chasing away the ache in my ribs. Whether or not this psycho was the same guy who'd abducted Melanie, he needed to be stopped.

And he wasn't going to touch my girl.

CHAPTER 31

Luke

THE WHISPER WAS all anyone in Tilikum seemed to be able to talk about. And it was driving me up the wall.

A shadow of fear hung over the whole town, and the gossip line had gone wild. Everyone had a theory, and the list of supposed suspects was as long as it was outlandish. Stop into any shop or restaurant, and there'd be someone ready to give you their take on it.

My personal favorites, for their absurdity, were aliens or Bigfoot. Aliens at least made a bit of sense, if you believed in that sort of thing. But Bigfoot? Apparently Tilikum Bigfoot lore had expanded to include creatures who drove cars and could use duct tape. They might as well have blamed it on the squirrels.

Melanie was staying with me, and with the exception of a rather heated discussion over who was responsible for the toothpaste splatter on the mirror—no matter what she says, I still maintain it was her—things were great. She slept peacefully every night, untroubled by nightmares. And I slept soundly, knowing the psycho would have to go through me to get to her.

Days were more tense. The third and fourth victims had

been taken during the day. The Whisper wasn't skulking around in the dark to hunt for his prey anymore. It made me feel like I had to be vigilant every time we set foot outside the safety of my house.

Our evening promised a bit of respite. My parents had invited us and Melanie's parents to their place for dinner. There was something about the trek up the long gravel driveway that lifted the weight from my shoulders. No whispers up at the Haven homestead.

The sun blazed red through the smoky haze in the air as we parked outside their house. Melanie seemed more at ease, her smile relaxed. I took her hand and led her up to the porch and in the front door.

"Mom! Dad! We're here."

We found them in the kitchen, and the way Mom stepped away from Dad, her cheeks flushing slightly, made me glad I'd announced our arrival. I had a feeling we would have walked in on something I didn't particularly want to see.

It was great they were still in love, but no one wants to see their parents making out.

"There you are," Mom said with a smile. She held out her arms to give Melanie a hug. "Welcome."

Dad scowled at me, obviously annoyed that we'd interrupted them.

"Hi, Marlene." Melanie hugged my mom.

Seeing the two of them embracing made my throat feel a bit tight. I hugged my mom and tipped my chin to my dad. His irritated expression melted when Melanie gave him a hug, the big softy.

"Thanks for having us," Melanie said. "Your house looks exactly the same, and I mean that in the best way. It feels so homey and cozy."

"Thank you," Mom said. "I'm so—"

"Knock, knock!" Krista's singsong voice came from the front of the house. "Can we come in?"

"Yes," Mom called. "Come in!"

Melanie's mom came down the hall clutching her hands to her chest and smiling, as if she couldn't contain her excitement. Anton followed her, carrying several pizza boxes.

"Luke, you handsome man, you!" She grabbed me and planted a kiss on my cheek.

"Hi, Mom," Melanie said. "Inside voice, maybe?"

Krista hugged her daughter, then made her way over to my parents. "Marlene! Don't you look lovely tonight. Paul." She held out her arms and my dad flinched backward, but her embrace was light and friendly.

Melanie swiped her thumb across my cheek, and I wiped off the rest of Krista's bright pink lipstick with the back of my hand.

"Thanks," I said quietly.

She just smiled.

Anton set the pizza boxes on the counter.

"We brought dinner!" Krista gestured like a game show model showing off the prizes.

"Thank you again," Mom said. "What a treat."

"It's our pleasure. Or Anton's pleasure since he did all the work. But he was happy to, weren't you, honey?"

"Of course," Anton said with a slight nod.

"There should be something for everyone," Krista said. "We know Paul loves all-meat, so we brought one of those."

Dad grunted his assent.

"There's also a pepperoni and a margherita for something a little lighter. Mel, we brought a personal-sized fried pickle pizza just for you."

"Doesn't anyone else want the pickle pizza?" Melanie asked.

Mom was too polite to make a face, but Dad was not. He grimaced.

I leaned closer to Mel. "I think that one's all you."

She shrugged. "Their loss."

We all dished up in the kitchen and took our plates to the dining table while Mom poured wine. I followed my dad's lead and took some of the all-meat. The toppings were so thick, my plate felt like it weighed ten pounds.

The Andolinis knew how to do pizza right.

Melanie's pickle pizza, on the other hand, looked like a culinary abomination.

"I can't believe you're going to eat that," I said as we sat down.

"Fried pickle pizza is one of my dad's greatest inventions."

"I didn't invent it," Anton said.

"Okay, but you perfected it," she said around a bite. "This is amazing."

He smiled at her and took a bite of his pepperoni.

"So how's the pizza business?" my dad asked.

"Business is good," Anton said.

"We just love it," Krista said. "Everyone who comes in feels like family. Except the ones who complain. They can bite me."

My mom laughed and Dad grunted his agreement.

"Although, things have been so tense lately." Krista cast a worried glance at Anton. "Because of… you know."

"Mom, maybe let's not," Melanie said.

"Sorry, sorry." Krista put her hands up. "But if they don't catch him soon, I don't know what."

"They will," Dad said. "A guy like that won't be able to keep it up for long without making a mistake. He'll get caught."

"Maybe he'll move on," Krista said. "Just disappear, and this will all end."

"Or get hit by a train," Anton said.

"That'd be too good for him," Dad grumbled.

"Something slower," Anton said. "Like a fall off a cliff that doesn't kill him instantly."

"Bear attack," Dad offered.

Anton nodded. "Or cliff and then bear—"

"Stop." Krista put a hand over her heart. "Don't be so morbid. At least not at the dinner table. We're guests here. It's my fault. I shouldn't have brought it up."

Anton smiled at her.

"Yes, new topic please," Melanie said. "Politics? Religion? Anything but The Whisper."

"Anton, do you have any new pizza flavors in the works?" I asked.

"I'm always trying new things." He glanced at Krista. "What was that idea you had the other day?"

"Oh, listen to this," Krista said, gesturing with her hands as she talked. "Chicken and dumplings meets pizza. White sauce, chicken, peas and carrots, topped with little golden dumplings. What do you think? Discuss."

Melanie shook her head with a soft laugh as a conversation about chicken and dumplings pizza took off. She glanced at me with a grateful smile and mouthed, thank you.

I put my hand on her thigh and squeezed.

Thankfully, the rest of the meal went on without the conversation returning to The Whisper. After we came to the conclusion that Anton could probably make chicken and dumplings pizza work, the topic turned to cars. I doubted Melanie was interested in muscle cars the way our dads were, but she leaned closer to me and put her hand on my leg.

After dinner, we brought our dishes to the kitchen. I was going to help clean up, but Dad elbowed me out of the way while Mom put away the leftovers. I stepped out of the kitchen and into the family room so Dad wouldn't bark at me to move.

Melanie stood in the hallway, gazing at the family photos on the wall. I was about to ask her what she was looking at when Anton moved next to me and hesitated, like he had something to say.

A hint of nervousness tightened my shoulders. He'd given me a stern dad-lecture back in high school, one I'd never forget. Although her parents had been friendly, I wondered if they had misgivings about their daughter dating me again. I didn't have kids, but if one of my nieces had an ex-boyfriend, I'd probably hate him by default.

"Take care of her," he said, finally, his voice low. "We almost lost her once. Can't let that happen again."

"I will."

He reached out his hand, and I shook it. His grip was firm, and he nodded once before releasing my hand and walking away.

Like my dad, he was a man of few words. But those hit me right in the chest. What must Melanie's abduction have been like for them? To find out their daughter had been brutally attacked and barely escaped with her life.

Like a movie playing backward, events flashed through my mind, taking me back. Me and Melanie, still basically kids, cruising down the highway with the windows rolled down. The arguments, the fights, the blowups. Slamming doors and feet stomping away. Tires peeling out in her parents' driveway.

All those moments had led to her being outside that apartment in LA. If we'd only gotten our acts together—if only I'd fixed things back then—she wouldn't have been there.

She would have been with me. And her abduction never would have happened.

I let out a long breath. It wasn't my fault some psycho attacked her. Not directly. But indirectly?

And everything she'd been through since. Her marriage to that asshole. Her divorce. Moving back home to start her life over.

All those years, all that time, gone. How much of it was my fault? How much could I have prevented if I'd done things differently?

It was a lot to take in.

Ever since I'd finally admitted to myself I didn't hate her —and that I might actually be in love with her—I'd left the past where I thought it belonged. Mostly forgotten.

But how much of that past was going to haunt our future? What was I supposed to do with all that regret?

Melanie had made her way to the front door, where she and her parents were busy saying goodbye to mine. Or more accurately, Krista and my mom were exchanging a series of *thank you, we should do this agains*, and other effusive declarations of mutual gratitude, while Anton and my dad waited patiently for their wives to finish.

I glanced at the photos where Melanie had been standing moments before. There was one with the six of us boys with baby Annika in the middle. Another showed all seven kids playing outside with bare feet and dirt on our faces. But it was a slightly more recent picture that caught my eye—one from high school.

It was me and Zachary posing in our tuxes on the front porch before prom. Melanie would have been my date that night. Mom must have taken the photo before I left to pick her up.

"Luke, you ready?" Melanie asked.

"Yeah, coming."

Krista was still saying her goodbyes, but with a few soft words, Anton gently ushered her outside. I gave my mom a quick hug and a nod goodbye to my dad, then left with Melanie.

After hugging her daughter a few more times, Krista finally got in the car with Anton. Melanie and I got in mine, and she leaned her head back and sighed.

"I love my mom, but she's intense. And yes, I realize that's ironic coming from me."

"Your mom's great."

"It would be nice if she could get her goodbye routine

down to less than half an hour, but that's probably too much to hope for at this point. At least your parents are easygoing. Mine don't freak them out."

"Your mom and dad aren't as weird as you think they are."

She laughed a little. "Thanks."

I started the car and headed home. Melanie was unusually quiet. She watched the scenery go by with a pensive look on her face that made me wonder what she was thinking.

"What's going on?" I reached over and twined her hand in mine as I drove. "You all right?"

"Yeah, just thinking."

"About what?"

"I don't know. Lots of things."

I wasn't sure what that meant, or if it were good or bad. But she didn't seem to want to talk about it, so I let it go.

Still, the unsettled feeling inside me persisted. Even after we were at my place—in my bed—content and sated in each other's arms, I felt it. The sense that something was not quite right, something was missing.

Something unfinished.

And I wasn't sure what I was going to do about it.

The Whisper

ROSWELL MILLS

MY PARKING SPOT outside the Timberbeast Tavern was in the shadows, away from the pools of illumination cast by the streetlights, but where I still had a good view of the entrance.

Indecision gnawed at me. To go in or not to go in. That was my burning question.

She was in there. My Melanie.

And she wasn't alone.

I'd seen her with him more than once. Since I'd decided to start tracking her, learning her routine, it had quickly become clear that the small-town mechanic had wormed his way into her life.

She was even staying with him, basically living at his place.

My lip curled in a sneer. It was an unintended consequence of my activities. Fear permeated the town, and it seemed to have driven her closer to him. I didn't like it, but it was something I'd have to deal with later—eliminate her feelings for him.

I glanced at the copy of the *Tilikum Tribune* sitting on the passenger seat. Quaint little newspaper. And I'd made the cover.

THE WHISPER STRIKES AGAIN

I was front-page news. My sneer melted into a smile. That was also an unintended consequence. When I'd taken Melanie the first time, if it had made the news, I hadn't seen it. I'd been too scared, fleeing like a child to my mother's place in Tennessee. Like a scared little boy.

The sneer was back. I hated who I'd been back then. Truthfully, a part of me hated who I was now even more. But I shoved that part down into the depths of my consciousness where I couldn't hear its protests. Couldn't hear its pleas for someone to stop me before it was too late.

It was already too late. I'd come too far to back out now.

Especially after the last one.

Killing her had been a necessity. She'd woken up before I was ready, and she'd seen my face. My rehearsals had been enough of a risk. I couldn't let one go who could identify me. My plans would fall apart, and I'd never have the opportunity to take the one I really wanted.

The one I'd been waiting for.

I wouldn't take another. It was Melanie's turn. I was ready.

All that was left was deciding when and where. That wouldn't be easy because the idiot she was with never left her alone. It meant I wouldn't be able to plan the exact moment I took her. I'd have to be flexible. Stay close, and wait for a window of opportunity to arise, however small.

My practice runs had helped. I'd gotten faster. In less than a minute, she'd be mine.

And I was a patient man. Despite the way I ached for her, I could wait.

She was going to be worth it.

My eyes strayed from the door to the headline on the

newspaper again. The Whisper. I both loved and hated that they were calling me that. I loved that I'd made them afraid— that they'd taken notice of me. But whisper? I knew what I was, knew that no one saw me. That in the eyes of the world, I was nothing.

But she'd see. Soon, I'd no longer be a whisper. I was going to be a shout.

CHAPTER 32

Melanie

STARING AT NOTHING, I absently fiddled with the SPS whistle while Luke got our drinks from Rocco at the bar. Something about the nineties grunge playing in the background was oddly soothing. Maybe it was the familiarity of old songs and good memories.

Mostly good, at least.

Luke set our drinks on the table, then pulled his chair around next to me and sat. We'd chosen a spot against the wall. Neither of us seemed to want to have our backs to the room lately.

Living in a constant state of tension was getting exhausting. And we weren't the only ones who were tense. The whole town was on edge. A nervous hush had settled over Tilikum, making people side-eye each other and cast worried glances over their shoulders.

I took a sip of my beer. In any other context, I wasn't a beer drinker. But for some reason, at the Timberbeast, I was.

Luke put his hand on my thigh and leaned over to kiss my temple. I loved it when he did that. I really did. Although the fact that our town was being terrorized by a killer was starting to get to me, because I flinched.

"Is this worse?" he asked. "Maybe we should have stayed in."

"No," I said emphatically. "This is fine. I needed to get out."

I'd been going a little stir-crazy. Ever since the most recent victim had been found, Luke had been stuck to me like a magnet. We mostly went to work, then his place, with the occasional stop at a restaurant or store. He'd even been finding excuses to pop into the lobby at the garage more often than usual, as if the perpetrator might come in and grab me from behind the desk.

The Luke-magnet wasn't bothering me, but feeling like I was trapped was making my skin crawl.

"I'm just so tired of feeling like a prisoner," I said. "I can't walk up the street to grab a coffee or stop at the store by myself."

He squeezed my thigh. "I don't mean to stifle you."

"No, it isn't you. I was too paranoid to take the trash outside yesterday. I keep looking around and thinking he could be anywhere."

"Do you want me to call Garrett again?"

"It's tempting, but he'd have called if he had news he could share."

"I know. I'm just so fucking frustrated. I hate feeling like there's nothing I can do."

I leaned my head against his shoulder. "Yeah, me too."

A guy in a baseball cap wandered in and joined a few people at the bar. I remembered him, and several of the others, from high school.

Which reminded me of the other thread in my tangle of emotions. It was bright red, weaving in and out of the rest, a painful reminder of a once-broken heart.

Ever since our dinner with Paul and Marlene the other night, I'd been inundated with memories. Maybe it was because their house hadn't changed. From the knit throw blankets on the blue couch to the hint of pine and lemon in the air, it felt like stepping back in time.

Or maybe it was all the photos displayed on their mantel and walls. So many of those memories were adjacent to my own, times that I remembered too.

Like the photo of Luke and Zachary in suits before prom. I'd been his date that night. His bow tie and vest had been pale blue to match my dress.

It was a night that hadn't ended well.

But why was I letting that bother me? Who cared what had happened back in high school? I kept telling myself it had been so long. What we had now was different. We weren't going to fall into the same traps, the same patterns.

Except what if we did? What if Luke Haven was a colossal mistake? What if I was attaching myself to him out of fear, like I had with my ex?

After all, I'd moved in with Jared because of the abduction. There I was again, basically shacking up with my boyfriend out of fear.

I took a drink of my beer, trying not to give in to my frantic emotions. But what if I was repeating the past, rushing headlong into another heartbreak?

The door opened again, and my back tightened. It was only Theo, but I wished people would stop doing that. Every time someone new came in, I wondered if it was going to be The Whisper.

Not that I'd know who he was. But if it wasn't someone I knew, I'd have to wonder.

Then again, what if it was someone I knew? What if The Whisper was one of the townspeople? A regular member of society no one would ever have guessed was capable of murder.

Oh my god, was it Theo?

He grabbed a chair and pulled it up to our table.

"It's not you, is it?" I asked.

He sat and his eyebrows drew in. "Is what not me?"

"The Whisper."

Luke turned to me. "Seriously, Mel? My brother isn't a murderer."

"I'm sorry, I know you're not. I blurted that out without thinking." I shook my head. "It's just, every time the door opens, I wonder if he's going to walk in. And then I was thinking that I wouldn't know if he walked in because no one knows who he is. Which made me think, wait, what if he's someone we all know?"

"That is a weird thought," Theo said.

"It's like that cold case Garrett solved last year," Luke said. "No one saw that coming."

Theo shook his head. "That was crazy. Hey, have you talked to Mom and Dad?"

"No, why?"

"Dad's been tailing Mom everywhere she goes. He even went to her knitting group. I guess he stood there with his arms crossed, glaring at everyone in the store, like a bouncer outside a club."

"Sounds like Dad."

"My dad isn't letting my mom out of his sight either," I said. "She claims it's driving her up the wall, but she secretly loves it when he gets protective."

"This whole thing is wild," Theo said. "One guy has the whole town held hostage."

"They'll find him," Luke said. "There's no way he can keep getting away with it."

I wished I shared his confidence. "Whoever attacked me got away with it."

Theo cast an uncomfortable glance at Luke.

"Yeah, well they didn't have a Haven in their department." Luke squeezed my thigh again.

"You're not leaving her alone, are you?" Theo asked, gesturing to me. "Like, ever?"

"Nope."

Theo nodded. "Good. Too many weird things have happened in our family."

Luke took his hand off my leg and draped it over the back of my chair. I appreciated him so much, but I kept coming back to the fear that we were moving too fast. That his feelings were as mixed up as mine, and we weren't being honest about it.

If it weren't for The Whisper, I wouldn't have basically moved in with him. We wouldn't have been spending every waking moment together.

How much longer would he want to?

I was vaguely aware of Luke asking if I was done with my drink. And if I wanted to go home.

Home? Not my home. His.

I nodded without saying much. My insides were such a tangled mess, for once in my life, I didn't have anything to say. I knew I was spiraling. That I probably wasn't thinking rationally. But I couldn't seem to stop. My thoughts were on an endless loop, repeating the same fear over and over.

When was he going to get tired of me? When was he going to realize I was too much?

CHAPTER 33

Luke

MELANIE WAS tense and it was making me furious.

Anger seethed inside me as we drove back to my place from the Timberbeast. She hadn't been herself for days, and it was only getting worse. I wanted to find the piece of shit who was responsible and make sure he couldn't hurt anyone ever again—especially not my woman.

Shadowing her every move was probably starting to make her mad, but what else was I supposed to do? Someone was out there attacking women, and Melanie was not going to be one of them.

In the meantime, I wanted to rearrange his face. He was victimizing her without even targeting her directly. She was anxious and scared. And who could blame her? With everything she'd been through, I wouldn't have been surprised if she decided to bail on Tilikum forever.

That thought made me pause as I pulled into my driveway. Would she? And if she did, would she bail on me, too?

We got out of the car in silence, tension snapping between us. Despite all my confidence—all my bravado about being the one to marry her—deep down, I was worried. Maybe even afraid.

And that kind of pissed me off too.

She went up the stairs ahead of me and unlocked the door. I followed her inside and locked it behind us—something I didn't always used to do.

"I know it's early, but do you want to just go to bed?" I asked.

Stopping in the kitchen, she didn't turn around. "You know that's not going to fix anything."

"I'm not trying to fix anything. It's just been a long day."

She hesitated for a moment. "I don't know if I'm going to sleep here tonight."

If I'd been in a calmer frame of mind, that statement might not have felt like a punch in the face. But I wasn't, so it did.

"What? Why? You can't go to your place alone."

"I'll go to my brother's house. Or my parents'." She dug her phone out of her purse. "I'll see who's around."

"You don't have to do that."

"Yeah, I think I do." She started walking down the hall, her eyes on her phone.

"Why?"

She disappeared into the bedroom without answering.

Rolling my eyes in frustration, I followed her. "What's going on?"

"What do you mean, what's going on?" She had her bag on the bed and was stuffing things in it. "A psycho murderer is terrorizing the town, and I can't even stay at my own house. That's what's going on."

"We can sleep over there if you want."

"That's not what I mean," she snapped.

I was trying, and probably failing, to keep my voice from rising. "Then what do you mean? Why can't you stay here?"

"What are we doing, Luke?" She started gesturing wildly as she spoke. "We decide to start dating again because we both got jealous. What is that about? And then you move me in because you're afraid I'm going to be the next victim. So here we are, playing house, like this is all a great idea and our lives aren't spinning completely out of control."

"What am I supposed to do? Leave you alone and let you be an easy target?"

"This isn't about him!"

I was ready to tear my hair out. "Then what the fuck is it about?"

She opened her mouth like she was going to answer, then shut it again and started shoving more clothes in her bag. Without bothering to zip it closed, she grabbed it off the bed and shouldered her way past me.

"Where are you going?" I asked, following her into the living room.

"My brother's house."

"At least let me drive you."

"No."

"Mel, just let me drive you over there."

"I'll call him on the way and he can meet me outside, since this stupid town is so insane I can't even walk from my car to someone's front door without an escort."

As soon as she put her hand on the doorknob, a strange sense of panic seized me, making my chest tighten. It wasn't just fear, it was a memory—an awful memory. One that I'd tried very hard to forget.

For a second, it left me frozen. She was going to walk out and that was going to be it. It didn't seem like we'd just had a breakup argument, but it hadn't the first time, either. I'd been blindsided then just as hard.

And I'd let it happen.

I wasn't going to make the same mistake twice. Teenage me had figured she'd get over whatever had made her mad. That we'd get back together in a day or two and everything would be fine.

We hadn't. And there had been nothing fine about it. Not that day, or in any of the days since.

In that moment, everything became so clear I almost laughed. My anger melted, even as I watched her open the door and start to leave.

"I love you," I said.

She stopped in her tracks, her back to me.

My beautiful mess.

"This isn't about me being jealous of some other guy. I mean, I was. But I've loved you since high school. I never stopped. And if you think I'm going to let you walk out that door and out of my life, you're very, very wrong. I'll pick you up, fling you over my shoulder, and carry you, no matter what it does to my ribs."

Slowly, she turned to face me. "I'm not leaving you. I…"

"Aren't you?" I asked, my voice gentle. I moved closer. "I think you're trying to run. Baby, I'm not the one you need to be running from."

"How do I know that?" she asked, her voice almost a whisper.

"Because I love you."

Her eyes were wide, full of vulnerability. "You said that back then. And you didn't."

"Of course I did."

"Then why did you break up with me?"

I looked at her like she'd just asked me why I'd murdered her entire family. "What? I didn't break up with you."

Her forehead creased in confusion. She marched back inside, closing the door behind her, and dropped her bag on the floor. "Excuse me? Yes, you did. And I have the marriage to another man to prove it."

"You broke up with me."

Her mouth dropped open, her expression full of offense. "Excuse me, Luke Haven, I did no such thing."

"I'm sorry, did I just teleport to an alternate universe? Because yes, you did. You broke up with me. I was fucking devastated."

"No, you weren't." She put her hand on her chest. "*I* was devastated."

I stared at her in disbelief. "After prom, we were out at that party and we started arguing about something. I don't even remember what it was, but you got mad and said you were leaving. That someone was taking you home. I thought you were going to cool off and we'd be fine in a day or so, like usual. But you weren't fine, and apparently that was it. You were done with me."

"That's not what happened." Her voice was indignant. "We were fighting, and you said you were sick of it. And I said fine, I'd get a ride home. And then… I don't quite remember what else we said, but I left crying because you broke up with me."

"I didn't break up with you after prom. Is that what you thought?"

"Yes, that's what I thought. Why else would I have stopped answering your messages?"

"Because you broke up with me."

"Don't make this my fault." She put her hands on her hips. "It took you all of a week to start going out with Melody Torres. And then you were making out with Becky Green not long after that."

"I never went out with Melody Torres. Who told you that?"

"I don't know, everybody."

"Let me get this straight. You left that night thinking I'd just broken up with you. And then you heard a rumor that I went out with someone else."

She glanced away. "I didn't know it was a rumor."

I ran my hand through my hair. "Let me guess. When you heard that rumor, you immediately believed it and burned all my stuff and then made out with Derek Kelly."

"How did you know I burned your stuff?"

"I think Zachary heard it from someone and told me.

Which was why I kissed Becky Green at a party in front of as many people as possible. I felt like I had to prove I didn't care what you did."

"And you kissing Becky Green was why I kissed Derek Kelly at a bonfire. And why I didn't call you when I got my dorm assignment, even though I wanted to."

"And I didn't call you when I got an apprenticeship."

"And I avoided you at Christmas when I came home to visit my family."

"You avoided me every time you came home to visit your family."

"Yeah," she said, her voice softening. "I did. I thought you hated me."

"I guess I convinced myself that I did. Mostly because I thought you hated me. And because when we broke up, it gutted me."

"Me too."

I stepped closer. "You've always been the one who got away. You know that, right? I think I've spent my entire adult life comparing every other woman to you. And they all fell short."

She laughed softly. "I have a hard time believing that. I'm a hot mess, Luke. I'm too much."

"That's what this is really about, isn't it?" I moved in and brushed her hair back from her face. "We broke up back in the day. Your marriage fell apart. So deep down, you're waiting for the other shoe to drop. And if you walk out now, maybe you'll save yourself from having your heart broken again."

When she lifted her eyes to meet mine, they glistened with unshed tears. "I'm afraid of this."

Slipping my hands around her waist, I drew her against me and leaned my forehead down to touch hers. "Don't be."

She held my arms. "But what if we mess it up again?"

"We might. But messing it up in the short term doesn't mean we fall apart. It doesn't mean we give up."

"So… we can be grown-ups and actually talk about our problems?"

My mouth lifted in a smile, and I kept my forehead touching hers. "Exactly."

"That seems awfully reasonable. What's the catch?"

"There's no catch."

"Are you sure? You know me, better than anyone. You know I'm a lot."

"Baby, I don't know who convinced you of that, but they're wrong. You burn bright, and maybe that's a lot for other people, but I love it. I love how I feel when I'm with you —like I'm alive."

Her body softened and she draped her arms around my shoulders. "I love that you get me. That I can be myself with you, even when I feel messy. And how you stay so calm, even when things are hard."

I brought my mouth to hers and kissed her softly.

"I love you," she whispered when I pulled away. "I love you so much."

Warmth spread through my chest. Hearing those words chased away any lingering doubts. "I love you, too."

"Doesn't it make you mad, though?"

"What?"

"That we could have been together all this time."

"Believe me, it's crossed my mind that if I hadn't let you go, you wouldn't have been in LA that night. You wouldn't have married someone else and been through everything you've had to deal with in the last couple of years. But maybe this is how it was supposed to be. We both had a lot of growing up to do."

"And maybe instead of worrying about the mistakes we made in the past, colossal as they might have been, we should focus on the future."

"And be grateful we found our way back to each other." I

kissed her again, deeply this time. "I'm ready to love you the way you should be loved."

"And I'm ready to love you back."

She lit me up, like a spark catching dry tinder. Heedless of the twinges of pain that still tightened my midsection, I picked her up and tossed her over my shoulder.

"What are you doing?" she asked with a laugh.

I strode to the bedroom and dropped her on the bed. "Claiming you. Don't move."

She bit her bottom lip. "Yes, sir."

I shucked off my clothes, but took my time undressing her, kissing her skin as I removed each piece of clothing. Touching her and teasing her, I worked her into a frenzy, making her pant and beg.

"Please, Luke. I need you."

My fingers brushed her soft center. Groaning, I licked off her taste before climbing on top of her and settling between her legs.

Our bodies came together in a rush of heat and pleasure. She wrapped her legs around my waist and clutched my back, moaning with every thrust. Her skin was silk, her shape molding perfectly to mine, as if we'd been made for each other.

Pressure built, every sensation intensifying.

"I love you," I growled into her ear as I thrust hard. "I love you, I love you, I love you."

Her answer was almost breathless. "Yes, Luke. I love you. Don't stop. I love you."

"Don't hold back, beautiful. Let me hear you."

Her climax overtook her, and it was all too much. I came undone, exploding inside her, pushing her up the bed with the force of my hips.

As the intensity subsided, I kissed across her shoulder. She held onto me, as if she were still afraid to let me go.

"Stay here a minute," she whispered.

I held there, still inside her, burying my face in her neck. For a long moment, we just breathed.

Finally, I propped myself up so I could look at her. "How do you feel?"

"Amazing. Is that what I-love-you sex is really like? Because that was incredible."

My lips turned up in a grin.

"You might just convince me to stick around if you keep doing that."

I kissed her and nibbled on her bottom lip. "Baby, we're just getting started."

And that was the truth. In moments, I was ready again. We lost ourselves in each other, in the heat and passion and pleasure.

After all, I had to make up for a lot of lost time.

CHAPTER 34

Melanie

THE OPPRESSIVE HEAT was finally beginning to abate, but the haze of wildfire smoke still tinged the air. On the plus side, it made for spectacular sunsets. The mountain peaks rose against a sky streaked with purple and orange as the red sun sank behind them.

Luke and I got out of his car at the stadium behind Tilikum High School. The excitement was contagious as students and families poured out of their vehicles and made their way to find seats, ready to cheer for the Tilikum Timberwolves in their first home game of the football season.

It was nice to be out and about and not feel like the entire town was giving each other the side-eye. It had been a couple weeks since the last attack, and while Luke and I weren't holding out hope that it was really over and the perpetrator was gone, the tension had eased. Town chatter had shifted, centering around the wildfires and whether they were going to get close enough to cause problems.

Not that I wanted a fire to threaten Tilikum, but it was a welcome respite from all the whispers about The Whisper.

Luke took my hand as we made our way toward the bleachers. It was a little bit strange to be back on the campus of our old high school—so fraught with memories—especially with him. But there was a newness to it, as well. We weren't the kids who had crept around corners to steal kisses between classes or had stomp-away-from-each-other arguments in the parking lot.

I wasn't so naive as to think we wouldn't have problems or make mistakes. But I wasn't afraid of that anymore. Luke knew me inside and out. He'd seen me at my best, and my worst, and he still loved me.

I'd never felt so peaceful with anyone.

"Are your parents coming?" I asked.

"Oh yeah. They go to all the games. Especially since Owen started playing last year." He pointed at a spot in the stands. "There they are."

It wasn't just his parents. The Havens practically took up an entire section. Josiah and Audrey sat just behind Paul and Marlene. Josiah had their daughter Abby in his arms. Next to them were Garrett and Harper with little Isla.

Zachary and Marigold sat next to Paul and Marlene with their baby, Emily. And behind them were Annika and Levi with all four of their kids.

Just behind the Havens, the Bailey clan took up several more rows. In the middle of all five families and their kids was Gram Bailey, the matriarch of the bunch. She had a big Tilikum Timberwolves foam hand and was already waving it around.

None of the Baileys had kids in high school yet, but Tilikum was a tight-knit community. Win or lose, the stands were always packed.

We made our way over and claimed seats. Moments later, Nathan and Sharla showed up, Lucia, Zola, and Nico adding to the chaos of excited children. My parents were with them and my mom was decked out in a Tilikum Timberwolves T-shirt and knit hat.

"What is all this?" I asked, gesturing to her swag. "You don't have any kids or grandkids who go here."

"What does that have to do with anything? They're my home team. I can still represent. Besides, we're all practically family." She gestured to the rows of Havens.

"Practically family?"

She patted my cheek. "You know what I mean."

I rolled my eyes as she and my dad found spots. Luke just grinned.

"What are you smiling about?" I sat down and he took the seat next to me.

"Nothing."

I nudged him with my elbow.

"I heard from Andrea earlier today. Did I tell you that?"

"Is she coming back to work?"

"She'd like to."

"The timing is perfect. I have to start recording next week."

"I know." He put his arm around me and scooted me closer. "But I like having you there."

"You just want to be able to keep an eye on me."

"I do, but I like having you there either way." He kissed my temple. "I'm going to miss you."

That made me smile. "I'll miss you too."

I would miss him, but it was for the best, especially long term. Voice acting was what I loved, and it would be good for us to have our own things—give us a little space from each other. I had a feeling we'd appreciate our time together even more.

And we'd be less likely to try to kill each other over something stupid.

It wasn't long before the announcer's voice boomed over the sound system, welcoming the crowd to the game. He announced the opposing team's starting lineup to cheers from the visitors' section and polite applause from the home crowd.

Theo stood on the sidelines with his clipboard in hand. He tucked it under his arm to clap for his team as the Timberwolves starting lineup was announced.

The home crowd went wild, standing and clapping for each athlete. When he got to the last student, I almost had to plug my ears.

"Number thirty-three, Owen Haven!"

Our entire section, from the Havens in front to the Baileys behind us, erupted in cheers and whistles. The noise only quieted for a moment, until they announced head coach Theo Haven, and we cheered again, just as loud as if he'd been the star athlete on the field.

I'd gone to a lot of the games back in high school, but I'd never been much of a football fan. Now, the excitement was infectious. I didn't have to understand everything that was happening on the field. I could tell when to cheer, and the Timberwolves gave us plenty of opportunities.

Especially Owen.

Every time the quarterback gave him the ball—which was often—we yelled and applauded. And when he scored a touchdown, we all surged to our feet and screamed our brains out.

I almost felt bad for the other team. Almost.

People made trips to the concession stand and passed out popcorn and hot dogs to everyone who wanted some. I passed on the hot dog, but happily shared a bag of popcorn with Nico and Zola and a lemonade with Luke. It was only mildly disappointing that the concession stand wasn't selling pickles. I thought it was a missed opportunity. Luke didn't agree.

By halftime, I was well on my way to losing my voice.

"I'm not going to be able to talk after this," I said to Luke.

"Oh, no," he said, his voice dripping with sarcasm. "Mel without a voice? That's terrible."

I elbowed him. "Hey."

He grinned. "Do you want some water?"

"Yeah, that would be good. And I need to use the restroom."

"I'll walk you over there."

"Aren't they inside the school?"

"No, they built new ones on the other side of the concession stand a few years ago."

That was handy. When we were students, we had to go all the way inside the school building to use the restrooms on game nights. Luke took my hand, and we made our way down the bleachers and toward the concession stand. Sure enough, there was a gray stone building a short distance away.

Luke paused outside the entrance to the ladies' room, eyeing the door like he wanted to go inside and inspect it. A mom with two young kids walked in ahead of me and an elderly woman walked out. The regular traffic of typical townspeople seemed to appease him.

"I'll meet you right here," he said.

I popped up on my tiptoes to give him a quick kiss. "I'll only be a minute."

Inside, there were two rows of stalls, and no line. That was nice, seeing as my bladder was increasingly giving me danger signals. That lemonade was going right through me.

I used the restroom and came out of the stall. It took me a second to find the sinks around the corner. I didn't see the mom with her kids, but I could hear her talking softly to one of them while I washed my hands.

With that taken care of, I checked my teeth for bits of popcorn in the mirror, applied some lip gloss, and went out the exit.

Luke wasn't there, which was odd. I took a few steps and

glanced around the back of the building. He wasn't there, either.

In fact, no one was there, and neither was the concession stand. I paused for a second, confused, and tried to get my bearings. Where the heck was I? It felt like I'd just been sucked through a space-time portal.

Turning around again, I realized the noise of the crowd was on the other side of the building. I must have gone out the wrong door. The interior of the restroom was a bit maze-like, with the rows of stalls and separate sink area. I tried the door, but it was locked from that side. That figured. I'd just have to go around.

Out of nowhere, an arm wound around my neck, cutting off my air. Terror exploded inside me, and I kicked and flailed, gripping at the arm, trying to break free. He was too strong. The edges of my vision went dark, the world closing around me rapidly.

The last thing I heard before my consciousness failed was a soft whisper in my ear. "Shh. Don't struggle. There's my good girl. Everything will be okay."

CHAPTER 35

Luke

I HOOKED my thumbs in the pockets of my jeans as I waited outside the women's restroom. A knot of giggling teen girls went in and a mom with two little kids came out.

Melanie was taking her time, but I wouldn't pretend I understood the inner workings of the female restroom experience. For all I knew, she'd run into someone she knew, and they'd be in there for a while chatting. That was a girl thing, right?

Guys would never do that. Dudes understood the iron-clad rules of the men's room. In and out, no talking, and absolutely no eye contact.

The scent of popcorn wafted from the concession stand and the stadium lights lit up the field. It was a good game so far. Awesome to see Owen kicking so much ass. He'd been the first player in years to start varsity as a freshman, and as a sophomore, he was already their star running back. Theo was convinced he'd be college bound on a football scholarship.

I was a damn proud uncle. He wasn't just a great football player, he was a great kid.

The group of girls came out, and my brow furrowed as the door shut behind them. Where was she? Maybe she was having digestive issues. That would suck. No one wanted that in a public restroom. I'd have to see if she needed me to take her home where she could be more comfortable. Maybe put a heating pad on her stomach the way my mom used to have us do when we had stomachaches as kids.

But seriously, where was she?

I didn't want to make it weird, but I was getting worried about her. I was pretty sure she had her phone with her, so I sent her a text, asking if she was okay.

No answer.

That didn't necessarily mean anything. If her phone was in her purse, she might not hear it.

I waited another minute, fidgeting a pair of high school girls went in the restroom. They came out and still no Melanie.

Screw it. I went to the door, opened it, and stuck my head in. "Mel, are you in there?"

No answer.

"Melanie?"

"Um, excuse me?" a female voice said behind me.

Letting the door shut, I stepped aside. "Sorry."

"It's okay." She was probably around my age, with a long brown ponytail, glasses, and what looked like flecks of paint on her shirt. "Are you looking for someone?"

"Yeah, my girlfriend. She's been in there a little longer than I expected. I don't want to embarrass her or anything, but I want to make sure she's okay."

"What's her name?"

"Melanie."

"I'll check for you."

"Thanks, I appreciate it."

"No problem," she said with a smile and went in.

Less than a minute later, she came out, her forehead creased with confusion. "There's no one in there."

My heart stopped dead in my chest. "What? Are you sure?"

"Positive. I checked every stall. They're all empty."

I barreled my way inside. "Melanie?"

"I'll just guard the door, I guess," the woman said behind me.

I ignored her, madly going from stall to stall, looking under each door, then opening them, as if somehow she'd be hiding with her feet out of view. But the woman was right, they were all empty. No one was by the row of sinks. I even checked the door to what was probably a supply closet, but it was locked.

There was one more door, on the far side, past the sinks. At first, I thought it must be another closet, but it opened. I stepped out and found myself on the other side of the building, facing a tall chain-link fence near the outskirts of the parking lot. There was an entrance to the lot, but not many people parked on that side since it was farther away from the bleachers.

My stomach dropped right through the ground at my feet, and I was seized with dread.

"Melanie? Are you out here?"

No answer. Nothing but the roar of the crowd behind me and the hint of popcorn in the air.

Fuck.

Half of me wanted to panic—to run through the parking lot shouting her name. But I knew I wasn't going to find her that way. I had to stay calm and think it through.

I called Garrett.

"Yeah?" he answered.

"Melanie's gone."

"What?"

"She went in the restroom and didn't come out. There's a fucking door on the other side, leads out by the back parking lot. She must have gone that way."

"Are you sure?"

"I went in. Checked every stall. She's not there. She's not out here, either."

"All right, stay calm. If she went out the other exit, she probably just walked around the building, and she's on her way back here."

It made sense. I didn't believe him, but I jogged around the building anyway, looking for any sign of her.

"Come back this way," Garrett said. "We'll start looking over here in case she's talking to someone in the stands. Don't worry, man. She's around."

Forcing myself to a walk so I could look at every person I passed, I made my way back to the bleachers. The student section was packed with kids chanting with the cheerleaders. The rest of the stands looked like a chaotic mess of people—too many faces, too many colors.

Where was she?

I pulled out my phone again and called her as I scanned the crowd. Still nothing. It rang but went to voicemail.

Fuck.

I hurried over to my family, but there was no sign of Melanie there, either.

Garrett stood at the bottom of the bleachers, holding Isla with one arm. "Harper and Marigold went back to search the restrooms, just in case."

"I told you, she's not there."

Josiah stood and made his way down to us. "We should spread out. She's gotta be around here somewhere."

Garrett's phone rang and he put it to his ear. "Find her?"

By the look on his face, I already knew the answer.

"Okay, come back here. And stay together." He ended the call and pocketed his phone while Isla chewed on her fingers.

"Asher," Josiah called, and Asher Bailey looked up. He had his youngest, a girl, in his lap. "We can't find Luke's girl."

As if they were all a single unit, Asher and his brothers handed their kids off to their wives and stood.

"Where was she?" Asher asked as he came down the bleachers.

"Restroom," I said. "I was waiting outside but she must have gone out the other door. I can't find her anywhere."

Krista's eyes were wide, and Anton put an arm around her. Garrett started organizing an impromptu search, giving everyone an area to cover. He assigned Anton and our dad to stay in the bleachers and keep watch for her there—and keep watch over all the wives and kids. There might have been some protests from the women—mostly Logan's wife, Cara—at being told to stay where they were. But we all knew the real threat was to them, not us.

If The Whisper was out there, he attacked women.

But I had the horrifying feeling he wasn't a threat to any of them. Because he was busy with mine.

Rage and adrenaline pumped hot through my veins, burning away my fear. I wanted to scream at Garrett for being so calm and reasonable, reassuring everyone we'd find her. Assigning search areas, as if she was going to turn up on the football field or was simply chatting with someone near the concessions.

As if we wouldn't have found her already if she were there.

When Harper and Marigold came back, Garrett passed Isla to her mom. Dad and Anton stood at the bottom of the bleachers, one on each side of the section, as if they were the last line of defense, protecting the women and children. I half expected Krista to freak out or push past her husband to look for her daughter. Instead, she caught my eyes and clasped her hands to her chest as if to say, '*Find her for me. Please.*'

Garrett and I headed back toward the restrooms. The game continued, and I was vaguely aware of the announcer declaring another Timberwolves touchdown.

"We should have him make an announcement," Garrett said, bringing out his phone again. "I'll see if Harper can get him to do it."

I knew we wouldn't find Melanie inside the restroom building, so I veered around it to show Garrett the side door. He finished his call to Harper and started looking around. There wasn't much to see, as far as I could tell. Just some shrubs around the building and a gravel path leading to the gap in the fence.

He stopped about halfway to the fence and crouched down. Before I could ask him what he was doing, he took a picture of something on the ground with his phone.

"What is it?"

"Syringe cap." He stood and put his phone to his ear. "Sheriff, I have reason to believe The Whisper has another victim."

I ran to the parking lot while Garrett gave Sheriff Cordero his report. I didn't know what I was doing—she wasn't there. How long had it been since she'd gone in the restroom? Ten minutes? More? If The Whisper had her, she was long gone, stuffed in the trunk of his car.

And he was going to—

No. No, he wasn't. That disgusting psycho piece of shit was not going to hurt her. I'd burn down the whole fucking world before I let him touch her.

I was going to find them. And he was going to pay.

CHAPTER 36

Melanie

MY HEAD SWAM with an almost pleasant buzzing sensation, and I vaguely wondered why my eyes were closed. A jumbled mess of thoughts vied for attention, and I couldn't make sense of any of them.

A second later, the fear hit. Something was very, very wrong.

Confusion and panic made it almost impossible to think. My eyes flew open, but nothing made sense. Why was it so hard to breathe? My mouth wouldn't open.

Closing my eyes, I tried to breathe through my nose. My body wanted to panic—to flee, to run, to lash out. But I couldn't. My limbs were too heavy, my brain too fuzzy. Unconsciousness beckoned to me, the bliss of sleep almost too tempting to resist.

No. I forced my eyes open and took a deep breath.

I was lying on my side, on a soft surface. A mattress, maybe? The room was dark. I stretched out my legs, but they were stuck at the ankles.

The sensations plodded through my groggy brain like thick mud. Duct tape. There was duct tape over my mouth and around my ankles. My wrists were bound, and when I lifted my hands and tried to move, I met resistance. I looked up, squinting into the darkness. Was I chained to a wall?

Panic rose again, sharp and overwhelming. I wanted to flail and scream, but it was so hard to move. Where was I? How did I get there?

More deep breaths. I needed to think, not have a mental breakdown. But why couldn't I seem to fully wake up?

Wait. I knew that feeling. The grogginess, the strange shadows at the corners of my vision, the desire to sink into unconsciousness, or maybe just stare at the wall and float for a while. I'd been drugged.

The football game. We'd been at the high school. I'd gone to the restroom and exited the wrong door, on the far side of the building. No one had been around, and the door to go back in had been locked.

But no. Someone had been there. I just hadn't realized until it was too late.

He'd been so quiet, sneaking up on me like a silent predator. For a second, I'd had the awful realization that it was happening again. Someone had me, and my attempt to fight back was quickly neutralized as I lost consciousness.

I couldn't remember anything after that. I didn't know where I was, or how I'd gotten there. But I had a feeling it involved the trunk of a car.

Anger flared through me, burning away some of the haze. I didn't know how this had happened to me again. Could lightning strike the same person twice? Apparently so. But I'd fought my way out once. I'd just have to do it again.

Fucker didn't know who he was dealing with.

A sound sent a jolt of fear through me. A click, then a slight squeak, like a door opening on old hinges. The creak of stairs. Someone was coming.

"Are you awake?" he asked.

That voice. It sent a chill down my spine. But my stubborn

streak was stronger than the fear or the drugs in my system. I didn't move, even to nod.

His footsteps seemed to disappear, although I could feel him draw closer to me. How was he so freaking quiet? A light flipped on, and I had to squeeze my eyes shut against the brightness.

As he came around the mattress, I blinked, trying to adjust to the light. He peered down at me with something like curiosity in his gaze. He looked oddly plain, almost generic, although he was vaguely familiar. Blond hair cut short, eyes that were a dull blue-gray. No facial hair. Gray T-shirt and jeans. He was wiry rather than bulky, but the memory of his arm around my neck flashed through my mind. He was stronger than he looked.

His mouth turned up in a slow smile. That was when my still groggy brain registered an alarming fact. He was letting me see his face.

That couldn't be a good sign.

"Look at you." His tone was almost reverent. "I've waited so long for this. It's even better than I imagined."

With my mouth taped shut, I couldn't reply, even if I'd wanted to.

Shadows seemed to move behind him, but I couldn't tell if they were real or hallucinations. He had something small and black in his hand, and as he lifted it, he seemed to point it at me. A flash went off.

A camera. He was taking pictures.

I glared at him. If he wanted me afraid, he was going to be disappointed.

Not that I wasn't scared. I was terrified. But screw him. If glaring at him was the only act of defiance I could manage, I'd glare with the fury of a thousand suns.

Lowering the camera, he crouched next to me and tilted his head. "Don't worry. I don't want to hurt you. I didn't want to the first time, but you never gave me the chance to explain."

The first time? Whether it was the drugs in my system or the shock of what he'd just said, it took me a few seconds to process what he was saying.

Was it *him?*

"You really don't remember me, do you?" he asked. "Not from our time together, before, of course. We didn't get this far last time. I underestimated you. Believe me, that won't happen again."

Remember him? How could I remember? The man who'd taken me hadn't shown his face. I'd never seen him. It was why he got away. There'd been no way to find him.

But something tickled at the edges of my memory. That face. I'd seen him before. Where?

"Of course you don't remember." His expression darkened, a spasm of anger distorting his features, and he lowered his voice. "No one remembers me. They don't even see me."

He stood and started to pace back and forth in front of the mattress, opening and closing his fists. "You were supposed to know. I've been waiting for this. I wanted the moment when you knew. When you realized it was me all along."

I watched him while he muttered to himself, still walking back and forth. I didn't know what he wanted from me. He'd taped my mouth shut, what the hell did he expect me to say?

"Fine. I'll show you."

He grabbed the camera and disappeared. The stairs creaked, followed by the soft swish of a door opening. Craning my neck, I could see a set of wooden stairs behind me. The light from the bare bulb hanging from the ceiling hurt my eyes, but I kept watching the door.

A moment later, he came down again, his footfalls making more noise. He crouched and held something in front of my face.

I blinked a few times, trying to get my eyes to focus. It was a playbill, old and slightly faded. Sunset Community Theater presents *P.S. I Adore You*.

I'd been in that play, back when I'd still been doing live theater. In fact, it was the last one I did, because it was right before…

My eyes moved to his face again. I did recognize him. He'd been part of the stage crew. Lighting and effects, maybe? A quiet guy, rarely talked to anyone. In fact, we'd hardly noticed him.

"Yes," he said, his voice low. "You remember now, don't you? We worked together for months. You were the highlight of that job, Melanie. So talented. So beautiful."

Bile burned the back of my throat, and my stomach felt queasy. I really hoped I didn't vomit with tape over my mouth. I'd probably choke to death before this guy could take me out.

There'd be some irony in that, though. The predator watching his intended victim gurgle and suffocate before he could finish the job.

Apparently, my flair for drama wasn't diminished by mortal terror.

Which gave me an idea. Or at least, the beginnings of an idea. I wasn't sure how to make it work, and my brain was still struggling to keep up. I didn't think I'd be able to fight my way out. After my admittedly lucky blow to his nuts the first time, he'd be ready for that. It was why I didn't remember how I got there. He'd kept me unconscious long enough to put me somewhere secure.

But I was a trained actor. Maybe I could use that.

"Unfortunately, there was another man." He stood and tossed the playbill aside, as if it were no longer important to him. "I would have liked to have been able to do things differently, but I knew it would never work. He was a suit. A lawyer who made good money. I was just a lowly stagehand making minimum wage. Not even good enough to be cast in the ensemble."

A lawyer? Had he known about my ex? Jared and I had only just started dating when I'd been in that production.

My confusion must have shown on my face, even with my mouth taped shut.

"Don't look so surprised. Of course I knew about your boyfriend. I probably knew more about him than you did, Melanie. I knew you weren't the only woman. You would have thanked me, eventually. I would have saved you from him."

The fact that Jared might have been cheating on me when we were first dating would have hurt, once. But it didn't even surprise me. And I had much bigger problems.

"I know about your new boyfriend, too."

Don't react. Don't react. I wanted to fly off the mattress and castrate him for just the mention of Luke. But I didn't want him to know that. I wanted him to think I was still groggy. So I kept my face as neutral as possible, just watching, waiting for him to continue.

"I thought I might have to get rid of him. The arrogant jerk wouldn't leave you alone. But he doesn't matter now. I'm sure he'll try to find you, but he won't. I've been careful. And we won't be staying here long anyway."

My stomach churned again. I really wanted the tape off my face. Character voices, each with their own persona, swirled through my head. What did he expect? Even more, what did he want? Who was he hoping I'd be?

Quiet guy. We'd hardly noticed him. *They didn't even see me.*

The stagehand. What was his name? Damn it. He had a weird name. One I'd never heard before.

Roswell.

It popped into my head out of nowhere. I wasn't sure if it

was some kind of auditory hallucination or if I'd actually remembered his name. But it seemed right.

I made a small noise, lifting my voice as if I were trying to ask a question.

Tilting his head again, he blinked. "Don't ask me to untie you. That's not happening."

I gave my head a little shake. I'd be innocent and afraid. A little bit defiant, because he'd expect that, but also in awe of him. He wanted to be seen. Remembered.

He watched me like he was considering what to do next. I let my fear show, pleading with him with my eyes.

After a long moment, he pulled something out of his pocket and held it up.

A syringe.

"Don't try anything." He crouched next to me. "I don't want to put you to sleep again, but I will I if have to."

I nodded.

He ripped the tape off my face. It hurt like hell, but I pressed my lips together, determined not to cry out in pain. My mouth was so dry, I would have given a kidney for a glass of water. Well, not to him. But to someone who really needed one.

When I raised my eyes to meet his, I wasn't Melanie Andolini. I wasn't Queen Ione, with her maniacal laugh and haughty contempt, or the Southern belle with her sass, or any number of other characters I'd played whose voices were still in my head.

I was a damsel in distress. Helpless and docile. Who'd lashed out at him once and scored a lucky shot. But who would quickly learn her place and cooperate.

"Roswell," I whispered.

The grin that stole over his features spoke volumes. I was right about his name and couldn't have chosen a better opening line.

"I don't use that name here. You remember?"

I nodded. "LA. You worked for the Sunset Theater. One of the regulars on the crew."

The second part was a guess, but a reasonable one. Sunset had been known for retaining their crew members rather than hiring new ones for each show.

"That's right." There was a hint of pleasure in his voice.

I kind of hated not having a script for this, but I could ad lib with the best of them. "I thought you didn't like me. You always ignored me."

"No." He lowered himself onto the floor and crossed his legs. "Is that what you thought?"

I nodded.

"Sweet Melanie." He reached out and brushed a lock of hair from my forehead.

It was all I could do not to flinch.

"I never disliked you," he said in that eerie soft voice that made my skin crawl. "I wanted to be close to you, but you were so beautiful. So unapproachable. You weren't the star of that show, but you were the star of mine."

Rude. Way to rub it in that I'd missed out on the lead.

"I followed you. I knew where you went, every day. That coffee shop up the street from the theater before rehearsals. The market on the corner where you bought groceries. I thought about stopping to talk to you, but you never saw me."

"How could I? You were hiding from me."

His mouth lifted in a grin. "I suppose I was."

I shifted, pulling at the bonds at my wrists. "This hurts."

His smile disappeared. "No. I'm not untying you so you can kick me in the balls again."

"I didn't know." The hint of panic in my voice wasn't an act. It was hard to keep from losing it. "I didn't know it was you. You didn't tell me. I didn't see your face."

"No one sees me." He closed his eyes for a moment and took a deep breath. "You'll love me eventually, my sweet

Melanie. You'll learn. I'm a very patient man, and I've been planning this for a long time. There's no need to rush. Eventually you'll understand."

"Understand what?"

"That you're mine."

Those words in Luke's mouth had set me on fire. The same words from that psychopath turned my blood to ice.

"You've always been the one who got away. But you won't get away from me again." He glanced toward the stairs, as if something had caught his attention, and got to his feet. "I'd planned to stay here longer, but I think we're going to have to leave soon. The more I think about it, the more I realize it's the right thing to do. I need to get you away from here."

"Where?"

"That's not your concern." He bent down and met my eyes. "I don't want to hurt you. But I will, if that's what it takes. If you can be a good girl and stay quiet while I go upstairs, I'll bring you a drink of water. If you can't—if you make any noise at all—I won't."

He turned and went back up the stairs, quiet as a whisper.

CHAPTER 37

Luke

AFTER THE LONGEST night of my life, the sun had finally shown its face over the mountain peaks in the east. And Melanie was still missing.

My brothers and I—along with Anton, Nathan, and the Baileys—had spent most of the night searching. We'd checked the area around the high school, my place, hers, my parents', her parents', my shop, the streets downtown. Nothing. No sign of her except that syringe cap.

We'd talked to as many people at the game as possible, but no one remembered seeing anything suspicious. No one hanging around the restrooms or driving out of the parking lot too fast. Certainly no one carrying an unconscious woman and putting her in the trunk of a car.

He'd taken the other victims without a trace, too. The guy was a fucking ghost.

Garrett was at the sheriff's office, doing his job. Which was exactly where I wanted him. He had access to resources I didn't. And I knew my brother. If there was something I needed to know—whether or not he was supposed to tell me —he'd call.

But I also knew law enforcement might not be able to move fast enough.

Sometime in the middle of the night, most people had gone home to catch a few hours of sleep. Feeling angry and helpless, I'd gone to Melanie's parents' place and crashed on their couch. We had no new leads, and there wasn't much we could do in the dark.

Anton, Krista, and I had been up before the sun and come to Home Slice to start organizing the search. People had started showing up soon after, including my brothers and a growing group of SPS members.

I stood next to the table where Anton had a map of the area spread out with broken crayons to mark the search teams. He looked like an old-school general preparing for war. He'd sent my dad and Josiah to search the area around the high school again. Zachary and a few other guys, including some of the Baileys, were heading toward Echo Creek, while another search party had already been sent east of town.

"Once we have a few more people, we'll get a group searching the north end," Anton said, placing a blue crayon on his map.

I nodded my assent, but it was hard to stand still. He kept insisting we had strength in numbers—that if we covered a large enough area, we'd find her. I wanted to share his confidence, but every minute that ticked by increased my dread.

She'd already been gone for hours.

But I didn't have a better plan.

"What about here?" Krista pointed at the map. She'd been strangely calm since Melanie had gone missing. All business.

"There's nothing out there," Anton answered. "Not even any roads."

"No cabins or anything?" she asked.

"The terrain is too rough." He pointed at another area,

closer to Echo Creek. "Here, though. We probably need a second group here."

"What about in town?" she asked. "Why assume he's been taking his victims somewhere isolated?"

"That's the problem," I said. "We don't know. The other victims remember being chained to a wall, but all that tells us is that he has a place to take them. Even if every SPS member shows up to help, we can't check every house in town. Not to mention Echo Creek and Pinecrest."

"Isolated makes the most sense," Anton said. "Otherwise, neighbors would hear."

I was glad he didn't finish his thought out loud—what the neighbors would hear. We knew what he meant.

A few more SPS members showed up. I wandered away from the table while they conferred with Anton. She was my woman, but she was also his daughter. For now, I was letting him take the lead—at least when it came to organizing volunteers.

I paced around the restaurant and checked my phone. I kept hoping Garrett would call with a new lead, a clue, a rumor—anything that would give us some direction. I understood Anton's need to do something, and sending out search teams was certainly better than nothing. But we weren't going to find her that way. Even if the whole town turned out to help look for her, they weren't going to find her if The Whisper had her chained to a wall in some basement.

Theo came in, so I went over to talk to him.

"Any word from Garrett?" he asked.

"Nothing yet."

"Fire department got called out to help with the wildfire. So we lost some guys."

"Fuck," I muttered.

"They weren't happy about it, but I guess the wind picked up or something. It's not threatening Tilikum, but it's getting close to Echo Creek. They might have to evacuate."

"It doesn't even matter." I kept my voice low so the others wouldn't hear me. "I appreciate what everyone's trying to do, and we can't sit around doing nothing. But how did this guy not leave a single clue? How did no one see anything? Hundreds of people were at the game last night."

"It's dark on that side of the parking lot."

"Yeah, and everyone was busy watching Owen kill it on the field."

Anger and fear churned in the pit of my stomach. We'd been through the possibilities at the scene. Whoever he was, he'd taken a big risk. As far as we knew, his other victims had been taken from more isolated places. This had been different. Why?

"Why?" I repeated the thought aloud.

"Why, what?"

"Why did he take her there? Why take anyone right then, when there were people around? Why not grab another jogger or a hiker on a trail or someone coming out of another bar at night?"

"Maybe because we were ready for those things." He paused, his brow furrowing. "Or maybe he's escalating. Isn't that what Garrett said? First victims were at night. Then the others were during the day. Maybe taking a woman from a crowded place was his way of upping the ante."

"Some kind of sick challenge."

The door opened and my heart almost stopped dead in my chest. For a split second, I thought it was Mel. But it wasn't. The woman who walked in had long dark hair and a similar build, but it wasn't Melanie.

Except... I did recognize her. She was Bella Lewis, The Whisper's second victim. There were still signs of bruising on one side of her face and her arm was in a sling.

One of the SPS members rushed to the front to intercept her. Roy Lewis, if I remembered correctly. "Bella, what are you doing here?"

"I want to help, Uncle Roy." Her expression was determined. "There has to be something I can do for her."

I had an almost irresistible urge to hug her. She'd survived the unthinkable, and there she was, full of defiance and strength.

She was also a link to him. The last thing I wanted to do was traumatize her by asking questions. She'd already talked to law enforcement, but if she knew something—anything— that could help us find Melanie…

"You should go back home," Roy said to her.

"No," she said. "Let me help."

"Wait." I put my hand up and walked over to them. "You're one of the survivors, aren't you?"

She nodded.

"He has my girlfriend."

Concern flashed across her features. "You've got to let me help."

"Bella—" her uncle said.

"No. I'm not going home. I can't sit around while this happens to another woman." Her expression darkened. "Someone needs to catch this asshole."

I led her to the first open table, just a few steps behind me, and we both sat. Theo and Roy took the remaining chairs.

"I know you already talked to the police, and I don't want to make you relive it," I said. "But we've got hordes of people out there searching aimlessly."

"It's okay, I can talk about it," she said, her voice clear and strong. "I did talk to the police, and I don't know if there's anything else I can tell you. But I'll try."

"Do you have any sense of where he might have taken you?"

"Not really. I don't remember a lot after he grabbed me."

"Is it okay if I ask about him?"

"Yes, but I didn't see his face. He had a ski mask on the

whole time. He didn't seem very big. Kind of skinny, actually. I was surprised he could carry me as easily as he did."

"You remember being carried inside?"

She nodded. "I was groggy, but awake. My wrists and ankles were bound and there was tape over my mouth. He picked me up out of the trunk and put me over his shoulder. We went inside a building, but I couldn't see much. There were stairs, though, I'm sure of that. Once we were inside, he carried me down a flight of stairs."

"What about the car? Did you get a look at it?"

"I keep trying to remember something about the car that might help, but I was so out of it. I saw it for a second when he put me over his shoulder, but I'm not even sure what color it was."

"And I assume you didn't see anything when he brought you out again."

"No, he drugged me before he even unfastened me from the wall. I don't remember anything. I woke up in the woods."

"The sheriff's department has been searching the areas where the victims were found," Theo said.

"I know, but they're all random. He left them in different places." I rubbed my forehead and raked my fingers through my hair. "Melanie could be anywhere."

"Melanie?" Bella asked. "Is that her name?"

I nodded. "Melanie Andolini.

"That's so weird," she said, her tone taking on a tinge of fear.

"What's weird?"

She opened her mouth, then closed it again with a slight shake of her head. Roy put a reassuring hand on her back.

"Sorry, I didn't remember it until you said that name," she said. "But he was calling me Melanie. He wanted me to answer to it. It made him angry when I didn't do it right."

"He called you Melanie?" I asked.

"I think so. I could be remembering wrong. So much happened and I was so scared."

I looked past her, my eyes unfocused. "It is him."

"It's who?" Roy asked.

I stood, my brain spinning, trying to piece things together. "Anton, I think it's him. I think it's the same guy who took her in LA."

Anton looked up from his map. "Why?"

I walked over to his table. "That's Bella Lewis. She was one of the victims. He called her Melanie and tried to get her to answer to it." Leaning closer, I lowered my voice. "And she looks like Mel. A little bit, don't you think?"

His eyes flicked to Bella. "Similar."

"Even if you're right, what does that tell us?" Krista asked.

"It tells us she was the target all along." I started pacing again while I thought it through. "And it tells us he's not a local. He followed her here."

"How?" Krista asked. "And why now? It was eleven years ago."

"I don't know. Right now, there's no way to know what he's been doing for the last eleven years. But I think he came here to finish what he started." I kept moving, walking back and forth between Bella's table and Anton's. "Melanie moved back in June, and the abductions started after that. But that doesn't help much. Tilikum is crawling with tourists all summer. One more new face wouldn't stand out."

"If he's an out-of-towner and he followed her here, where's he staying?" Theo asked. "Rentals book up for the summer at least six months in advance. Just ask Josiah. How did he get a place?"

"Good question. It would have to be something off the beaten path. Not in town." I stopped and looked at Bella. "You said you woke up when you were still in the car?"

She nodded.

"Any idea how long you were in there?"

"No, I don't know how long I was unconscious."

"Do you remember anything else about being in the trunk?" I asked. "Was it big or were you cramped?"

"Cramped." She paused, her forehead creasing. "I think I woke up because I was bouncing around so much. But that stopped, and the road got smoother again. Not smooth like a highway. But better than the bumpy part."

"Gravel road, probably," Theo said.

"I'm not sure if it was." Bella paused again, her eyes on the table like she was trying hard to remember. "Gravel roads can be bumpy, but this was different. We kept going up and down, up and down, like he was driving over something. It was rhythmic, not random like potholes or driving off-road."

For a moment, I stared at her, and my ribs ached with remembered pain. "Did it feel like driving over railroad ties? Like following the actual tracks?"

"Yeah, that's exactly it," she said. "The bumps were regular, in a pattern like a railroad track."

"I think I know where that is," I said, not sure who I was really talking to. My mind was racing, trying to remember exactly where that had been.

"Where?" Theo and Anton asked at the same time.

"There's a railroad bridge near the old racetrack. Has to be out of service. I don't think it connects to anything. The guy who drove me to the hospital took us over it, said it was a shortcut to Echo Creek. I thought it was going to kill me."

"Where is it?" Anton asked.

I hurried over to his map and pointed. "The racetrack is roughly here. There are a couple of old dirt roads that lead to it from the highway, but obviously they're not on here."

Tilting my head and gazing at the map, I tried to make sense of the hazy memories from the night of the crash. Which way had we gone?

"It's gotta be around here." I pointed at a thin blue line

that snaked across the terrain outside Echo Creek. "It was dark, so I couldn't see much, but the bridge crossed over a ravine. There could be a creek at the bottom. Over on this side, it's pretty flat. There could easily be a hunting cabin or something in this area."

"Maybe even something abandoned," Anton said.

"Luke," Theo said, and the alarm in his voice caught my attention.

"What?"

"That's where the fire's headed."

He handed me his phone, open to a map of active wildfires. The main burn was east of there, but if it was moving toward Echo Creek, that bridge—and any dwellings in the area—were right in its path.

Without a word, I tossed Theo his phone and ran for the door.

Questions were shouted at my back, but I didn't have time to answer. In seconds, I was in my car, tires peeling out in the parking lot.

I didn't know if I was right. Maybe the bridge was a dead end. I'd have to trust Garrett and his crew—and everyone else who was looking for her—to act if they discovered better information. If the trail led somewhere else, they'd follow it.

But that psycho had her, and if I was right, the fire was headed straight for them.

CHAPTER 38
Melanie

THE COMBINATION of thirst and a full bladder were almost unbearable. My mouth was so dry, my tongue felt thick and sticky. And if I didn't pee soon, my bladder was going to pop like an overly full water balloon.

I had no real sense of time, but it seemed like Roswell had been gone for hours. And while my head was clearing as the drugs wore off, thank goodness, I still found myself zoning out occasionally. But as the minutes ticked by, and my discomfort grew, the sensation of being disconnected abated.

Did he *want* me to pee my pants? Because that's where things were headed.

The chain holding me to the wall didn't have much slack. And no way could I break the duct tape around my wrists. He'd wound and twisted it, securing me to the chain. After my first abduction, I'd practiced breaking zip tie and duct tape bonds. I'd gotten pretty good at it. But I hadn't accounted for the lack of mobility from being chained to a stupid wall.

I was able to move around enough that I'd taken stock of the room. Not that there much to see. Based on the window set high in the wall, and the musty smell, I was in a basement. The floor was finished—some kind of vinyl—but the walls looked like plain plywood. There was a small bathroom in the corner, but it didn't appear to have a door.

The subtle creak of the stairs made my back clench and my stomach churn. I maneuvered myself onto my other side so I could see.

Roswell came down the stairs carrying a water bottle with a straw. I wanted it so badly I was willing to do... not anything. But a whole lot of things I wouldn't under different circumstances. Beg being the foremost among them.

He crouched and tilted his head, gazing at me with those dull gray eyes. "You've been quiet, just like I told you."

I decided more silence was likeliest to get me a drink of that water, so I just nodded.

"Good girl." He held out the bottle and put the straw to my lips.

It took an enormous amount of self-control not to fight back in defiance. To spit on the bottle instead of drink from it and refuse to cooperate with anything he said. But that wasn't going to get me out of there. I had to stay in character—be the damsel in distress. And my mouth didn't have any spit.

Lifting my head, I winced at a stab of pain in my neck. I took a small sip from the straw, hoping it was water. It didn't taste like anything else, so I took another.

"Is that better?" he asked, his voice eerily soft.

I nodded again and laid my head back down on the mattress.

He smiled, as if he were pleased with himself. Or me. It was hard to tell.

What I needed to do was turn this thing around somehow. Keep him feeling like he was in control but get him to give me something I wanted. The bathroom was a good enough place to start. It wasn't merely a want, it was becoming a desperate need.

I raised my eyes to meet his. "Thank you."

"You're welcome."

"Roswell?"

He lifted his eyebrows.

"I feel shy about asking this, but…"

"It's all right. What do you want to ask?"

I lowered my gaze, as if I were embarrassed. I was about to say, *I need to use the bathroom,* but at the last second, I decided to phrase it as a request. "May I please use the bathroom?"

"Of course. I'll be right back."

He disappeared up the stairs. I knew it wouldn't be my opportunity for escape. I wanted him to think he could trust me—that he could give me more freedom.

But I also knew what he'd done to his other victims. He'd killed the last one.

Was that why I was there? Was he planning to kill me?

He came back down, quiet as ever, and knelt beside the mattress. Using a small pocketknife, he cut through the duct tape, freeing me from the chain, but kept my wrists and ankles bound.

"I'll help you up." He took my hands and hoisted me to my feet.

With my ankles tied, I couldn't walk. He seemed to have already thought it through and picked me up like a baby, with one arm behind my back and the other behind my knees. I wasn't overweight by any means, but I had some curves, and he carried me to the bathroom like it was effortless.

Definitely stronger than he looked.

He set me down in front of the doorway. "I took the door down. Maybe in our next place, if you're a good girl, you can have a door."

It was a half bath with a pedestal sink and toilet. Nothing I could use to hit him over the head. No surprise there. He'd obviously put a lot of thought into everything.

My bladder screamed at me, but I also had an idea. I did

not want this guy pulling my pants down. But letting him would go a long way toward convincing him I wasn't a flight risk.

"Roswell? I, um… I need your help."

His face lit up with a smile.

Bingo. The damsel was exactly who he wanted me to be.

He came over and paused, his hands poised near my waist. By the shuddering breath he took, he was totally getting off on the prospect of touching me.

I took slow breaths through my nose. *Don't punch him in the face. Don't punch him in the face.*

Yet.

He pulled my pants down, and thankfully, he stepped back. Turning sideways, he looked toward the stairs, apparently to give me privacy.

Lowering myself onto the toilet was tricky, but I managed, and even with Roswell standing right there, I had no trouble releasing my bladder. The rest of the process was awkward, and it made my skin crawl to turn my back to him to wash my hands, but I was glad it no longer felt like my internal organs were going to burst.

Like a compliant child, I lifted my arms out of the way and let him pull up my pants, my nose wrinkling at the scent of cigarettes. How hard would I have to hit him to knock him out? A blow to the temple was probably my best bet, but would I have the chance? I'd only get one shot. If I tried and failed, I didn't know what he'd do to me.

Still, I noted the presence of the knife in his pocket. And I assumed he still had a full syringe handy.

"Feel better?"

"Yes. Thank you."

He reached out and held his hand next to my face but hesitated. Without breaking character, I leaned my cheek into his palm.

"Don't worry," he said. "I'm going to take such good care of you."

I didn't trust myself to look him in the eyes, so I kept my gaze on the floor. But I nodded.

He smiled at me, his face full of twisted affection. I didn't know how far I could push him before he got angry or how long I had before he assaulted me in one way or another. One thing I did know—I couldn't let him move me. I needed to get away before he took me somewhere else. Somewhere farther away and more difficult to find.

Which meant I needed to get out of these bonds. I couldn't ask him to untie me yet, but maybe I could convince him to give me something else I wanted. Take some of my power back while still making him feel like he was in control.

"Roswell?" I asked in my damsel voice.

He lowered his hand. "Yes, Melanie?"

"I'm hungry."

"I thought you might be soon." He picked me up again and set me down on the mattress—seated, instead of lying down. "I'll be right back."

He didn't chain me to the wall, but I could hear him lock the basement door at the top of the stairs. It wasn't time to make my move, so I didn't try to get up. I'd be right where he left me.

A minute or two later, he came back down with a bag of potato chips and a small plastic bowl in his hands. By his expression, I could tell he was pleased to find me sitting in the same spot. He sat next to me, opened the bag, and poured some into the bowl, then held it out to me.

I took the bowl and positioned it between my knees, but didn't take a chip. I felt like my damsel in distress character needed a bit more credibility—a reason I was being so docile.

"You were right about him," I said.

"About whom?"

"The guy. The lawyer. It was awful." I kept my eyes downcast. "He was terrible to me."

Roswell let out an angry breath. "I knew it. I knew he would be."

"You don't want to hurt me, do you? The way he did?"

"No." He put his hand on my back. "I don't want to hurt you like he did. I told you, I want to take care of you."

"Did you hurt those other women? Was that you?"

"I had to. They were part of the process. You don't need to worry about them." He paused for a moment, as if deciding how much to tell me. "It was their fault. I would have just let them go if they'd done what I said."

"But you're not going to let me go, are you?"

"Melanie, I did all of this for you. So I could have you. So we could be together."

Well, that was the creepiest thing anyone had ever said to me in my entire life. A sick feeling spread through my stomach. I wasn't sure what was worse, being abducted by someone who wanted to kill me, or someone who wanted to keep me.

Stay in character, Mel. Keep up the act.

"I was going to break up with the guy in Tilikum," I lied. "I just hadn't done it yet."

"Good." He rubbed slow circles across my back. "You were more ready for me than I thought."

My heart started to race in anticipation of what I was about to do next. If he'd watched me all those years ago, he knew I wasn't quiet and meek. All too quickly, he was going to realize it was all an act.

Plus, I felt like I needed to push him. Get under his skin. Mess with his head.

"These aren't the chips I like," I said.

"What?"

That had caught him off guard. Good.

"I don't like these."

He hesitated, and my heart beat so hard, I was surprised he couldn't hear it. I kept myself still, breathing through my nose so my body language didn't give away my fear.

"Just eat them," he said, finally.

I lifted my gaze to his and looked him dead in the eyes, my lower lip protruding in a slight pout. "I need something else."

His brow furrowed in confusion. "Melanie—"

Grabbing the bowl with my bound hands, I threw it across the room. As it clattered against the far wall, I collapsed onto the mattress, twisting away from Roswell, and started to sob.

"I can't eat those," I said between shuddering breaths. "I can't."

"But…"

I kept crying, tucking my knees so I was in the fetal position and balling my fists against my eyes. "I'm so hungry."

"Okay, okay," he said, a hint of alarm in his tone. "You don't need to cry. I'll be right back."

Instead of creeping up the stairs on silent feet, he hurried, his footfalls echoing in the mostly empty room.

As soon as the door shut behind him, I took a break from my pretend tantrum. Propping myself up on my forearms, I glanced around again. The bowl was still on the floor, surrounded by broken chips. A plastic bowl wasn't going to be of any use to me, so I didn't bother trying to retrieve it.

I could hear Roswell's footsteps upstairs. I was surprised he'd given in so easily, although I wasn't going to assume a little display of hysterics would get him to untie me. Still, it might be something I could use again.

A scent tickled my nose. What did I smell? It was almost like a faint whiff of campfire. He couldn't be up there cooking, could he? And it wasn't the scent of burning food on the stove or in the oven.

The smell didn't last, disappearing as quickly as it had

come, replaced by the basement mustiness. Maybe I'd imagined it.

As soon as Roswell opened the door, I lay down, curling into a ball. My eyes were still wet with tears, and I sniffed loudly, as if I'd been crying the entire time.

"Melanie?" He sat on the mattress. "Sit up."

Because I was nothing if not a drama queen, I didn't. Just curled up into a tighter ball and let out a whimper.

He touched my back again. "I brought food. Aren't you hungry?"

I turned over, and he helped me into a sitting position. He had indeed brought food. In fact, he'd made a sandwich.

Why I found that so funny—considering I was still tied up and at the mercy of a murderer—I have no idea, but I almost laughed out loud. One little tantrum and he'd gone from offering me no-effort snack food to preparing a meal. A simple meal, to be sure, but it had worked.

I thought about asking him to free my hands so I could eat, but my instincts told me I should wait. The damsel would be sweet, compliant, and thankful. For now. I just needed a little more time, and I was pretty sure I could convince him to untie me.

The hint of campfire tickled my nose again, but I was too preoccupied with my makeshift plan—and staying in character—to pay attention to it.

As long as he didn't try to move me too soon, I might have a chance to get away.

CHAPTER 39

Luke

I RACED down the highway in my Chevelle, heedless of the speed limit, taking every turn as fast as I dared. My ribs ached and my neck was knotted with tension, but I ignored them both. My discomfort didn't matter. I just had to get to her.

The sun had long since risen over the mountain peaks, but the sky was thick with a dingy haze. Wildfire smoke. It got worse the farther south I went. I didn't see the actual fire—it was too far east of the road—but I could tell I was getting closer.

My plan was to drive to Echo Creek and backtrack from there, finding the road that Kyle had taken after my crash. That would be faster than going all the way to the old race-track and following the dirt road to the bridge. I didn't want to waste a minute.

Echo Creek was about a thirty-minute drive from Tilikum —if you were going the speed limit. As long as I didn't get pulled over, I was going to make it in a lot less than that. So far, luck had been on my side. I didn't give a shit about a ticket, I just didn't want to stop.

Ash swirled through the air, and I had to turn on the

windshield wipers a few times to deal with the buildup. Urgency flared in my gut. If the fire was bearing down on them, would he know? Would they have any warning?

I was approaching a sharp bend in the road, so despite my desire to keep it floored, I had to let off the gas. Blue flashes of light seemed to glint off the haze and I slowed down just in time. As I came around the corner, the road was blocked by a police car.

Slamming on the brakes, I came to a stop, hope and dread surging in equal measure. Had they found something?

Had they found her?

I rolled down my window as an Echo Creek police officer walked over to my car.

"Sorry, sir, the highway is closed."

"Did you find her?" I asked.

His brow furrowed, like he had no idea what I was talking about. "Find who?"

"Melanie Andolini. She's missing from Tilikum. The Whisper got her."

"No. I'm just here to stop people from going through. Highway's closed due to the fire."

"It's this close?"

"It hasn't hit the highway yet, but the winds aren't on our side. Echo Creek is under stage three evacuation."

"Listen, I need to get by. I think I know where he took her."

"Sorry, sir, I can't let you do that."

"Do you even know what I'm talking about? The Whisper, the guy who's been abducting women? He has my girlfriend, and I think I know where they are."

He glanced over his shoulder, like he wasn't sure what to do. "I really can't let anyone through. It's for your safety."

I was about to tell him to call Garrett, but I didn't want to wait. And if the fire was that close, I might not be able to get through from that direction anyway.

"All right, I'll turn around." I rolled up my window and the cop backed away toward his vehicle.

Since there was no other traffic, I did a U-turn in the middle of the highway. Despite my deepening sense of urgency, I didn't floor it. I needed to find a turn. Another road that would lead me in the direction I needed to go.

Toward the fire? Probably. Toward Melanie? I hoped so.

I followed the highway back northward, watching for a road leading in the direction I wanted to go. There was a web of old logging roads in the area, crisscrossing the forest through the low hills at the base of the taller mountain peaks. I'd been through them a million times, exploring the wilderness, dirt biking when we were younger, and even off-road racing. I just had to hope I could find a way through that didn't lead me miles in the wrong direction.

Finally, I came to an almost invisible dirt road stretching off into an area of sparse pine trees. I turned, slowing so my car would handle the bumps and I wouldn't accidentally drive over a fallen log or other large debris.

The road continued straight for a while. I needed to turn south and debated going off-road and cutting through the trees. But something told me to wait, and after topping a low rise, the land went down again, and the road forked—one side turning south.

My tires spit dust into the dry air as I flew around the corner. The trees opened up, and the land rose and fell in a series of hills. Ash drifted down from an increasingly smoke-filled sky, and I wondered if I would run headlong into the fire or the wildland firefighters working to contain it.

A string of possibilities ran through my mind as I navigated the narrow dirt road. What if the wildland crew found his hiding place? Would they have any idea he was holding Melanie hostage? What if he fled with her, either to avoid discovery or to get away from the fire? How would I find her then? They might already be long gone.

Or what if he had no idea the fire was coming, and I didn't get there until it was too late. A forest fire could rip through an area in minutes, trapping anyone who hadn't left.

No. That wasn't happening. He would not have time to hurt her, and she was not going to die in that fucking fire.

The danger to the woman I loved sharpened my senses. Adrenaline flowed through my veins, but it was a tool, not a drug. My grip on the steering wheel was supple, rather than tight. The world seemed to slow, the roar of the engine fading into the background, and every obstacle stood out.

The road curved to the left and a fallen branch appeared, almost out of nowhere. I swerved hard, avoiding it, leaving more dust in my wake. I had to make snap decisions whether rocks or other debris were passable. It was like navigating the track amid a host of other drivers, some of whom wouldn't hesitate to clip you.

Emerging from a narrow thicket, I pushed my speed, almost catching air as I went over another hill. A loud roar almost made me slam on my brakes. Was there another car? I looked around but didn't see anything, even as the noise grew.

Glancing up, I saw a plane flying over the treetops. It was a water scooper, an aircraft designed to skim the surface of a body of water and drop it onto a wildfire. It was flying at low altitude, which probably meant I was getting dangerously close to the fire.

Didn't matter. I had to find Melanie.

With the sun obscured by the smoke in the air, it was tough to keep track of my direction. The road forked again, and I slowed to a stop. Which way? Leaning forward, I looked out the windshield, trying to find the sun.

Like a song surging into my brain out of nowhere, Melanie's evil queen voice popped into my head. *The glove box, you imbecile.*

"Thomas," I said out loud and opened the glove box.

The blue drawstring bag with the present he'd given me was still there. I got it out and dumped the contents onto the seat. The toy Lambo and the flashlight rolled toward the seat-back. I grabbed the compass and opened it, hoping it actually worked. The needle wobbled a bit, then settled. The right fork led south.

"Buddy, I'm going to have to help pay for your college or something," I said as I hit the gas and turned right. "You might have just saved my ass."

Using the compass, I navigated the back roads through a thicker section of forest where the pine trees crowded the road on either side. There was room for me to pass, but only just. I had to hold tight to the center of the road, otherwise I risked hitting the branches. Scratches were one thing—didn't care—but a large branch could take out my windshield if I wasn't careful.

Finally, I emerged on a wider section of road. The trees thinned out and another road joined the one I was on—coming from the direction of Echo Creek.

Was I on the road that led to the bridge?

Pushing my speed, I went as fast as I dared under the conditions. Birds flew overhead—hundreds of them going in the opposite direction. Probably fleeing the fire. If things had been different, I would have worried about driving in the opposite direction of a mass exodus of wildlife. I was heading straight into danger, and I did not care.

Finally, I saw it. The old railroad bridge. There was nothing on either side—no wall or guardrail—and the ravine plunged down to the creek bed below. I had to slow down just to get across and it was every bit as bumpy as I remembered. Rhythmic bumps, just like Bella had said. This had to be right.

With my teeth rattling in my skull, I made it across. With every foot of ground I covered, the smoke got worse. The fire was getting closer. Not far from the other side of the bridge, I saw what I'd been hoping to find—a turn. If I went left, I'd wind up at the old racetrack. But turn right, and hopefully I'd find Melanie.

With my heart in my throat and ash falling from the sky, I took the turn and drove as fast as I dared.

CHAPTER 40
Melanie

WITH MY WRISTS and ankles still bound, I dutifully ate some of the sandwich Roswell had made me. I wasn't actually hungry, and it was hard to swallow around the lump of fear in my throat, but somehow, I pulled it off.

The worst part was the way he watched me, his dull gray eyes intent on my face and the trace of a smile on his lips. He seemed to be enjoying himself, which made me want to throw the sandwich at him.

But I stayed in character. The damsel was happy with what he'd brought her.

"Thank you," I said, putting the rest of the sandwich back on the plate. "I'm finished."

He slid the plate out of the way and gave me another drink of water.

Without meeting his gaze, I shifted on the mattress and fidgeted to make it clear that being tied up was uncomfortable.

"What time is it?" I asked.

"Don't worry about that."

Keeping my face lowered, I nodded. "What's going to happen next?"

He ran a finger down my arm and, as abhorrent as it was, I didn't flinch away. "It's hard to keep myself from you."

Bile burned the back of my throat again. *Stay in character. Stay in character.* "I'm not ready yet."

"Yet?"

"I need you to understand, I've been through a lot. These last few months have been so hard. I went from one bad relationship to another. I didn't know how to get out."

"But that's the thing, my sweet Melanie. I got you out. I rescued you."

Nodding again, I slowly lifted my gaze to meet his. "You did."

"We're going to leave. I'm going to take you far, far away from here. Once we get there, we can start over. We'll be together, and you won't have to worry about anything ever again. You just have to be good for me, and I'll take care of you."

"I can be good."

"I know you can." He traced his finger along my arm again. "You'll be my good girl forever."

Like hell I would. I was nobody's good girl, least of all his.

Drumming up some silent tears, I let them fall down my cheeks. When he didn't seem to notice immediately, I sniffed.

"What's wrong? Are you still hungry?"

I shook my head and kept crying.

"Then what is it?"

"I'm fine."

His brow furrowed. "You don't seem fine. You're crying."

"I'm fine," I said again, my tone more insistent, and I twisted my wrists, pulling at the duct tape.

"I don't understand."

Time for another outburst.

"This hurts," I sobbed, thrusting my arms out toward him. "Why are you doing this to me?"

"Melanie." His tone was stern, but I didn't miss the hint of doubt in the background. "I can't let you free yet."

Twisting away from him, I collapsed onto the mattress and went fetal again. "I thought you wanted to help me. You were supposed to save me, not hurt me like they did."

"Like who did?"

"My exes. I thought you were supposed to be different, but you're not."

"No, Melanie, that's not what's happening."

"Yes, it is." I took my hysterics down to a whimper. "Why aren't you different? Why aren't you better than them?"

He was silent for a long moment. I stayed curled up in a ball, hoping I hadn't pushed too hard. I didn't want to make him angry, just confused and off-kilter.

I didn't bother suppressing the shudder as he leaned close to my ear.

"You're mine, Melanie," he whispered. "Don't ever forget that."

Reaching over me, he grabbed my hands. I rolled onto my back so I could stretch my arms out. Oh my god, it was working. He had the pocketknife. He was going to cut the duct tape.

Something seemed to catch his attention. He paused, the knife still poised in one hand, and his gaze darted toward the stairs. I scarcely dared to breathe. Had he heard something?

Had someone found me?

Roswell's eyes widened in alarm. He closed the knife and stuffed it back in his pocket, then grabbed the duct tape and tore a piece off.

"No," I pleaded. "No, please—"

Before I could even think about how to resist, he'd taped my mouth shut again.

"Be quiet." He wound more tape around my wrists and re-fastened me to the chain. "I'll be right back."

There was a faint noise upstairs that might have been

knocking. It was hard to tell. Roswell ran up and shut the basement door behind him. I had no idea if he'd locked it, but it wasn't like it mattered. I couldn't get free.

Please be help. Please be help.

Another noise sounded like voices, but after a second, I realized he'd turned on a TV or music or something. Probably to drown me out if I decided to yell. With my mouth taped shut, any semblance of a scream would have been too muffled to hear anyway. I just had to hope it was law enforcement, and they searched the place.

I couldn't be certain, but I might have heard Roswell talking to someone. The noise was dull, and everything seemed to mingle together. My heart beat wildly in my chest and it took every ounce of my self-control not to completely lose it.

Breathe in. Out. In and out.

After what felt like an eternity—what was he doing up there?—the basement door opened. I looked, desperately hoping to see people in uniform descending to get me out of this mess.

My heart sank right through the floorboards and into the ground below. It was Roswell.

"We have to go," he said on his way down the stairs. "The fire is getting close."

The scent of smoke followed him. He crouched in front of me and ripped the tape off my face.

"I'm sorry, Melanie. I didn't want to have to do that. But I can't let them take you away from me."

"Who was it?" I asked.

"Firefighters. They're evacuating the area."

"But they don't know I'm here, do they?" I tried to make it sound like I hoped they didn't.

"No. They left, but we have to go."

"Where are we going?"

He huffed out a frustrated breath as he cut me loose from

the chain, leaving my wrists bound together. "I don't know yet. I haven't had a chance to make the proper arrangements. We were supposed to stay here until you were ready."

Now. I had to get him to untie me now.

I met his eyes and lifted my arms, holding my wrists out to him. "It'll be easier for us to get away."

He hesitated, his gaze moving from my face to my bound wrists.

The tears that filled my eyes weren't an act. They were real —tears of desperation. I had no idea if another tantrum would get him to untie me or if he'd decide he was tired of my antics and just drug me again. But I had to risk it.

"Fine, just leave me here," I sobbed. "You might as well let me die."

"I'm not leaving you."

I rolled away, curling into a ball. "I stayed quiet when you answered the door. I didn't even try to make noise. And you don't trust me enough to let me walk on my own. Just go."

"We don't have time for this. We have to get out."

Making no move to reply, I kept crying. He let out a frustrated growl, and I was sure I'd feel the prick of a needle. I'd gone too far.

But I hadn't. He moved around me, grabbed my arms, and sliced through the tape. Then he did the same to my ankles.

As much as I wanted to throttle him in every way possible, I didn't. I was lying down with no leverage. I'd only get one shot. I had to time it just right.

So, I stayed in character. The damsel in distress didn't get up. She wiped her eyes and smiled gratefully at her captor as if he'd just given her everything she'd ever wanted.

"Thank you," I whispered.

He grabbed my hands and helped me to my feet.

Hesitating, he held my eyes and shifted his weight slightly. I could read him like a book. He was waiting to see if I was going to kick him in the balls again.

As much as I wanted to, he was ready for it.

When I didn't lash out at him, he smiled and grabbed my wrist. "Let's go."

I let him lead me up the stairs and through the door. It opened into a small kitchen with an olive-green refrigerator and range and only a scrap of counter space. A black wood stove, the kind with a cooktop, sat on the other side. The air was smokier upstairs, even indoors, and through the window there was nothing but white haze.

Without letting go of my wrist, he paused to grab a set of keys and stuffed them in his jeans pocket.

My eyes darted around, looking for something I could use to get away. Anything. The remnants of his sandwich making were still on the counter, but paper plates and a loaf of bread wouldn't do me any good.

"Do you need to pack your things?" I asked, hoping he'd let go for even a minute.

"I already put what I need in the car. The rest can burn."

Burn. The wood stove. Was there anything—

"Let's go," he said, tugging on my wrist.

I couldn't let him put me in that car. I was dead if he did. Desperation and panic tightened my chest. Without really meaning to, I took a gasping breath, my control slipping. The breath turned into a cough, and Roswell's eyes widened in alarm.

Running with it, I bent forward, pretending to have a coughing fit, as if the smoke was already too much. It wasn't, but I put on a good show, and Roswell let go of my wrist.

Without hesitation, I lunged for the wood stove. There was a set of black tongs and a poker in a stand beside it. I grabbed the poker, spun around, and with as much strength as I could, I hit Roswell on the side of the head.

He crumpled to the ground, and on the edge of blind panic, I ran.

Still holding the fireplace poker, I flew out the door into

the smoke-filled air. As I passed the car, I wished I'd had the chance to get his keys. But they were in his pocket, and there was no way I was going back. Maybe I could get to the fire-fighters. I didn't know where they were, but at least one had been there.

I could hardly think. All the terror of the past day rose up, dark and overwhelming. I didn't know where I was going or what to do next. I just had to get away.

So I ran.

CHAPTER 41

Melanie

FILLED with fear and with smoke stinging my eyes, I raced down the uneven dirt road. For all I knew, I was heading toward the fire. Visibility was low, the trees shrouded by a thick haze of gray, and ash fell from the sky.

My throat was dry and scratchy. I wasn't going to be able to run for long in the smoke. Should I turn off the road? Go into the trees? I had no idea if I'd knocked Roswell unconscious, and if I had, I didn't know how long he'd stay that way. He had a car. He could catch up to me any second. Somewhere along the way—probably right outside the cabin—I'd dropped the fireplace poker, so I no longer had a weapon.

If I left the road, I'd probably get lost. Was lost in the woods in wildfire territory better than held captive by a man who wanted to keep me for his pet?

Yeah, it kinda was.

My throat tightened. Stopping, I ducked behind a tree before the coughing fit overtook me. The dry, acrid air was brutal on my airways, and it took me a moment to catch my breath.

A noise came out of the gloom. It sounded like the rumble

of an engine. Bracing myself against the trunk, I took another ragged breath as I listened. Where was it coming from? Was it Roswell?

I was about to dart away through the trees, anything to get away from Roswell, when I realized it wasn't coming from the cabin. Someone was approaching from the other direction.

Firefighters again? Would they come back?

I didn't know, and I didn't particularly care. I stepped out into the road so I could wave them down. Headlights gleamed through the smoke, and a second later, a blue muscle car appeared.

Tires skidded, kicking up dust into the smoky air as the car came to an abrupt stop. I froze in place, mid wave, and my eyes widened with shock.

It definitely wasn't firefighters.

The driver's side door swung open, and Luke flew out of the car. Without a second's hesitation, he ran to me, scooping me up in his arms. My feet dangled above the ground, and his strong arms held me tight.

"Luke?" I asked, scarcely able to believe he was real. "You found me."

With his arms still around me, holding me close, he set me down and pulled back just enough to look at me. "Are you hurt?"

"Not really. How did you find me?"

"It's a long story." He cupped my cheeks and planted a hard kiss on my lips. "We need to get out of here."

The sound of another vehicle carried in the air. It was coming from behind me—from the direction of the cabin.

My eyes widened with fear. Luke's narrowed with resolve.

Without a word, we raced to the car and got in. I tugged on the seat belt and fastened it while he backed up to turn around in the tight space.

"I hit him with a fireplace poker, but I don't know if I

knocked him out or what," I said. "He had the car keys in his pocket."

Luke nodded. He made a quick forward maneuver, backed up a couple feet, then cranked the steering wheel and got the car turned around. A second later, we were on our way.

His eyes flicked to the rearview mirror. I twisted to look behind us and saw the flash of headlights approaching through the smoke.

"Faster," I said. "Go faster."

He didn't respond. He faced straight ahead, and his jaw was tight as his hands gripped the steering wheel.

I looked back. Roswell was catching up.

We bounced around with every bump, and Luke let go of the steering wheel with one hand to grab the seat belt and wrench it across his body. I took it and clicked it in place so he could keep driving. We hit another bump, and if we hadn't been strapped in, we probably would have banged our heads on the ceiling.

My heart raced, and my throat still hurt from running in the smoke. Bracing myself with both hands, I tried not to shriek in terror every time a tree branch jutted out over the road or debris seemed to block our path. Luke handled it all with expert finesse, steering around every obstacle without crashing into anything.

A jolt hit us from behind, and I whipped around. Roswell had bumped Luke's car.

"Is he trying to run us off the road?" I asked.

Luke kept his eyes straight ahead, and his voice was calm. "Yep."

"He goes from chaining me to a wall so he can keep me forever to trying to kill me."

"If he can't have you, no one can."

Luke was right. I could almost hear the words as if Roswell were whispering in my ear: *You're mine.*

A shudder ran down my spine.

"Shit," Luke said under his breath.

"What?"

"Hold on to something."

I braced myself again as he took a sudden turn, then glanced behind us again.

"He's still there."

"I know. But if I went straight, we'd have to cross an old bridge with no sides or railings."

My stomach dropped. And Roswell could have hit us from behind again and sent us careening over the edge.

No thanks.

"But there's a problem with this road," Luke said.

"Other than the man trying to kill us?"

"Yeah. I think we're heading straight for the fire."

"Get pushed off a bridge or drive into a wildfire. I don't like these options."

He cast a glance at me. "I'll get us through."

I nodded. "I trust you."

Adjusting his grip on the steering wheel, he pushed on the gas, and we surged forward.

The smoke thickened, turning a darker gray, and the road curved, winding through trees and up and over hills. I'd lost all sense of direction, but I meant what I'd said. I trusted Luke to get us through.

Roswell hit us again. I jerked in my seat, but Luke maintained control. Another bump threw me forward, the seat belt digging into my collarbone.

"Fucker," Luke muttered. "Hold on again."

I braced myself as he took a hard right. Looking backward, I was hoping to at least see some distance between us and Roswell, but he was right there, bearing down on us through the dust and smoke.

The world seemed to go dark, as if the sun had set. The smell of smoke was intense, and my eyes felt the sting of it.

When we rounded the next corner, it looked like we were heading straight into hell itself.

Massive clouds of black smoke billowed into the air, and the entire forest on both sides of the road glowed red. Flames licked the sky from the tops of trees in the distance, and the ground all around was scorched.

"Can we get through?" I asked.

"We can make it."

Roswell bumped us from behind, and the car jerked to one side before Luke regained control.

"Asshole!" I yelled. Not that he could hear me. But I'd played the part of the damsel in distress for too long. I had a lot of pent-up rage. "I hate you and your stupid face!"

"There's my girl."

Roswell hit us again—harder—and we narrowly missed the smoldering remains of a tree.

We crested a hill, and as we started to come down the other side, the red glow intensified.

"This looks worse," I said. "Sorry, I shouldn't keep talking."

"It's okay. I'll get us out."

Pressing my lips together and keeping myself braced in case Roswell hit us again, I watched as Luke navigated the scorched road. Ash whirled in the air, and some of the trees were still burning, the flames bathing the forest in an eerie orange light.

Luke swerved to one side, then to the other. I looked back. Roswell kept surging forward, trying to smash into us. My heart felt like it might burst, and my stomach was sick with fear.

Roswell sped closer, and Luke veered aside just in time. The road took a sudden turn, and just as we darted around the bend, Roswell seemed to miss, his tires skidding on the uneven ground and spitting dirt behind him. I gasped as his car slammed straight into a burning tree.

My eyes widened, and I clapped a hand over my mouth as the tree broke, the tall trunk smashing the top of Roswell's car.

"Holy shit," Luke said.

Slowly, I turned around, my eyes still wide with shock. "I don't think he's making it out of that."

"Probably didn't survive the impact."

I put my hand to my chest. I didn't know whether to feel relieved, horrified, or just stick with abject terror, since we were still on the edge of a raging wildfire with no end in sight.

"Hang in there, baby," Luke said. "I think we're almost through."

Another road branched off, and Luke took the turn. Around another bend, and over the top of a low hill, the trees returned to normal. Some showed signs of scorching on their trunks, but their branches were intact, and the worst of the smoke was behind us.

"Do you have any idea where we are?" I asked.

"Actually, yes. This should take us back to the highway. Probably south of the closure, but at this point, it doesn't matter."

Leaning my head back, I took a few deep breaths. Although the road was still bumpy, Luke was able to slow down, and it wasn't long before we came to the highway. I'd never been so happy to see pavement in my life.

He stopped on the shoulder, unfastened both our seat belts, and hauled me across the bench seat into his arms. We stayed there for long moments, just breathing. Gratitude overwhelmed me until I found myself sobbing into his chest. Not the fake sobs of the damsel trying to manipulate her captor, but the relief of having survived and knowing that an evil man would never hurt anyone again.

It was over.

After a long embrace, Luke called Garrett to let him know

they could call off the search—I was safe. I used his phone to call my parents. For once, my dad did most of the talking. My mom was too overcome to say much. I assured them I was okay, and I'd see them soon.

When I ended the call, Luke gently touched my face. I melted into him as he kissed me, slow and deep.

After more kisses and whispered I love yous, we set out again, this time heading for home.

CHAPTER 42

Luke

THE MORNING after Melanie's rescue, we stayed in bed late while she told me the whole story of her captivity.

I held her while she talked, gently stroking her skin. I hadn't pushed her to tell me anything, leaving it in her hands whether she shared the details. She'd insisted that she wanted to. That she needed to speak the truth of what had happened to her. Bring it into the light so it wouldn't fester inside her.

It wasn't easy to hear. But in the end, I was so fucking proud of her.

And so grateful she was with me, and it was over.

After lingering in bed, our limbs tangled, we got up and it was like stepping into a new reality. The past wasn't gone, and it certainly wasn't forgotten. But it wasn't as heavy as it had once been. And I knew that somehow, after everything we'd been through, we were free to move forward.

I went to the kitchen to make coffee while she poked around the cupboards and refrigerator, looking for something to eat. I loved the sight of her in nothing but one of my old Haven Auto T-shirts, her legs bare.

She pulled a jar of pickles out of the fridge and opened the lid.

"Really?" I asked. "First thing?"

"It's midmorning. This is a brunch pickle."

I made a face. "A brunch pickle?"

She took a bite. "It's a thing."

"I don't think it is, but you do you, baby."

"I should probably put some pants on."

My brow furrowed. "Why would you do that?"

"How long do you think it'll be until people start stopping by? And by people, I mostly mean my parents."

"We saw them yesterday."

"What does that have to do with anything?"

I shrugged and poured our coffee.

When we'd arrived in Tilikum after our ordeal, I'd wanted nothing more than to fall into bed with Melanie and shut out the world. But there were people who loved her too who needed to see her—hug her and see for themselves that she was all right.

We took our coffee—and her jar of pickles—to the couch, and she nestled against me. I kissed her hair and leaned my face against her head, just breathing in the moment. She was there. She was safe. She was with me.

And I was never going to let her go.

Not like the psycho who'd taken her. He'd wanted to chain her up, hold her captive. I wanted her free—free to be the chaotic, dramatic mess I loved so much.

Free, and also mine.

My phone buzzed with a text. Somewhat reluctantly, I reached over to the coffee table to check it. It was Garrett asking if he could stop by. I replied that it was fine.

"I guess you should put on pants." I stroked her bare thigh a few times. "But I don't have to like it."

She laughed a little. "You can probably talk me into taking them off later."

"Your wish is my command."

"My every whim is your command," she said in her

Queen Ione voice as she got up from the couch.

"That probably shouldn't turn me on, but it's so hot when you're an evil queen."

"I'll allow you to please me later," she said, still using the voice. "For now, I have duties to attend to."

Grinning, I shook my head and adjusted myself as she sauntered to the bedroom. If Garrett hadn't been on his way over, I would have followed her.

She came back a short time later, dressed in my T-shirt and joggers, her dark hair down. We'd cleaned off most of the duct tape residue, but there was still redness around her wrists from being bound. I drew her back onto the couch and kissed the insides of her wrists a few times.

There was a knock on the door, so I got up to answer it. Garrett was dressed in street clothes, carrying a pink Angel Cakes Bakery box. He came inside and took off his aviators.

"Sorry to bug you guys," he said as I closed the door behind him. "But Harper sent cookies."

I took the box and set it on the coffee table, then took my seat next to Melanie. "It's fine. Are you here on official business or just checking in?"

He sat in the armchair. "Both. I wanted you to hear it from me. The suspect did not survive the crash."

I could feel the tension leave Melanie's body.

"Thank freaking goodness," she said. "My imagination was going a little wild, thinking he might show up here, all black and burned, like something out of a horror movie."

"No chance of that," Garrett said. "We were also able to search the cabin where he took you."

"The fire didn't get it?" I asked.

He shook his head. "The winds shifted last night so we were able to get out there early this morning. Between what we found there and the contents of the vehicle, we've been able to piece things together. He had photos of you from before the first abduction. And one from…" He hesitated. "During."

She shuddered. "That's so gross."

"We also figured out where he's been for the past eleven years. Or at least for ten of them. From what we can tell, after you escaped his first attempt, he fled to his mother's residence in Tennessee. While he was living there, he was caught and convicted of credit card fraud. It was pretty substantial, so he went to prison. Served a ten-year sentence."

"Holy shit," I muttered. "That must be why he didn't go after her before."

"Exactly," he said. "Based on when he was released, he left almost immediately. Came here."

"How did he find her?" I asked.

"We don't know. There are a number of ways he could have tracked her down."

"It's not like I've been in hiding or something," she said.

"The good news is, it's over," Garrett said. "He's out of the picture and won't be coming back to haunt you."

"We should celebrate," she said. "With cookies."

Garrett gestured to the box. "Those are fresh."

"Tell Harper thank you so much." Melanie opened the box and gasped. "Oh my god, they're pickles!"

Sure enough, Harper had made pickle-shaped sugar cookies, complete with green icing.

"They're not pickle flavored, are they?" I asked.

"Don't think so," Garrett said.

Melanie picked one up and took a bite. Moaning, she closed her eyes as she chewed. "These are so good. Whoever said cookies can't solve your problems has never tried Harper's baking."

"She'll be glad to know you like them." Garrett stood and put on his aviators. "I should get back."

"Thanks for stopping by," I said.

"I'm just glad I had good news to deliver. And that you two are okay."

Melanie picked up a second cookie. "I'm sure I have enough unresolved trauma to keep my therapist employed for the next decade. But that's okay, because therapy exists! And so do cookies, and pickles." She glanced at me. "And other things."

Garrett said goodbye, and as he closed the door behind him, Melanie handed me a cookie. Thankfully, they were not pickle flavored.

A short time later, her mom called to announce they were bringing us lunch. Then her sister-in-law called to see if we needed anything, and my mom called to ask if she could bring over dinner later. Theo texted to see if we wanted anything from the store, as did Annika a few minutes later. Then Audrey and Marigold both texted the same thing.

"I feel like we should host an I'm-okay-and-all-is-well reception," Melanie said as she set down her phone. "Probably a weird reason for a big family get-together. So, what are you doing tonight? Oh, you know, a family member was abducted and could have been killed, but her boyfriend saved her and now we're all going to eat pizza and breadsticks."

"You know, if we play this right, we could get free food for a week." I leaned over and brushed her lips with a kiss. "And I don't know that I did a lot of saving. You were well on your way to saving yourself."

She smiled and kissed me. "I think it was a team effort. Just the way it should be."

I kissed her again, savoring the feel of her lips on mine. "How much time until your parents show up?"

"Probably an hour. Why?"

"I think the queen deserves someone who will please her." I licked my lips. "With his tongue."

She shifted to her queen voice. "Do your worst."

Pushing her onto her back, I took off her clothes and went to work pleasing my queen, just the way she liked it.

Later, we lay on the couch together, our bodies sated. My mind wandered as I traced idle circles on her skin. We'd laid ourselves bare, sharing our memories and wounds—even the ones we'd given each other. But there was one thing unresolved between us.

I still had a bet to win.

CHAPTER 43

Melanie

FALL WASHED over Tilikum like a cleansing shower. A solid week of rain helped control the wildfires and clear the smoke from the air. After the storms, the sun came out and the sky had never seemed so blue. The leaves turned, and the temperature was cool enough for a sweater.

With glee, I got out my favorite knee-high boots. Their time had come.

On a bright, crisp, Saturday afternoon in October, Luke and I arrived at Lumberjack Park. I was delighted to be wearing a cardigan with jeans and my boots. I'd missed my fall clothes, especially after such a long, hot summer.

Luke walked next to me, holding my hand, dressed in a dark orange flannel and jeans. It was a good look on him— gave him a lumberjack meets small-town mechanic vibe that kind of made me wish we were going home so he could take *off* my boots and cardigan.

But there'd be time for that later.

My parents were already there, as were Nathan, Sharla, and the kids. Lucia and Zola were decked out in full princess attire, plastic crowns and everything. Lucia was probably getting close to outgrowing her dress-up and play-pretend phase, but I was glad she hadn't quite left it yet. Nico wore a black cape that had been serving as villain, superhero, prince, captain of the guard, or whatever character his sisters gave him.

Zola caught sight of us first. "Luke! Auntie Mel!"

The other two gasped and all three of them beelined for us. I wasn't even mad that the girls hugged Luke first. I could hardly blame them.

"Look at you," I said, as if I hadn't seen them in costume a hundred times. "What beautiful princesses."

They did their obligatory twirls.

"Grandma got us new crowns," Lucia said, touching hers and fluffing her hair.

"They're lovely," I said.

"What an awesome grandma," Luke said. "They're perfect."

We walked to their picnic table and said hello to the adults. My parents still looked at me with a certain anxiety in their expression, as if they expected me to fall apart any second. That seemed like a normal enough response to their daughter being abducted for the second time by the same psychopath. I gave them each a hug.

"How are you?" Mom asked. "I'm not pressuring you to talk about anything, I'm just wondering. But really, how are you? Do you need anything? Chocolate? Pickles? Chocolate-covered pickles?"

"I was about to say no, I'm fine, but chocolate-covered pickles? Do those exist?"

"Please, no," Nathan said, and Luke chuckled.

"I don't know, but if they do, I'll find them." Mom got out her phone.

"It's okay, Mom, I can research later. And I really am fine. Probably more than I have any right to be, all things considered." I glanced at Luke. "But everything is… really good."

With a sigh, she put down her phone. "I'm sorry. I'm trying not to project my anxiety onto you. But it's not easy."

Dad gently rubbed her back. "You're doing fine, my love."

She smiled at him.

"Honestly, right now, I just want pumpkin spice everything," I said. "Does anyone know if Angel Cakes has pumpkin spice muffins? We need Harper to get on that."

"I think there are, actually," Sharla said.

I grabbed Luke's arm. "I know what I want to do after this."

"What my girl wants, my girl gets." He grinned at me. "Pumpkin spice it is."

"Luke, can we do our play now?" Zola asked.

"What play?" Mom asked, looking curiously at Luke.

"Oh, it's just a little something I helped the kids come up with," Luke said. "Lucia, did you bring our scripts?"

"Yep!" Lucia held up a few small stacks of papers stapled together. "Got them right here."

I nudged Luke with my elbow. "When did you help them write a play?"

He winked with a casual shrug and Lucia handed him the script. "There's a part for you."

"Oh yeah? Who am I playing?"

"Queen Ione," Zola said.

"Of course. I should have guessed. Do I need to rehearse or are we just doing this?"

Luke gave me a copy. "Just read along. I'm sure you'll get the hang of it."

There weren't any lines for me on the first page, so I started to look through the rest of their script.

"Don't read ahead," Luke said.

"Why?"

"Because spoilers."

"There aren't spoilers when you're in the show."

"Just don't." Luke walked over to the other side of the picnic table. "Ready, girls?"

"Mom, take a video!" Lucia said.

"Got it." Sharla held up her phone. "And… action."

Lucia's expression changed, her smile disappearing as she read from her script. "I am Princess Persephone, and my realm is threatened by the evil Queen Ione, who lives in the forest."

Zola stepped up and twirled. "I am Princess Iris, twin sister of Persephone. My sister, we must find a way to stop the queen."

"But how?" Lucia said, putting the back of her hand to her forehead. "She is too powerful. Our magic is no match for her. And her minions are pouring over our borders."

"What does she want with our kingdom?" Zola asked. "She has her own realm."

"I do not know," Lucia answered. "But we must find a way to stop her."

They paused, and everyone looked at me. I'd been watching them instead of reading along with the script. I turned the page and realized my line was next. "Sorry!" I cleared my throat and began in my Queen Ione voice. "The princesses are plotting against me. I must discover their plans so I may thwart them."

Nico marched over to me and bowed. "My queen."

According to the script, he had more lines. I paused, waiting to see if he'd remember.

"What are your orders," Lucia whisper-yelled at him.

"Oh yeah," he said. "What are your orders?"

"Spy on the princesses and discover their plans."

He bowed again and walked away. He was so cute, it was hard not to break character.

Taking a few steps, I kept reading. "Their power is nothing compared to mine. But I fear they have a secret weapon that could be my undoing."

The scene shifted back to the girls, so I moved out of the way.

"Princess Iris, I know what we must do," Lucia said.

Zola gasped dramatically. "What?"

"We must enlist the help of Queen Ione's greatest nemesis."

"Do you mean?"

"Yes." Lucia pointed at Luke. "King Lukonidas. His power rivals the queen's. He is the only one who can stop her."

"Will he help us?" Zola asked.

"I do not know. But we must try."

The girls marched over to Luke and curtsied to him. While I'd been looking down at the script, someone had handed him a gold crown. It was slightly too small, balancing precariously on his head. He stood straight and put his hands on his hips.

"Princess Persephone. Princess Iris." He bent his head to each of them, and I could tell he was having trouble keeping the crown on his head. "To what do I owe the honor of your visit."

I couldn't stop smiling at his king voice—his tone low and serious. It sent a little shiver down my spine.

"We come to you with great need, King Lukonidas," Lucia said. "The evil Queen Ione threatens our kingdom. You are the only one who can stop her."

"For you, sweet princesses, I will do this." His crown slipped off and fell to the ground, but he kept going. "I warn you, however, once I have begun this quest, I will not stop until it is accomplished, come what may."

"You have our thanks," Lucia said, and the girls curtsied again.

I had to wipe the smile off my face and get back into character as Luke strode over to me. But it wasn't easy.

"We meet again, Queen Ione," he said.

"Foolish king. You think you can defeat me?"

"We have done battle many times and always come to an impasse. This time will be different. I will prevail."

Nico ran up and handed us toy swords. The script said we were supposed to do battle with magic and swords. Holding the plastic weapon in one hand, I clashed it with Luke's a few times, then stepped back and stretched out my arm, as if casting a spell. He deflected my magic with his blade, then cast his own.

I glanced at the script. "Your power has grown, Lukonidas."

"So has yours, Ione." He lowered his sword a little. "As has your beauty."

"My…" The slight flush in my cheeks was no act. It was so silly, but something about Luke's king voice was getting to me. "You try to distract me."

"No." He stepped closer. "I came here seeking to defeat you. But now I know the truth. I love you."

"How could you possibly love me?"

He moved in, closer still, and his voice gradually shifted to his own. "For long years, I have loved you, my beautiful queen. Fate has kept us apart, but it will no longer be so."

I lowered the script and met his eyes as he continued.

"Your spirit burns bright, a fire that devours all in its path. It has consumed my heart, melting the ice that once encased it."

"The girls wrote this?" I asked, totally breaking character.

"Shh." He put a finger to my lips. "Though we once faced each other as enemies, I see now our mistake. It is not hatred that fills our hearts. It is a love beyond imagining."

I stared at him. Part of me wondered if I had more lines, but I couldn't quite make myself break from his gaze to look at the script.

"Melanie," he said softly, and it occurred to me that he'd used my real name. "I want to be the man who loves you forever. The king to your queen."

He lowered himself to one knee. The script slipped from my hand and fluttered to the ground as he pulled a ring from his pocket.

My lips parted in shock. My mom was already sobbing while my dad tried to hush her.

Meeting my eyes, Luke lifted the ring. "Will you marry me?"

I started nodding before I regained the use of words. He stood and slipped the ring on my finger.

"Yes," I said. "Oh, this is happening. Yes. Yes, I'll marry you."

My family erupted in applause as Luke scooped me into his arms and held me tight. The kids surrounded us, jumping up and down and cheering.

Tears stung my eyes as Luke pulled away. He swiped a tear from my cheek and placed a knuckle beneath my chin to lift my mouth to his. The kids' cheering turned to exclamations of disgust as he kissed me.

It was perfect. Absolutely, completely perfect.

He slowly broke the kiss and grinned. "I love you."

"I love you too. You planned all that?"

"I had a little help. Although Nico wanted you to turn into a dragon."

I glanced at my mom. She was sobbing into my dad's shirt. "She didn't know, did she?"

"Would she have kept it a secret?"

"Oh my goodness, no. Krista Andolini couldn't keep a secret to save her life."

Dad met my eyes and winked.

"You talked to him first, didn't you?" I asked, nodding toward my dad.

"We Havens are a bit old-school like that. I let him know my intentions with his daughter."

I wound my arms around his neck, and he dipped his head to mine, our mouths meeting in a delicious kiss.

After everything we'd been through, the long road we'd traveled to get there, I was going to be Luke Haven's girl —forever.

There wasn't anything in the world I wanted more.

Epilogue

LUKE

THE FOLLOWING SPRING...

Racing muscle cars had nothing on getting married.

I stood at the front of the room, my heart pounding with anticipation while I waited for my bride. Adrenaline coursed through my veins, giving me a heady buzz. My brothers stood next to me, decked out in suits, and I had to say, the Havens cleaned up good.

Melanie's bridesmaids fanned out in the other direction, holding bouquets and anxiously watching the back of the room. We were at Salishan Cellars—the fire last fall had been contained before it got there—in their largest event space, and it was packed. Andolinis, Havens, Baileys, and a host of other people from various parts of our lives filled the rows of seats.

You don't realize how many people you know until you plan a wedding.

The doors opened, and Melanie appeared, her mom on one side and her dad on the other. My focus sharpened to a point, the world around her going hazy and indistinct. She stood out as if a spotlight shone on her and her alone.

Her strapless white gown molded to her curves, and her hair was pinned in an elaborate updo. Instead of a veil, my beautiful drama queen wore a big, sparkling tiara.

I grinned at her, thinking about how much I wanted to kiss that red lipstick off her full lips.

She beamed at me as she walked up the aisle, her shoulders trembling like she was holding back a giggle. I smiled back, drinking her in.

The woman was everything.

My heart beat harder as her parents hugged her and took their seats. But it wasn't fear. It was excitement. She stepped up next to me, and as I took her hands, electricity coursed between us. Her eyes met mine, bright and beautiful. She'd felt it too.

The ceremony was straightforward, and the only thing that took me by surprise was how deeply I felt the words of our vows. They speared through me, right in the chest. I meant every word. No matter what life threw at us, no matter how things changed, she belonged to me, and I belonged to her.

We'd face it all together.

Her eyes misted with tears as we both said I do. And then it was done. I drew her in for a kiss.

Melanie was my wife.

Taking her hand, I led her back down the aisle. We stopped just beyond the last row of guests, and I hauled her against me, kissing her again. I couldn't help myself.

I'd never been so happy in my entire life.

The reception began. We'd decided on a midday wedding with wine and hors d'oeuvres, followed by cake.

Guests mingled, chatting as they sipped their wine, and coming over to share their congratulations and hugs. Our older nieces and nephews ran around, and the babies were passed from person to person. Nathan stood guard in front of the cake table so none of the kids smashed into it. He was a smart dad.

When it was time for the best man to give his speech, Theo clinked a fork against his wineglass until everyone quieted. I stood with my arm around Melanie's waist.

"Hey, everyone," Theo said. "When Luke asked me to be his best man, I thought about getting up here and cracking some jokes about their relationship back in high school."

Even without a joke, there was a murmur of laughter.

"But the truth is, it wouldn't be fair to either of them to judge who they are now based on who they were at seventeen or eighteen. Let's face it, we're all a little stupid at that age. Trust me, I work with high schoolers every day." He glanced at Owen. "No offense, kid."

Owen smiled and lifted his glass of Coke.

"These two had to travel a long road to get where they are today. But the thing is, I think it was probably exactly what they needed. They grew up and, for a while, went their separate ways. But they didn't grow apart. In fact, they grew closer together without even realizing it."

Melanie leaned against me, and I squeezed her closer.

"Luke and Melanie, you've shown us all how powerful love can be. You didn't give up on each other, and I know you never will." He raised his glass, and the guests followed. "To Luke and Melanie. Cheers!"

"Cheers!" all the guests said in unison.

Melanie and I held up our glasses and took a drink.

After cake—which was outrageously good—I pulled Melanie out into the hallway, where it was quiet. She let out a long breath and brushed a wisp of hair off her forehead.

"Amazingly, I think I like every person in that room. But I'm getting tired."

"Yeah, I figured." I pulled a little surprise I'd kept for her from my inside jacket pocket. A pickle in a sandwich bag. "Here."

Her eyes widened as I took it out of the bag and handed it to her. "You brought me an emotional support pickle?"

"Of course. You didn't think I'd let you go through an entire wedding without one, did you?"

She took a bite, closing her eyes as she chewed, her tiara sparkling. "So good."

I grinned. She was so weird. I loved it.

We stayed in the hallway, undisturbed while she ate her pickle. I'd already resolved to keep them handy in all places at all times. I even had a jar in the glove box of my car.

It was good to be prepared, especially when it came to Mel.

When she finished, I cupped her cheeks and leaned down, touching my forehead to hers.

"I love you, my wife."

"It feels so good to hear you say that," she whispered. "I love you too, my husband."

I was about to move in to kiss her when she pulled back.

"Wait. I owe you a hundred bucks, don't I?" she asked.

"What?"

"The bet. You bet I'd get married again within a year." Her lips turned up in a smile. "You didn't marry me just to win, did you?"

"Yeah, it was so important to me to win a hundred-dollar bet, I spent thousands on a wedding."

She laughed. "Okay, that's fair."

I touched her jaw, tilting her face up. "Thank you."

"For what?"

"Coming home to me."

She smiled. "Thank you."

"For what?"

"For wanting me."

Leaning down, I pressed my lips to hers. She wound her arms around my shoulders, and I took the kiss deeper, savoring her.

I'd almost lost her—twice. And I was never going to lose her again. There would be new challenges to face, but also new experiences, new joys, new adventures. No matter what, we'd be together. That was what it was all about.

She was the love of my life. I'd loved her then, and I loved her still. And it was the first day of our happily ever after.

Bonus Epilogue
MELANIE

SEVERAL YEARS LATER…

That whole starting over thing? It wasn't nearly as bad as I'd thought it would be.

Sure, I'd spent more years than I wanted to remember in a bad relationship. I'd been through a divorce, uprooted my life, and moved back to my hometown. And okay, I'd been so broke I'd had to take a job working for my high school ex-boyfriend.

And of course, there was the whole guy-who-wanted-to-keep-me-chained-to-a-wall-in-his-basement thing.

A lot of people would look at that and see failure. Or at least a trial to be avoided. But I didn't. I saw it as growth—the path I'd needed to take to get home.

Actually, I could have done without the guy-who-wanted-to-keep-me-chained-to-a-wall-in-his-basement part.

But the rest? It had led me back—to Tilikum, to my family, and to Luke.

And never did it feel more worth it than when I watched Luke with our kids.

Oh yes, kids. Plural. Four, as a matter of fact.

I didn't give birth to them. Finding and marrying the true love of my life didn't magically heal my reproductive system. There was no amount of positive thinking or wishing or hoping that would make it possible for me to get pregnant.

But Luke hadn't been kidding when he'd told me it wasn't a deal breaker. And I hadn't been kidding when I'd told him I was open to parenthood, although it would mean taking a different road to get there.

A different road. Kind of the story of my life.

I paused in the kitchen where I had a view of the living room. Luke was on the couch with our minions. Luke Haven, Jr.—we call him LJ—was six and obsessed with cars. He sat wedged next to his dad, driving a small toy sports car across the cushion. On Luke's other side, stretched out so his head was against the armrest, was four-year-old Daniel. And taking up Luke's entire lap, dressed in matching nightgowns, were our surprise twin daughters, two-year-old Ruby and Rosie.

How do you get surprise babies when you're adopting? Trust me, it can happen.

Luke's above-the-garage apartment had been left behind after our wedding, and we'd moved into a nice four-bedroom house not far from Nathan and Sharla. A few months after we'd bought it, on a lazy Saturday morning while we were still in bed, Luke had asked how I felt about filling those bedrooms with kids.

Because he knew me better than anyone, he'd had an emotional support pickle on hand.

My answer had been a resounding yes. So, we'd decided to see where that road took us. And just shy of a year later, we brought LJ home. Two years later, we adopted Daniel.

Daniel was such an easy baby, around his first birthday, we decided we were open to one more. That one turned out to be two. Rosie had been sneakily hiding behind Ruby during her birth mom's early ultrasounds. Once we found out there were twins on the way, we decided to embrace the chaos and move forward with the adoption.

Best decision ever.

Actually, all our children were the best decision ever. They hadn't grown in my belly, but they were the babies of my heart. My love for them was fierce.

And Luke? Fatherhood looked incredible on him.

After pausing for a long moment to watch while our kids climbed and leaned and shared closeness with him, I glanced at the clock. It was almost bedtime.

"Who's ready for a story?" I asked in a sing-song voice.

LJ raised his hand, Daniel scrambled to sit up and almost rolled off the couch, and the girls' cry of, "Me!" was loud enough that I wondered if we should start saving for Luke's eventual hearing aid fund sooner rather than later.

"Girls, don't blow out Daddy's eardrums," I said.

Rosie settled in his lap and Ruby jumped down. I scooped her up and balanced her on my hip.

"What story tonight?" Luke asked. "Whose turn is it to choose?"

The girls shouted, "Me!" again.

"No," LJ said. "It's Daniel's turn."

"I think he's right." I gestured to our bookshelf stuffed full of children's books and dropped into my Queen Ione voice. "Daniel, this task is appointed to you. Choose wisely."

With a big grin, Daniel slid off the couch and went over to the bookshelf. The girls watched, wide-eyed and open-mouthed, as if the choice of book was a momentous part of their day, while LJ kept driving his car, making engine noises.

Finally, Daniel pulled a book from the shelf and held it above his head with a look of regal triumph on his face.

"Excellent choice," I said, still using my queen voice, and gestured to the couch. "Take your seat."

Keeping the book above his head, he marched with his knees high, then spun and held the book out to Luke.

Okay, not biologically related to me, but so my son.

I sat on the couch next to Luke and moved Ruby so she was on one side of my lap. Daniel sat on my other side, and we all settled in for story time.

Daniel had chosen a fairy tale featuring a peaceful kingdom threatened by a fearsome dragon, and the warrior king and queen who stop it. We'd read it approximately eight hundred sixty-four thousand times. Fortunately, it was fun and well-written, so it never really got old. And Luke and I had most of the dialogue memorized.

"Once upon a time," Luke began in his normal voice, "in the peaceful land of Elderbarrow, there lived a king and queen in a mighty castle."

He kept reading and the kids all leaned in close to see the illustrations. The land of Elderbarrow was a place of beauty, surrounded by magical forests and meadows of wildflowers. The castle stood atop a hill, with white spires that gleamed in the sunlight. The king and queen held court there and welcomed guests from near and far.

One night, during a great feast, the full moon was briefly cloaked in shadow. A terrible fear swept over the guests.

"What can it be?" I read the queen's dialogue in a softer version of my Queen Ione voice. "Trepidation fills my heart, yet I do not know why."

"I feel it too," Luke said, his voice deepening as he read the king's lines. "Something draws near. Could it be the ancient evil of which my forefathers warned me?"

"My king, you can't mean…"

"I fear the worst, my queen. But take heart. Whatever assails us, we will face it as one."

Luke continued reading as the king and queen reassured their guests that all was well. In minutes, the haze of fear left, and the celebration continued. But the king and queen were not complacent. They knew trouble was coming to their peaceful realm.

The story continued, detailing the destruction the dragon began to bring to the outer reaches of their kingdom, burning villages and displacing the people who lived there. The king and queen knew they had to act to save their people.

On a cool morning, as dawn broke, the brave king and queen, both clad in shining armor, mounted their horses and rode out to confront the dragon.

I wasn't sure how much of the story the girls really followed, considering they were only two, but they loved the illustrations. When Luke turned the page to show the dragon with glowing red eyes and wings spread, they gasped. Daniel mouthed along with Luke as he read and gestured every bit as dramatically as I ever had, almost hitting me in the face as he acted out the story.

Over the next several pages, the battle commenced. The dragon was huge and powerful, breathing scorching fire. But the king and queen worked together to lure it into position so they could strike. Just when the dragon's fire breath was about to devour the king, the queen darted in and drove her sword through its foot. Its flame sputtered, and with its mouth open wide, the king threw his blade like a spear, piercing it through the back of the dragon's throat.

LJ lifted his arms in the air and cheered, like he was watching a sports team score. Daniel mimed the king's spear-throwing move, then hopped up from the couch and played the dragon, falling to the ground, dead. Ruby pointed to the illustration, and despite the epic battle, Rosie was already half asleep with her head resting against Luke's chest.

The king watched in triumph as the dragon fell, but his apparent victory was soon replaced with alarm. Where was the queen?

"Uh-oh," Ruby whispered.

"It cannot be," Luke said in his king voice. "My queen!

Has she been slain with the beast? Have I defeated my enemy only to lose the one that I love?"

"Nay, my love," I said as he turned the page. "I yet live."

The king ran to his queen and helped her out from beneath the dragon's leg. Luke glanced at me with a wink as the characters shared a moment of relief and happiness at their victory, and their love for each other.

It really was a sweet story.

Luke closed the book and handed it to Daniel. Rosie's eyes were half closed as she leaned against her daddy and Ruby was feeling heavier in my arms.

"Bedtime," Luke said in a gentle voice as he hugged Rosie against him and rocked back and forth a few times.

The boys knew the drill. They hustled down the hall to the bedroom they shared to change into pajamas while we put the girls to bed. If they changed and brushed their teeth without being told twice, they'd get another story.

Almost an hour later, after the girls were asleep, the second story read, and the boys tucked into bed, Luke and I collapsed on the couch together. Parenting was awesome, and also exhausting.

I nestled against him as his familiar scent washed over me. All the little stresses of the day seemed to melt away, and my body relaxed.

"Do you want to watch another episode?" he asked.

We'd been into a crime drama and only had a few episodes left. "Maybe in a little bit. I think for now, I just want to do this."

He tightened his arm around me. "This is good."

It was good. It was so good, sometimes it was hard to believe it was my life.

When I'd first come back to Tilikum, I hadn't realized the truth—I wasn't just moving to the town where I'd grown up. I was coming home.

And home wasn't just a place. Turned out, home was also a person. It was Luke Haven.

It almost made me laugh—maniacally, like Queen Ione herself—when I thought about how much I'd hated Luke. Or at least, how much I'd thought I hated him.

Really, I'd just missed him.

As teenagers, we'd broken each other's hearts. Our lives had gone in different directions, but in a strange way, the time we'd spent apart had prepared us to come back together.

And together—as a family—was where we were going to stay.

Dear reader

Dear reader,

I have a confession. I didn't know what to do with Luke.

He appears as a side character in Unraveling Him (Bailey Brothers book three, Evan and Fiona's story) and from that moment many of you were hooked on him, hoping for his story. But the problem was, I didn't know what his story would be.

That's not necessarily unusual. Sometimes I need to ponder for a while before a character's story becomes clear. But this one took a lot of pondering.

What was really going on in his life? What was holding him back? Why hadn't he found love?

And then I realized, he had. But he'd lost her.

Melanie not only blazed into Luke's life, she blazed into mine. She made the story make sense. Her fiery personality wasn't just what Luke needed, it was what I needed to write at the time. I love her for that.

I wanted to tackle a second chance romance again (it's been a while) and explore the dynamic of time. What happens when two people who had a young, passionate, but immature relationship mess it all up? And then get another chance, years later, to try again.

How does the time apart impact the new relationship? How have they grown? But how are they still incomplete without each other?

Those were my questions as I wrote and hopefully you found the answers satisfying.

And Roswell Mills? Yikes.

This suspense storyline had been in my head for a long time. I wanted to write an antagonist who seemed to disappear (because prison), and then reappears in an unexpected way, intending to finish what he started. This one required writing from his point of view, which meant I had to get in his head a little. Don't worry, I didn't stay long.

Shudder.

I hope you enjoyed Luke and Melanie's story!

Love,

Claire

Acknowledgments

Many thanks to everyone who helped bring this book to life!

Thank you to my beta readers and editorial team for your feedback and encouragement.

Thank you to Lori for another gorgeous cover and being a beautiful human.

Thank you to TeamCK, Alex, Nikki, and Stacey, for ALL your behind the scenes work. It's such a gift to have people I can rely on and trust. I love your faces!

And to my other admins and helpers, thank you for all you do! You make it possible for me to spend time doing what I really need to be doing—writing.

Thank you to the content creators, readers, superfans, and lovers of the Haven Brothers for your support, enthusiasm, and love. I appreciate you all so much.

And to the Melanie who inspired the heroine's name. I told you I'd make it up to you someday.

Also by Claire Kingsley

For a full and up-to-date listing of Claire Kingsley books visit www.clairekingsleybooks.com/books/

For comprehensive reading order, visit

www.clairekingsleybooks.com/reading-order/

———

The Haven Brothers

Small-town romantic suspense with CK's signature endearing characters and heartwarming happily ever afters. Can be read as stand-alones.

Obsession Falls (Josiah and Audrey)

Storms and Secrets (Zachary and Marigold)

Temptation Trails (Garrett and Harper)

Whispers and Wildfire (Luke and Melanie)

The rest of the Haven brothers will be getting their own happily ever afters!

———

How the Grump Saved Christmas (Elias and Isabelle)

A stand-alone, small-town Christmas romance.

———

The Bailey Brothers

Steamy, small-town family series with a dash of suspense. Five unruly brothers. Epic pranks. A quirky, feuding town. Big HEAs. Best read in order.

Protecting You (Asher and Grace part 1)

Fighting for Us (Asher and Grace part 2)

Unraveling Him (Evan and Fiona)

Rushing In (Gavin and Skylar)

Chasing Her Fire (Logan and Cara)

Rewriting the Stars (Levi and Annika)

———

The Miles Family

Sexy, sweet, funny, and heartfelt family series with a dash of suspense. Messy family. Epic bromance. Super romantic. Best read in order.

Broken Miles (Roland and Zoe)

Forbidden Miles (Brynn and Chase)

Reckless Miles (Cooper and Amelia)

Hidden Miles (Leo and Hannah)

Gaining Miles: A Miles Family Novella (Ben and Shannon)

———

Dirty Martini Running Club

Sexy, fun, feel-good romantic comedies with huge… hearts. Can be read as stand-alones.

Everly Dalton's Dating Disasters (Prequel with Everly, Hazel, and Nora)

Faking Ms. Right (Everly and Shepherd)

Falling for My Enemy (Hazel and Corban)

Marrying Mr. Wrong (Sophie and Cox)

Flirting with Forever (Nora and Dex)

———

Bluewater Billionaires

Hot romantic comedies. Lady billionaire BFFs and the badass heroes who love them. Can be read as stand-alones.

The Mogul and the Muscle (Cameron and Jude)

The Price of Scandal, Wild Open Hearts, and Crazy for Loving You

More Bluewater Billionaire shared-world romantic comedies by Lucy Score, Kathryn Nolan, and Pippa Grant

———

Bootleg Springs

by Claire Kingsley and Lucy Score

Hot and hilarious small-town romcom series with a dash of mystery and suspense. Best read in order.

Whiskey Chaser (Scarlett and Devlin)

Sidecar Crush (Jameson and Leah Mae)

Moonshine Kiss (Bowie and Cassidy)

Bourbon Bliss (June and George)

Gin Fling (Jonah and Shelby)

Highball Rush (Gibson and I can't tell you)

———

Book Boyfriends

Hot romcoms that will make you laugh and make you swoon. Can be read as stand-alones.

Book Boyfriend (Alex and Mia)

Cocky Roommate (Weston and Kendra)

Hot Single Dad (Caleb and Linnea)

———

Finding Ivy (William and Ivy)

A unique contemporary romance with a hint of mystery. Stand-alone.

———

His Heart (Sebastian and Brooke)

A poignant and emotionally intense story about grief, loss, and the transcendent power of love. Stand-alone.

———

The Always Series

Smoking hot, dirty talking bad boys with some angsty intensity. Can be read as stand-alones.

Always Have (Braxton and Kylie)

Always Will (Selene and Ronan)

Always Ever After (Braxton and Kylie)

———

The Jetty Beach Series

Sexy small-town romance series with swoony heroes, romantic HEAs, and lots of big feels. Can be read as stand-alones.

Behind His Eyes (Ryan and Nicole)

One Crazy Week (Melissa and Jackson)

Messy Perfect Love (Cody and Clover)

Operation Get Her Back (Hunter and Emma)

Weekend Fling (Finn and Juliet)

Good Girl Next Door (Lucas and Becca)

The Path to You (Gabriel and Sadie)

About the Author

Claire Kingsley is a USA Today and #1 Amazon bestselling author of sexy, heartwarming contemporary romance, romantic comedies, and small-town romantic suspense. She writes sassy, quirky heroines, swoony heroes who love big, romantic happily ever afters, and all the big feels.

She can't imagine life without coffee, great books, and the characters who inhabit her imagination. She lives in the inland Pacific Northwest with her three kids.

www.clairekingsleybooks.com

Made in United States
North Haven, CT
12 April 2025

67873307R00262